A Long Time Dying

By the same author

The Home Girls
Loving Daughters
Amy's Children
The Rose Fancier

Olga Masters

A Long Time Dying

W · W · NORTON & COMPANY
New York   London

Best Books for Public Libraries

Copyright © 1985 by Olga Masters
First published as a Norton edition 1989

All rights reserved.

Printed in the United States of America.

Library of Congress Cataloging-in-Publication Data

Masters, Olga, 1919-1986
  A long time dying/Olga Masters.
  p. cm.
  I. Title.
[PR9619.3.M289L55   1989]
823—dc19   88–34609

ISBN 0-393-02688-4

W. W. Norton & Company, Inc., 500 Fifth Avenue, New York, N.Y. 10110
W. W. Norton & Company Ltd., 37 Great Russell Street, London WC1B 3NU

1 2 3 4 5 6 7 8 9 0

To my brothers and sisters

Contents

A Long Time Dying

1 Scones Every Day

Cobargo was a terribly dull place in 1935.

There was only tank water, and no electricity. In the town there were two hotels, a police station, a post office, a few stores, a solicitor's office, two schools and three churches. Four miles along the road to the coast there was a butter factory.

Employment was a great worry. Many of the young people who left school at fourteen worked on their parents' farms. Sometimes it was a sharefarm, in which case there were no wages, so life did not change dramatically for them at all. One day they were in school clothes, with sandwiches in a brown paper bag, and the next (if girls), packing the sandwiches and seeing the bearers off, needing to look down on the working clothes they wore to be convinced they were not going too.

The boys rushed eagerly into farmwork, fooling the fathers into thinking it a permanent arrangement. They would sit for a long time over meals in this new found freedom, worrying mothers who were wiser to the ways of the young, and who watched for the friction that would develop when the sons became aware of carrying more than a fair load.

The Jusseps were such a family. There were ten children, the eldest twenty. They worked a sharefarm belonging to the Rossmores, who were Cobargo landowners and descendants of the pioneers of the district.

This particular branch of the Rossmore family had a fine house on a hill, and the sharefarmer lived in a more roughly built place tucked into the side of another hill.

1

The property was rather like someone handsomely dressed to all appearances, but carrying a shabby bag which he kept out of sight.

The Rossmores had a tree-lined drive to the main road while the Jusseps had only cartwheel tracks winding around the base of the hill. Wild weather saw the little Jusseps hanging to their hats, the wind threatening to tear their clothes from their bodies as they made their way to the road, with another mile walk to the school.

They went to the convent school, for the Jusseps, like the Rossmores, were Catholics. When the time came to look for a family for the farm, Bert Rossmore favoured Catholics, although the large families they had could become a worry.

When the Jusseps came there were five children. Ten years later there were ten. This made great inroads into farm produce like milk and eggs.

The parish priest, Father O'Malley, was one who approved the recurring births. He raised pious eyes to the sky when told of the arrival of a new Jussep by Bert, and on those occasions Bert felt he was in some way entitled to a share of the praise.

But he had a different view when alone with Mrs Rossmore.

"Where is it going to end? She's got years left in her!" (He had a tendency to class Mrs Jussep with his cows and mares.) "She could end up with fifteen! Fifteen! A damned disgrace!"

Mrs Rossmore, who had borne three in twenty years by restricting her favours to only a few days a month, ran hands down narrow hips to remind Mr Rossmore of what could be if she wasn't in control.

"No control, no control at all!" Mr Rossmore cried. "I'll talk to the man, I'll have to!"

But he didn't need to. Life changed for the Jusseps one day at scone making time.

Mrs Jussep made scones every day before the afternoon milking. Mary, the eldest (as good as a boy on the farm), Tom, Gordon and Mr Jussep ate them fresh from the oven, and a tea towel was thrown over the others for the younger ones when they came in from school. Cobargo talked about Mrs Jussep's scone making. The younger Jusseps came in for their share of harassment.

"Every single day? Every day? Supposing there was a great storm and the stove was flooded, would she make scones then?" This was asked of ten-year-old Patty, who was very fair, and her blushes showed up vividly against her pale forehead and hair. "And what about when she's at Mrs Patgett's? What happens then?" Mrs Patgett's was the local cottage hospital where Mrs Jussep went every second year to give birth.

Patty swung her fair hair away from the questioner, unable to bring herself to say Mr Jussep made the scones then. Admitting this would provide Cobargo with endless fuel for gossip and put Mr Jussep, whom the children loved, in an unfavourable light.

This day there was neither a raging storm to affect the function of the big fuel stove, nor was Mrs Jussep at Patgett's for a new birth.

After getting the cows in Mr Jussep came into the house with his mouth watering for hot scones, holding a picture in his mind of the brown tops and the steam flying when they were pulled apart. But Mrs Jussep only had the flour in the basin and was sitting on a chair at the corner of the table. She had starey eyes and deep grooves around her mouth. Mr Jussep was amazed first of all to see her sitting down.

"I feel crook, Joe," she said, and he noticed she held onto the table and seemed to be breathing strangely.

"Nothing much," she said. "I just feel winded."

"Lie down," he said. "I'll make the scones."

He was surprised that she went at once, and for some reason he was never to discover, she went to the front room to lie on the double bed there. The Jusseps had the best bedroom furniture in this room for visitors, rare though they were, and they took great pride in keeping it immaculate, not being as particular about the rest of the house. The family crammed into the other four bedrooms, but the good room (as they called it) was kept empty, swept, and dusted, with starched runners on the chest and bedside table, and the bed quilt not showing a crease nor the rag mats the hint of a wrinkle.

The first thing Mary noticed when she went to tell her mother the scones were ready was that Mrs Jussep hadn't removed the starched pillow shams but had her head with its straggly grey hair crushed into the hollow between them. Her dirty feet were already marking the quilt. Mary opened her mouth to say something then left it open to scream.

Mrs Jussep was dead.

Cobargo was shocked and although it was simply that Mrs Jussep's heart had stopped beating, there were many who blamed the scones.

"All that flour, all that dough, every single day must have clogged the arteries," someone said.

Others agreed, and some restricted their intake of scones as a precautionary measure, while reminding children wont to scoff down half a dozen with scarcely a pause of the fate of Mrs Jussep (of which they were well aware).

"One day you'll go off like Mrs Jussep and lie on the good bed and die with that bellyful of scones," one mother said.

There was even greater speculation on what would become of the ten children.

The Rossmores paid a formal visit after the funeral, which was well attended to the surprise of many, for the family was humble as well as poor and Mrs Jussep was hardly ever seen in the town. Mary tried to act as her mother would have, sitting the Rossmores in the best chairs in the sitting room which Mrs Rossmore, there for the first time, was surprised to see furnished with cane pieces in quite good taste and patchwork cushions, clean curtains and a nicely shined linoleum square on the floor. Mrs Rossmore went cold all over at the sight of a picture on the wall which appeared at first glance to be similar to one of hers. But on closer inspection the frame was inferior and the scene a little different, as if the Rossmores had the upper reaches of a river and the Jusseps a bend lower down. Mrs Rossmore decided though to move hers from the hall to the small sitting room, very seldom used. She managed to avoid looking its way for the rest of the visit.

She was further irritated when they were driving home in their Studebaker to hear Mr Rossmore murmur that very little seemed to have been achieved by the visit. What did he want? Mrs Rossmore to go down on her knees and scrub the kitchen floor well in need of it? She had taken a fruit cake and neglected other jobs to make it. And Madge, the youngest of the Rossmores' children, had begged to go too but had been refused. Just as well. She would have noticed and remarked on that picture. There she was, hopping from one foot to the other inside the big gate to the house, waiting for them. She lifted the loop of wire holding the two parts together and opened the gate with great care, her tongue making a mound of one of her cheeks.

Mr Rossmore thought of the one about her age at the

5

Jusseps, very pale and thin, like a ferret he thought, sitting on a chair, doing different things with her feet on the rungs until the big girl told her to go away and attend to the baby. There was a tribe of them alright! Lucky the eldest was a girl. If that wasn't the case Rene here might be called on from time to time, but she had enough to do in the big house. There it was by jove, veranda three parts of the way around, windows winking a welcome and his own young Madge breathing between his and Rene's faces from the back seat, having jumped in the car for the short run to the house.

The fact was, Madge wanted information on Patty Jussep, whom she would have liked to call her best friend but was afraid to.

"No, no!" Mrs Rossmore would reply regularly to Madge's request to have Patty to play on Saturday afternoons. "We can't start that. There'll be no stopping it!" (She sounded like Bert when he was on the subject of the Jussep babies.)

Naturally, Madge wasn't allowed to go to the Jusseps either. "You see the little girl at school. That should be enough!" Mrs Rossmore eased a mildly troubled conscience by telling herself she would never interfere with Sister Alfreda's running of St Joseph's. But Madge would go to boarding school in Goulburn when she was twelve and there would be a natural end to any unwelcome liaison of a social nature between the Rossmores and the Jusseps.

Mr Rossmore made up a fire in the sitting room when they were inside and, sitting by it for awhile, worried about the Jusseps milking seventy cows. Lucky it wasn't spring when there would be one hundred, he said to himself, putting the logs together and admiring his good work in getting a nice blaze so quickly.

The Jusseps would be in the yard now, or most of them, with that little light haired one keeping an eye on the baby and the kitchen fire. It was a boy just walking, he knew, because Jussep sometimes took it about with him in the paddocks, and Rossmore had been forced at times to praise something it did. A knowing little cove, Jussep frequently said.

He wondered now uneasily if he should have sent his Stan, the nineteen-year-old home from university for the midwinter holidays to give the Jusseps a hand this afternoon. He had put in milking machines though. The only sharefarm for miles with milking machines. You got through the milking in no time with machines. Besides, it was good for the Jusseps to keep busy. That big girl Mary who could plough as straight a furrow as any man would have to spend more time in the house, he supposed, which was a pity, but might not be necessary since another girl was about to leave school and there would be plenty for her to do now.

"Which is the one about to leave school?" he asked now of Rene, who was darning socks. (Who would darn all those Jussep socks?)

"Joyce!" cried Madge from her place on the floor rug, scraping stones from the long strands of wool, for she was playing a game of jacks and imagining Patty her opponent.

"She's fourteen," Madge said. Rene looked at Madge's long thin arms in a tight grey sweater and with her pleated skirt spread like a fan on the rug.

"Is she leaving school soon?" Bert asked.

Really, he's encouraging the child! "We don't know the Jussep's business simply because they work for us," Rene said. Madge fixed round blue eyes on her mother, then spreading the fingers of her left hand between the five stones, she put her head very much to one side to stare at them.

Rene's heart said she was lonely for company. She

7

would telephone a brother-in-law and suggest that their daughter Nancy spend one of the days in the holidays at her cousin's place.

"Would you like Nancy over to play jacks with you and stay for dinner one day?" Mrs Rossmore asked.

Madge decided to answer her father. "Joyce isn't coming back to school after the holidays."

Really, that was providential, Mrs Rossmore thought. And the woman died in the holidays which was convenient too (since she was meant to die). No doubt the quite large gathering in the church and at the cemetery was due to the timing. Children made crowds look bigger, Mrs Rossmore decided. Whole families appeared to go to the funeral, which Mrs Rossmore began to think might have been a tribute to themselves. Trangie, as the property was called, was after all the best in the district. So it would naturally follow that the Jusseps were the most fortunate of the district's sharefarmers.

She heard some noises from the kitchen. Madge heard them too. She scraped her jacks together and put them in the little bag with the drawstring at the top and got up. Now she was off to talk to Jessie, the girl who helped with the housework and who was now stoking the stove fire after her two hours off spent in her room with her fancywork, for she had a glory box though no boy friend. Mrs Rossmore laid her darning aside and decided to go to the kitchen too, not so much to supervise tea preparations but to supervise the talk between Jessie and Madge. Jessie was peeling potatoes and talking about the satin stitches in variegated purple thread she was using to embroider clusters of pansies on an afternoon tea cloth.

Madge would be shown the first completed cluster.

She dropped the subject when Mrs Rossmore appeared, looking for gossip from the funeral. Jessie would have

8

liked to have heard of sobbing and wailing from the Jusseps, the more harrowing the better.

In actual fact, Mr Jussep only blew his nose once and Mary was distracted by a feeling at the back of her knees, correctly attributed to the hem of her coat coming down. Only Tom, Gordon and Mary had gone with Mr Jussep, while Joyce, Malcolm (twelve) and Patty were left in charge of Bernie (eight), Nina (six), Joseph (four) and the baby Peter.

Mary had been busy making sure the others looked neat and respectable and had scrambled into her coat at the last minute with no time to look for defects.

It was the first thing she did when the Rossmores left after their visit: she spread the coat out at the end of the kitchen table while the others came inside to get warm around the stove. She found needle and thread in the drawer of the sewing machine (in the kitchen) and with her strong young hands stitched up the hem and tightened two buttons and, with time before milking, she gave the coat a good brushing and hung it on one of several pegs on the closed-in back veranda, known as the coat place.

When she came back into the kitchen and looked around the pensive faces she saw tears pouring down the face of Bernie. She looked away, then back, hoping no one else would see. Mr Jussep had the tin of flour on the table to make the scones and was about to grease the oven tray. So far he wasn't noticing. The baby was on Patty's knee, his hard round head seemed larger than her fair one and you could see he was pleased with all the attention he was getting. The others seemed intent on studying the line of scarlet around the stove door and the big black kettle setting up a thin song, sweet and soothing but with an edge of urgency as if to say it would do its job and boil if they did theirs and kept the heat up.

Tom and Gordon saw the tears, and with mouths

9

working in white faces pulled on their old felt hats and went outside to do things rather than hang around the kitchen. Mr Jussep saw them go with surprise and checked the time on the clock. Mary saw Bernie slide off the chair he was sharing with Nina and crouch on the floor. He wedged his face between his knees and crushed it there, as if the knees pushed into his cheeks would curb the flow of tears.

Nina wriggled into the centre of the chair, relishing the luxury of having it to herself. To add to her comfort she put her feet out and used Bernie's head for a footstool. He shook his head so that her feet fell, one on each shoulder. Mary, putting on her hessian apron, wondered if she should rebuke Nina. What would her Mum have done? She looked to her father with his hands in the flour, like a clump of dead dark trees rising out of snow.

Nina, rubbing her bare feet on Bernie's neck, felt the wetness from his tears. She removed her feet quickly and swung her head around to tell Mary with round eyes.

Bernie's head went down lower between his knees until he was a round ball on the floor, with one cheek turned upwards so the firelight made it glisten like a pool of water on a dark road.

Mary thought if they waited awhile he might stop. She put cups and saucers on the table for the tea.

Joyce put Joseph on her back and carried him off, Malcolm and Patty went with Peter swinging between a hand of each. It seemed strange to see the chairs empty with the firelight dancing on the slippery wooden seats turned to odd angles.

The round ball stayed on the floor.

"They're all gone, Bernie," Mary said. "So you can have any chair you like!"

"He can have the first scone too," Mr Jussep said, feeling pleased with the light dough as he set them out.

Bernie broke into loud unrestrained sobs, and Mary had to leave the cups and hold his shoulders.

His weeping was enough to satisfy even Mrs Rossmore's maid.

Mary's mending her coat had started it.

After a time, when she took him into the cold sitting room so that he wouldn't start up the others eating their scones, he asked her who else was going to die.

2 Stan and Mary, Mary and Stan

Both the Rossmores were worried about Stan but said nothing of their fears to each other.

He was soon to return to university in Sydney after the midwinter holidays, and was not saying a word about it. Mrs Rossmore kept checking his room to see if he had done anything with the books he had emptied from his case and put on his table when he came home. Exams would be in a few months after he got back. She had put a lamp there for him, but even it had not been moved to a new position and she was sure he had not lit it. She saw a light through his window passing (unnecessarily) along the veranda but knew it to be a candle by which he was reading a detective story.

"Where's Stan?" Mr Rossmore asked one night by the sitting room fire after tea.

"In his room with his books," Mrs Rossmore answered. This was not a lie, and it would not be necessary to mention it to Father O'Malley at confession.

Next day Mr Rossmore, coming up behind Stan's straight young back in the corn paddock, asked if he was all set to go back on the coach out of Cobargo on the Monday, a week away. (Even Rossmore acknowledged it a foolish question. What other way was there to go?)

Stan's shoulders wriggled and Mr Rossmore supposed he ducked his head, for he saw briefly a little more of Stan's sunburned neck. Inwardly he rebuked himself. He was paying good money for Stan's education; Stan wasn't taking it on himself to decide his future! He was going back alright. If his mother knew of any doubts there would be a nice old upheaval! And what would he say to Frank and Harry, his brothers with lesser properties and average children (very average). My son the doctor. Dr Stan Rossmore. Dr Rossmore. It had been his mother's dream since they found him reading at four years of age. Too clever for farming by far.

Eric, the younger son, could have two years at agricultural college if he did well enough with the Marist Brothers in Goulburn where he was a boarder. Stan was the brain. What was going on inside that head, covered with tight ginger coloured curls? Not with Eric's dark good looks, but with a freckled face with pale blue eyes that seemed to be strained, as if they did not see as well as stronger coloured ones. Mr Rossmore had to stride out to keep up with him, and when they reached their horses, tied to the old pear tree at the corner of the paddock, Stan swung onto his and Mr Rossmore had a job disguising an enormous effort to keep up. Stan manoeuvered his horse onto the single track up the last gully, galloping ahead and making it appear like a courteous gesture allowing his father a clear path. I'm a wake up, Bert said to himself, seeing the chestnut's rump bounding away between the line of poplars. Stan had to stop, though, when he was through the big gate and wait for Mr Rossmore to pass through. (A well mannered boy, I'll say that for him.) When the gate was closed there was only a short canter to the house, and too late to start anything up.

And at dinner there was Jessie coming in and out all the time and Rene in charge of things as always. She kept an eye on their plates and talked about Cobargo events, giving them more importance than they warranted. There was a ball soon in the School of Arts, the annual Catholic ball, which everyone worthy of a place in the sect and over the age of fifteen would attend.

Mary, Gordon and Tom Jussep usually went.

This year, a fortnight after the death of Mrs Jussep, they would be in a period of mourning.

Everyone thought of this. "Will the Jusseps be going?" Madge asked. Ah, here was something to cheer Mrs Rossmore, with most of her mind on Stan, eating his stewed steak and cauliflower and with an expression she could not read. Stan was allowed two dances with Mary Jussep aside of those in the progressive ones. This was only polite and Mrs Rossmore would have insisted, but she didn't need to, for few could fail to notice the eagerness of Stan when he bent over Mary, sitting on the bench against the wall, and the way her hand sprung out to go into his. She would stand quickly, but not without grace, and put her wrap (not warm enough for a cold June night) and shabby little bag on the seat, keeping her eyes away from those next to her who were looking hard for anything serious in this. Mrs Rossmore usually saw as well, for she was out of the supper room by this time and ready to take her place on the floor with Bert, despite his irritating habit of pumping her arm up and down as if it were a well handle.

The Jusseps would be missing from the ball, thank goodness, (only because it freed her of certain worries).

"Of course they won't be going!" Mrs Rossmore said, frowning on Madge, who had a cheekful of mashed potato. She laid her knife and fork evenly on her plate and stared until Madge, swirling the potato around a few times, finally swallowed it, ducking her head and turning red with the effort. Stan's very pale lashes batted his freckles a couple of times. "The Jusseps I'm sure would know better than that!" Mrs Rossmore murmured.

No more was said until they were up to the pudding. Then Mrs Rossmore said Eric might go this year.

"It would be something for Jim," she said. Jim was

Eric's school friend with whom he was spending the first part of the holidays on a property outside Goulburn. Jim would spend the last part at the Rossmores'. Madge was excited at the prospect. They were yet to meet Jim, and Madge was wishing she could see Patty and share speculation with her on what he would be like.

Stan thought of the School of Arts without Mary. The decorations drooped, the music sounded tinny and hollow, and the sandwiches tasted dry. He might not go. Mrs Rossmore read something of this in his face. Ever since he was a little boy his freckles had stood out when he was about to do or say something of a rebellious nature. No, she wouldn't press the point, just go ahead and air his suit and iron his best shirt and hang them in a conspicuous place on the day of the ball the following Friday.

"Mrs Jussep won't be cooking for the ball this year," Madge said. Her cakes had been among the most professional of those from all the Cobargo cooks. Mrs Rossmore felt cheered by the loss of rivalry and despondent at the loss of the cakes. She rose quite abruptly and began clearing the table as if she should start at once creating extra time for the added workload. Jessie, hearing the rattle of plates, hurried in worrying that she was at fault.

Mr Rossmore was displeased. He had wanted Madge to go off and play and he and Stan and Rene to engage in intimate conversation about Stan's next half year at university. But Stan was on his feet too and, shocking them further, announced he would ride to the sharefarm and ask Joe Jussep if there was anything he could do to help.

"Me too! Me too!" Madge cried, abandoning all parental ruling in her wild desire to see her friend. She stood, such a pathetic and eager figure in her wrinkled stockings and short wincyette dress, now pulled down and wrapped around her knees and held there in her excitement. Stan forgot his own worries and looked tenderly on her.

"Let her come," he said. "She can ride behind me." Madge began to race off after an ecstatic bound in the air, then had to stop and turn to her mother for direction. She was fearful of what she might see on her mother's face.

But Mrs Rossmore, with a swift glance at Bert, could find no grounds for objection. It would not be wise to cross Stan at this stage. She had a pair of little sausage lips that were parted when she had a glitter of concern in her eyes. This is how her eyes were now.

Then she lowered them and dropped the little stack of bread and butter plates onto the tray Jessie held. "Put on your warm skirt then," she said, "and your blue coat." (It was her second best.)

Madge flashed a triumphant look to Jessie, she couldn't help it, unwise as well she knew. She went off straight of back, suddenly sedate as if about to prepare for a formal and dignified occasion. Stan went off to put the saddle back on Larry and Mr Rossmore, suddenly deciding he did not want a conversation with Mrs Rossmore, took his tobacco and went to look at the new peach and apricot trees bearing for the first time this spring.

Mrs Rossmore was left to Jessie. To Jessie's surprise she took a tea towel and stood beside the draining board with Jessie at the sink, nervous that she might not be as thorough as she should under this unaccustomed scrutiny. They both heard the thud of Larry's hoofs die away and Jessie, with an odd air of satisfaction, wrung out the dishcloth to give the kitchen table its best wipe down in a week.

"There they go!" she said.

There they go! thought Mrs Rossmore, her throat thick, her shaking hands hanging up the tea towel. She went rapidly out, her back telling Jessie she was not returning. Jessie gaped after her. Well, I must say that didn't last long. I needn't have been so fussy after all. She gathered up the saucepans from the back of the stove where she put them to dry thoroughly, something Mrs Rossmore had been trying to get her to do since she came six months ago. She took off her apron and hung it behind the pantry door and went off to her bedroom to get on with her fancywork until four o'clock. She was happy about Madge. Do the little thing good, she said to herself, climbing into her unmade bed and reaching for the wicker basket that held her tea cloth and cottons. She decided not to go on with the pansies in satin stitch, but to have a change and do some stem stitch on stems and leaves. She bit off the first thread from a silky skein, a lovely moss green, with a feeling of excitement.

Madge had a similar feeling sitting behind Stan on Larry, bouncing along the cart wheel tracks towards Jusseps. She lay her face in the curve of his back. Like a little gully, she thought, the tiniest gully in the world, rubbing her cheek there to make sure there was a ridge. "You alright there?" Stan said with his face turned just enough for her to see his pinkish cheek and the freckles. She had freckles too and her hair was a little darker than his and not as curly. She hated both. Patty Jussep's hair was like a beautiful creamy silk table runner thrown over her head. Madge admired it, especially when it swung out then settled back exactly as it was before. Her straight fringe did the same.

"Let me," Madge would say, giving it an unnecessary smoothing down when she and Patty were reading at playtime under the school pines, and Patty had both hands pushing the fringe up from her forehead.

Most of Cobargo favoured curly hair, which made Patty something of an oddity. "Absolutely the straightest hair I've ever seen. Absolutely" a Cobargo matron said.

"Draw a line, straight as Patty Jussep's hair," a big rough Thompson boy hissed to his equally rough classmate in school.

"One day she'll be mistaken for a haystack and come to school with half a head where a sickle got her," the classmate hissed back.

Madge wanted to tell Sister Joan on them, but Patty's scarlet cheeks and drowned blue eyes made her decide she wouldn't, and spare her friend the humiliation of hearing the words repeated.

In sight of the Jussep's house, Stan and Madge saw Patty in the yard, her hair showing out like a white handkerchief on a dark bush.

"You'd know that hair anywhere," Stan said. It was different the way he said it. Acceptable. Madge placed a small but passionate kiss in the hollow of his back.

She slid off Larry's back and stood quite close to Patty, barely able to believe it was real. Mary came down the back steps and crossed to them. Stan had no hat to remove, but nodded to Mary over Larry's neck, his fair chin bobbing in the thick, dark brown mane as if he had suddenly sprouted a beard. Mary smiled her big wide smile over her splendid teeth at the sight, and the two girls looked with joy on Stan and Mary's delight in each other.

"Come somewhere with me," Patty whispered, as if Stan and Mary should be left alone. Patty turned towards the house holding Madge's hand in one of hers, with the other across her mouth in acute embarrassment. She was taking Madge into their shabby, untidy old place after the grand Rossmore house! Where would she take her?

To the kitchen, where Joyce was washing the dinner things in slapdash fashion, anxious to be done and Malcolm and Bernie were wiping up, it being their turn to do it? If Patty had been visiting the Rossmores, she would most likely have been taken to Madge's room, kept neat by Jessie, the bed beautifully made and the latest holy pictures displayed on the chest of drawers or bedside table, Madge having told her this is where she put them. Patty felt great shame that hers could only be tucked into the frame of a picture of the Sacred Heart on the bedroom wall. She always thought the face of Jesus took on a wistful look when this happened, as if He were losing credibility. Patty shared the room with Joyce and Nina, she and Nina in a double bed and Joyce in a single one. They were made, but the dressing table would be littered and the one chair piled with clothes, even shoes, not with a cushion on a lovely slant as she imagined Madge's bedroom chair. She knew what she would do. Take Madge to the good room! Mary had washed the quilt after Mrs Jussep's feet marked it when she had died there. Madge would know she didn't sleep there, but there would be no need to mention this, and they could sit on the two chairs, and Patty, although it would be difficult, could avoid looking at the bed.

But reaching the sitting room, Patty saw the door of the good room was closed, not wide open as it always used to be, showing off the brass bed and the big hooked rug and the lamp with the pale pink base and pearly white chimney her mother would never allow anyone to light.

"We'll sit here," Patty said, taking one half of the cane seat in the sitting room, pleased with the nicely plumped cushions, though wondering if Madge thought the patchwork terribly old fashioned. Madge saw the picture.

"Exactly the same as ours!" she cried, writhing her hands on her lap, fighting to control her excitement.

"Is it? Is it too? Is it truly?" Patty said, fearful that Madge's generous heart might be making this up.

"It is," Madge said solemnly. "Cross my heart and hope to die. It is the very, very same."

They both glanced at the closed door at the word "die".

Madge spread her pleated skirt with downcast eyes and Patty did the best she could with an old serge tunic handed down from Joyce, worn now over a grey jumper, skimpy and badly matted with constant washing. Patty wondered if it could be improved with a belt, if she could find one. Madge, pink of face with her freckles turned a rusty brown, looked pointedly to the doorway leading to the veranda, keeping the door of the good room well out of her vision. She wanted to know Patty's feelings about her mother and those of all the others. Were they still crying on and off? Everything looked normal, except that Mrs Jussep was missing. Madge had never seen Mary smile so wide. It was terrible not to know, but she couldn't ask.

"I should have brought my jacks," she said, now looking at the rug in front of the fireplace. More shame invaded Patty. Her jacks were in a bad way, two of the five with sharp edges liable to cut you when you came to the part of the game where you picked them up from between spread fingers.

"I've thought of something!" Madge said getting to her feet. "We'll go to the creek and get us a set!"

Find smooth round stones just right for jacks, in the creek bed with Madge? Nothing could be better! They would slip away before Joyce saw them, for she considered herself in charge of the house now and might find something for Patty to do, humiliating as it would be with Madge there.

"Come on!" she cried, hand out. They took the way that lost sight of the house almost at once, plunging down an embankment to the cartwheel tracks that ran from the cowbails and dairy to the main road. Crossing the tracks they tore down the slope so steep you had to run, you were liable to tip over at any other pace. Patty led the way, sure of her footing through a spreading blackberry bush, hopping from rock to rock, around which the bush rambled, and looking back to see that Madge was following. They scrambled onto a log fallen across the creek and together jumped onto a dry patch of the creek bed. Madge was in charge now, digging with her shoe into a crusty edge of stones bordering a shallow water hole, picking up and pocketing any that were likely jacks. Patty with no pockets had to hold hers in a bulging hand.

"Let's spread them out somewhere and pick a set," Madge said. They found a place, a patch of short grass, a new growth which had sprung up under a low growing wattle defying winter. They had to break the ends of several branches to fit underneath and sit, one on either side of the patch, a small soft green rug spread by nature for the very purpose of a game of jacks. This discovery shone simultaneously in the eyes of Madge and Patty.

"You go first," Patty said, remembering Madge was the guest.

The eyes of the two of them following the flight of the first stone thrown upwards caught sight of two figures on a grassy slope on the opposite side of the creek, a couple of hundreds yards away.

It was Stan and Mary sitting in the sun with Larry and Mary's grey, named Jock, behind them, reins trailing on the ground.

"Oh, look," breathed Madge. "Can they see us, do you think?"

The two of them slid deeper under the wattle. The feathery fronds tickled their faces but they got a good view of the reclining figures, with the sun behind making a red brown fire of Mary's hair and a lighter one of Stan's.

"They can't see us," Patty breathed.

"What are they saying, I wonder?" said Madge. "Oh, I wish we could hear!"

Stan was telling Mary he didn't intend going back to university. He hated the course, lectures were agony. He wanted to be a farmer, not a doctor. He slid down on the grass, and curved an arm over his head as if he were in bed and getting ready for sleep. Madge and Patty watched fascinated, half expecting Mary to slip down too and fit herself into the hollow of his body. But she put her hands farther back behind her, both supporting her and pinning down the reins of Larry and Jock, who were starting to fidget.

"I'm supposed to feel nerves with my fingers," Stan said, "real nerves. I can feel nothing." Mary saw his hands smallish, with short fingers twitching in the agony he felt at their uselessness. She wanted to take hold of one of them but was embarrassed about her own hands. She never seemed able to wash them clean of milk after stripping cows twice a day. A sticky substance lingered between her fingers despite the thorough scrubbings. When she went to dances her pleasure in the dance was spoiled by wondering all the time if her partner was offended by her hands. She formed the habit of jamming her fingers together, causing the young Cobargo men, several with an eye on Mary, to want to inspect her hand to see if she had something wedged there.

So now, much as she wanted to, she couldn't take Stan's hand, just rub one of hers on the grass between them. Through half-closed eyes Stan was admiring her long fingers and clean nails cut level with her finger tips, for he hated the new fashion of long nails on women and hoped it never reached Cobargo.

Stan, with his eyes on Mary's hand, said she was the first he had told about his plan for abandoning his medical

22

course. When she turned the hand over he took hold of it and she began to squeeze the fingers together, but he threaded his fingers between hers, so dry and cool she was filled with envy and mortification. Gradually she loosened the fingers, and when she freed her hand and clasped both around her knees, he left his lying on the grass almost as if it didn't belong to him. His eyes were nearly shut. Was he crying? Mary felt tears prick at her own eyes. She began thinking of her mother. Stan would open his eyes and take her hand in a moment and say he was sorry Mrs Jussep had died. He did not go to the funeral, so he hadn't yet spoken to her of it. Mary moved throwing her long nearly straight hair down her back. Stan put a hand out and twisted a fistful, without opening his eyes.

"You have the loveliest hair of any I've ever seen," he said.

"I couldn't have," Mary said, although believing him. "All those girls you see in Sydney!"

"There's some in the course," Stan said. "One has this great awful moustache."

Mary with her lovely smile was grateful for the moustache.

Stan put out a hand and touched her waist. He kept his eyes shut.

"I have to tell her, Mary," he said. "My mother."

Mary went stiff. His mother. Mrs Rossmore with those lips she hardly ever put together. She looked briefly and swiftly on Stan and saw his lips were folded back, showing a gold filling between his two front teeth. Tom needed to go to the dentist. Mrs Jussep, just before she died, had been trying to arrange for the two of them to go to Bega and have some fillings done, staying overnight with a married cousin. Mary's face warmed. She had started to think of Stan at home all the time. With him at the dances and tennis matches. Stan and Mary, Mary and Stan. Stan Rossmore and Mary Jussep, Mrs Stan Rossmore, Mary Rossmore.

Stan opened his eyes and saw the deep pink of her cheek. "Mary!" he said. "How will I tell her?"

Mary saw her own mother, her face like grey mud in a creek bed long dried up, her hair a different grey, the face dead, the hair still with life there. Looking over the paddocks, some pale chocolate squares ready for spring planting, Mary found it hard to believe all this was still here and her mother gone. She jumped up rather quickly and put both arms over Jock's neck to climb on. When she was turning Jock she saw Stan mounting Larry with a sulky face.

"They're going," Madge breathed to Patty. "Where?"

"Somewhere to kiss passionately," Patty breathed back. Madge tore a piece of bark from the tree and chewed it, then scrubbed her mouth free of the black and bitter taste.

"We might find some gum to chew," Patty said, for the wattles often oozed a thick, pale substance encased in a crust that had to be picked with a sharp fingernail to release the gum, which was neither sweet nor savoury like a flavourless honey. Madge shook her head and scrambled into the clear, as if dismissing gum chewing as something belonging to a childish past. Her small face was tense, her chin up; she was striding away ahead of Patty who had to run to keep up. She put out a hand and took hold of the hem of Madge's coat.

"What will your mother and father say, do you think?" Patty said.

Madge dropped her head and slowed down. "She musn't know," she said.

"If there is a wedding she'll have to know," Patty said. Madge shook her head quite violently. She had a vision of her mother's little sausage lips parted and her eyes quite wild.

24

"Madge!" Patty cried urgently, for Madge was hurrying again along the creek bank and Patty had the terrible feeling she was hurrying out of her life as well. They crossed the creek on the log and up the hill, Madge sure of her footing now, Patty following, unsure of everything, most of all Madge.

"Will you tell your mother?" Patty asked, aware that it was a foolish question, for Madge had already answered more or less.

Then suddenly Patty stood still, holding out her arms to balance herself. In a moment she collapsed to the ground folding her legs under her and clinging to the tops of tussocks. Madge looked back and sat too, then slid down near her.

"I know," she said. "Your mother." Patty lifted the hem of her tunic and scrubbed her face, only caring a little that she had no handkerchief.

Madge bowed her head until it touched her knees around which her arms were wrapped.

"Don't cry," she said to Patty's neck, which was like the rim of a frail white china cup above her collar.

Patty cried on. Madge put a hand to her back running the tips of her fingers down the tunic. Then Patty flung herself around and lay her head against Madge's coat, one button cutting into her forehead and another scraping her chin.

This is how they were for a minute or so, like two abandoned puppies, separated from a pack of wilder, stronger dogs and uncertain whether to take up the struggle to rejoin them.

Then Madge called out "Look!" and Patty lifted her head and there two or three hills away were Stan and Mary bringing the cows home for the afternoon milking. Stan was behind the herd and Mary on the lower side. Madge and Patty watched, urging them with their small beating hearts to swing their horses and come together. But Stan moved Larry around to the higher side, and Mary turned Jock to ride where Stan had been. Stan then urged Larry into a trot until well clear of the herd and several yards in front. The pummelling hearts of Madge and Patty said they had quarrelled. Perhaps not. Stan stood in the stirrups and flung an arm across his head in a large wave. Mary did not wave back. His back was to her so it would be a wasted effort.

Oh, gallop up to him, gallop up to him, cried Patty's heart. But if Mary had any such thoughts, the black cow Helen took charge of them, and decided then to break away and with her silly canter make for the clump of quince trees. Mary sent Jock flying after her.

"Quick!" Madge said, scrambling to her feet and pulling her away up the slope. "Stan is going! He might go without me!"

Patty reached the cartwheel tracks first and helped hoist Madge up by the shoulders of her coat. Madge wriggled the coat back into position again and flew ahead. "Stan might forget me!" she cried.

They saw him talking to Mr Jussep near the back gate to the house. Madge, as if still in fear of being left behind, ran faster, throwing her arms over her head like a swimmer.

Stan pulled her up onto Larry and she was crushed behind him, closing her eyes in her small glowing face as if the visit had now reached a peak of perfection. Mr Jussep stood back courteously to acknowledge the departure and Madge, when Larry moved off, flapped an arm in Patty's direction.

They rode in silence until within sight of the Rossmores' house. Madge freed her mouth from against Stan's warm and quivering back.

"Will you marry Mary Jussep?" she asked.

26

Stan kicked Larry into a canter and Madge needed to put her face back and cling tighter.

"I'm marrying no one!" Stan threw over his shoulder.

Madge saw behind her shut eyes Mrs Rossmore's little sausage lips come together and her eyelids fall.

It was like a window closing suddenly on a celebration inside a room, for fear some of the jubilation might escape.

3   The Little Chest

One of the general stores in Cobargo was owned by Andy
Colburn, who had brought his family from Sydney in the
mid-20s and had taken over a house in the main street.
The front veranda was so close to the street, the posts
still bore the marks of bridle reins where farmers had tied
their horses when they rode to town when the place was
first settled.

Andy had turned the front parlour into a shop selling
whatever he could come by, and this included some of
the family's furniture since the reduced space gave them
a surplus.

A fine mahogany chest of drawers that had been Mrs
Colburn's mother's was sold for three pounds to a man
named Schaefer who worked at the post office and
occupied a house bought by the government for the
married postal assistant.

The eldest Colburn girl, a schoolmate of the eldest
Schaefer girl, came often to the Schaefers' house to play.
She sometimes brought a younger sister, Elsie, who would
invariably point to the chest and say it used to be theirs.
The child, although only seven, wore an expression that
said the chest had no right in the Schaefers' house, where
it was set off with a doily and a sepia picture of
grandparents taken on their wedding day.

"This part is the brown toffee and this part is the creamy
toffee," Elsie said with large accusing eyes, referring to
the wood, for there was a smudging of a lighter colour
at the edge of the drawers and around the knobs. Elsie
had loved the chest, and when it went had to be content

with a butter box for her clothes, one of four put together by Mr Colburn. The boxes had a curtain in front made by Mrs Colburn, who silently mourned the loss of the chest too while she constantly tidied the children's clothes, for they jumbled everything together when they took a garment out.

Mrs Schaefer thought about moving the chest from the end of the hall to somewhere less conspicuous, where a door could shut it away from view. But it fitted beautifully between the parlour and the kitchen doors and was the first thing you saw when you opened the front door. It was a centre piece for the whole house.

Mrs Schaefer thought about banning the little Colburn girl from the house. But this gave rise to complications, for the Schaefers were Methodists like the Colburns, and Mrs Colburn took a Sunday school class with the Schaefers in it. It was feasible that they might be deprived, not so much of religious instruction, but bounty at the annual Sunday school picnic, if dissension arose between the two families.

So the little chest stayed where it was and little Elsie Colburn continued to rush for it when she went to the Schaefers, and sometimes put her arms around one end and lay her face on the top.

"I'll box her ears, I really will, if she keeps this up!" Mrs Schaefer said. Mr Schaefer, picking his teeth after dinner, said the solution was a simple one.

"Give her a good kick up the arse," he said. He was a fattish young man, only thirty, with four children already. He had a big face with a poor complexion and thick sandy hair. He was known as Sandy Schaefer, rather than Keith, his given name.

Mrs Schaefer was a very particular housekeeper, sweeping and scrubbing and shining her house, washing curtains when they showed the slightest sign of soiling, and she was fanatical about cleaning windows. When they moved to the house, the first thing Mrs Schaefer looked for was the height of the windows from the ground. When she found she could reach the highest with the help of a carpenter's stool, she was overjoyed on two counts. She was in control of the windows and could keep them scrupulously clean, and she had insisted on the stool's going with the furniture, although Keith (she did not call him Sandy) had wanted it tossed in with the rubbish they had left in the corner of the yard in the old place for the succeeding postal assistant to deal with.

Sandy was not a man to work around the place, with the excuse that it wasn't his own. He liked to play sport, and belonged to the local tennis and cricket clubs. He helped organize the football, since he was not fit enough to be on the team, and he went fishing and shooting when farmers invited him.

Mrs Schaefer was left at home with the children, and would often, on a Saturday afternoon, fill a large dish with hot soapy water and wash every piece of good china and glass she possessed, although none of it had been used since its last washing. Another of her Saturday afternoon jobs was to polish the little chest. She took everything out and removed the three long drawers and two smaller ones at the top, and polished each individually, with particular attention to the wooden knobs, using a cloth stretched between her hands to give them such a lustre, they were like eight little lamps gleaming in the dark shadows at the end of the hall.

Elsie Colburn or no Elsie Colburn, Mrs Schaefer thought when she was finished, there was no other place for the chest but there.

There was another fairly regular Saturday afternoon activity for Mrs Schaefer. Providing the glass and china were washed and stacked on clean, fresh paper in cupboards, the house was without dust, and of course the little chest shined, she would put the smallest Schaefer in the pram, and with another clinging to the side ready to go in when his legs grew tired, and with two more straggling behind, she would join the crowd of spectactors at the tennis court.

She kept a fairly frugal table at home and avoided as far as possible contributing to the fare for afternoon tea at the tennis. Cooking messed up her stove and kitchen table, and she would rather spend money on sandsoap and washing tablets than on butter and sugar.

Most of Cobargo knew this, and on this particular Saturday afternoon she arrived at the court right on afternoon tea time. Foolishly and fruitlessly she slowed her steps to a creep to try and encourage the children, round eyed at the sight of food, to hold back too.

Sandy was playing at the end of the court near the wire gate that let his family in, and was losing his match.

"You bring any tucker?" he asked, giving a ball a great whack to send it down for the server.

Mrs Schaefer shook her head.

"A pity you can't eat soap and drink turpentine, then we'd live like fighting cocks!" Schaefer said.

There was a titter from the tennis shed and those who gossiped freely about Mrs Schaefer's domestic habits blushed in their guilt. Now that it was openly acknowledged by he who should know best, they wanted to rush to Mrs Schaefer's defence.

One of the women players in a tennis dress that showed knees like large uncooked buns held up a plate of scones.

"A scone for the little ones?" she called out. The small Schaefers nodded with shining eyes, which they averted from the mounds of cakes they preferred.

Sandy, his match over, came off the court and took a seat opposite his family, Mrs Schaefer having sat

31

gingerly on the edge of the plank near the exposed end of the shed, as if this showed she was not there to eat.

"Only tea for me, Daphne," Sandy said to the young woman piling a plate with sandwiches and a variety of cakes obviously intended for him.

"After all those rallies only tea!" cried the scone-bearing woman, halted on her way to the line up of Schaefer children. (Sandy had lost nearly all the rallies.)

"We had dinner," he said, his pale blue eyes in fiery rims fixed on his family. Then he stood, and gathering up the balls near his feet, slogged them hard with his racquet to the service end of the court. "Whiting and beeswax and washing blue, but it was dinner!" he said, the fury of the flying balls emphasizing his words.

The older Schaefer children, wriggling to crush their backs against the wall, asked with their eyes that no one believe this. But they felt a dryness in their mouths like the powdery taste of whiting.

Schaefer swallowed his tea, for it had cooled quickly in the wintry air, and set his cup down on one of the folding card tables holding the food and tea, making it shove other plates and cups aside for a space. They rattled angrily in reply. His children watched in fascination while he pushed towards the centre of the table a fat, uncut sponge cake and fussily wiped his fingers clean of the cream they would have gladly licked. The woman with the scones screwed herself until her back was to the Schaefer children. She put the scones down, frowning, and found something else to do.

Little Elsie Colburn looked on in pain. She saw Mrs Schaefer's face was very red, showing the tears up more. The two older Schaefer children, both girls, left their mother's side and went and stood backs pressed to the outer side of the wall out of everyone's sight. The wind whipped their skirts around their thighs and made their eyes water too.

Jack Hines, the president of the club, brought his hands together like a clap of baby thunder. "We should get the doubles going!" he said.

"We should eat!" said his wife Hilda. "For goodness sake!" She took up plates of food to pass them around. Sandy moved his feet and his body with his eyes on the court, to allow her to offer the food to a knot of shy players from the opposing team clustered around the net post.

Elsie Colburn, under cover of her mother preparing to go on the court, slipped into the place the Schaefer girls left beside their mother.

She went with Mrs Schaefer and the children just after the doubles started.

The children walked crushed close to the pram and Mrs Schaefer cried openly, with tears running under the neck of her dress.

Inside the house Elsie flew around, bringing a clean napkin for Mrs Schaefer to change the baby on the kitchen table, and then snapping kindling wood into little pieces to help Mrs Schaefer get the stove fire going.

Mrs Schaefer mopped her face on the dry part of the baby's soiled napkin and that was the end of her crying.

Elsie did not go near the little chest.

And hardly ever did as long as the Schaefers were in Cobargo.

4　The Brighter Arnold

Fred Rossmore had the largest general store in Cobargo and was a cousin of Bert, Frank and Harry's.

He had learned the business under his father, who had a store in Petersham, a suburb of Sydney. The family lived above the shop, and Fred as a school boy spent holidays with his cousins in Cobargo. When Fred's father, in his sixties, decided to sell out, he gave Fred a share of the profits. Fred, then in his thirties and married to Betty, whom he had met through the local church fellowship, left the city and opened what became the main Cobargo store.

It was formerly an abandoned blacksmith's shop on the junction of two roads leading in and out of the town. Fred had it pulled down and rebuilt, backing over the Cobargo Creek which flowed through the town, dividing it into two parts. The store followed the angle of the road, which turned sharply when it crossed the bridge and ran towards the coast. The grocery section looked across at Andy Colburn's store facing Cobargo's main street. The drapery faced the road to the sea, fourteen miles away, and looked on the side of the only bank in town, also facing the main street.

Fred had one seat placed under his drapery window and another around the corner, facing his bowser, for he was the first in Cobargo to sell petrol when the first cars came to town.

The seats had little use except by school children. Fred was a Catholic, so children from the convent school felt they had the right to the better seat with a display of dress materials, men's and women's shoes and hats, buttons, laces and ribbons at their backs behind the glass.

The public children (called public pimps by the convents, who in turn had the name convent whackers) had to be content with a wall at their backs and spilled petrol at their feet. Fred did not approve of this discrimination. Busy as he was in the shop, he would sometimes come out and stand between the two seats, trying to draw the children together in a talk.

He had little success. Being interested in sport, he raised the subject of challenge matches between the schools. The publics favoured the idea of tennis, because there was a court at their school, but the convents, without one, shook their heads and shuffled their feet.

"Basketball then?" Fred asked, for both schools had posts in the playground.

The convents said "Yes, yes!" for they played regularly, but the publics exchanged knowing looks and kicked their school cases. Their basketball ground was overgrown, and the teacher who had played the game with skill had moved away.

Fred didn't pursue the subject of football or cricket. That would exclude girls, and he was fond of them. He and Betty were childless, a great disappointment there. But Betty had been a bookkeeper in her single days and, unencumbered with a young family, unlike most other wives in Cobargo, she spent several mornings a week in the shop working on the accounts.

Fred indulged in a dream of having a family, say, three girls (for him) and a boy for Betty, for he believed women favoured sons. When there were only girls on the seats, or mainly girls, waiting for lifts to their farms, or taking a spell before setting out on foot, Fred put his hands in his pockets and stared down on their young knees coming out from tunic hems while he talked to them.

He found to his surprise the girls on the public seat more to his liking. The Arnold girls in particular. They were olive skinned with thick dark bobbed hair cut with a fringe across the forehead. They were so alike strangers took them for twins, but they had been born eleven months apart. Both were in the same class at school, to the chagrin of the eldest, Nancy. Nola was the younger.

Their similar appearance gave Fred something to talk about this wet Wednesday afternoon when they were the only children on the seats. They were there hopeful of a lift home in the mail car that went in and out of Cobargo every day except Sunday. In fine weather it went through just before school came out, but on wet days, with progress slowed on a slippery road, it could be up to ten minutes late. The Arnolds, if spotted by the driver on Rossmore's corner, would be invited aboard. Their farm was three miles out along the Bega road.

Fred was teasing Nola now, accusing her of eating more porridge than Nancy because she was slightly heavier, and the girls giggled, but in a distracted way, looking through the rain towards the post office where the mail car stopped first. Fred swung around and looked too, up the deserted street, for the weather had kept the crowd from packing around the post office door, closed while the mail was being sorted.

"It sneaked away on us, I think," Fred said, frowning and bunching his hands in his trouser pockets, rippling his knuckles so that the eyes of Nancy and Nola were drawn there.

He waggled his fists, causing the cloth of his trousers to stretch.

The edges of the buttons on his fly were suddenly exposed.

Nancy and Nola looked away, red like the bowser in front of their eyes.

The rain began to come down sharply, and they needed to move their feet, for it was sprinkled liberally around the base of the bowser like someone peppering a plate of food. The Arnolds, even in their anxiety about getting home, watched in fascination the spilled oil, showing rich purple, green and blue as the rain bounced off it.

Fred sat on the seat beside them and watched too. He had a long face and a slightly jutting chin, which he pointed first up the main street, then to the right along the road leading to the coast. His house, a modest place into which he and Betty had moved (then bought) when he came to Cobargo, was a few hundred yards away, just on the rise. Betty kept a fine garden, which, with the store accounts, was her main interest.

Fred blinked his eyes, owlish behind his glasses, and the Arnold girls blinked too, and looked at their feet suspended above the water now running under the seat. They saw Fred's large thick-soled shoes untroubled by it. It raced to their edges then ran back as if afraid of them.

Then Fred stood up and looked back at the shop where young Percy Brothers, the fortunate boy of fifteen, chosen by Fred to work for him when his assistant of long standing, Ted Parker, performed the dreadful deed of opening a small general store of his own (on the wages Fred paid him and the experience Fred gave him), was sweeping out the storeroom. Pearl Prosser, equally fortunate but much older, was tidying drawers of underwear in the drapery.

"It's wet, and quiet in the shop," Fred said. "I might drive you home."

He put his head to one side to see the effect of this on the Arnold girls. Nancy looked to Nola (the brighter Arnold) to confirm that this was acceptable (and real). Nola looked to Nancy, the eldest, to thank their benefactor, as their parents would have expected. They both examined their shoes, and were surprised that Fred was examining his too.

"Wait here," Fred said. "I'll tell young Perce."

Young Perce came grinning to the door when he heard the news, and Fred left to get his car from the garage next door to his house. Betty, with a colander of broad beans on her hips, went from the garden to the front gate to see the back wheels of the Ford moving carefully down the wet road. Fred glimpsed the top half of her body bent over the gate in his rear vision mirror and realized he could have asked her to come for the run but didn't want her to agree.

He worked up a frown, due to a feeling of guilt, and Percy, still in the doorway excited about the unusual turn of events (putting him in charge of the shop for the first time in mid-afternoon), thought the frown was for him and rushed back behind the counter.

Fred opened the car door in front and the Arnolds climbed in. Nola was next to Fred and that pleased him. If he had a choice to make on the matter he liked Nola slightly more than Nancy. She was a little rounder, like a brown bear, cuddly, and with eyes that seemed to know in advance what was on your mind. They were a treacly brown, and so were Nancy's, but the treacle of Nola's eyes appeared to have been in the sun and, melting there, it had acquired a softness, while the treacle of Nancy's eyes had stayed in the tin, with nothing to see deeper than the dark and heavy surface.

The Ford set the bridge rattling as they went across. The brown water, swirling under it, was beginning to rise already, an indication that there had been heavy rain in the mountains.

"Ooooh," said Fred with pursed lips and an indrawn breath, sharing a fearful prediction with the girls that the bridge might be covered by morning. Their chests felt tight

38

as drums while the car negotiated the bridge without falling through, and they marvelled at the unconcern on Fred's face.

He shifted gears to climb the hill past the last clump of houses, where surprise showed on the faces of women wandering their verandas, looking at the rain, seeing the small black heads of Nancy and Nola under Fred's elbow.

He needed to change gears again soon and slid a hand with the gear stick along Nola's thigh, causing her tunic to rumple up and Nola to pull it down in great haste. Fred smiled past Nola to Nancy, who felt she had to smile back, and Nola put a smile on her face too, feeling troubled that she might have offended Fred. When he changed gears again she would be ready, she decided, with her tunic pinned firmly under her leg.

But she wasn't, or rather the ruse did not work. Fred changed gears about half a mile from the Arnold's gate, a grinding elaborate change, and Nola's tunic went with the knob of the gear stick so high, the mole on her thigh was exposed in all its shame.

"See that!" Fred said, the Ford wobbling on the road, for he temporarily lost control. He decided to let the wobble end in a stop by the roadside. He looked down on Nola's thigh covered now by her tunic. She was red of face and staring ahead through the windscreen, un-hopeful of any help from Nancy.

Fred leaned back against the seat, and draped his arms across the wheel.

"What I would like to know," Fred said, pausing but serious, "have you both got one in the same spot?"

He frowned on them, as if he were an examiner and the examination of great importance.

Nola put her hands between her knees and giggled a little with her head to one side, raising a shoulder to touch an ear. Nancy lifted her chin and her still eyes and gazed directly into Fred's face. By George, Fred thought, she would be a beauty one day! Her jawbone was more defined than Nola's, her skin smoother and creamier, her hands, holding her crossed knees, a woman's hands.

Nola was the brighter Arnold, everyone said. It was obvious to him Nancy was overlooked. Fred had no intention of overlooking her.

"Are you both eleven years old now?" Fred said.

Nola answered, sliding her red lips back to show little fat teeth. Were Nancy's teeth the same? He would get her to smile. "Nancy's thirteen, I'm twelve," Nola said. "In June I'll be thirteen too. For four weeks we'll both be thirteen."

"Who is the boss for those four weeks?" Fred said with his eyes over Nola's head on Nancy.

Nancy turned her face to look at the branches of the gum tree under which the car had stopped. She saw the rain had left a shine as if someone had polished them, and she saw too the leaves quiver downwards like eyes laden with tears. The trunk of the tree looked like a leg in a pale grey stocking, and the branch from the fork like the other leg, raised white and waiting for its stocking.

Nancy swung her head towards Fred. "We could walk from here," she said. "It's not too far now."

Nola didn't want to. The car was warm and dry and she had never ridden in the front seat of one before. She put her legs out straight in front of her, holding them stiffly to indicate she had no intention of walking.

"The rain has stopped," Nancy said. It had eased to a drizzle.

"We could get out and have a look to see how the creek has come up," Fred said. He got out on his side and went around and opened the door for Nancy. She slid out, without even a cursory glance at their school case on the back seat. Fred shut the door smartly and for a moment his large long face seemed to fill the opening as he looked in on Nola.

"Stay cosy there, if you'd rather," Fred said. "We won't be long." He took hold of Nancy's hand, looking up the road as if they were on a busy street, but wondering if she might pull her hand away, and ready to grip it hard if she tried. It lay passive in his, as if she were unaware of it there, so he squeezed it and he felt, or thought he felt, a slight curling of her fingers. He squeezed again to say he was pleased she was leaving her hand in his and liking it. He had to let go while he pulled the wires of the fence apart for her to climb through. He flung a leg across like a boy, letting the wire caress his crotch before it flew up taut again. She walked ahead through the long grass and he looked back to see the small head of Nola in the car. Even from the distance Fred saw a question in her eyes.

"She'll stay there alright?" Fred said. "Not take off home?"

"She loves riding in cars," Nancy said. "Even when they're stopped."

"I thought so," Fred said.

Closer to the creek there was a wall of rocks, one rising well above the others, with a small square platform on top. Children scaled the side with ease, but it was awash now with rivulets of water shining brown, and Nancy put a hand up as if she might stop the flow.

"You'll slip if you try to climb it," Fred said.

As if she didn't hear, she made her way around the base, climbing part of the way up to avoid a sprawl of blackberry bush. Fred, unable to follow, looked mournfully on his big shoes. When he looked up there was her black hair and pale oval face appearing over the top of the rock, followed by her body.

In a moment she stood reared against the sky. The wind

flicked at the hem of her tunic, and she linked her hands behind her back, pinning it there but allowing it to dance and billow above her knees in front. She looked up and down the creek, which was swollen with rushing brown water, carrying sticks and branches urgently along, flinging off foam that formed into tiny islands and raced with an urgency too. Nancy appeared fascinated by the fence on the other side, three parts submerged, the posts blackened by the rain, lined up crookedly, like people watching a race, so still they might be dead.

"Look down here!" Fred called and put both hands to the top of his fly.

Nancy looked, folding her arms across her waist, allowing her tunic to billow and blow at will. The fascination she had for the creek and the fence posts was transferred to Fred's hands. Her chin jerked down with every button he opened.

Something white contrasted with black. Flesh or a piece of clothing? Nancy wanted to raise her eyes and look for a piece of matching cloth somewhere else on Fred. But her eyes stayed there where Fred's hands were poised to tear his fly wide open. Inside her chest she began to whimper like a new born pup hating the world, not wanting to be part of it.

But in a moment there was a noise, unmistakable, from the road.

Nancy raised her head and swung it around.

"Dad!" she cried, and looking carefully at her feet, made her way down the rock and waded with big steps through the grass towards the fence. Fred screwed his body towards the creek to button his fly. Then he walked briskly and straight of back, smoothing at the front of his clothes, appearing to remove any twig or grass seed, but checking that his fly was fully closed, and hailed Mr Arnold as he climbed the fence.

"It's coming up fast, Leo," he said. "It's worth a look!"

Mr Arnold turned his horse to meet Fred, the horse walking so slowly it hardly needed to change pace when Nancy scrambled on, with a foot on the toe of her father's large boot to help her.

Nola was out of the car by this time, not forgetting the school case from the back (she was the brighter one), and across to climb via Mr Arnold's other boot to sit in front. In spite of the encumbrances, which included two dry coats under his macintosh for his daughters, Mr Arnold was able to lean down and shake Fred's hand. His face glistened like the oilskin of his coat in gratitude for Fred's kindly deed. There was just a shade of embarrassment there, in respect of the Arnolds giving their custom to Ted Parker, on Mrs Arnold's insistence, for she was a Presbyterian like Ted.

Nancy put her arms around her father's waist, but when she felt the buckle of his belt where her hands met and the ridge of his fly, she dropped her arms to her sides.

She could ride quite well without hanging on.

Nancy closed her eyes when they moved off, letting the horse's flesh ripple into her flesh. She felt rocked, as if in a cradle, a gentle jerking rhythm. Worth a look, worth a look, worth a look, worth a look, she said to herself, keeping time with the rocking.

She saw in her mind the brown racing water, the floating twigs and foam, and the black, watching fence posts.

Anything else she refused to see.

5 The Christmas Parcel

Christmas in 1935 would have been a dreary affair for the Churchers but for a parcel, more like a small crate, sent from the eldest, Maxine, in Sydney.

Maxine was eighteen, and had been away two years. The first Christmas she sent a card, and the Churchers were delighted with this and stood it against the milk jug on the table for Christmas dinner, which was baked stuffed rabbit, for they were plentiful, but money was not.

The next Christmas Eve the driver of the mail car gave several long blasts on the horn passing the paddocks where the Churcher children were standing, spindly legged among the saplings and tussocks, trying to invent a game to ward off disappointment that there would be no presents.

Their mother had warned them. Sometimes she cried softly as she told them, sometimes she was angry and blamed their father for his inability to find work, sometimes she was optimistic, indulging in a spasm of house cleaning, washing curtains and bed clothes, whitewashing the fireplace ready to fill with gum tips, and scrubbing the floorboards until they came up a grey white, like sand on some untouched beach.

Who knows, something might turn up, she would say as she worked. Her better off sisters in distant towns might send a ten shilling note in their Christmas cards, which would buy lollies, cordial, oranges, bananas, and raisins for a pudding, and be damned to Fred Rossmore who would expect it paid off the account, owing now for half a year.

The clean house gave her spirits a lift, as if they were cleansed too, and she would finish off the day by bathing all the children in a tub in front of the stove, adding a kettle of hot water with each one, washing their heads as well, and sending them out to sit on the edge of the veranda and share a towel, very threadbare, to dry.

Their old skimpy shirts and dresses were usually not fastened properly; it didn't matter, it would be bedtime soon.

The young Churchers would feel lighter in spirit too, sniffing at the soap lingering on them, although it was the same Mrs Churcher used to wash the clothes. They would look forward to fried scones for tea, and some stewed peaches, a small greenish variety, sour near the stone, eaten bravely while trying to avoid thinking of the sugar and cream that would make them so much more palatable.

Mr and Mrs Churcher were sitting on the woodheap when the mail car driver blew the horn through a cloud of dust.

"And a Merry Christmas to you too!" Mrs Churcher shouted. She was in a black mood, and Mr Churcher feared it and feared for the children, soon to trail home, not giving in readily to the futility of hanging stockings. While she angrily shuffled a foot among the chips, he looked at the children like stringy samplings themselves, some like small scarecrows, for they were playing a game with arms outstretched, their ragged old shapeless clothes flapping in the wind that had sprung up, kindly cooling the air after one of the hottest days of the summer.

Mr Churcher watched as one of them suddenly tore off to the track that led to the road. It was Lionel, racing hard and soon lost to sight where the track disappeared into a patch of myrtle bush. Mr Churcher was surprised at the energy with which Lionel ran. He worried about the children's not getting enough to eat, but perhaps they were doing better than he thought. Anyone who could run like that after tearing about all day must be suitably fuelled. He felt a little happier, and looked at Mrs Churcher, surprised she was not sharing this feeling. She looked over the top of their grey slab house at some puffed up clouds, but not seeing them, he was sure, for the clouds had a milky transparency and he foolishly thought they would have a softening effect upon her. But her face wore a cloud of another kind, dark and thunderous. There was mutiny in her dark eyes, creased narrowly, not wide and soft, not even her body was soft, but gone tight in the old morrocain dress, practically the only one she owned.

"I'll chop the head off the wyandotte," Mr Churcher said. He was proud of his knowledge of poultry, and they had a cross breeding in their meagre fowl run, comprising cast offs from other, fussier, farmers who pitied the impoverished state of the Churchers.

They rented their old place from the Heffernans, who had built it as their first home when they settled on the land fifty years earlier. Heffernan bought an adjoining property as fortunes improved and used the old place to run cattle. Since the house wasn't fenced in it was difficult, due to wandering steers, to grow produce to feed the eight children, or seven, now that Maxine had gone.

Mr Churcher was in constant conflict with Jim Heffernan. He (Mr Churcher) considered the five shillings a week rent unreasonable; he was actually doing the Heffernans a favour living there in a caretaking capacity, stopping the house from falling into ruin. He never tired of pointing out the work he put into the fowl run, although he had actually stolen some wire netting from a bundle delivered to the roadside for the Heffernans to extend their kitchen garden. Mr Churcher saw the heap

46

and sent Lionel for pliers to snip a length from a roll, which he was sure would escape the notice of the Heffernans.

Mrs Churcher was distressed to see the children a witness to theft, but put those feelings to one side when she saw Mr Churcher had made a good job of the pen and more eggs appeared, since the fowls did not continue to lay in obscure places like inside blackberry bushes and up hollow logs.

Mr Churcher was thinking now of making some reference to the fowl pen to expose (once again) a more commendable side of his character and get him into his wife's good graces, although he did not think there was much chance of this. He took up the axe and spat on the blade, rubbing the spittle along the edge.

"I'll chop off its head before they get here," he said, seeing the ragged little army, still several hundred yards off.

"It'll be tough as an old boot," Mrs Churcher said looking at his. Her own feet were bare.

"It'll make good gravy and there's plenty of 'taters," he said, injecting cheer into his voice.

Mrs Churcher was going to say the dripping to roast the fowl in was needed for their bread, for they had not eaten butter in weeks, when a shrill cry made her look towards the myrtle patch on the rise.

Lionel came screaming out of it, like a brown leaf bowling along, aided by a strong wind, his feet beating so hard upon the earth, Mr and Mrs Churcher expected the vibrations to be felt at the woodheap. They stood up.

"He's bitten! A snake's got him!" she cried out. (Her mood would not allow for anything but the worst news.)

But Lionel had stopped yelling to fly towards the wood-heap, with the other children breaking into a run and shouting wildly too.

Lionel flung himself upon his father. He was a skinny boy of eight, so red of face now his freckles had disappeared in what looked like a wash of scarlet sweat. His brown straight hair, in need of a cut, was standing upright in spikes or plastered to his wet ears. His chest, no bigger it seemed than a golden syrup can, heaved and thudded and his little stick-like arms were trembling.

"It's a parcel! The biggest I've ever seen! With Dad's name on it! Mr Barney Churcher, it says. And there's a million stamps!"

That was as much as he could say. He breathed and puffed and held his father's waist for support.

"Barney Churcher! That's me!" Mr Churcher said. He stroked down his front and looked up the track. "That's me alright!"

Lionel sat panting on a block of wood. "Oh, it's big, it's so big!"

The other children, all six of them, had reached the woodheap by this time. Ernestine was first. She was thirteen, and fairly fleet of foot too. "The mail car left us a parcel!" she called back to the running knot.

"Big!" Lionel cried now, with enough breath back to stand and throw his arms wide. "Take the slide for it!"

"Hear that boy!" said Mr Churcher looking at Mrs Churcher, watching for the film of ugliness to slide from her face. He's a smart boy and he's ours, was the pleading message in his eyes.

"Go and get whatever it is, and I'll stoke the stove, for God knows what we'll eat," Mrs Churcher said, walking off. Mr Churcher told himself her body was softening up a little and that was something.

"Come on!" he called, sounding no older than Lionel, and seizing the rope attached to the slide standing on its end by the tank-stand. The slide flew wide with the great tug Mr Churcher gave it, and the children laughed as they jumped out of its way.

"Lionel should get a ride!" Ernestine cried. She was brown haired and slender like Maxine, and would be a beauty too.

"He should and will!" Mr Churcher shouted and steadied the slide while Lionel climbed on and made a small heap of himself in the middle. Raymond, who was fifteen, took a part of the rope, and like two eager horses with heads down, father and son raced ahead, the slide flying over the brittle grass, barely easing its pace up the rise.

The parcel was from Maxine. They knew her writing. The contents were enclosed in several sheets of brown paper, then the lot wedged into a frame of well spaced slats. Mr Churcher's name and their address was written on a label nailed to one side. Above the writing was a line of stamps, some heavily smudged with the stamp of the post office through which it was sent.

Mr Churcher and the children crowded around it, sitting by the slip rails, the gate long gone, unhinged by the Heffernans and used on their new property. All of them, even four year old Clifford who had ridden to the road on Ernestine's back, bent over the parcel, stroking the paper, patting the wood, jumping back to keep their eyes on it, as if it might disappear. How different the road, the sliprails, the deeply rutted track leading to the house, looked with it there. Leave it, leave it! cried part of the minds of the Churchers. Take it away and the emptiness will be more than we can bear!

"Come on!" called Mr Churcher, as if he too had to discipline himself to break the spell. He flung the parcel onto the slide and put Clifford beside it.

"Not too fast!" cried six year old Josephine, who was not as sturdy as the others and suffered bronchitis every

49

winter. Ernestine took her on her back for she was no heavier than Clifford. She whispered into Ernestine's neck that the parcel might be opened before everyone was there, for Mr Churcher and Raymond were flying down the track with the wind taking all of Clifford's hair backwards.

"No, no!" cried Ernestine, breaking into an energetic jog. "We'll all be there!"

Mrs Churcher was watching the track. "There's Mum!" Clifford shouted.

"We got it!" screamed Lawrence, who was nine and between Gloria and Lionel in age. (Which accounts for all the Churcher children.)

Mrs Churcher watched, as if mesmerized, the parcel sliding to a stop at the edge of the veranda. Mr Churcher took his eyes off it to fasten them on her face. A crease at each corner of her mouth kept any threatened softness at a distance.

"From Maxine," Mr Churcher said, pleading. He looked down on it beside Clifford, who was still on the slide reluctant to climb off.

"The stamps," Mr Churcher said, touching them with his boot. "Look what it cost even to send it."

"It's a parcel for us for Christmas, Mum!" Ernestine said, brown eyes like her mother's begging with some impatience for her excitement.

"There'll be nothing to eat in it," Mrs Churcher said. "Toys and rubbish, I'll bet." She looked hard at it, perhaps to avoid the eyes of the children, every pair on her she felt.

"I'll knock the old chook's head off!" Mr Churcher said.

"Not Wynie!" came in a chorus from most of them.

Gloria, who had wild red hair, sat on the edge of the veranda and held her bare feet. "We can eat anything," she murmured dreamily.

"Anything you'll be eating too!" Mrs Churcher said.

50

"It's soft," Lionel said. "So I reckon it's clothes. Clothes." The light in his eyes ran like a small and gentle fire setting alight the eyes of the others.

"It's heavy, even for Dad," Ernestine said. "There's something in there for you Mum, I reckon. New plates, like you want."

"Plates! They'd smash to smithereens. We'll be sticking with the tin ones!" Her eyes rested briefly on Mr Churcher. It's your fault they're only tin, they said.

Mr Churcher looked down on his hands wishing for a cigarette to use them, but he had no tobacco. There might be tobacco in the parcel. Yes! A packet of Log Cabin and papers. Two packets. Maxine used to sit on his knee and watch him roll cigarettes when she was a little thing, no more than two and the only one. They thought there would be no more and life would be fairly easy with the Great War finished and not too many joined up from Cobargo, thank heavens, to show him up. (He had no sense of adventure where war was concerned, no inclination to join in fighting.)

They had rented a little place in the town for six shillings a week (one shilling more than this and a palace in comparison, as he was always threatening to inform Jim Heffernan) and he had work, stripping bark, cutting eucalyptus, navvying on the road now and again. But the Depression came, and so did the children. Sometimes he went away for work, down as far as Moruya, coming home with his clothes in one sugar bag and some produce in another, oysters one time which the children had never tasted and passionfruit, which had been growing wild on the side of a mountain cleared for a new road. Mrs Churcher waited hopefully for him to produce some money, but there was always little of this. Once there was a pound note which the children looked upon as a fortune. It was a terrible disappointment to them when Mrs

Churcher gave it to Fred Rossmore to ensure credit for a few more weeks.

Mr Churcher was thinking of past homecomings now, looking at the parcel, still on the slide with Clifford, irrelevant thoughts, for they concerned Maxine, not likely to come home herself, spending all that money on things for them. The children saw. They found other things to look at momentarily, but in a while their glances strayed back.

"Did any of you find any eggs today?" Mrs Churcher said. (For the fowls had found means of escaping the pen and were reverting to former laying habits.) They had not, it seemed. They stared at the parcel, as if the remark had insulted it.

"Then what do we eat?" Mrs Churcher said. She did not look at Mr Churcher, who turned his face towards the paddocks, hard and dry like his throat.

"You'll find something, Mum," Ernestine said. "You always do."

"There comes a time when you don't!" Mrs Churcher said. "It's come at Christmas. A good time to arrive!"

Her voice, hard as the baked, brittle paddocks, gave the words a ringing sound like an iron bar striking earth it couldn't penetrate.

Mr Churcher longed for an early evening, for long striped shadows to bring a softness to the hard, harsh day.

"Will we have nothing for Christmas dinner?" Clifford said, huddled and dreamy on the slide. The others felt their bodies twitch, hungrier suddenly than they were before.

"Remember last year?" Gloria said. "We had baked rabbit and Maxie's card."

"This year is better," Lionel said. "We got the parcel."

"If Mum will let us open it," Gloria said.

Mr Churcher looked at Mrs Churcher's set face.

"It's not addressed to me," she said.

Mr Churcher slapped a top pocket as if tobacco were already there. "It's not Christmas yet," he said. They looked at the setting sun filling the sky with salmon and peach jam and beaten egg white.

"We'll go into town and ask Fred Rossmore for some stuff!" Now he was patting his pockets as if money were there. He put his hands down and his face away. "We can pay after Christmas."

"With the endowment money I want for something for the kids to wear back to school!" Mrs Churcher cried.

The children wondered briefly which of them might have got something new.

"There might be things in here we could wear," Lionel said, with a gentle toe on the brown paper.

"Come on!" Mr Churcher said, and began to walk rapidly off. He was taking the short cut through the bush, cutting off a quarter of a mile of road. Lionel ran to him and they both stopped and looked back to see who else was coming. Even with distance Mr Churcher's face showed he wanted Ernestine.

"I'll get my shoes and carry them!" she said, and was in and out of the room where the girls slept before Mr Churcher turned his head towards the track again. She ran to her father, not looking back.

Raymond, after standing with legs apart for a moment, holding his braces with fingers hooked in them, let the braces snap back into place and followed, racing past the little group to sit on a log some hundred yards ahead and wait, picking up bits of dead wood, rabbit dung and anything big enough to throw at nothing.

After a while they were lost to sight of those on the veranda, the gums and wattles and grey white logs, their roots exposed like a mouthful of rotten teeth, swallowing them up.

53

"I wonder what they'll bring back?" murmured Gloria. Clifford stood up and jumped off the slide, a very small jump he tried to make big. Lawrence moved along from his place on the veranda and put both feet on the slide.

"I'll stay with the parcel and mind it," he said.

Mrs Churcher padded to the kitchen, opening the stove door and shutting it with a clutter of metal so loud Gloria came uneasily inside.

"Did you see that?" Mrs Churcher said, sitting with her knees spread, stretching the morrocain until you saw through it.

Gloria did not know what she should have seen.

"Him!" Mrs Churcher said.

That meant Mr Churcher. That much she did know.

"Do you know why he made Ernestine go?"

No, Gloria didn't. Her chest went tight. Perhaps Ernie was his favourite. She (Gloria) was ugly (she thought). She and Lawrence were the two heavily freckled and with bright red hair. She had only sandshoes and could not have gone to town on Christmas Eve. Not that she would cry about it. There might be shoes in the parcel for her. She sat forward in her chair so that she saw a corner of it, watched by Lawrence, Josephine and Clifford, close together on the veranda edge. She was sorry she had come inside. Her mother strode to the stove now and put in a piece of wood Gloria thought too big and green to burn properly.

When Mrs Churcher went back to sit by the kitchen table she put her head on her arm and began to cry. "Rotten men!" she said, sitting up suddenly and wiping her eyes with her fingers.

A thin smoke began to bathe the log in the stove and some of it ran out of the stove door. "You need some chips," Gloria said, anxious that her father should not be blamed too harshly for the wood he had brought in.

Perhaps it was the smoke that sent more tears running down Mrs Churcher's cheeks.

"He took her with him to get stuff easier from Fred Rossmore!" Mrs Churcher said. "I know Fred Rossmore!"

Of course, Gloria thought. Everyone in Cobargo did. Even children knew he was a powerful man in the town.

"He's fond of girls," Mrs Churcher said. That seemed alright in Gloria's view, except for the tone of her mother's voice (like an iron bar on hard dry earth it couldn't penetrate).

"Huh!" Mrs Churcher said, which could be interpreted as meaning that Gloria knew precious little about Fred Rossmore's character. "Not for their good, but for his!" Mrs Churcher said.

Gloria pondered this. It appeared to mean that with Ernestine there, Fred Rossmore would not be handing out goods from his shelves. Her heart was troubled for her father coming in empty handed.

"He touches diddies if you let him," Mrs Churcher said. "And up here." She touched the morrocain stretched across her chest.

Gloria considered this a small price for butter, bacon, tinned peaches and biscuits, but dared not say so.

"And that parcel," Mrs Churcher said. "I wonder about that."

Gloria bent forward again to see it, the most innocent thing in all the world.

"To start with, a man would put it in a frame like that. Not her."

I wish she wouldn't say her, Gloria thought. Maxine had the nicest name of them all. Ernestine was next. After that it seemed Mrs Churcher's selection of names was clouded by her worries at feeding and clothing them all. Gloria had been told an aunt, a sister of her father, had named her after the film star Gloria Swanson. Gloria felt

55

a deep shame that she failed to turn out looking anything like Miss Swanson.

The green wood was filling the kitchen with smoke and Mrs Churcher got up and rubbed it into the hot ashes for it to burn quicker.

"For all we know a man might have bought what's in it. I reckon he did."

"For touching her diddie?" Gloria said.

Mrs Churcher was across the room in a second with a slap across Gloria's face so violent, Gloria lost her balance on the chair, and the noise brought the three from the veranda running to the door. They returned almost at once.

"Only Mum whacking Gloria," Clifford said, sitting down even closer to the parcel.

"There!" Mrs Churcher said, working the legs of the chair into the floor as she sat down. Gloria lay her face on her knee and cried softly. Mrs Churcher also cried. She allowed the tears to run in a great hurry down her cheeks, and when Gloria lifted her head she was surprised to see her mother's eyes quite bright and her face quite soft. She left her chair and went and sat on her knee. The fold of her stomach was soft as a mattress, and her shoulder a pillow, a fragrant fleshy pillow.

Mrs Churcher began to rock Gloria and this appeared to set them both crying without sound. When the others came in, tired of waiting by the parcel, Gloria lowered her face and Mrs Churcher turned hers. But they saw enough to make their eyes water too, so they moved together in a little bunch and stood giving all their attention to the stove fire.

Lawrence went off and returned with his old hat full of peaches. Gloria brought in some spindly wood that helped the green piece burn. Josephine asked if she could set the table, and Gloria, frowning on her, said to bring in some clothes from the line. The peaches were not as small and hard as those usually found, and when they had rolled to a stop on the table and Gloria brought a saucepan and a knife, Mrs Churcher said: "You'd better let me."

The four of them pressed their small chests against the edge of the table as they watched the peeling. It was a miracle of thinness, the furry skin falling from the knife like pale green tissue paper. Look at our Mum, said their eyes to each other. If only there was sugar to shake on some spoonfuls, without spilling a grain.

Mr Churcher brought some. Clifford, going out to check on the parcel, saw them come out of the bush and start their troop across to the house. He yelled as loud as Lionel when he found the parcel.

"They've got something!" he cried, flying inside then out again. The others followed except Mrs Churcher, who went to the stove with the saucepan of peaches and stayed there, making sure the lid was tight and they were on the right part of the stove to cook gently. Gloria allowed herself a brief look at the returning party, then when her mother had hung up the hessian oven rag, she went and hooped both arms around her and lay her face in the hollow of her breasts.

"They're coming," Mrs Churcher said, not actually pushing her off.

"Sugar, Mum!" Lawrence cried, as Mr Churcher put the little brown bag on the table with two tins of herrings in tomato sauce, some cheese, cut into such a beautiful triangle it would be a shame to disturb it, and a half pound packet of tea and some dried peas.

"And look what Ernie's got!" Lionel cried, stepping aside from in front of her to reveal her holding clasped against her waist a paper bag. Everyone knew, by the little squares and rolls and balls making little bulges in the paper, it could be nothing else but sweets.

"Lollies!" screamed Clifford, and Mrs Churcher turned to the stove again and they saw by the neck showing under the thick straggling bun of her grey and black hair that she was crying.

"Stop crying, Mum," Joseph said. "Ernie will give you one."

"There for all of us to share," Raymond said, in case anyone should begin to think differently. He sat on the doorstep with a glance backwards at the parcel, the afternoon sun making diamonds of the tacks holding the label in place.

"Mum's not well," Mr Churcher said. He was standing in the middle of the room, one hand near his waist, the fingers spread as if a cigarette was there. "She's having another one."

Mrs Churcher sat and found the hem of her petticoat to wipe her nose.

"It'll be the last," Mr Churcher said.

The eyes of the children said this might or might not be so. Ernestine put the bag of sweets at the end of the top shelf of the dresser and snapped the glass doors shut. She moved to the table and put the other things from Fred Rossmore's inside the food safe. Mrs Churcher's wet eyes followed her. Ernestine's old sleeveless print dress showed her round tanned arms, and her hair heavy as a bird's nest showed bits of her neck, pure white inside dark brown slits. She brought out flour to make fried scones, holding the bag between breasts beginning to pout. Tears ran over Mrs Churcher's cheeks as Ernestine lowered the flour to the table and took a mixing bowl from a crude shelf above her head.

"There's four boys and four girls in this family," Lionel said. "So the next one can be anything it likes."

Mr Churcher was on a chair with his elbows on his knees. "Well said, Lionel. A smart boy that." He longed to be brave enough to look into Mrs Churcher's eyes. "You're all smart, all of you," he said.

Raymond looked at the kitchen floor boards between his feet. He had left school a year ago, and still had no job except for trapping rabbits in the winter and selling the skins, a great pile of them for only five shillings. The tips of his ears were very red.

"Next year things are going to be better," Mr Churcher said. Everyone half believed it, and Mrs Churcher, as if her mind were on something else, took out the sugar, and carrying it to the stove tipped a little onto the peaches. They all watched her fold the top of the bag down letting nothing escape.

"Yes, I reckon next year will be better," Mr Churcher said, putting a hand to a back pocket and moving it around there, as if making room for a packet of tobacco.

"And there's the parcel!" he said, throwing back his head suddenly like a terrier about to bark.

Josephine flung herself on Ernestine, as if the excitement was too much to bear alone. Raymond drew himself into a tight ball with his face crushed between his knees.

Lionel and Lawrence went to the veranda to each put a light foot on the parcel. Clifford climbed onto his father's knee, and Gloria leaned against her mother, with the cheek still red from the slap rubbing gently into her morrocain shoulder.

"And it's Christmas tomorrow!" Mr Churcher said, with his head back again and the words coming out like a terrier's bark. Out of the corner of his eye he saw Mrs Churcher's face start to go soft, then tighten again. She stood, taller than normal, he thought and looked across at him. Her eyes swept the children to one side. She might have sent them from the room, though all were there, faces tipped up at her, eyes begging for harmony.

"That parcel was sent from the place where the bad girls are," she said.

There was a rush for the veranda to look at the parcel again. Even Mr Churcher screwed his head towards it, but turned it back almost at once. His face did not believe it.

Gloria had a vision of a great mass of girls with pinched and sorrowful faces and their skirts dented deeply in the region of their diddies. She looked at Ernestine, who was measuring flour into a bowl with lowered eyes, but there was nothing to be seen past her waist, which was level with the table.

"Make sure you sift that flour properly," Mrs Churcher said. Then she sat on a chair with her head up, not looking at Mr Churcher. "You can see on the stamps where it was sent from."

"She could have given it to anyone to post. It's a great thing to lug herself," Mr Churcher said.

"She never writes," Mrs Churcher said.

"She was saving up for all those stamps," Mr Churcher answered. He got up and went and pulled the label from the parcel, looking at the stamps and postmark.

"You see it? Kings Cross! That's where she is!" Mrs Churcher took the bowl of flour from Ernestine and buried her hands in it. She began to cry again.

Mr Churcher put the label in the dresser next to the lollies from Fred Rossmore.

"Now it doesn't matter where it came from," Lionel said. Mr Churcher's eyes told Lionel this was wisely said.

Josephine went to Ernestine to cry into her waist. "We'll never know what's in the parcel!" she wailed.

"That's right!" Mrs Churcher was mixing dough fast

60

with a knife, her tears temporarily halted. "We'll send it back!"

Josephine wept louder and Ernestine, checking that her mother's hands were covered with dough, and Josephine seemed safe from a blow, held her very tight.

Raymond went pale, and the freckles stood out on Gloria and Lawrence for their faces had a pallor too. Lionel, sitting suddenly beside Raymond, turned the sole of one foot up and looked long and intently on it.

"You're a cruel woman, Maudie," Mr Churcher said.

The children were not as frightened by his words as they might have been. He called Mrs Churcher Maudie in the soft moments.

Mrs Churcher, her face clear of tears, tossed her head high and banged the frying pan on the stove. It was not a terribly loud bang though.

"I know my Maxie," Mr Churcher said. He was seated with his elbows on his knees. He held two fingers near his face and the children looked hard to be sure he had no cigarette.

"Your Maxie!" Mrs Churcher said.

"Our Maxie!" Mr Churcher said. "A good girl!"

"Yes, yes, yes!" came in different voices, Josephine's the strangest, for she was laughing as well as sobbing. Ernestine wandered outside, still holding Josephine, and Gloria followed.

Under the old apricot tree, from which the fruit had been early and hungrily stripped, they put their backs to the trunk.

"I'm frightened," Gloria said. "If there are gold and jewels in that parcel, what will we do?"

Ernestine tried to shrink the parcel in her vision. Mr Churcher came to the back door and filled the opening. Ernestine, Gloria and Josephine went and sat at his feet on the slabs laid on the earth to make a rough veranda.

Ernestine bound her body in her arms and rocked herself a little while, looking away to the mountains gone black to show the sunset up all the brighter.

She lifted her face, no less lovely, to her father. "You open the parcel, Dad. Like Mum said, it's addressed to you."

"By jove I think I might!" Mr Churcher said, loud enough to swing Mrs Churcher's face from the food safe to which she was returning the flour.

"I'm setting the table here," Mrs Churcher said. "Without any help as usual!"

"Leave the table setting!" Mr Churcher said. "I'm bringing in the parcel!"

He didn't go through the kitchen but strode around the house with Ernestine, Gloria and Josephine clinging to him.

Raymond, Lawrence, Lionel and Clifford were around the slide when they reached it. Mr Churcher lifted the parcel as if it were a pillow.

"Our Dad's so strong!" cried Lawrence. They stepped back like a guard of honour for him to go to the kitchen. He laid it on the table end.

"Don't break the box!" Lionel said. "It'll be handy for something!"

"A doll's cradle!" Gloria said. "If there's a doll in there for Josie!" Her eyes then sent an agonized apology to her mother.

There was no doll in there. But Josephine forgot her disappointment when the paper was pulled away and Ernestine held up a quilt, a snowy while fringed quilt with the honeycomb pattern broken up with a design of roses as big as cabbages, and trailing stems and leaves.

"Look at that!" someone cried.

"For Mum's bed!"

"And Dad's!"

Ernestine put it tenderly on a chair.

"Towels!" shrieked Gloria as four were found inside and four sheets with only a little fraying at the hems.

After that came a tablecloth, heavy and white, a beautiful thing for Christmas dinner, and several tea towels.

Ernestine held them up against the open doorway and there was hardly any wear showing.

"Give them all to Mum!" Gloria cried.

Mrs Churcher was on a chair, hands on her thighs, trying to keep the hardness in her eyes.

Mr Churcher sat on the door step where Raymond had been. He was watching Ernestine, Gloria and Lionel come to the end of the parcel.

Lionel shrieked when he held up a single page with Maxine's writing on it.

"I hope you like these things," she wrote, "I work for these people called Pattens. Mr Patten has a shop. He brought home some new sheets and things, all in colours which is the new fashion now. Mrs Patten decided to give me the old ones, or some of them, to send to you. She is not paying me this week, but says she has a Christmas present for me. They are having roast pork for Christmas dinner here, but I would rather be having what you are."

Lionel read the letter and everyone hearing it was quiet.

Mrs Churcher bent down to look into the stove fire, which was smoking again, so she needed to find her petticoat hem to wipe her eyes and nose.

Mr Churcher stared at his hands as if for the first time he realized they were holding nothing.

6 Tea With Sister Paula

St Joseph's Convent was half a mile from the post office in Cobargo, which was considered to be the centre of the town.

When you started up the hill you reached the public school first on the same side of the road. Like the convent, which had the Catholic church next door to it, the public had the schoolmaster's house beside it. The church and convent were in red brick with white trimmings, and with neat gardens both looked sparkling bright, while the public buildings, though brick too, were painted over in an ochre colour.

They were like a bright sister and a sombre one, which was appropriate, for the younger nun of the three at St Joseph's, Sister Paula, was black eyed, with a white skin and a full figure, spreading the pleated bodice of her habit, and her sturdy legs flung the skirt in and out as she worked about the convent. The bands of her wimple pushed her plump cheeks forward, and made a crease at either side of her mouth, deepening when she smiled.

The schoolmaster, Dan Russell, and his wife, Emily, had one daughter, Dorothy, who was about the same age as Sister Paula. Dorothy wore glasses under a straight fringe of hair, neither black nor brown, which despite Emily's constant washing maintained a greasy look.

While Sister Paula was pleasantly plump, Dorothy Russell was fat, though corseted by her mother and dressed in dark clothes, which Emily believed gave an illusion of slimness. They succeeded only in making

Dorothy look an older, dumpy spinster, when in fact she was a young, dumpy spinster.

She had not been able to learn at school, and this was a great disappointment to Dan, for she was the only child born ten years after marriage, when Emily was thirty-six. One day in school, Dan was berating a boy who could not master long division. "You're a half wit!" he shouted, and in the silence that followed someone hissed: "He's got one hisself!"

The room of fifty children in five different grades (placing great strain on Dan's capabilities) expected a major explosion, and a solid caning for the culprit. But what followed stunned them even more. Dan put his chalk in the little hollow below the blackboard and left the room. His assistant, a young woman whom everyone (the children and the town) called Miss Kelly, witnessing Dan's departure through the glass door connecting the two classrooms, opened it to keep an eye on Dan's children as well as her own roomful of infants.

Dan had nowhere else to go but to the house, for Emily was inside the back gate leading to it, stirring the earth around the young beans. She was five years older than Dan, and it being a windy, wintry day, her hair was flying about, nearly as white as the may bushes which were threshing long flowery stems back and forth.

Dan could not sit foolishly in the weather shed under Emily's curious eye, so he went briskly up the steps as if on an errand for material from the bedroom he used as a study, for school houses were built for families much larger than Dan's.

Dorothy was in the kitchen on the couch, cross legged, ogling through her glasses as she cut pictures from a magazine. She quivered inside at the unexpected sight of her father, and removed her tongue from the corner of her mouth but did not close it.

Dan saw her round, like a child's top that had spun itself out and was waiting lopsided to be wound up again. Her top half was like one too, for she wore a boldly striped pink and white blouse Emily allowed for indoors only. A younger sister of Dan's visiting once had left the blouse with Dorothy when she formed a deep attachment to it.

Dan went to his study and closed the door. Dorothy gave a little jump. Emily, although she could scarcely have heard, put the fork into the earth, and went up the steps into the kitchen. Dorothy blinked on her mother, though without fear. Emily, washing her hands in the porcelain sink, which she kept in a white and gleaming state, expected to see Dan pass through the kitchen on his way back to school by the time she had hung up the hand towel, making the two ends meet in a perfect line over the rail. But he was still there after Emily had gathered up scraps of paper Dorothy had let fall with her scissors, and burned them in the stove.

She looked briefly on Dorothy, checking that she did not offend Dan too greatly, then went and tapped on the study door. Dan stirred the legs of his chair which Emily took as permission to enter.

"Have you found what you want?" asked Emily. She and Dorothy were forbidden to disturb anything in the room, Emily dusting around papers and exercise books, even hesitant to put a cap back on an ink bottle. It was unlikely Emily could help if Dan was in search of something. He stood up scraping the linoleum with his chair. Emily wanted very much to tuck it neatly under the desk if Dan was finished with it as he appeared to be. There was another chair in the room, on the edge of which she sat, looking up at him, trying to read his face. Dan frowned around the chair legs and Emily's impulse was to stand, which she did not obey.

"Is the inspector coming?" Emily asked, unwisely, for she usually kept hidden from Dan her awareness of his great discomfort on these occasions.

"The inspector!" Dan nearly shouted and flung off his glasses and put them on again almost at once. "A normal human being?"

It was Dorothy then.

Emily had thought she would be finished cutting out by half past three when school was over for the day. Dan sometimes came straight to the house so Emily made sure his afternoon tea was ready. Or he might turn up an hour later, having found work to occupy him in the school, or having pottered in the school garden. He left Emily to attend to the house garden, never interfering, not out of respect for her creativity, but to keep their lives on separate courses. Emily had borne Dorothy, and Dorothy was her responsibility (and fault).

Dan took his glasses off again, and chewed angrily at the end that hooked over his ear.

"The Bunfield boy," Dan said, "said — said in class — " And he waved his glasses at the door.

Emily had an idea what the Bunfield boy said. Sometimes small knots of children gathered around the fence separating the back garden from the playground and watched through the palings if Dorothy was sitting on the grass exposing her legs, short as they were, like fat logs against the green. Emily would bang on the top of the fence with her little gardening fork and the children would scatter, and Dorothy, too late, would pull her skirt down.

"Did you cane him?"

Cane him! The woman was a fool! No wonder the girl — ! Would it go away with a caning of the Bunfield boy? The silly, simple thing there on the chair in the shelter of the house he provided. Little or nothing to do all day. Worse still, she liked the girl. Actually liked her! Emily saw Dan had whitened around his nostrils and under his lower lip and was chewing at his glasses again.

She stood as dignified as she could, the way she was when showing her face in Cobargo, particularly when Dorothy was with her, lips pressed together, giving her a look of severity, brows drawn down, causing people to think she's a hard one, a sour piece if you ask me, and old Dan such a good bloke too.

She knew Dan blamed her for Dorothy, but she did not deeply resent this, surprising herself that she felt this way. Dan was holding his chair back now, and Emily remembered when he was a young teacher, troubled about school matters, or warring with parents, and she would unclench his hands from the chair back, and put them around her, smoothing out the fingers, holding them there at the back of her waist, pressing his thumbs down to knead the top of her buttocks.

It would have been twenty years easily since anything like that.

She had been terrified for months before the birth of Dorothy that bodily activity might affect her.

Afterwards she was sensually satisfied feeding the child. She secretly hoped too that the flow of milk from her breasts might turn the snub-nosed, slant-eyed little creature into something resembling the babies of her sisters and sisters-in-law and those wheeled in prams about the little town where Dan was teaching (after Dorothy she did not look at them).

Thankfully, Dorothy was fourteen and past school age when they moved to Cobargo. Her condition could not be kept from the townspeople but a great deal of embarrassment was avoided with Dorothy out of the classrooms. Cobargo people did not use terms like retarded or mentally deficient. They called Dorothy a cromp. The

Russells have only got one and she's crompy, they said. Those with a big tribe of mentally alert youngsters said the words with certain relish. They've got a good house to live in, and he's got a good job, but they've got a cromp, so which of us is the better off?

Dan took a book from a shelf and went out. Emily had to move her legs to let him past. Her heart went with him past Dorothy in the kitchen, listening to the steps that made rapid progress without pausing. Emily saw him keeping his eyes from Dorothy on the couch.

But when she went to the kitchen, Dorothy wasn't there. The pages pulled from the centre of the magazines, stood like small tents about the floor, between them paper shapes, strips and curls, some so fine it looked like a hail storm had hit a camp site.

Emily tidied the area, making sure no uncut pages were discarded, putting these inside uncut magazines and then in a box under the couch, closing it hastily as was her habit for there were toys there from Dorothy's childhood which she still played with, and although Dan knew about this, Emily tried to keep the evidence out of sight.

She was a few minutes more putting the kitchen straight before going to the back landing to look for Dorothy.

She was nowhere to be seen.

She is below the creek bank, Emily thought, willing the round, dark head to bob into view. I will see her in a moment.

But when she didn't, Emily went into the bedroom and tidied her hair and relaxed her worried face in the mirror, telling it to be sensible. It was not a good thing to leave Dorothy alone in the creek bed. Once when there with Emily, Dorothy had stopped and lifted handfuls of brackish water and drank, spilling quite a lot down her dress but swallowing enough to worry Emily, who took her home and made her drink a strong draught of senna tea, causing further complications with turbulent bowel action during the next twenty-four hours.

Emily, frowning up and down the creek, saw Mrs Keaton in her back garden, for the Keatons' was one of three homes between the public and the convent schools. Mrs Keaton saw Emily and pointed her garden fork — one on a long handle — in the direction of the convent.

Emily went inside angry. Mrs Keaton pointing a rake after Dorothy as if she were a dog with a habit of losing itself! She went into the sitting room and, raising a blind sharply at the front window, sat near her cane sewing stand and took out her embroidery. She was working a cloth with fine spoke stitch, impressing the class of girls she taught sewing one afternoon a week, Dorothy given a back seat, a book of pictures and many long, pleading looks not to make a fool of them both.

It took awhile for Emily's hands to steady over the fine linen, mainly because she was not shaking off an image of Mrs Keaton's expression, believing it to be a mixture of pity and scorn. The Keatons had one daughter who was a nurse, another in a bank, and two sons at home who were among Dan's best pupils.

Unfair, unfair! cried Emily's heart, her hands spreading a worked corner on a trembling knee, trying to draw comfort from the perfection of her stitches. She would not walk past Mrs Keaton to find Dorothy. Mrs Keaton would stay in the garden watching for Emily to appear, knowing Emily couldn't walk up the creek bed, the banks thick with blackberry bushes until almost level with the convent.

Dorothy will take a little walk then come home, Emily told herself, lifting her eyes from her work to eye off the piano and picture the new cloth draped across the top.

"A piano scarf," she told her class, many in homes without pianos, even those with them without such elegant touches as scarves for adornment (the children of richer Cobargo families went to boarding school).

Emily liked to see envy trickle into the eyes of the girls, although some, to get even, would turn their heads and look hard at Dorothy, who might be picking her nose or twisting her face into grotesque shapes.

She was doing neither now. She was hurrying on her sturdy legs towards the convent fence, already aware of the movement of Sister Paula's brown habit between the palings.

The convent had beans growing too, and Sister Paula was stirring the earth around them as Emily had been in her garden. Dorothy put the fingers of one hand through a gap in the palings and waggled them.

"Guess!" she called.

Sister Paula raised her head and checked the faces of the convent and school. Both blank. She let her hood fall to help hide her face as she dug faster than before.

"You know I'm here!" Dorothy said. "I'm your visitor!"

"Take a seat!" Sister Paula dug harder.

Dorothy sat and giggled, stretching her legs out, half burying them in the grass.

"I'll make the tea in just a moment," Sister Paula said, though not pausing in her digging. "And there'll be sandwiches!" She took a handful of beans dangling from a bush, no bigger than darning needles, and held them out in Dorothy's direction, beautifully green on her small roughened hand.

"I'll eat two hundred!" Dorothy cried. Sister Paula took another guarded look at the buildings and moved so that her brown rump cut Dorothy from view, although she was unlikely to be seen, squinting through the paling cracks, except that her blouse bobbed about like a pink and white flag lowered to ground level.

"I thought of something just now," Sister Paula said.

"I'll ask Sister if I can dig a garden along the fence," (she waved her fork in its direction, and Dorothy saw her white arm run up inside her wide sleeve) "and then I can see your face better while we talk!"

"My face!" Dorothy said. "It's like a cow's bum!"

Sister Paula dug her fork deeply into the ground and clung to it while she put her head down and laughed. Dorothy saw her hood rippling too with her laughter.

Her face grew smaller and whiter and she pulled at tufts of grass.

"You're laughing!" she said, not so much accusing as sorrowful.

"No, no!" said Sister Paula (worrying too about lying) "Who would say that?" (She very much wanted to know.)

Dorothy was a long time answering. "I don't know. Someone."

Sister Paula went back to digging, making up for lost time.

"I'm hungry," Dorothy said, a trifle sulky.

"Visitors don't say they're hungry. They just wait. Politely."

She allowed herself a brief glance at the back of Dorothy's neck, a lot of it showing. And sad. "But you can help by getting out the plates."

More of Dorothy's neck showed. "You know!" Sister Paula said, and turned a bean leaf towards the fence.

Dorothy's face caught a draft of joy and held it trapped. "The best green ones!" she said, standing and pulling leaves from the big Moreton Bay fig.

"You clever girl!" cried Sister Paula.

A little wind, wandering among the branches, snatched up Dorothy's chuckle and took it to the top of the tree.

Sister Paula stood and looked at the school. Sister Alfreda pulled a window down, making a shrieking noise, and brought one of Dorothy's eyes, winking alarm, to a crack in the fence. Sister Paula cocked her head to one side in listening pose. When "Now the Day is Over" started up in the infants' room, it meant only fifteeen minutes before Sister Alfreda and Sister Joan would be closing the school doors. Then, hands in sleeves and heads forward, like dolls dressed as nuns, they would cross the piece of ground where the girls skipped and would soon be inside the convent for afternoon tea.

Sister Paula already had the cups out, covered with a cloth against a stray fly or two, and the bread and butter cut paper thin as Sister Alfreda had taught her.

The two senior nuns took their tea at the end of the long table in the refectory, and Sister Paula, who by this time had started on the soup and pudding for the evening meal, drank hers in the kitchen, setting her cup down from time to time among the vegetable peelings.

"The cups out?" asked Sister Paula now, back on her haunches and at the end of the last row of beans. Sliding her eyes past the edge of her wimple, she saw Dorothy look around for what was expected of her.

"On the top shelf where they're always kept!" said Sister Paula.

Dorothy's head tilted back on her little fat white neck and her face like a small moon wore a great watermelon of a smile. All her teeth showed like little white seeds.

Her expression sobered almost at once, as with great care she took down a line of acorns on the top rail and arranged them, awkwardly, with her fat fingers on the bottom rail.

Sister Paula dug her fork into the ground with an air of finality, and rubbed dirt from her hands on the grass. She pulled a handful of beans, hearing a whispering wince from the bush and wincing herself, checked the school again, where windows were going down, wincing too under stout nuns' arms.

"Pass your plate," she said, and Dorothy pushed a leaf through the fence with a finger tip. Sister Paula laid beans across it, folded it and pushed it back.

"Munch and crunch away!" she cried. "Delicious!"

Dorothy ate. The beans twisted about inside her open mouth like little green snakes thrown on a bed of burning coals.

Sister Paula bit a bean, delicately, and with almost a dreamy air. Then her hand flew to her mouth and her eyes flew first to the convent buildings, then to Dorothy.

Dorothy pressed an eye and an open mouth to the space in the palings.

Sister Paula's eyes above her firmly pressed hand said don't be alarmed, this I have to do, Sister Alfreda insists no nun be seen eating in a public place.

When the last of her bean had been chewed away, she stood and smoothed her habit down and settled her hood by lifting it from the back of her neck as another girl would settle her hair.

"Time for us both to go!" said Sister Paula.

"No, no!" said Dorothy, pushing her stretched out legs about.

"Yes, yes!" said Sister Paula, quite gaily, hearing the school doors slammed shut.

Without looking back she went briskly up the back steps into the convent kitchen.

Dorothy ran home past Mrs Keaton, who said, "Hullo, Dorothy, your mother's looking for you," thinking how virtuous she was bothering with a poor half wit. Dorothy as usual did not answer.

Dan and Emily were having tea at the kitchen table. Dorothy slid onto a chair, not pulling it out, but wedging herself against the table, the edge squashing her breasts.

She took a piece of cake and Dan, as was his habit, screwed himself sideways to avoid seeing her eat.

Emily saw her mouth with the cake inside, beaten and flung about as if a mincing machine was at work.

She lowered her eyes to her plate, but in a second, missing the sucking noise Dorothy made, she looked up and saw Dorothy with a hand pressed to her mouth.

See Dan, said Emily's heart. See she is improving. Look at her. Look at her now!

But Dan got up and left the room without looking.

7 The Teacher's Wife

After the Russells were transferred to another town, the Carrolls came.

They were very different. There were six children and Marie Carroll was a small, dark, busy woman who did not bother with Emily's garden, gave sketchy attention to household chores and got herself out of the house as often as she could.

She played tennis, darting about the court in a dress shorter than those the other women wore, and was not content to dress herself and the children for show and sports days, but worked instead as an organizer, although, being a woman, her ideas were not always welcome.

No woman had ever been on the Cobargo Agricultural and Horticultural Committee, and Marie Carroll gave serious thought to being the first.

"Why not, Percy?" she asked her husband in the school house kitchen one midday Saturday when the *Cobargo Chronicle* had a notice calling for nominations for the forthcoming annual meeting. "You could nominate me, now why not?"

She tied a bib, too late, on the baby in its high chair, who had already filled the space between its neck and collar with potato and gravy. The sink, no longer in the state in which Emily had kept it, was loaded with dirty plates and cups, and Marie, in her tennis gear for a match on the town courts, was washing and leaving to drain some of the china and leaving the saucepans to soak.

The water left the sink with a gurgling sound of relief, as if it too were anxious to be away.

Marie caught up her racquet, propped by the dresser since her last game, and tried the tautness of the strings with a bunched fist. Then she touched the baby on the forehead among its silky curls with the handle and told it to be good for its father. On her way out the front gate she passed three of the other children making mud pies in a flower bed of Emily's that once grew prize pansies.

She hoped the three year old would not stand up and wail and rub mud into his eyes, but he did. She hurried through the gate, calling "Mumma won't be long!" and to get the cry out of her ears as quickly as possible, ran fast towards the town, leaping over the ridges of roots spread by the bank of pine trees, the tops worn smooth by the feet of school children.

All through the match, smacking balls harder than usual, causing the Cobargo supporters to say Marie's belting into them today and no mistake and marvel at the six children coming from such a quicksilver of a body, moving too fast, it seemed, to have a seed germinate there (and Percy such a slow, dreamy poet of a man), Marie thought about the show committee.

Jim Clancy's father, Harold, was the chairman (and had been for twenty years) and as Marie was Jim's mixed doubles partner, she had good reason to sit with him while the men's singles was on, and, to all appearances, exchange strategies. In fact Marie talked about the way the show was run.

"Why have the grand parade last thing of all?" asked Marie, beating her racquet on the upturned toes of her tennis shoes and sending dried powder flying about, for she tended to cake it on in her hurry.

Jim, who was twenty-two, and the eldest of the three Clancy boys and educated at agricultural college, smiled on the shoes, thinking a little irreverently (since the subject was the show) of his own efforts at college at cleaning his shoes (now his mother did it for him).

"Don't you think it would be better to have it much earlier so that the farmers don't have to rush away to milk straight after?"

"Aw," said Jim, for in spite of his higher education he had a slow, country way of speaking. "Most of the prize winners have sharefarmers."

"But the sharefarmers like to see the parade!" Marie said. "They would be just as pleased, even if they don't own the stuff!"

"Own the stuff," said Jim, mocking and smiling.

"Well, why not?"

"And why not?" Jim, still smiling, was mocking again. "You always say that." He looked away, then down, his straight brown hair falling between his eyebrows. "I like it."

He saw with half an eye a peak of Marie's bobbed hair pushing gently at a dimple.

"I'd like to get on the show committee and change a few things," Marie said. I said that out loud, she thought. Some pink was running into her cheeks, she knew. Oh dear me, whatever will he think? She saw him looking at nothing again.

"I can imagine what your father would say!" Marie said.

"I'm trying to," said Jim.

"I told Jim about going on the show committee," Marie said when she was at home in the school house kitchen after tennis, and Percy and all the children were there too, eager for a meal.

Percy had let the stove fire die down, and Marie, with a flushed face, was reviving it.

She had stepped over a boot box of tomatoes on the back step as she came in, left there during her absence by a school parent, and almost at once she flung a large black frying pan over the coals.

She would fry the tomatoes and have them with eggs and bread. She had meant to buy a bag of cakes from the bakery on her way home. She couldn't remember passing it, and wondered that the smells had not reminded her.

I'm getting strange, she thought with a little smile that puzzled Percy, who was on a kitchen chair nursing Tommy (the three year old) and the baby.

"Pack up all my cares and woe, here I go singing low, bye, bye blackbird," sang Percy, performing the quite amazing feat of jigging Tommy on one knee and swaying the baby on the other. Marie poured a column of tomato breathing scarlet fire into a bowl plucked from the draining board by the sink. She set it on the middle of the table and Percy and all the children were there in an instant, the baby in the high chair, the other three younger ones on a stool, and Martin and Lorna, aged ten and eight, with the status of their years, on chairs and inclined to look with scorn on the occupiers of the stool.

Marie didn't want to take her end; she would have liked to have slipped into her bedroom where there was a mirror to look at her face. She expected to see it different, prettier. She looked down on her tomatoes, such a big serve, she would never get through it and away.

"What would you young ones think of Mumma a show woman?" Percy said.

The round eyes of the children and their mouths, which were open and ringed with tomato, asked questions.

Did this mean a woman in tight clothes walking a tight-rope as they had seen one in a circus that came last year to Cobargo? She would not be their mother! Lorna began to cry.

"Stop it, you sook!" Martin said, beginning to dream of living in the caravans and not having to go to school.

"She wouldn't leave us," Percy said. "She would just go to meetings after tea some nights."

"Don't cry, my lovely biggest girl," Marie said, wanting to cry herself.

"I see no reason, Percy," Marie said the following week when Percy was in one day for lunch, "why I shouldn't go to Clancy's myself and talk to Harold about getting on the committee."

Percy couldn't see any reason why not himself. He stood a little in awe of Harold Clancy, who had nothing to do with the school since his sons were not educated there but went to boarding school, then to "ag" college, as Cobargo called it. Harold was able to set them up with farms, if and when they married, although it would mean moving sharefarmers away. The children of the share-farmers were among Percy's pupils, and this caused Percy to relegate himself to a status below the Clancys, although he thought himself foolish to have this attitude. But he did not want to approach Harold about Marie joining the show committee. He would feel like a servant begging a favour. She could go herself and see him. She seemed not to be afraid of anyone, a quality Percy secretly envied.

When school was out the following day, Marie backed their old Ford onto the road and sent it wobbling along, children scattering out of the way, looking through the dust to see who was in the car. Marie saw their faces in the rear vision mirror, memorizing tales for their mothers at home. Mrs Carroll with an empty car going somewhere without any of the children, Mr Carroll minding them when he would have schoolwork to do, marking books and getting blackboards ready for next day, not like Mr Russell who might have had a crompy daughter, but spent more time at his job, and didn't do women's work like carrying the baby about while she was off somewhere and other Cobargo women were beating tough steak with a mallet to make a tasty braise for tea. Not the housekeeper Emily Russell was by a long chalk.

Marie Carroll only got to the start of the Clancy property. For Jim was rounding up a steer that had wedged itself into a corner, a wild-eyed thing with a coat like dark blood splashed with white, stubbornly pawing at the stout Clancy fence in preference to swinging around and going the way Jim wanted.

The car's stopping agitated it further, and it plunged its chest onto the top rail, putting its front legs over and hanging there, scraping its chest and belly on the lower rail, sliding its neck on the splintery wood, foam around its black lips.

"Woa there!" Jim cried, standing in the saddle and cracking his whip in magnificent fashion, then when the steer remained clinging to the fence, sent his horse flying into the corner, brushing the rail with its chestnut body, and worrying Marie that Jim's leg in its beautiful high riding boot might suffer some injury.

"Mumma is not bothering about the show after all," Percy said later that afternoon, with Marie dodging among the children as she set the table for tea, and the saucepans of vegetables pressed together on the stove to get what heat was available from Percy's poor fire.

Tea was going to be late, and this fact was reflected

81

on the mournful faces of the children, only the baby given a crust, eating it sleepily against Percy's chest, smearing his shirt with the soaked and swollen end.

"Mumma saw this big, red steer," Marie said, putting out the children's mugs and two cups for herself and Percy.

Martin and Lorna and Jean, who was next to them in age, gave their attention to the loaf of bread on the board with the knife beside it, hoping for an early slicing.

"This steer was so wild!" said Marie, throwing out her arms and making her eyes wild too. The baby was roused from her half sleeping state, and flung out a hand holding the crust, that was worn to a sloppy stump and appeared to grow from her fingers.

The five year old, Isabel, half sitting on the stool, half believing this might hasten the meal, turned her mouth downwards with cranky eyes.

"Oh, come now, don't have the miseries!" Marie cried. "Look! I'll be that wild red steer!"

She turned the four kitchen chairs about to form a line, and flung herself over their backs, breathing loud, snorting, blowing out wind from her puffed up cheeks, kicking and sliding her feet on the linoleum and beating them on the rungs of the chairs.

Marie had also formed the dramatic society in Cobargo, and acted in most of the plays. There were many who said she should be at home caring for her husband and children like a normal wife.

8 Not The Marrying Kind

No one in Cobargo expected Millie Clarke to marry.

In 1935 she was about twenty-four, considered a spinster in those times, although she had looked much the same since she was seventeen.

Every Sunday afternoon, except when the weather was very bad, Arthur and Amy Clarke, with Millie between them, went for a walk along one of the four roads leading out of Cobargo.

Sometimes families at Sunday dinner, at very dull times, speculated on which road the Clarkes would take come half past two. You could set your clock by their setting out, and almost to the minute they would be home again at five o'clock.

Many years earlier, Arthur and Amy had taken the same walk with their daughter, Annie, until circumstances surrounding Millie's birth caused the practice to lapse.

Arthur and Amy passed Millie off as their daughter (although the town knew differently), since Annie vanished after Millie was born.

When Millie was about five, by which time Arthur and Amy had grown used to the stares and the references, in case they were forgetting Millie's origin, the walks were resumed.

The little Millie held Amy's hand while in the town, and Arthur's as well when out of it. On the way home, when Millie's little legs grew tired, Arthur carried her until the houses started, then passed her over to Amy for the last quarter of a mile.

The Clarkes' house was next to the bridge, cowering

half beneath it, with the garden on one side going right to the edge of the creek. It had a shamefaced look about it, the roof of the veranda almost low enough for a long-legged man to step onto from the bridge approach. Certainly you could jump from the bridge rail and land on the veranda roof.

It seemed after Annie's disgrace the roof went lower, but it just happened that a wistaria, planted by Amy, took off all of a sudden, and by the time Millie was twelve or thirteen there was a tangle of trunks like so many writhing snakes, and at blossoming time the mauve flowers packing the veranda roof could be seen for miles. The vine looked as if in time it would cover the house and push it deeper into the earth.

Millie played on the veranda, looking up from the wooden blocks Arthur had cut for her, through the feathery leaves and weight of flowers dropping petals on Amy's scrubbed boards, at people passing along the bridge.

Amy (for Arthur's sake mainly) kept Millie out of the Cobargo eye but of course the time came when Millie had to be exposed, and the wistaria was a help in this breaking-in process.

Half a dozen other houses straggling out of the town on the Bega road had their quota of school children, and the children gave the most attention to the little Millie with her blocks behind the wistaria.

"Old Arthur must have made her those," one mother said when the blocks were described to her by her daughters. She frowned while she said it, as if disapproving, for it appeared that Arthur was condoning Annie's terrible sin by making toys for her child.

Millie was pretty as a baby, then plainer as she grew older, or the constant frown between her eyes robbed her face of a girlish softness. Her frown always seemed particularly heavy when walking on Sunday afternoon with Arthur and Amy.

The Cobargo people who disapproved of everything about Millie, her birth, and the care Arthur and Amy gave her, were pleased to see she did not become a beauty. Some (naturally) were worried that sons when looking around for wives might take Millie into consideration.

This was unlikely, for when Millie left school, she did not go anywhere without Arthur or Amy. Arthur had the bootmaker's and saddler's shop, next to the butcher's, on the road to Bermagui. It was an untidy place, with his saddles, some half made, and big pieces of beautiful pinkish leather, smelling of cattle and wet bush, piled up inside the door, and his boot lasts and boots and shoes taking up so much counter space there was barely room for the shoes you wanted mended or the money for those that were done.

Arthur had a brown skin, black hair and dark brown eyes which he flashed briefly on customers before he bowed them over his work. Cobargo blamed Annie, Amy and Millie (in that order) for the scandal. They had pity for Arthur, giving him the role of the innocent caught in a women's trap. It was an odd attitude, especially for the women, since a man had been responsible for the sixteen year old Annie's downfall.

The problem for Cobargo was that no one knew the man. They guessed wildly, and as Millie grew, looked for Rossmore eyes, a Greaves nose, the walk of a Parsons.

Annie had started going to dances at fifteen.

She used to fly around the hall. The boots Arthur made for her were lighter and more slender than those the other girls wore, fighting it seemed with the hem of her skirt. The skirt kicked out and swishing back, slapped at the boots, like a firefly teasing a pair of playful kittens.

"Who is my father, Ma?" Millie asked at fifteen,

noticing Arthur was slower than he used to be, making his way up the incline to the road, returning to the shop.

"Pa is your father," Amy said from the doorway, half looking backwards at a smear of dust on the little table by the piano. Millie was getting careless with her dusting.

"My real father," Millie said with her face against the wistaria trunk, allowing it to rough her cheek. Amy felt her heart contract in a troubled way. Millie might have been caressing the cheek of a man.

"You wouldn't find a better father anywhere than Pa," Amy said, with so much passion in her voice, Millie was afraid to continue the conversation. She pulled a bunch of wistaria over her black hair, so that it looked like bridal headgear.

"Dust the little table again," Amy said sharply. "You missed most of it, swiping at it the way you do."

Millie got up from the step and went through the house to the pantry for the duster.

Amy went with Millie to the dances and the pictures, which were shown three or four times a year in the School of Arts.

At the dances Amy sat on one of the seats ranged around the wall with Millie beside her most of the time. Amy, most of the time, thought about Annie, remembering how she had abandoned herself to the dance, her face showing up when she danced under a lantern, still and pale as the light itself, coming in and out of the shadows like a creamy oval plate, tipped back so the eyes were lost under a thick thatch of hair dark as Millie's and Arthur's.

Amy tried to remember if she had missed Annie at a time when Annie would have conceived Millie.

One night Amy took over the washing-up after supper when a regular helper, Mary O'Shea, had a fainting turn.

"This is kind of you, Mrs Clarke," said one of the

Rossmore women, not in kindly tones, but stiffly, not succeeding in keeping disapproval out of her voice, for it was a Catholic dance and the Clarkes were not of that faith, nor any other followed in Cobargo.

Amy kept her head over the washing-up dish (like Arthur over his saddles and boots) until she was done, then pulled her black crepe skirt straight with thumb and forefinger of each hand and went back to watch the dancing.

How long was she in the supper room that night? She couldn't remember seeing Annie on the floor immediately she took her seat again. Had Annie slipped away long enough to . . .?

Amy never said aloud what Annie had done, not even to Arthur. It was nearly six months before Annie's condition was confirmed. Amy and Arthur took Annie to Bega when her stomach started to swell and dosing with bicarbonate of soda would not bring it down, for Amy was convinced Annie had inherited Arthur's wind laden bowels, an acute embarrassment to her, for Arthur was known to relieve himself among his saddles while looking for a suitable piece of leather, with a customer coming noiselessly into the shop.

"If he talked with his arse, he'd burn the ears off our heads!" said old Mrs Gladys Watt, for Arthur's poor vocal record was a source of annoyance in Cobargo.

When Amy and Arthur decided to take Annie to the doctor in Bega, they hired a horse and buggy from Jack Caldwell, who was the town's blacksmith and who had his shop on the other side of the bridge from the Clarkes' house, the shop pulled down years later for Rossmore's store. Arthur had never hired the buggy before and was appalled at the cost. In a state of shock on the way home, his thoughts were channelled mainly towards the seven shillings he had paid out, a good portion of his week's profit.

"Get up, get up!" he said to the horse, slapping at its sweating rump, as if its lazy pace was added proof of the one-sided deal.

"Don't tell me who the man was!" Amy cried passionately, allowing herself only half a glance of Annie's thighs which, like her stomach, appeared to have expanded since they left Cobargo that morning, her own body sweltering in her hot clothes on the November day. The buggy seat was wet with their perspiration and Annie's face wet with tears.

"Don't say the name! I don't ever want to know!" But what Amy was really saying was, I want to blame you, and only you. I want to punish you all the rest of your life, and only you.

"Get up, get up! Move for God's sake!" Arthur cried to the horse, although he and Amy thought simultaneously there was no great advantage in arriving home early. Cobargo had to be faced, and from then on they knew that all their lives would change.

One of the big changes and challenges was keeping Annie out of view during the months remaining before it was time to give birth, the projected date a problem in itself since Annie could not, or would not, give any indication of the time she last menstruated, or had the "things", as Amy said.

"I wish I could remember when I washed her rags," Amy said to Arthur in their bedroom.

Arthur made no reply, flashing his eyes away as he did when he had a customer with whom no further talk was necessary.

Amy could not believe her own stupidity that she had not noticed an absence of Annie's rags, stiff with blood amongst the dirty clothes, although Annie had menstruated irregularly since she was thirteen. Because Amy had to soak the rags with a good handful of salt (sometimes finding them weeks old jammed between the mattress and the foot of Annie's bed) Amy supposed she was glad to be spared the job over a long period.

"I didn't see any dirty rags for a long time," Amy said one day to Annie, who was sitting on the back step, very big now and trying to keep her stomach turned towards the kitchen, should Jack Caldwell see her from the rear of his shop, or some children from the creek where they often wandered on a Saturday afternoon.

"I didn't have any dirty rags for you to see," Annie said, folding her skirt back on her young thighs, to cool them in a breeze from the water, little of it as there was in the February drought.

Amy was preparing to open up on one of her tirades, more frequent now as Annie's time grew closer and Amy's worries increased with the prospect of a child to rear under such painful circumstances, when Annie got up with a strained face and went into her bedroom.

Amy heard the door shut and scrubbed harder at the pots in the washing up dish, using up the energy she would have put into words. After a while Amy, unable to hold back some new accusations that had come to her, fuelling the savage fire of her anger, went and flung open Annie's door.

Annie was holding onto the towel rail of the washstand with sweat running over her cheeks.

Arthur had to close the shop and ask Jack Caldwell for the horse and buggy again.

"Five shillings will do this time," Jack said, working speedily with shafts and harness.

Arthur was pleased but wounded. It seemed that he was regarded as a regular customer to whom a discount was due.

89

It was a dreadful trip to Bega, with Annie writhing and sobbing and twice asking to stop to fling herself down on the grass, legs apart and dress up around her thighs, Amy in terrible fear that she would give birth then, and in her fear, more abusive than she intended to be.

She hauled Annie to her feet and forced her back into the buggy telling her it could be days, even weeks before the actual birth.

"This is your punishment! Like it or not, it's your punishment!" Amy cried, and Annie turned sideways and clung to the back of the buggy seat and kicked Amy's legs, whether intentionally or in pain was not clear.

Millie was born about two hours after they reached Bega hospital. Faces bowed in their deep shame, Amy and Arthur were prepared to leave as soon as Annie was shut away in the labour ward.

"You may as well wait," the matron said, a cold glitter in her grey eyes running over Amy and Arthur which they interpreted as blame for Annie's downfall. "She should be delivered quite soon."

Arthur felt compelled to mention the hired buggy and the need to return to Cobargo as soon as possible.

"I got a cut price on the hire," he said.

"Two shillings off," Amy said. Both pairs of eyes raised to the matron's starched cap said we haven't been totally shunned, we have friends at home, whatever you may think of us.

But they stayed and saw Annie, white of face on the white pillow, her rich hair spread all about, and the tiny child with its reddish skin and thin wisps of wet hair fastened to Annie's body with her round, childish arm, about which there was a looseness and a detachment even then.

They waited for Annie to open her eyes. When she did they were still, like water waiting for the tide. Then came a wash, like flotsam brought in by the tide, no treasures, just sharp edged ugly objects, the sight chilly to Amy in her hot clothes, so that she turned and started from the room, Arthur more hesitant, but finally following.

In two weeks they hired the buggy again. Jack Caldwell didn't mention the charge, expecting Arthur to take for granted the normal price, since the drama had passed and the disgrace brought upon Cobargo must now be paid in full.

Annie was gone when they got to the hospital. The matron, with eyes as cold as the tide of Annie's, washing more on Amy than Arthur, told them Annie had gone into service in Bega.

"A nice respectable place," she said, making it sound as if Amy's and Arthur's was not.

Amy's initial reaction was relief. They could turn around then and go home and anyone in Cobargo asking of Annie (and including the baby without using words) would be told Annie was well settled in a job in Bega.

The matron's next words shocked Amy so deeply she had to cling to the back of the chair by which she stood. (Neither Arthur or Amy had felt it proper to take the chairs they were offered.)

"The baby has been weaned," the matron said. "She's taken to the mixture, and you can take enough home to keep her going for a week. Your local store will stock it, I should hope."

Amy had a crazy vision of shelves piled high, running through the ceiling, of navy blue tins with grey lettering, which she knew to be a new product for infant feeding when mother's milk failed. Her brain worked sufficiently to see the matron wore an expression of doubt that Cobargo would be abreast of the times in infant feeding.

"And she wants her called Kathleen," the matron said.

The two dark figures with the white-wrapped baby

drove towards Cobargo in the glaring February afternoon without speaking.

In sight of Cobargo bridge, Amy, grateful that Arthur could set her down and cross it alone and thus spare her the glare of Cobargo from Caldwell's shop, grateful that the buggy hood came forward enough to hide her from eyes at the edge of window curtains and in door slits, grateful for all of this, spoke at last.

"She's not getting the name she wants! Make no mistake about that! I'm not naming her the way she says. I won't do what she asks! Why should I?'

She carried the baby down the incline, awkward in her long black skirt, and was glad to be in the cool house. When Arthur came in she told him the baby would be called Millicent. It was a name she remembered from girlhood, that of a girl in her class at school whom she admired and longed to have for a friend.

Amy grudgingly conceded (to herself) that life was less difficult than she had expected. She bought flannelette (too late in the season for a lighter material) and made three nightgowns from a paper pattern she had kept for seventeen years, thinking briefly of Annie when she found it in the bottom of a hatbox.

Old Fred Grant, who had Cobargo's only general store then, made a neat parcel of the cloth, shutting the smell of newness inside the brown paper, making Amy think of the newness of little Millie at home, sleeping in the care of Arthur home for midday dinner, urging her to hurry back.

Fred made out the docket carefully (the Clarkes were good payers) and spiked the duplicate and said good afternoon to Amy without hinting about the baby. A woman would have said something, Amy thought, with a rush of love towards all the men of the world.

Millie was still sleeping when she got home, and Arthur

was finishing his cold meat and tomatoes on Amy's starched white tablecloth. She was impatient for him to go back to the shop for her to lay the flannelette and pattern on the bare table and start cutting. Her sewing machine was one of the few in Cobargo, the wheel turned with a little handle, running down a whole seam in a few seconds. She had made Annie's clothes by hand, but she wouldn't think of that, but concentrate on the feather stitching in pink thread with which she would trim the sleeves and hem.

I'm happy, Amy thought. It's hard to believe, but I am actually happy. She turned the wheel so hard, it ran by itself for half the seam.

Millie's first years were spent almost entirely behind the wistaria. All Amy needed to do if someone was passing to whom she didn't wish to speak was to tilt her head so that a leaf or bloom obscured her eyes. Little Millie stared back at them, answering their curiosity with a curiosity of her own, and if it was a knot of school children stopping and hanging over the bridge rail to watch Millie, Amy would scoop her up and stand where the wistaria was thickest, until the little group straggled off, Millie turning her neck to watch until they were out of sight.

"Silly old kids," Amy would say, carrying Millie off inside.

When Millie was seven, Amy had to decide about sending her to school.

"She's been having the Sunday walks with us long enough now to be ready for something more," Amy said.

Arthur didn't reply, his silence indicating acceptance of the logic.

But Millie's introduction to school was not a success. Her shrill weeping at the strangeness of her surroundings had barely died away when it was replaced by another variety, a low sobbing inside her small hard chest, escaping in half strangled breaths from her dry mouth.

She was in the centre of a group in the playground, which fell away, leaving her, a pathetic sight in a dress that almost reached the top of her boots, for Amy tended to dress Millie as she had done Annie at the same age.

The girls in senior classes had informed Millie that Amy and Arthur were not her real parents, but that she was the daughter of Annie, who had abandoned her and had never been heard of since.

Amy had feared this, and when the bewildered and incoherent Millie had given Amy the trend of the accusations, Amy shouted angrily at Millie, unable to understand herself why she could not be gentle. (Perhaps it was because Millie sat in the very spot on the kitchen doorstep where Annie had sat before they took her to hospital to give birth.)

Millie got up and washed her face as she was told, and changed her clothes as she was sternly bid. Then she was sent to Grant's store for half a pound of mixed biscuits, a rare purchase, causing Millie to be torn between pleasurable anticipation and fear that she might run into her tormenters on the way.

She went to school white faced next day, lowering her frightened eyes in the presence of the older Parsons, Henrys and the Gillespie girl. But the tormenting thinned itself out in subsequent weeks, mainly through Millie maintaining a silence when accused of the circumstances of her birth, unaware though she was of the wisdom of this course. To weep and carry on brought down Amy's wrath, and for Millie the taunts of her peers were the more acceptable.

She was about twelve when the old Pinkertons left the bank and a new family came. They were called Chalinor. There was a boy Millie's age who went to the public school, but would be sent to boarding school in a couple of years' time.

One day Millie, on her way home from school, dawdling, because once inside Amy did not let her out again, saw young Kevin Chalinor watching the creek water from the bank below the bridge approach on what Cobargo called the town side. Millie watched Kevin unobserved (or so she thought), seeing a side of his face with a sweep of straight dark hair against a freckled cheek. Freckles were considered a social blight in Cobargo, and Millie's smooth unblemished skin was envied by freckled Rossmores, Rankins and O'Reillys. And now the new bank family, with a red-haired father, had freckled Kevin and a three year old who looked as if she had started out with a plain white face, and then someone took to it with a brown pencil, liberally marking the forehead, the bridge of the nose and the centre of fat round cheeks with spots.

Millie did not share the Cobargo view of freckles. She thought Kevin's cheek a lot like the wing of Speckly, a favoured hen among the few kept by the Clarkes in a pen near the vegetable patch on the edge of the creek bank. Millie felt the cheek of Kevin would be as soft to touch as the wing of Speckly, and was thinking this when Kevin lifted his eyes, very brown.

He looked away almost at once, pressing his boots into the blackish sand, forming a crusty edge to the creek. She watched, for it was something she liked doing, and he moved along, deciding now to break the crust, stamping his foot harder with each step. Then a foot went down deeper where the edge was softer, and not only did he raise a sodden boot, but fell on his bottom, leaping up hurriedly, and slapping at dark sand clinging there. He might have looked back at the bridge but Millie couldn't be sure. She stuffed a handkerchief into her mouth to stifle the laughter he could not possibly hear. He began to run, whirling his arms to help his balance like a wind-mill threatening to topple over.

At tea that night, Millie remembered and put her head back and laughed suddenly under the lamp swinging above the table. Amy, remembering Annie dancing under the lantern, got up and unhooked the light and set it on the food safe behind her chair.

"Don't laugh at nothing," Amy said. "Only crazy people do that."

Kevin tore past Millie next day on the way home from school.

See this, said his straight back in his school shirt, billowing like a blue sail. See how fast I run. Never a slip of these sure feet! Woosh! Down the bank. A pity Millie could see only the top of his head if that. Millie took her time walking by the railing that started several panels before the actual bridge, ducked under to her own surprise, and ran or rather slithered down the grassy slope, pretty sure of foot too. When she pulled up she sat, not flopped down, and putting out both feet, with the toe of her boots broke away some sandy crust, wishing she were wearing her best shoes, a tan pair with a strap across the instep and two rows of punching, beautifully curved on the toe cap. Kevin was breaking the new crust too that had formed overnight, for a shower of rain had fallen, widening the water a couple of inches. He was putting one foot in front of the other carefully so that only a pinch of sand, like decoration at the edge of a pie crust, marked the space between the toe of one boot and the heel of the other. When Kevin was getting quite a distance from Millie he looked back at the artistry, his head on one side giving it all his attention and none at all to Millie.

She saw the pinched edge like a pie of Amy's and thought of a slice now, not for herself but for Kevin.

Across the creek was the back of her place and the kitchen window up a few inches, a space good enough to slide a pie through.

Then Amy came down the steps, a dish balanced on her hip, and her free hand stirring at the grain ready to throw to the fowls, who were beginning to go crazy with anticipation, massed into a corner of the pen. Amy had her eyes on them, and Millie had the crazy idea of flying across the creek and into the kitchen for a slice of pie for Kevin. But she turned quite suddenly and scrambled up the bank, adopting a sedate walk across the bridge for Amy to see on her way back to the house.

Kevin was not at school next day, and a younger sister gave out the news that he was sick in bed.

Millie did not take the turn to the bridge that afternoon, but walked rapidly and diagonally across to the bank to sit on the steps. They were marble, cool through her school bloomers, and Millie wondered at this for it was a warm day. Above her on the first floor of the bank the Chalinors lived. The bedrooms faced the main street, and Kevin's room was the second from the end, the parents occupying the end room which had a second window on the wall facing the road to Bermagui. Such luxury of two windows for one bedroom and a whole house, bathroom too, reached from inside the bank up a satiny brown staircase, and the choice of outside steps leading to a back veranda, securely windowed too against the weather, was a talking point for sixth class at Cobargo Public, although Millie made no contribution to it.

Kevin, at a quarter to four, was ready to get up, having slept and sweated through most of the day. Out of bed, he wandered to his shell collection on the chest of drawers and touched the shells, in particular a creamy one smooth as a girl's skin, the edge dimpled like the sand in the creek which he had broken with his boots.

Millie.

He went to the window to look where the bridge rail ran emptily along, staring as if at any moment a small dark head would sail into view.

Something (he did not know what) made him look directly down and there she was. A button was half fastened at the neck of her dress, showing a little piece of her back, and her peaked shoulder blades with plaits of hair that were like twin glistening snakes resting on the dark grey stuff of her dress, rougher textured than the material of his sisters' clothes.

He banged his forehead on the glass of the window, and the plaits were gone, flung to her front, as if they were ropes tossed by an expert hand. The back of the neck was gone and, in its place, a cup of a face, square at the chin, a face puzzling Cobargo and causing peevish anger at the unknown origin.

Millie unfolded her legs and stood quite tall, and Kevin shrunk downwards so that his chin was on the window sill and his shameful pyjamas out of sight. His sister Eileen came into the room, craning her neck at the window to see Millie too.

She drew in her breath, like wind inside a chimney flue, fanning a fire eager to blaze. "Mumma!" she cried, and Mrs Chalinor, a thin, harassed little woman, came running in with a handful of cutlery, for she was setting the table in the dining room early, nervous about a visitor for tea, a bachelor customer of the bank whom Bob was anxious to please.

"Oh, back into bed!" she cried, seeing Kevin. "There in bare feet you'll die of double pneumonia!"

"But look, Mumma!" Eileen said, pointing down to the top of Millie's head, for Millie did not dare look up any more.

Mrs Chalinor stretched her neck, her eyes snapping impatience and worry. "Oh, go home, go home! Home to your mother at once!" she said, snapping the window shut.

Eileen crushed herself against the wall, hand to her mouth, eyes big enough to write Millie's history in them.

Kevin got into bed and turned his back to the window.

When Millie was eighteen she met a boy named Andy Cummins.

He began to hang around Arthur's shop, liking the smell of new leather, and trying to get Arthur to explain how he cut pieces for saddles and shoes guided only by a tilted black eye.

Andy, sitting on a pile of leather folds and old saddles to be mended, saw his own hands, hanging from long, bony wrists resting on his knees, as the most useless things in the world.

Millie came in one afternoon he was there, bringing Arthur a billy can of tea and a teacake warm from the oven, wrapped in a serviette. She was embarrassed to be seen with such a load, although pleased at the look in Arthur's eyes when he saw her. She wished the young man there could see the little leather bag Arthur had made for her. It was shaped like an envelope with a button fastening the flap, which Arthur had made too from leather strips so finely plaited it looked like a lovely crinkle-topped chocolate. She wished to be carrying the bag, or that there was some way of telling Andy that she possessed it. Millie knew who Andy was and Andy knew who Millie was, although she had rested briefly in his arms only once in a barn dance.

Andy was spending a few weeks with one of the Rossmore families, a relative on the wife's side. He was not long orphaned with the death of his father, his mother dying when he was born. He would go to university the following year. Meanwhile, helping around the farm was seen as a contribution towards easing his loss. He didn't know what he would study to be, a doctor or a teacher he supposed, but he really wouldn't mind making saddles like Arthur.

He told Millie this one day when she was crossing the bridge going home from Rossmore's store. Andy had walked to town and had spent some time on the seat outside Rossmore's, not doing more than looking across at Arthur's shop, for he was beginning to feel sensitive about spending time there, and he thought Arthur was lowering his head more over his work and saying even less then he used to.

But he was glad he hadn't gone there for he might have missed Millie, who had taken her little leather bag and gone into the drapery for some cotton for Amy and had been served while Andy was out the back with Fred, who had not long had his new storeroom and was packing the shelves, spinning the job out to take pleasure in blowing out wood shavings and fragments of sawdust as he worked.

Andy told Fred he would leave for his uncle Harry's to help with the afternoon's milking. This pleased Fred, for he considered most young people were lazy, although without children of his own for first hand experience. Fred, however, did not approve of the way Andy mooched past the counter and hesitated by the bowsers with half a face towards the other side of the road, and still seemed hesitant about which way he was going.

If Fred were as young as Andy (although he should make allowances for his newly-orphaned state, he supposed) he would put his shoulders back and walk off with a brisk air and purpose in his step. He would know where he was going, and he would go there cheerful and grateful to the Harry Rossmores for taking him in, for he was only a nephew by marriage, not a real Rossmore of Cobargo.

Andy smartened up when he saw Millie. He did put his shoulders back and pulled down the cuffs of his shirt sleeves, hoping this would disguise the length and thinness of his arms. Millie was at the bridge approach walking ahead, her little bag swinging elegantly from a soft, round arm.

Andy lessened the space between them, hoping he did not imagine Millie slowing down, fearful lest she begin to hurry and reach her house before he reached her. Imagine if she went inside and slammed the door to let him know she didn't want anything to do with him! Girls were like that, he had been told. He plunged out in his nervous state at the prospect of this, and Millie put her square chin over her shoulder briefly and, dangling her little bag over the bridge rail, stood still as if the Cobargo Creek was as worthy of admiration as the waters of Venice.

Andy saw the beautiful shine on the reddish brown leather of Millie's bag and wished for enough courage to feel it and study Arthur's work at close range.

"Did he make it for you?" he asked, aware that he could not say your father, and hating himself for the disrespect to Arthur, whom he respected as much as anyone he knew.

Millie's chin went up quite sharply, and Andy, more miserable now, blushed a deep red. He was even more distressed to see how quickly they reached the other side of the bridge.

"I'd like to be able to make that kind of stuff," he said, sniffing the air as if it was filled with the pungent smell of Arthur's leather.

Millie's face was still, and Andy could see that as much as she loved Arthur, she had ambitions for a superior occupation.

"I'll be studying for a teacher or a doctor though," Andy said and he was sure her eyelids falling over her dark eyes was a sign of approval.

"I'll be back for holidays," he said. "There are a lot."

Just then Amy opened the front door, and bits of her skirt and pieces of her face were visible through the wistaria.

Millie swung her little bag out towards Amy indicating that the cotton was inside.

Andy, not knowing what else to do, walked off, quite fast up the hill on his way to Harry Rossmore's, a good walk, for the Bert Rossmores came first, more than a mile from Cobargo, and Harry's gate was another two miles away on the opposite side of the road.

Where was Millie standing when he turned his back? What look was on her face? He hurried, aware that he had no chance of knowing, hating himself for his foolish action in running from her. When he neared the bend that would take Millie and all Cobargo from his view, he went to the middle of the road and turned fully around. There was nothing of her and little of the house except the fronds of the wistaria, spread out by a wind as if it were conspiring to shut her away.

He turned then and ran hard up the middle of the road, as if he were taking part in a race, and indeed he looked over his shoulder from time to time as if to see where his competitors were.

He took a rest at Bert's gate, sitting in the cream box, not comfortable, for he was too tall for it and the top edge forced his neck down onto his knees. He was there thinking about starting on the next stage of his walk when Bert came down to the gate, his curiosity aroused from a front window of the house at movement seen through cracks of the cream box.

Andy scrambled out when he saw Bert, not straightening up at once, aware that the bowing posture was quite pleasing to Bert.

He gave Andy's face a swift but penetrating look before he sat on a wattle stump, the remains of a tree which had been removed lest the branches scratch Bert's newly acquired Studebaker, the first motor in Cobargo.

Bert looked down between his feet. Rene, he saw with the left side of his face, was on the veranda, and sitting on the steps were Stan, ten then, and Eric three years younger. Their tiny new one, the girl Madge, was sleeping in an upstairs room.

Only twelve years before, Bert had been hanging around the Murchisons, out on the Wandella Road, favouring Rene among the tribe of girls, old Vince Murchison (only old to the youthful Bert) pleased to see one of them off his hands, and into the keeping of a Rossmore. Good stock the Murchisons, the mother from a Goulburn family of graziers, meeting Vince when he was there at a Catholic boarding school, the same Stan and Eric would attend when they were older. Good stock all round! Bert raised his eyes to his cattle dotting the ridges. The distance made them appear better bred than they really were.

Bert sprang up and put out a hand. "You'll be off to Sydney in a week, son. Goodbye in case I don't see you."

Andy was walking in the direction of Harry's when he remembered it was more than two weeks before he was due to leave.

Millie hoped no one would notice her dressing much earlier than was necessary for the walk the following Sunday with Arthur and Amy.

She had on a fine silk cigar-coloured blouse with many

of Amy's beautiful pintucks, and Amy frowned disapproval from her side of the table at the raised spoon of quivering blancmange threatening to plop from Millie's spoon.

When they left the house, Arthur took the lead, climbing the incline with a show of energy and walking to the middle of the road.

Amy came up with a flutter of her black skirt, but from Millie's, still at the edge of the road, there was barely a whispering of pleats. Millie watched Arthur's back, the grey in his hair under the brim of his hat like silver needles stuck in black cloth.

Last Sunday they had gone the Bermagui way, the Sunday before they had taken the road past the schools, and the week before that had climbed the hill towards Tilba, resting as they usually did by the cemetery fence, looking down on Cobargo over the row of pines, planted when that was a new road, making a second highway to the coast.

This Sunday they would surely go the Bega road. Millie turned her face that way thinking of Andy somewhere in the direction waiting (perhaps) on the Harry Rossmore gate, long legs dangling beyond the middle rail.

But Arthur began to cross the bridge, and Amy began to break into a half jog to reach him. She called back to Millie. "We all walk together. People will think we're fighting, straggled out this way."

Cobargo always said Millie Clarke (although she wasn't entitled to that name) would never marry.

She didn't either.

9   In Cobargo Now

The Boyles were almost as poor as the Churchers and there were a number of other similarities.

There were nearly as many Boyles as Churchers, and the father, Les, was frequently out of work. In Cobargo if you did not own a shop, work in one, or the post office or the bank; if you did not own a farm or sharefarmed, were not a nun at the convent, or a teacher at the public school there were few opportunities for employment. It had been years since any new roads were made, so work was intermittent there, only repairs at infrequent intervals, and these restricted mainly to the Bega road, where there were Rossmore properties. This was attributed to the influence of Bert, who was friendly with the president of the shire incorporating Cobargo.

Les Boyle talked a lot about work and a large, grand house for his family of seven, much of the time sitting in the kitchen doorway, dangling his legs and scraping his feet on the patch of worn earth below.

The house had only four rooms and a front veranda. The back should have had a veranda too, but the building was stopped when a Twyford girl decided not to marry one of the O'Reillys, and the O'Reilly went off and enlisted in World War I and died in France.

The Twyford girl left home too, and went into service in Sydney, eventually marrying the baker who delivered the bread to the fine house on the harbour foreshores, about which she wrote at great length to her relatives in Cobargo, so full of praise for the beauty of the furniture, the quality and abundance of the food and the ease of her life there, it was surprising that she went to live in the slums of Darlinghurst, with only a metal teapot from the family she served so devotedly.

Old Hector O'Reilly, who had been building the place for his son, did not have it finished, and it was empty a long time, then finally let to the Boyles, who moved to Cobargo after a sojourn of camping at Wallaga Lake, where Les fished and sometimes sold a catch to guest houses at Bermagui.

Most of the population of Wallaga Lake, as the name implies, were Aborigines, so Mrs Boyle and the four children (and a baby too young for social discrimination) were pleased to have white neighbours, and to look up inside the house to a ceiling.

"Look at it!" Mrs Boyle would cry (sometimes to help cheer her when she did not know where the next meal would come from). "Isn't it the most wonderful thing you ever saw!"

The children (two more were born after the move to Cobargo) would raise their bright eyes to the ceiling, which was made of narrow timber boards, and Beryl, the eldest, would sometimes say: "Twenty-four boards, aren't there Mum? And twenty in your room!"

There a wider board had been used, but the two back rooms had a naked iron roof, supported by beams in their raw state, but with the advantage of taking nails, a great many for they were practically the sole means of hanging clothes in the children's room, and pots and oven rags in the kitchen.

"Thank you Dad, for getting us a real house!" little Ella, aged six, said one day to Les who was at the head of the table eating a plate of tomatoes and shallots grown by the tank-stand, safe from meandering cattle and horses, for there were usually enough little Boyles around to chase them off, should they cross from the opposite bank, the creek often in a dry state in the summer months.

"Yes! Thanks, thanks, thanks!" ran around the table from Beryl to two year old Connie. The baby, Leslie, the only little Boyle not contributing to the outcry, was asleep across the middle of his parents' bed between their two pillows removed from the bedhead.

"Hush, hush!" said Doris, the mother, holding the bread up like a baton. The noise rippled to nothing, most pairs of eyes swung to the door behind which the baby slept.

"I want him to have a good, long sleep," Mrs Boyle said to the table, apologizing for curbing their high spirits.

"He's a beauty, that boy, isn't he now?" said Les.

The children would have liked to have bellowed a great chorus of agreement, but had to be content with deep nods and wide smiles.

"And these tomatoes?" Les said. "What do you think of these tomatoes? Could anyone in Cobargo grow better tomatoes than these?"

Mary, who was eleven, slipped from her chair and ran and gave her father a kiss on the neck, the most accessible place she could find, for the dinner table was not that big, and Les had Connie on one side of him, and on the other side John, aged nine. John's place was the corner of the table, but Les's arms, being long, made it difficult for John to lift food from his plate to his mouth. He had to time the movement to coincide with Les's raised elbow, when he could duck swiftly and get a mouthful before his father's arm was lowered.

John, who was bright of eye with a mind to match, would on occasion entertain his mother and sisters (the mother trying to keep a straight face) exaggerating the eating process, sometimes missing the opportunity of getting his spoon or fork to his plate, for his father, engaged in a passionate monologue, would eat very fast to match the speed of his words.

John would then feign great sorrow and display advancing faintness through lack of nourishment, but in a while would poise himself, fork raised, aimed at his plate, ready to spear a morsel when his father's arm went high.

This time he speared his father's arm in error, followed by a contrite cry of "Sorry, Dad!" his sisters falling on their plates in their mirth, the mother going very pink and pushing her features into sternness with great effort.

"Just when Dad was up to such a good part in his story, too!" she cried, trying hard to frown on John.

Les put his knife and fork together on his plate and left the table. He sat in the doorway, the back of his neck plainly expressing his hurt. John moved into his place, throwing his elbows to their widest and flapping them up and down, working his mouth in time, whether to indicate an intake of food or a flow of words, was not clear. No matter which, the girls around the table threatened to explode with laughter, except Connie, who left her chair and went and lay along her father's back, rubbing her yellow silky hair into his neck.

"Carry on from there, Les," Mrs Boyle said, frowning very hard on John now without effort. The girls immediately grew serious and sat up very straight.

"Look it's raining!" Ella cried, her place at the table allowing her a clear view of outside. "Don't get your legs wet, Dad!"

"I'll pull Daddy in!" Connie said, with both arms under his armpits and a giggling show of dragging him into the kitchen.

"You knew it was going to rain, didn't you, love?" Mrs Boyle said.

Les swung his legs inside and sat sideways. "I knew it

would rain alright!" he said, taking his tobacco tin out of his pocket and beginning to lift shreds from inside, cupping his other hand and poking the tobacco down under the tin.

"Let me!" cried Connie, and he gave her the tin to hold. The others watched his brown fingers roll the cigarette up to the delicate pinching of stray threads of tobacco from each end. Mrs Boyle wasn't awestruck like the children, she thought of the butter, sugar and cheese the money spent on tobacco and cigarette papers would buy in a week. Never mind, she told herself, he must have some pleasure, as she got up to clear the table and thus avoid seeing too much of the wasteful puffing.

There was no pudding to finish the meal, the children saw, and Mrs Boyle read disappointment on their faces.

"Pudding tomorrow!" she said cheerfully.

"What?" asked John, a shade suspiciously.

"Let it be a surprise!" Mrs Boyle said, gathering plates with energy, avoiding John's face and craning her neck to see the rain, falling hard now.

"Oh, look at it!" she said, unable to resist looking to the ceiling, marvelling at the beautiful dryness.

"Remember the storm at Wallaga when the tent came down?" said Beryl, which was usually said by one of the children when it rained on the new house.

"Every single thing, even the bread was drenched in a minute!" Heather said, who did not actually remember, being the baby at that time, but since this was also recalled by one of the older children every time it rained following the move to Cobargo, she was now wise to the sequence of events that followed the downpour.

"Did you know it was going to rain that day?" asked John innocently to this father. (This hadn't been said before.)

Mrs Boyle frowned on him again, and Mary, the pretty

one, crossed both hands over her mouth, her face around the hands very pink.

"No silly laughing now," Mrs Boyle said, thankful that Les wasn't listening, but smoking dreamily, with Connie on his lap curled up, taking advantage of the music the rain made on the roof to fall asleep.

"The blacks took us in," Ella said (who did remember).

Les heard that. "They built them humpies and were too bone lazy to dig drains. The first thing you do before you start buildin' a place is to drain the land. If there'd been drains to take that water, we'd been high and dry. As it was they damned near drowned us. If I hadn't moved fast — " He took out his tobacco tin as if there were the need for a soothing agent, the memory sending him into a state of agitation.

The children agreed with half their minds. The other half recalled the warmth inside the humpy of the man called Wallaga Wal, who hustled the women to fry pieces of sourish bread dough, which puffed beautifully in the pan and was fed to the children dripping with golden syrup.

The taste came into Ella's mouth now, and she put her head on the table tiredly. It was a long time to wait for tomorrow and pudding.

"Let's not talk about the blacks," Mrs Boyle said. "We're in Cobargo now!"

Ella thought of Lottie, Cyril, Pearl, Rose and Angus with whom she and her sisters and John played at the lake. A picture of the water came into her mind. Beneath it the sand sloped away, pearly grey like the inside of an oyster shell. The black children's mothers and aunts sat on a log to see that no one drowned, bare feet stretched out, bluish black, making their toenails show up very pink. They seldom smiled, and seemed hardly to talk at all. Sometimes one or another would get up and saunter

110

to the lake and dive in, clothes not removed, swimming far out, soon nothing more than a speck.

The black children took no notice, the little Boyles were fearful she would never return. But she would soon be back, her body changed now, the buttocks like twin loaves of bread, the belly round like a pie, risen in the centre, the naval a dent, like an opening for the steam to escape, the thighs like submerged logs, their covering of thin wet cloth giving them a shine. The thighs vibrated as she walked, and the breasts waggled, nipples defined, large, like candle stumps in saucers.

Ella looked down on the creek, her chin on the table. The rain stroking hard upon it, wrapping it in a grey blanket. It might not have been there except for three or four cows from Coady's farm (with the creek for one of the boundaries) standing on the bank mourning the threat to cut off their way across.

Mrs Boyle saw Ella's face, mourning too. "When the rain stops and the boy wakes, you can take him for a walk," she said.

"Now!" cried Heather, who at four did not see weather as a handicap, no matter what kind.

They had an old cane pram, coloured a battleship grey, having weathered six little Boyles, which squeaked its way up what Cobargo called the cemetery hill regularly, with two Boyle girls behind it and Leslie inside. The girls would bend forward, the hems of their dresses in front nearly scraping the ground, their faces invisible to the boy at times, who expressed his disapproval with eyes flashing from side to side, bluer with his tears and with his mouth pulled into a piteous shape, which changed to a wide grin when the heads went back and the faces showed and kisses were showered on plump legs, pumping up and down.

But there was no walk that afternoon, when the boy

woke rosy and good tempered with several pairs of skinny, young arms eager to hold him.

The rain continued, and Les put on a macintosh with *Department of Main Roads* stamped heavily up one seam. Les should have returned it after a job of three weeks, two years ago, but failed to, claiming he had done extra hours for which he wasn't paid, and the coat was his entitlement.

Mrs Boyle tried without success to fade the lettering, and she was deeply embarrassed when he took every opportunity to wear it, especially this day when the post office crowd would be gathered to collect their mail after sorting.

The Boyles received very little mail, but this did not deter Les from standing wrapped in his wet and glistening coat, hands under the cape, flirting with the younger and prettier of the women and teasing the children, and raising his eyes every now and again to the top of the door where the inside bolt was, the rattle of which would be the first indication of the door's opening to let in the flood of mail seekers.

Les stood well back, taller than most of the others, to allow everyone else to be served first, upholding his reputation for courtesy. (The Cobargo opinion of Les was that he was a useless bastard, but you couldn't help liking him.)

It was fortunate because Bob Lumsdaine, a farmer at Quaama, about seven miles in the Bega direction, came into the post office on business. He was well, (and legally) covered in an oilskin, and the look he sent towards Les said he wanted a word with him. Les followed Bob onto the porch, a gesture to the postmaster on his way out, saying the business of mail collecting was of little importance, there was another matter awaiting his urgent attention. (The box marked "B" was now empty anyway.)

112

Bob offered Les a day's work at the Quaama sports about three weeks off.

Last year the work had been too heavy for the voluntary committee and they were running between organizing the foot races, the steer riding and the tug of war, as well as keeping someone on the gate and the fires burning under the row of kerosene tins boiling water for the gallons of tea served in the refreshment tents.

Les was offered fifteen shillings to be general rouse-about for the day.

The main job appeared to be looking after the fires and keeping children away from them, as the children tended to light sticks and paper twists and chase each other with these, which they appeared to enjoy more than events on the sports arena.

Black children in the party from Wallaga Lake were the main offenders. Wallaga Wal owned a lorry and drove up the coast, stacking the rear table top with relatives and other residents, most of them standing clinging to each other to avoid being flung out, exhilarated by the risk, looking in their bright clothes above long, thin black legs like ragged flowers defying destruction while their stalks suffered the effects of a raging fire.

The little Boyles did not immediately think of the Wallaga Lake people at the Quaama sports, for they had never been. They screamed and jumped nearly to the ceiling when Les came home and shed his macintosh and told them they would all be going, getting admittance free of charge, since he would be on the gate.

But Mrs Boyle said she wouldn't go. She would stay with the boy and make sure he got his good, long sleep and it would be a chance of getting all the ironing done.

In their feverish excitement the little Boyles overlooked the thinness of this statement. There would be little ironing to do, since they owned few clothes and these

113

would be mostly on their backs for the day at Quaama sports.

They put every effort into persuading their mother to go on the rare outing.

"Oh, Mum!" said Mary. "Please, please, *please!*"

Mrs Boyle put more wood on the stove as if she were starting already to build it up for the marathon ironing.

She wanted to say she had only her old grey voile, very shabby now, but didn't want to draw attention to Les's failings as a provider.

"I'll make you a big parcel of sandwiches and you can all have a lovely day," Mrs Boyle said. "But we'll be watching out for you from five o'clock, the boy and I!"

"You don't have to bother with sandwiches," Les said grandly. "We'll all eat in the tea tent!"

This brought howls of joy from the children. Never before had they eaten anywhere but at their own table. They had been told at school, after the sports each year, of the long tables spread with white paper and, running down the centre, plates of sandwiches and cake, some large and whole, others small, iced or oozing cream, little tarts, puffs and eclairs, great slabs of buttered currant loaf, some of it iced too, and filmed with shredded coconut. The little Boyles could not get enough cake.

"Did you hear what Dad said?" cried Ella, who had jumped and screamed with the others, but wanted it confirmed and repeated.

Les had said too much already.

Bob Lumsdaine had not offered free food to the Boyles, nor said anything about free admittance. Les was troubled by a vision of the little Boyles miserably outside the tin fence, hearing the excited din from the other side. They well may be hungry too. Well, he would get them through somehow, and would approach the women in the tea tent for a plate of the rougher sandwiches and crumbled cake,

114

saying a dog had got their lunch, and it didn't matter about him, it was the children he was worried about.

Les worked this out while the joy of the children simmered down to an occasional squeal, collapsing wherever they could find a seat, curbed by the rain, for they would have liked to run outside and use up their exuberance whirling their thin arms about and crying out to each other: "The sports! The Quaama sports! We're going!"

Then Les took a seat by the stove to extol the virtues of Bob Lumsdaine, which surprised the children (who had barely heard of him) and puzzled Mrs Boyle, who had heard (from Les) tales of his parsimonious practices in relation to families who worked his sharefarms.

"He was coming up here to the house to see me," Les said. " 'There's no one else we'd trust with the job, Les' " he said to me. One of the few real gentlemen left in the world."

He saw himself with a Gladstone bag on a long strap over his shoulder, the money falling into it, as he juggled change and tickets and a cigarette between his lips, greeting everyone, mostly by Christian name, for it was Les's proud boast that he knew and was known to practically everyone from Eurobodalla in the south, north to Bega.

"How will we get there?" John asked suddenly. No one else, not even Les, had thought of this.

"Bob'll have something arranged," Les said. "There'll be dozens of cars through Cobargo that day." He took out his tobacco and opened the tin quite sharply, as if this helped erase some small doubts that had arisen.

The children assumed serious expressions. Heather, who was given to easy tears, saw herself separated from the others, travelling with strangers. She ran to her father and clung to him like a burr as if to indicate this was the way she was travelling to the Quaama sports and no other.

Mary took Connie on her knee, arms wound around her, the old couch their mode of transport, the scene through the back door no longer the tank-stand and the track to the creek, but the cars, the noise, the dust, the smells, the people, the excitement of Quaama sports.

Those people without means of transport to the sports gathered on Rossmore's corner to be taken on board a car or lorry by courtesy of the driver. The little knot around the bowsers early in the morning of sports day usually comprised the impoverished Cobargo families, youths from the poorer sharefarms, who had been spared, reluctantly, for the day, and two or three old men who had been going to the sports this way for years. Some were picked up by the same cars year after year. Others hung outside the crowd, looking away to hide their disappointment when seats were found for others, and soon there would be no one left but their embarrassed selves, and the day rushing away, and the terrible prospect of having to return home, or undertake the seven miles on foot. This was unthinkable, because it meant arriving when the programme was all but ended, and if you couldn't get a lift to the sports there was little chance of a lift home.

By midmorning there was normally no one left at the bowsers. Wallaga Wal was through by then, and anyone waiting was hauled onto the table top, backs to the gathering around the cabin of the lorry, holding hard to the edge, very little else to grip, and what the travellers might be carrying like a box of sandwiches and a rolled overcoat, abandoned to slide and rush about the space left, terrifying the owners that it would be flung over the side, but better it to go than themselves, or any children, straddled on their backs, almost choking the adults with a stranglehold of terror.

116

Les saw Bob Lumsdaine only once before the sports day, but neither mentioned transport for Les, not Bob because all the necessary arrangements were made as far as he was concerned, and he was a busy man, his taxes paying the child endowment for people like Boyle. He was reminded of this, seeing Les on the seat outside Rossmore's, but was a little envious of his leisure at the same time, causing him to cut short Les's threatened monologue.

Les felt his independence was on the line if he sought Bob's help in getting to the sports, best to let Bob think there was car, lorry, horse and sulky or motor bike at his disposal. For all Bob Lumsdaine knew, such could be housed in the tumbledown shed at the side of the house, which in fact held some old suitcases and rotting tea-chests tossed there after the move from Wallaga Lake.

Les's dreams saw a vehicle there at times, a motor when he felt a surge of love for his family, seeing himself at the wheel, motoring cap at a jaunty angle, the back seat filled with the ecstatic children. Other times when he wanted to free himself of the shackles of his marital state (Doris had been pregnant when they married) he saw a bike and himself riding it, bent sideways, the engine roaring as he took a bend with Cobargo looking on in awe and admiration.

As time drew closer to sports day, he was forced to put his dreaming aside and concentrate on fact.

He had no way, it appeared, of getting to Quaama with six children, except by the method of waiting at the bowsers, and this was as humiliating in thought as in deed. They would probably be left to be collected by Wallaga Wal, for it was unlikely any other vehicle would have space for the seven of them.

He should have announced he was going alone, not burst out with an invitation to them all, fool that he was.

117

Now he hadn't the heart to disappoint them since they talked of little else but the sports and had told the school they were going, and that their father was on the gate, information that brought about some toadying from the Casey family, whose mean parents gave each of the four money to get in but nothing to spend, urging them to look on the ground for droppings from the pockets of the careless, particularly the men drinking at the bar. To keep their threepence for a spending spree would have been glory indeed.

"The Caseys and no one else will be getting in for nothing," Les said, when Ella, more naive than the older ones, repeated the Caseys' faint hopes. "And Wallaga Wal with his lorry load hasn't a chance, neither."

Ella jumped and screamed.

"We might see Cyril and Rose and them!"

Mrs Boyle hushed her quite sharply. "Remember the boy!" she said, forgetting the boy had recently wakened and was being nursed by Beryl in the doorway, to give him a view of the outside world and for Beryl to check the movements of some Coady heifers, making their way down the bank of the creek with unsure legs and wobbling udders.

"You'll all need to be on your best behaviour, won't they Dad, between now and sports day?" Mrs Boyle made her mouth prim.

"And when they get there too," Les said darkly, "keep clear of that Wallaga Lake lot. We're in Cobargo now."

Les decided, at that moment, that whatever happened they would not travel to the sports with Wallaga Wal. He would be down at the bowsers hours before the lorry was due to go through, and they would take the first transport offered, and would split up too, this seemed certain.

"We might be travellin' separate," Les said, looking for

118

his tobacco on the shelf, not seeing the rounded eyes of the children, all, except John's mistrusting lids, fixed on a bootlace in his hand with which he was flicking at flies that were raiding a scatter of breadcrumbs on the corner of the table.

"Clear the table and there'll be nothing to bring the flies!" Les cried. "All of you gather up the cups and things and wipe the table clean!"

He sat himself in the one easy chair to make his cigarette. "We wouldn't have wanted to stay a day longer at Wallaga Lake!"

John took his father's bootlace and hung it on a nail, and the others made a rush for the table, assuming serious, industrious expressions, and Beryl brought the boy in and sat him in his highchair, calling for the dish cloth to wipe down the little wooden tray in front.

On the days approaching the sports, Les was frequently seen walking about the town, putting out feelers (as he expressed it to himself) for possible lifts, but the only trucks or lorries bound for Quaama appeared to be those to be loaded with livestock for the rodeo events. While Les might have been squeezed into a cabin of these, or a seat found in a car, spaces for all the Boyles seemed impossible to come by.

He went home to open his heart to Doris.

"I'm too good hearted," he said. "It's been my trouble all my life. I should be going off for a day on my own. I'll have to keep an eye on all those kids all day and work like a black as well! A man's a fool!"

Doris winced and reddened as she easily did. "Them kids'll die if they don't go," was all she said.

With the boy in her arms she waved them off from the front veranda on sports day.

It was barely seven o'clock, and she had been up since half past four finishing a false hem on an old dress of

119

Beryl's for Ella to wear, scorching her face over the iron, rubbed over everything the children were wearing, and making a parcel of sandwiches, "in case" as she said.

There was difficulty in finding a pair of hands willing to carry the parcel, as it was seen as a threat to getting into the tea tent.

"Take them one of youse!" Les cried testily. "Or there'll be a belt across the ear all round!" John took them under an arm.

"Now go off happy!" Mrs Boyle said. "The boy and I would love to be going!"

They trooped down the hill to the bowsers, where old Bill Sawyer was already waiting in a mismatched coat and trousers, sucking on his pipe, the bowl of which sat under his chin, the stem having such a deep curve. The little Boyles were glad of the opportunity of studying this at close range, and did so until Les beckoned them with a large, sharp bend of the head to range themselves on the seat and wait.

The Albert Perrys came first and took old Sawyer into the back seat, the three girls not pleased as they tried to save the skirts of their new dresses from a crushing. They looked briefly out on the gathering of Boyles, their expressions saying thank heavens we have been spared that, at least. All the Boyles looked away in case their expressions showed the envy they felt.

Les walked around the bowsers and smoked and, passing the row of little Boyle knees, frowned on them, causing Ella to hastily cover a dirt mark on her white sock, a legacy of a game of chasings.

Then Alex Parsons stopped and offered Les a seat, to be gained by Ted and Charlie, strapping farm youth, sharing the one, and the two girls doing the same. Les, becoming very worried about the nearness to nine o'clock, went back for Connie, but Heather sprang from the seat and stood stiff as if frozen, and screamed so loudly she drowned out the noise of the Parsons engine, kept running lest it fail to start again once it stopped.

Les turned and slid Connie to the ground, and there was a new noise, two pairs of pounding feet belonging to Frank Barrington and his younger brother, Sydney, who had walked in from their place on the Bermagui road, their parents and sisters to go to the sports by sulky when the morning farm work was done. Alex Parsons saw problems with the Boyles and shouted above the noise for the Barringtons to climb in, and, starting the car moving, he called out to Les that the next car along would be sure to have room for them all.

Beryl took Heather on her knee, pale of face herself at the violent shuddering of Heather's body, and Les sat at the end of the seat, Connie fastened weeping to his coat sleeve.

John suddenly threw the parcel of sandwiches in the air and caught them like a football.

"We'll go home," he said.

"No, no!" shrieked Mary and Ella in one voice, and Les called sharply to them to quieten down.

"Youse never seem to learn how to behave in public," he said (sad and bitter were his tones). "You should've been left back there at Wallaga Lake."

The children looked about the deserted streets (shops did not open to allow everyone to go to the sports), puzzled at this status bestowed on Cobargo, since there was not a person in sight.

But it did not remain that way for long.

There was a rattle and a roar defined as coming from the cemetery hill, and growing louder by the second, and would have brought the little Boyles to their feet if they had dared to move. They had to be content with a modest wriggling and a gentle clapping of their feet together.

It was Wallaga Wal at the wheel of his lorry, pulled up by the bowsers before the children could scream a greeting had they been game to. They just went scarlet of face, Ella crushing her hand to her mouth, wide eyes on the lorry load. There were some squeaks and giggles among the crowd hanging to the cabin roof, for the sudden stop sent them swaying, threatening to loosen their hold.

Wal, who was generally called a "flash black" by the white population, climbed from behind the wheel and went to Les hand outstretched.

"Laas!" he said, showing big teeth, yellowish with tobacco, and a vast amount of pink inside mouth. "Laas, you wanna ride to Quaama?"

"I'm on the gate," Les said, making a hitching movement with his arms, as if he were already holding the bag.

Wal flung open the lorry door and might have pulled out a large black woman nursing a child, and a youth of about fifteen, if they hadn't scrambled down, the woman tossing the child to another, sitting with her back to the cabin, and following up herself with a foot on the wheel. The youth sprang up, black legs flying over the side to sit hunched and joining big hands between his knees.

His expression was sad, but resigned.

Les gathered up Connie, and Heather clung to his trouser leg, as if she were a small monkey about to climb a tree. That way the three got into the front seat.

"We can take another one in here!" said Wal, looking Beryl, Mary, Ella and John over with black eyes under grey eyebrows, thick as caterpillars. His hair was grey too, and his skin a greyish black with a shine on the cheeks and the flattish nose, going flatter when he smiled.

Beryl went into the front, and Mary and Ella and John

climbed on the back helped by Wal grasping a leg of each of the girls.

The feeling stayed after the lorry went roaring off. Each of the girls looked at her leg, wondering if they reached down and plucked at their skin would they be free of the feel.

Wal had instructed several of the black children to form a circle around the little Boyles. They sank to their haunches like mushrooms, turning their eyes up shyly, suggesting they might meet the eyes of Mary, Ella and John, given a little more time.

"How is the time about?" Les asked Wal, slapping a breast pocket as if a watch were there as a rule, not just at present.

Wal flicked his eyes towards the sky and back to the road. "You on the gate?" he said, very respectful.

"I'm on the gate!" Les said. "Other things too. Seeing that everything goes smooth."

"That's real good, Laas," Wal said, driving faster.

This caused the engine to roar louder, and Les had to yell to make Wal hear. "Drop us off before you turn in. I'll take the kids into the bush for a minute. The wife said to."

"Don't be listen' to women," Wal shouted back. "There's places for them to go inside!"

"I'll have to get off though," Les yelled. "I'm on the gate!"

"We got our money," Wal said. "The bream are runnin' in their thousands. You should be back there!"

Les wanted to say he was in Cobargo now, but he was distracted by the stares of a truck load from Bemboka, at the sports for the first time, pulled up and uncertain about driving through the open tin gates.

"You go right through!" Wal called with authority, stopping so suddenly the load on the back bent low, as if a wind were worrying a patch of mixed growth on a small, flat-topped hill. Mary and Ella, although seated, fell back on top of Cyril and Pearl, and Rose began to laugh so hard, her chin and shoulders and budding breasts all shook. Even the mothers and aunts smiled.

Les looked through the opening at the back of his head. "I'll haul them kids off," he said to Wal. "Up to some fool game back there!"

Wal was right by the gate now, and Bob Lumsdaine was there with the money bag and a cold glitter in his eye.

"Get the fires going," he said, ignoring the hand Les stretched towards him (hopeful the bag would be placed in it). "Half fill one of the tins too, the women want to make a few pots of tea early."

Les started to run towards a part of the ground where there was a line of iron posts and cross bars from which hung chains to take kerosene tins of water. The tins were lying about, crusted with black grease on the outside, liberally spread with rust inside. Les would need to scour them before they went on the fire. The only wood available had been too green to burn last year, and looked as if it required several more years of seasoning.

It was not going to be an easy day for Les, and there already was an unfortunate start.

Connie had run squealing after Les, and Heather ran too, wailing loudly, falling into the end of a seat for spectators, screaming at injuries or imagined injuries. Beryl raced up, worried that she was through the gate without paying, pursued by Mary, Ella and John sharing the same concern.

Rose was not prepared to suffer separation from her former friends so soon after the reunion and raced to join them, her thin black legs working furiously under the hem of a white voile dress with loops of blue ribbon through the hem. Just about every child on the lorry had soon swarmed around the Boyles, giving Beryl and Mary a harder job calming Connie and Heather, who were terrified of the black faces, unprotected by their father.

Beryl saw, across the head of Connie burrowed into her chest, that Wal had a pound note waved in the air, and it appeared to be sourly acknowledged by Bob that it would cover the cost of admittance of the lorry load, black and white.

After a while, with Connie giving a succession of dry sobs and Heather clinging to Mary and Ella for dual protection, the little Boyles broke away and joined their father at the fires.

He was not a good firemaker, Mrs Boyle doing the job at home most of the time. Beryl and John saw he was trying to get too large a piece to light.

"You need some small stuff, Dad," Beryl said. With John and Mary she stood in a line looking on Les at work.

Les shouted and broke up the line as surely as if he had thrown a detonator at their feet.

"Get in and help me!" he cried. "Useless, lazy beggars you are! Half an hour with that mob and you go just like them!" He looked darkly and warily about in case Wal, the women and children were within hearing.

But they were all grouped by the enclosure where steers were thrashing about, already wild of eye, snorting and bellowing and working themselves into a frenzy, helped by an occasional crack of a whip over their backs from Sandy Hopkins, seated on the top rail, one eye reflecting pride in his job, the other daring the Wallaga Lake people to interfere.

Ella ran for some dry brambles not too far from the steer pen, and Rose, seeing her, broke from the others and ran to help her break off twigs, then ran behind Ella to Les and the fires.

They flung their twigs on the fire sending flames licking at the kerosene tins, greedy for the grease.

"Don't forget one half full like Mr Lumsdaine said, Dad," Beryl said gently.

Les had forgotten and seized a can and sent a flood of water across the ground, some of it running back to sizzle at the edge of the coals and quite a lot rushing around the feet of Rose and Ella, who jumped back laughing at their wet shoes.

"Don't hang around the fires!" Les said. "You can do that at home! Beats me why you can't find more to do after all my trouble gettin' youse₁ a day out!"

Ella soberly joined her sisters on a log a few yards away, where Beryl had not totally succeeded in pacifying Connie, who kept her head pressed on Beryl's shoulder and her eyes entangled in Beryl's hair, as if the sight of the Quaama sports crowd, now building up, was too much to bear. Rose sat at the end of the log, legs apart, staring at the ground through her voile skirt.

John went and sat midway between his sisters and Rose. He was still attached to the parcel of sandwiches, which were now showing patches of wetness and a loop of string had loosened, exposing one end.

John poked two fingers in and drew out a mangled sandwich, tomato turning the bread to pulp, only a scrape of butter used. His tongue sought it without success.

Les was beginning to feel a little happier. A coat of steam was forming on the can half filled with water. He glanced back at the tea tent even more cheered. He would soon be able to put his head in and call for teapots. There would be a cup for him. Some younger women, like Alma Hill and Grace Hopkins, were good for a joke and a laugh.

Then he saw the little Boyles were each eating a sandwich with a melancholy air, contrasting with his mood, and as he looked John was passing the parcel towards Rose.

"Them sandwiches are not to be eaten!" he shouted. Every mouth was stilled, and Rose's hand, like a black tarantula springing away from a heavy boot, went back into her lap.

"It's not dinner time!" Les said. "It's hours from dinner time! How will people think I brought you up, hoeing into tucker at this time?"

His voice, as much as the odd practice of eating sandwiches at ten o'clock, brought some stares from passing groups, directed also at small black Rose on the log seat with the Boyles. They measured the distance from the Wallaga Lake group. Quite a way off, said the raised eyebrows of the Perry women, under their new straw hats.

Bob Lumsdaine came up, having passed the gate bag to one of his sons, freed from marking out and pegging the start and finish of the footraces. Bob's expression said plainly that Les had been long enough at the fires and it was time for something else.

The job coming up next was to shovel manure from the path leading into the steer riding arena, agitated animals given to relieving themselves, plunged into a confused state with a gate opened suddenly, misguidedly believing it led to freedom, followed by a spasm of terror when a body landed without warning on their backs.

The shovelling operation had to take place not too far from the Wallaga Lake people, and Les saw with the brief glance he allowed himself Wal's nose had flattened and many of his big, yellow teeth were showing. Les looked across at the fires and saw, too, there was no space now between the little Boyles and Rose.

He sent the shovel savagely under a pile of dung and flung it into a kerosene tin, the clatter causing the steers in the pen to rear up and straddle each other, and Sandy

127

Hopkins to roar "Steady there!" as much for Les's ears as those of the cattle.

The shovelling went on until there was a break in the programme at midday, and Bob Lumsdaine came up and ordered Les back to the fires to keep the boiling water up to the tea tent.

"Empty that on your way over," Bob said of the tin of wet manure swarming with flies.

Les, calling Bob under his breath a bandy legged bastard, flung the manure into a bank of wattle trees.

Immediately there was a shriek from behind.

The growth was thick, there was nothing to see, but Les detected movement, branches trembling, muffled giggling, then more laughter, louder, out in the open now, joined by other cries, and a shout of "Look at you! What did you cop?"

It was John, calling to Rose, flushed out as she was from her hiding, her white voile bearing a generous scattering of green spots. She stood, flicking the wet tops off, aiming them at the others who ducked, and laughed themselves into a state of near hysteria.

Les went rapidly and angrily through an opening in the trees to find all the little Boyles with Rose and Pearl interrupted during a game of hide and seek.

"Well, look at youse" he cried, and went into further shock to see Stella, one of the older Wallaga Lake women (one that would swim in her clothes) on the grass, legs stretched out before her, nursing the sleeping Connie.

An old yellow cotton jacket of Stella's was draped across Connie's body. Stella lifted large, sad eyes to Les, and Beryl and John stood between her and Les, as if one or the other needed protection.

"There's nothing to do here, Dad," John said.

"Nothin' to do!" Les cried. "There's steer ridin' over there! I don't have a chance to look at it, shovellin' muck for hours on end. Gettin' youse a day out while I work like a dog! A man needs certifyin'!"

"Boyle!" cried the voice of Bob Lumsdaine from the fires.

"Coming, Bob!" Les answered with his tin rattling.

Bob was standing near the opening of the food tent in the company of two women with teapots hanging from their hands. The card table by the tent flap was manned by another, Mrs Irene Howard, very straight of back behind little stacks of coins, from two shillings to halfpennies for change. All looked coldly on Les.

He kicked half-burned bits of wood into the centre of the fire and flung extra wood on and seemed uncertain of what to do about the tins, until Bob told him to transfer the contents of those partly empty into one, and fill the others with fresh water.

"There's buckets there to carry it to the women in the tents!" Bob said. "They shouldn't be dipping it out. We'll look good if there's a scalding accident!"

Then the little Boyles and Rose came up, Rose with a new air of confidence, as if the manure on her dress had established a bond between her and Les. They had all brought sticks and threw them on the fire.

Wal came up with a flat cardboard box under his arm and took it to the tent, standing at a respectful distance. Mrs Perry came out, knowing the ritual from past years, and took the box and filled it with sandwiches and cake.

Wal had his money ready, rolling about in a large, sweaty hand, and he counted it into a heap on the table, Mrs Howard looking pleased she did not have to pick it up to check it, she could see there was enough, and needed only to scoop it into a metal box there for the takings.

Rose suddenly jumped from the log where she sat with the Boyles, Connie there too, red of cheek and sweaty of hair, still not certain of her whereabouts since her sleep,

Beryl having scooped her from Stella's arms when Les appeared.

Rose ran to Wal, trotting beside him, wanting to, but not looking back at the Boyles, her thin black neck forward and her hands behind her.

"See that?" said Les. "She's goin' where the tucker is! You won't see her again till her belly's full. Good riddance too. No one decent wants you while you hang around blacks!" He flung some wood together with his boots, then stamped the ash from them. "That's one thing you learned today, anyway, after all my trouble gettin' you here!"

"How will we get home, Dad?" John asked. The children looked from the receding backs of Wal and Rose to the knot outside the tea tent, afraid to look at each other.

"I got you here!" Les said. "Now I have to think about gettin' you home! A great day out for me, I must say!"

He sat on the end of the log where Rose had been, and looked mournfully at his feet. Connie, now the day was almost over, was losing her strangeness to her surroundings, and ran from Beryl to wedge herself between his knees. The children looked on fearfully, but Les bowed a terribly sad face over Connie's head, and held her with a hand on her stomach.

"It's been a terrible day," Les said. "One of the worst days in all my life."

Mary, with tears coming to her eyes, was afraid he was going to cry too.

"It's been good," John said. "We saved a sandwich for you."

He took the parcel, now almost flat, from a hiding place under the log and dusted it off before pulling the wrapping back. There was a sandwich left, the heel of the loaf which did not get any butter at all. It was pale

pink with tomato juice and very wet. Les had to eat fast
to avoid having it fall away on Connie's head.

"A flamin' man could just about drink this," he said.
Bob began to walk past him, very fast, emphasizing
his bandy legs.

"The footraces, Boyle!" he said. "Ask Albert Peck what
he wants you to do!"

Les sat on the back of the lorry on the way home, nursing
Heather and Connie, and with Ella making a rest of his
back. That way she faced Pearl and Rose and Cyril, Stella
and the other women, and a number of youths, one of
whom, named Jed Stubbings, was successful in the steer
riding.

The cry of the crowd was still in Jed's ears, and his
eyes still held in them the magic of flying high, landing
close to the steer's tail, clinging to no more than some
stubbly, silky hairs, but cling he did, sliding eventually
down over the back legs of the animal, which threshed
them in a new terror, sending the lad bowling into the
dust.

Pearl had won the footrace for children under twelve,
and every now and again held up her sixpence, her teeth
showing very white in the gathering dusk.

Ella wanted to say again that Pearl had been three yards
at least ahead of the rest of the field, and John would
have liked to have recounted the good fortune of hearing
Wal shout that Jed was coming up next in the steer riding,
and miraculously they all reached the rails in time to see
him.

But Wal was driving even faster than he had on the
way to the sports, and they were almost in Cobargo now.

131

10 A Spread of Warm Blood

Frank Cullen had owned the butcher's shop in Cobargo for close on forty years.

For the past twenty he had told his wife, Jane, he would sell up and move to Sydney. Their only daughter, Doreen, was there, married (coincidentally) to a man who worked at big abattoirs. Frank could get a job with the son-in-law, so the son-in-law said in family letters and on his infrequent visits to Cobargo.

"Sell up everything and go to the big smoke," Frank said, very often at four o'clock in the morning with sheep bellowing in the pen at the back of the house, which was two miles from Cobargo on the Bermagui Road.

He did not mind waking Jane. He thought she should be up with tea made for him, instead of leaving him to build up the stove fire and get his own, as well as making up a fire by the killing sheds, no more than some slabs of stone, a sheet of corrugated iron propped up over a rough fireplace where water was boiled for cleaning up after the killing, all inside a wire fence, a bank of orange trees on one side for a wind break.

The fruit was small and sour, and a beast, unaware that death was at hand, would take a mouthful of leaves, perhaps an orange, slobbering with its large lips, a hint of surprise in black, unblinking eyes at the foreign taste. It would sometimes throw a look to Frank, who was in a bad temper with the fire, and follow it with a casual swing of the neck. The beast had an air of pity and part sorrow as if it were Frank about to die.

Jane's sister Martha lived with them.

She had, for twenty years, coming some years before Doreen went to Sydney to work and ultimately marry her Clarrie.

Doreen and Clarrie were childless, Doreen filling her spare time with work for the Catholic Church, her tepid approach to her religion under the influence of Frank boosted when she found Clarrie a member of a devout family. Frank, with no religion, and bent on weaning Jane away from the church, called him a bigot.

Martha made her home with Frank and Jane by accident. At twenty, Martha had been the only child remaining at home with her widowed father in a small grey house on a small grey farm off the Tilba road. They ran a few cattle, mostly sold for Frank's butchering, raised lucerne and corn, and grew vegetables and fruit. Frank put a few boxfuls in his shop, for his customers to select some onions or carrots or a bundle of beans, and ask at the counter for a price on it.

After a while Frank grew resentful. Instead of the vegetables encouraging customers to buy extra meat for wholesome stews and soups, with times very hard, they bought only the vegetables, some claiming that red meat brought on high blood pressure, heart attacks and death.

It was a fact that old Mr McTaggert did die suddenly at his plough, the horse taking fright and flying down the furrow at a pace no one believed possible under normal circumstances. The horse dragged McTaggert quite a way, but his body bore no injuries apart from a few scratches, so it was thought he had had a heart attack, and fell into a furrow, the reins tangling him up and jerking so violently at the horse's mouth it fled in panic.

That was the end of the McTaggert vegetables in Frank's butchery, and as old McTaggert had bought large quantities of meat (feeling obliged to) and some blamed over-indulgence for his death, Frank was guilt ridden on

133

two counts, the meat he sold quite forcibly at times and the vegetables he tried not to sell.

To appease the guilt, he did not object when Jane took Martha in. She never returned to the little grey house, the bank taking it over since McTaggert had not paid the debt on it.

Jane found room for the better pieces of furniture in their house, and the remainder crumbled away with the walls and veranda boards.

When there was a summer of bad bush fires, all that was left of the house was the brick recess that had held the stove and open fire. Lush rains followed, and with the earth nourished by the ashes, a pine near the front, surviving the holocaust, gave birth to a grove of deep green trees, turning the eyesore of the old tumbledown house into an oasis, causing travellers to exclaim at the beauty and watch with excitement for the village coming up, perhaps as a peaceful and pretty as the trees.

After a few weeks, Frank did not appear to want Martha there, but she stayed. When Frank stopped speaking to her, it made no difference and they lived that way for twenty years.

In 1935 Martha was forty, but she did not look that old. Her black hair was parted in the centre and coiled around each ear, like an illustration in a Dickens or Jane Austen novel. Not that Martha would have adapted her hair style this way. She did not read and, had she wanted to, this would have proven difficult, for there were no books in the Cullen house, Frank with no formal education and Jane leaving school when she was twelve.

Although Martha was born twenty years after Jane, conditions for education had not improved all that much, and the McTaggerts, living beyond the mile limit for compulsory education, did not have to send their children regularly to either the Cobargo Public or the convent only a few hundred yards farther away.

There had been four McTaggert boys between Jane and Martha: two were killed in the Great War, one had gone to Western Australia to look for gold and was never heard of again, and the other, named Joseph, went to Melbourne, and when last heard of he had been driving a tram there. Joseph sent letters to Martha a couple of times a year, only a few lines hoping she and Jane were well, the weather was cold so far south, but his little driver's cabin (he said once) was cosy and he was issued with a macintosh reaching to his feet.

"Probably trailing down the steps and dragging on the road," Frank had said at the kitchen table when Jane showed him the letter, for the Cullens were tall and the McTaggerts short, and this provided grounds for Frank to look down on his in-laws, physically as well as mentally.

Jane folded the letter and put it on the dresser for Martha to take to her room, when Frank had cranked up his old lorry and left for the shop, for he closed it for an hour at midday to go home for dinner.

Jane never answered Frank back when he was scathing about any of the McTaggerts and never asked why he did not speak to Martha, or voiced, in any way at all, the misery she locked up inside her.

Jane had a goitre, sitting above the neck of her dress like a turkey egg in a human skin. Sometimes she pressed it in with the fingers of both hands, as if the goitre were a storing place for her pain and this was a way of easing it.

Martha had no goitre in which to store her unhappiness.

She had, in fact, a slim white neck, which Jane envied. Both of them, in Martha's bedroom, getting ready to go to Confession on Saturday afternoon, would share the mirror over Martha's dressing table. Jane made dresses with collars standing as high as she could get them and spent a lot of time pulling and straightening the cloth, in a vain bid to disguise the goitre, while Martha slapped at the revers of her dress, to make them lie flat, the better to show off her neck.

But Jane did not begrudge Martha that redeeming feature. In fact, the two women were more like mother and daughter (bearing in mind the twenty years between them) than sisters.

When Doreen (only six years younger than Martha) came home for a visit, Jane and Martha had to accommodate her, metaphorically speaking, and this was difficult, especially if she was not with Clarrie.

After a day or two, they tended to lapse into their old ways, talking about the ripening state of the pears for jam, the suitability of a piece of meat Frank brought home for baking or braising, or the gravity of the last heart attack of old Mrs Annie Moore. They did not bother to explain any preliminaries for Doreen, who was unaware of the nearness of the Cobargo show, Frank's habit of bringing home the poorer cuts of meat for them to deal with, and the fact that Mrs Moore's heart condition had deteriorated since Doreen's last visit.

Doreen leaned towards Frank on these visits, going with him to pick up a sheep or a beast from one of the farms, keeping an eye on them through the rear window of the lorry in a makeshift pen. She slept on a cane-framed sofa in the front room, this causing added resentment since Martha's residency left no spare room. When Clarrie came too, Martha had the sofa and Doreen and Clarrie her three-quarter bed.

With Frank and Doreen paired off, Jane and Martha went back to normal, working in the vegetable patch together, sitting on the front steps to drink afternoon tea and going into town, as they called Cobargo, to shop at

Rossmore's and walk up the hill to St Joseph's to pay a visit to the nuns, taking them a few nearly budded roses, or fresh picked beans or tomatoes, for the Cullen garden could be relied upon to yield the district's earliest crops, Jane and Martha with a reputation to uphold, not with any great difficulty, for they were as eager to get their seeds in the ground as it was to take them, after lying chilled and barren through the long winter.

Without the garden it would be hard to imagine any sort of life for Martha.

Housekeeping for old Mr McTaggert from the age of fifteen, she slipped into old maidhood, only going to church, and working in the supper room with Jane at dances and balls. She never learned to play tennis and dressed frugally, from the money Jane could spare from time to time for a dress length from Rossmore's. Her shoes gave her a lot of worry, needing half soleing frequently, for she walked everywhere, it being nearly twenty years since she rode in Frank's lorry.

Frank and Doreen this particular Saturday (Doreen home on one of her visits) were on their way along the Wandella Road to buy a steer from one of the farms. They passed Jane and Martha, climbing the hill to St Joseph's, the wind tearing at their dark clothes.

They had been gone from the house since midday, and it was now after four o'clock. They had visited old Mrs Moore in her small cottage up past the post office, finding her in bed on the veranda, the gold rim of her glasses and her dark moustache showing up on her white face. The bedcovers were very white and the pillow cases shining with starch, Jane observing how the iron had been pressed with such force, the eyelet holes in the embroidery were large enough to see through. She resolved to give her own linen similar treatment, feeling an itchiness there on her chair to be up and about it.

Mrs Moore's daughter-in-law was out the back in the kitchen making a stew, expressing her annoyance that she was there, and not playing tennis on the town courts, by leaving Martha and Jane on the veranda all the time, only coming out to complain about the toughness of the meat, bought of course from Frank's shop.

"I'll put a rock in another pot and when the rock's soft, you'll know the stew's ready," she said, going back to the stove, her house slippers making a slapping noise, as if in contact with those putting her in this miserable situation.

She made no tea for Jane and Martha, causing old Mrs Moore embarrassment, and Jane to grow uneasy at the blue pinched lips of the patient, and the eyes, she feared, taking on a slightly glassy look.

Jane got up, followed by Martha, and they left to go to Confession. Both were considering whether they should tell Father O'Malley they overstayed a visit, and might have brought more trouble to a sick old woman, and did this constitute a sin, when Frank and Doreen went past.

"There they go!" said Frank. "Look at them! Bending their bloody knees already!"

"It's the wind," Doreen said. "Look at the way it's bending the trees!"

She felt unhappy seeing Martha and Jane out in the wind when she was having it easy in the lorry, although Frank would never have Martha aboard, no matter what the circumstances.

Doreen looked past Frank's set face to the church coming up, the peppercorn tree swishing green fronds about, reminding Doreen of the innocent days of her childhood, getting in a brief game of chasings before Sister Agnes saw, and came swooping down the convent veranda like a great brown bird to shoo the children into the church for Confession.

There was a ritual of kissing the feet of the statue of Jesus on the cross outside the confessional. The feet became affected after years of young mouths pecking at the plaster, causing a flaking of the indent where the nail fastened Jesus' feet together.

"Kiss the scab, kiss the scab!" young Peter Hanrahan hissed one day, sending the little knot of kneelers into a state of wild giggling, but with the unfortunate result of Peter's being told on by his cousin Letty, and the younger nun of St Joseph's, who came in for all the rough work, being assigned in future to guard the statue, standing by with head bowed in prayer (ordered by Sister Agnes to spend the time profitably repenting of her own wrong doings) and the offending abrasions filled in with plaster of paris.

"Let me out!" Doreen said, with a hand out suddenly on Frank's knee. But it might have been the changing of gears on the hill top that drowned out her words.

"I could wait for them, and walk home with them!" Doreen shouted as they tore along the road towards Wandella. Frank pushed his chest forward, crouching over the wheel, holding it tight as if there was a threat of separation.

"Frank!" Doreen all but screamed (she called him by his Christian name during their holiday intimacy), "I said I wouldn't mind getting out!"

"We're going for a steer, I thought you knew!" He appeared to drive faster, and Doreen had to put her head back against the seat, for her hair was blowing so wildly, it might have been torn from her head. She was a white-faced young woman with very black hair and brown eyes that appeared protruding, but this was due to her heavy lids, a short nose and a small tight mouth, causing the eyes to overshadow her other features.

There was some resemblance between Doreen and

Martha, except that Doreen had a more modern look and her thick hair was bobbed to just below her ears. People speculated on what each would look like in the other's clothes, and with their hair styled similarly. But it was unlikely Doreen would exchange clothes with Martha, who had very few, sewn by herself at the dining room table (when Frank was not around). Doreen, fond of smart dressing, saved her latest purchases in Sydney to bring home and show Cobargo, and was usually on the last dress, skirt, blouse or hat when it was time to go home, the social events in Cobargo so limited she was hard pressed to air them all.

When she and Frank got back with the steer, having taken, Doreen suspected, an unnecessarily long time over negotiations with the farmer selling it, Jane and Martha were home with tea ready, and there was a hurrying air about it, soon attributed to an evening of euchre in the School of Arts. Jane and Martha had only been reminded of the event when they had seen the calico notice on the door of the building, passing it on their way to Mrs Moore's.

Jane played cards, Martha didn't, an earlier attempt bringing down the wrath of Frank, with whom she had been unfortunately paired, in the week following the death of Mr McTaggert. Jane and Doreen had been partners against Frank and Martha.

Martha, still confused and jumpy since her father's accident, had trumped Frank's ace, then played a club, thinking it was a spade, and Frank went to great pains to draw a diagram of the four kinds of cards, printing the names boldly beside each and propping it against the table lamp directly in front of Martha. Then when the game was over he slid it in the box with the pack. It served no purpose (intended to be dealt out to Martha in future games), for Martha never played again.

But she and Jane decided to go to the euchre this Saturday night, Martha to sit with the few onlookers and to allow the games to carry on right up to supper time, boiling up the water on the primus stove and setting out the sandwiches and cakes brought along by the people supporting the event, which was to raise money towards improving the School of Arts, nothing having been done to it since the Great War.

Doreen had a fuji silk blouse which she hadn't worn yet. It had a boat-shaped neck, finely bound, and sleeves eased gently into a similar binding at the elbow. The night was warm, it being February, and spreading the blouse over the foot of Martha's bed, Doreen thought this an ideal time to show it off to what representation of Cobargo there might be in the School of Arts. She could be sure that those who would not see the blouse would be told about it, most likely in exaggerated terms, the neckline more daring than that worn by even the more fashionable of Cobargo.

When Doreen returned to the bedroom with a jug of warm water from the stove to fill the wash stand basin, Martha, in her petticoat with all her white neck showing and her black hair tumbling down, was standing looking at the blouse.

Doreen remembered the walk up the hill to St Joseph's, and she and Frank going past in the lorry. They had been to Confession and she had not, and she felt that she should perform an act of self sacrifice, as penance for this (although she could have scarcely leapt from the lorry at the rate Frank was driving), and wear something to the euchre night that had been seen before.

She spoke up quickly before she changed her mind.

"Wear the blouse, if you like."

Martha picked it up and held it across her front before the mirror, making sure the neckline was positioned exactly right. Doreen knew she was admiring her neck and shoulders. But I'm six years younger, she thought, and the blouse is mine!

"The sleeves are a little tight," Doreen said. "Even on me." She smoothed her bare arms, seeing them slender and apricot coloured in the lamplight.

But Martha pulled the blouse over her head, and when it settled on her body, put her hair back with both hands, leaving it loose around her face.

"Thank you," she said. "I do like it."

"I was going to wear it to Mass tomorrow," Doreen said.

"You still can," Martha said.

Her words were only a little louder than the whisper of the silk as her sleeve stroked her breast, for she laid a hand near the neckline and shook her head, to loosen her hair a little more.

Jane, in her petticoat too, came in then with another lamp.

"That suits her!" she cried, laying her navy morrocain on the foot of the bed, not looking at it. "Wear it with your black skirt!"

"I will," Martha said gravely, as if the skirt were not the only one she owned.

Doreen went to where her new things were on hangers suspended from the side of Martha's wardrobe. The two lamps now threw her sulky face into relief.

"Wear the stripe," Jane suggested.

She had worn it to Mass the first Sunday she was home, and her expression said so. She moved it behind her ruby coloured light wool she had travelled from Sydney in to emphasize the point.

Martha crossed her arms in front to take the blouse off.

"Now don't!" Jane said. "It's nice for you to have something different to wear!"

She pulled on her morrocain with an air of great industry to say you both do the same, and have an end to this nonsense. Martha did get into her black skirt rather slowly.

Doreen left for the kitchen.

She was there, drinking tea with Frank, when Jane went for a cake, newly made and fortunately uncut, to contribute to the night's supper.

Doreen's elbows on the table, the teacup between her hands, and her eyes protruding enough to look like shaded windows on a wall, all said she wasn't going to the euchre.

Jane was about to tell her not to be silly, to put something on and come, when she saw her as a fourteen year old, when Martha first came to live, sulking because Jane bought a few yards of cheap muslin to make Martha a summer dress.

She put the cake in a basket and went through the hall to meet Martha coming out of the door of her room, holding the little worn tapestry bag she had had since girlhood.

"The same colour as the blouse, look," she said, and put it under her breast, the rust coloured pattern picking up the red brown of the silk.

"Yes, fancy," Jane said.

Frank and Doreen, from the kitchen, heard Jane's and Martha's heels on the steps. Nearly always people wore soft soles in the house, slipping with muted sound on the linoleum. When there was the ring of hard leather and iron clips, it challenged the quiet. The house seemed in charge of the people, until their quick steps were heard, speaking of a happening beyond the walls and roof, an urgent engagement, no certainty about returning, but please, come back, come back! Snap, snap, snap across the veranda boards. Goodbye, goodbye. Only feet spoke goodbye in the Cullen house.

"A pair of bloody fools," said Frank, getting up for the teapot on the stove. "Walking eight miles in one day. Mad as a meataxe." He saw Doreen's still face. "Both of them."

"I never saw anyone make it away so fast in that blouse of mine."

Frank sent a great stream of dark brown tea into his cup. "See the cake go off?" he said. "A man might've felt like a slice."

Doreen gestured with a tilted chin towards a tin on the dresser top, an old tea tin with a pattern of peacock feathers she had loved as a child, now watching it fade more each time she came home.

There was cake inside but Frank dismissed it by not looking. He swallowed the last of his tea and pushed his cup from him.

Doreen took it with her own and unhooked the washing-up dish where it hung beside the window, like a round dull light, flaring when the firelight hit it. She poured hot water in and washed the cups, hooking them back on the dresser, and wiping the dish out so vigorously the inside shone nearly as brightly as the outside.

"You should get a sink," Doreen said.

"I should sell out and go to Sydney," Frank said.

"Clarrie would get you a job," Doreen said. Clarrie was now a foreman at the abattoirs in Homebush, and they lived in Croydon on the same railway line.

"I know," Frank said, and in the silence the steer bellowed. "A man should get away from that. Get it easier. Before it's too late."

Doreen went and sat a buttock on one of his knees. He looped both arms around her, his hands joined at her waist. Unlike most other men in Cobargo he did not smoke, having been brought up in a Methodist home, but having long abandoned any other influence. He did not believe in God.

"Six feet under the ground and that's it!" he told Jane, who swallowed and pressed her goitre, and fixed her gaze on her vegetable patch outside the kitchen window, both to cover tears that came to her eyes, and distract her to something hopeful.

Frank rocked Doreen very slightly on his knee. Both bodies were a little tense at first, then loosened, and Doreen's cheek felt the warmth of his flesh near his shoulder.

"You'd swear you had a hot water bottle under there," she said closing her eyes. "A warm water bottle, anyway."

Frank tightened his arm, but only for a moment. He was the first to move, nearly spilling her from his knee.

"You know it's been twenty years," he said. "Not quite twenty, but nearly."

He wondered why he felt the need for accuracy. He could have exaggerated, made his case worthy of greater sympathy. Doreen, feeling her face warm, folded her arms, lightly holding each elbow.

"You and Clarrie alright?" asked Frank.

Doreen moved the lamp to the table end, making him a silhouette by the dresser, and herself a rag doll, a face round and white like a saucer, the features worn away.

"Oh, yes, OK," she said. "Not too bad. Waste of effort, though!" She patted the table edge, as she did when a child and Frank announced they would go to the sea for a picnic, and she wanted to make sure it was true. (They had never talked this way.)

"Why, Dad?" she said, thinking too late, she wasn't calling him Frank.

"Why?" repeated Frank.

"Yes, why?" said Doreen, in a little bark-like voice, sending the words to hit the washing-up dish and fly to

145

the cake tin and back and settle on the stretch of scrubbed table between them.

A creak of Frank's chair told her he moved.

"She got off in your blouse, eh?" Frank said. "Have I seen it?"

"That's the unfair part. I haven't had it on my back yet. Except in the shop."

Frank pulled his boots from beneath a chair and put his feet into them and bent down to lace them.

Doreen's face, though partly absent, was asking why. He stood and pulled down the sleeves of his shirt. They had deep cuffs, stiff with Jane's starch, and he felt along the top of the dresser for his links.

"Put on one of those other pretty dresses," Frank said.

He sat with his feet well out before him. "She never said 'What about coming to the euchre?' "

"We would have to give them half an hour," Doreen said. "I don't want to pass them twice in the one day."

"We can sit out on the veranda in the cool, until it's time to crank up the old bus," Frank said. He smoothed his jaw. "I don't need a shave, do I?" The light caught his thrust-out chin, making a ripple of silver, like melting frost on pale grass.

"No," Doreen said, taking up the lamp. "I'll put something on."

While she did she thought about Martha in the blouse, with her hair like a blackbird's wing, watching the cards, waiting for the time to go into the supper room.

"Honestly I'll feel like ripping that blouse off her back when I get there," Doreen said, screwing a wooden rocking chair to face Frank, who was on the long form against the wall, sharing the space with half kerosene tins, in which Jane and Martha grew ferns and geraniums. Frank looked at the plants as if they were foreigners on a railway seat whom he disliked on sight.

146

"Stuff growing everywhere," he said. "A man won't be able to get in the door soon."

Doreen looked out on the front garden, the rose bushes making long shadows, for there was a young moon tipped in the sky like a slice of pale watermelon. The borders of phlox had lost all their brilliance to the night.

"You come home and likely as not the two of them are out there with their bums in the air and the fire dead out inside," Frank said.

Doreen thought this would not be a frequent occurrence, but decided not to argue; she preferred to think it the behaviour pattern of Jane and Martha.

"Your little garden was looking nice when I was down last," Frank said. This had been five years ago. Frank went alone to Croydon as Jane would not leave Martha behind. Old Brigham Taylor, who used to be a butcher, killed a bullock and kept the shop open until Frank came home after a week.

"It's the same," Doreen said. "I'd never grow vegetables. A shilling's worth of peas does us for over a week."

"My God, eh!" Frank said. "Youse get six pods for that at Pratt's."

Pratt's was a cafe in Cobargo, and the name was not really Pratt, but Pratenousis, a Greek family with three daughters, Tina, Maria, and Constance. The girls were black haired, with dark eyes, smooth skins and very white teeth. Shortening their name saved them from total annihilation in Cobargo.

They kept a small stand of fruit and vegetables in the cafe, having them brought from Nowra on the mail car once a week. It was usually out of season produce for Cobargo like lettuce which ran to seed in the summer heat, and Pratt, a sad-eyed spaniel of a man, priced it highly to cover the freight charges. The locals overlooked his

147

efforts in providing what was unobtainable from back-yard gardens, and called him a dago rook.

"It's a great place, Sydney," Frank said. "Hopping on those trains. You could spend a whole day at Central Station, just looking at people.

"I been trying to get away for twenty years. Sometimes I think I'll just up and away. And bugger them.

"What do you say?" he said when she said nothing.

"You got room. Clarrie could get me on at the meat-works. Times can't get any worse, they must get better. The papers say there'll be more jobs soon. Reen!" He used a pet name from childhood, not spoken for a dozen years.

Doreen swung the rocker to rest against the wall. "We should go," she said.

They flew along the road again, a white road in the moonlight with dust flying around the tyres of the lorry, the lights boring into the wheel tracks, great shadows dancing on the bonnet, thrown by the taller gums. Doreen was pleased at the roar of the engine making conversation impossible.

A lighted lantern was hooked on either side of the School of Arts door, wide open, with some dark shapes inside unfolding card tables and slapping card packs in the centre of each.

Two Heffernan families, the Perrys and the Parsons were there, for the cars were lined up, square nosed like pigs at a trough, the headlight eyes blinking a warning to each other to keep to their own territory.

The Murchisons pulled up as Frank did, Mrs Bert Rossmore alighting from their car at the same time as Mrs Murchison, who was very stout, tumbled from the front seat to greet her daughter warmly. They stood close together on the uneven ground, as if they had not talked for half an hour on the telephone less than three hours earlier. Both looked as if they could easily have spent the evening there in conversation, and indeed might have preferred to. Mrs Murchison's arms held a large covered tray, quite obviously food, and Mrs Rossmore peeped under the cover and ducked even closer to Mrs Murchison, in appreciation, no doubt, of Mrs Murchison's doing the cooking for her daughter as well as herself.

Frank and Doreen went in with the little bunch of Rossmores, Murchisons, Perrys and Parsons, the dimness not quite smudging from their faces a lively curiosity in the Cullens, there in two parts as always, Doreen home and, as usual, taking Frank's side, and making matters worse, really. Nothing would change, it appeared, and eyes confirmed this, finding Jane and Martha together on a seat against the wall isolated from the little groups, and Frank and Doreen halted with Nora Keaton and Betty Perry.

Brighter were the eyes for the discovery, relishing sighs expanding chests, hard and soft, flat and narrow, wide and cavernous. Some looked on the euchre night as a dull affair to which they were dutifully committed, the feuding Cullens injecting interest. Oh dear me, said the half shakes of the wise heads, this is going on forever (may it never stop).

Nora and Betty were chatting with a show of brightness, partly covering their resentment that Doreen got away to the city and they didn't, but pursued a life that barely changed from school days, except for children and even longer working hours.

Frank was saying, no doubt about it, Sydney was the place to be and it wouldn't be long before he was there too.

This caused an unashamed swing of two pairs of eyes to Jane and Martha on the seat and, since the way was clear, a good view of Martha in the blouse, the lantern above her giving the rust colour a sheen and whitening

149

her arms and darkening her hair, dressed looser so that fine hairs escaped the coils on her ears and were burnished too, like fine grass turned gold by the sun.

"Martha's got a new blouse," Nora said. "Very nice."

Doreen wanted to burst out, like a spiteful six year old, that the blouse was hers, and looked swiftly to Frank to agree with her. But little of Frank's face was seen, tipped back away from the light, his thatch of silvery hair had a vigour like his body, teetering slightly on his heels. Nora and Betty saw too, not for the first time, his stomach flat where other men's bulged, his belt flat too at his waist, where other men wore braces.

They had danced with him when they were fifteen and he was forty. There was the first brush of his hips when they turned in a waltz, alerting them for the next turn, the touch deeper and longer this time, blood under their young faces, blood tingling their young hips, the side hall door open, the grass a bed to turn their shamed faces from, the lantern above the door swinging gently, or was it the moon beyond that was beckoning them?

"There might be dancing after the cards," Nora said. "Stella's here."

Stella Parsons played the piano for most of the dances in Cobargo, and took a few pupils that could make their way to the Parsons farm four miles from town, and were not Catholics, in which case they were taught by the musical nun at St Joseph's.

At that moment Fred Rossmore rapped the table at the end. As chairman of the hall committee, he had the job of organizing the games.

"And we'll finish at ten o'clock if everyone agrees, and Mrs Parsons" (he did not use her Christian name since he did not know her in his youth and she was of another faith) "will play for a few dances."

He had not asked her, but had seen the roll of music

tied to the handle of the basket that held her cakes for supper, and used his wide shopman's smile to gain her acquiescence, which was a lowering of her head on its long thin neck and a little frosty, martyred smile which said whatever would Cobargo do without me?

Nora brought her hands together in a clap, and Betty smiled very carefully, for she had a new denture she was not quite used to.

Frank, Doreen, Nora and Betty together made up a table, Jane playing with the Perrys and their son Roley, at another table.

Martha was left alone on the seat, glancing towards the supper room now and again, nothing to do there since the kettles were filled, one sitting on the primus stove ready for lighting and the food set out on plates, two for each table, the sandwiches mixed so that the roast beef and mustard from Heffernans was balanced with the scrape of hard boiled egg from the Paddy Moores. Ethel Moore was a very mean woman who was said to shave her corn beef servings with a razor blade and take milk separated of its cream, fed by other farmers to their pigs, to make custards and rice pudding.

Martha was not worrying about being alone, for she usually was at times like these, and in her place under the lantern she pitied herself all those other times she had sat in her old clothes, the black she had for her father's funeral, a mustard morrocain twelve years old and fraying at the button holes, a style like old Mrs Moore would wear, a voile blouse she wore with this skirt, with a pattern of grey flowers, the centres of those at the back faded right out.

This beautiful blouse, the colour of shining blood.

She stroked an arm and studied again the little button, blood coloured too, that fastened the sleeve at her elbow. There were similar buttons on one shoulder and on the

151

opposite side. Sitting beautifully on one breast was a tiny pocket with a button there as well. Seven in all, she said to herself, thinking how terrible to lose one. She gave each a gentle pull to make sure it was safe.

Doreen was seated with her back to Martha, Frank playing opposite.

She gave him a look of intimacy like a wife and pinched a piece of the cloth of her dress near her shoulder. "This is far too warm for tonight," she said.

He shuffled the cards high near his face, Martha watching too. They appeared to fly around his fingers and when he dealt them, they settled miraculously in a beautiful fan shape in front of each player, as even as fingers on a hand.

Suddenly Martha stood and walked across and put a hand on Betty's chair. Betty's free hand touched the silk.

"Very pretty," she said. "Suits you too."

Doreen slapped a card on others face up.

"Doreen loaned it to me," Martha said.

"And swelters in her old rag of bygone years!" Doreen said.

"Your clothes are lovely," Betty said. "We all like to see what you bring home. Don't we Nora?"

Nora frowned heavily on her hand of cards. It was not what Doreen should be told.

Martha stayed on, holding the chair.

Frank cut the pack with a flourish, noted the scores with a flourish, raised his silvery eyebrows, hummed a little, whistled a little, but never allowed his eyes to stray anywhere near Martha, not even the buttoned cuff of her blouse on Betty's chair, her round white arm and a bluish smudge where her wrist started.

Martha turned her head and Jane was watching.

She slipped around the tables then and into the supper room.

152

Frank pulled a card from his hand, flung it on the little heap on the centre of the table, and swept the lot towards him, so swift the action, there was barely time for the others to see his winning king.

At the supper room door Martha looked back and he was shuffling, harder than before, chin up, eyes down. There was nothing on his face to say if he saw a blur of red or not.

Betty and Nora looked too, and in a moment there was the hiss of a flame and a great blue dancing shadow on the wall of the hall. The primus was alight.

"Good old Martha! Don't take her to Sydney when you go, Frank," Betty said.

Frank picked up his hand, looked at it, and played a card.

"Cobargo wouldn't be the same without the Cullens," Nora said.

"So don't go," said Betty.

The chairs were scraping back. Jane and Mrs Murchison went to the supper room too, an unwritten law at euchre nights saying that a maximum of three work there to avoid crowding and confusion.

"If she gets grease on that blouse I'll be in the right frame of mind for murder," Doreen said.

But Martha held the plates away from her body and her head erect as she went among the tables, the blouse a red sail, only rippling gently when she was under a lantern, dipping her dark head down, saying nothing.

"You look smart tonight, Martha," said Jack Martin, sitting with his Hilda and giving as much attention to the dip of Martha's breasts as to the slices of sponge cake she set beside the stacked cards and Hilda's little beaded handbag. The Martins' sixteen year old son pulled his lips back on very big teeth and studied the table edge, giving it all his attention, and deciding he would wait for his

153

tea before taking a piece of cake. In a little while Martha brought that too.

Stella Parsons went up the two little steps to the stage and lifting the piano lid teased the keys.

The sound at first was like plops of rain on an iron roof. Then silence, with the talk murmuring at the end of the hall like water running over stones, then some ponderous notes, silence again, and boom, boom, boom, a thunder that jerked chairs, that caused two or three to stand, eager for a partner, then blushingly sit and fiddle with a teacup handle.

Kitty Martin, near to tone deaf, but desperate for the approval of her teacher, took her place to turn the music. She avoided the dancing this way. The big Hanrahan boys had said once she was like a chained tree stump, waiting for a pull from a pair of draught horses.

"We'll go before the dancing," Jane said, gathering her basket and plates from the supper room.

At home Martha took the blouse off and, in her petticoat, pressed it at the kitchen table, for the irons were always on the back of the stove, and even with the fire out, were usually warm enough for something light and silky.

She put it on a hanger and with Doreen's other things on the side of the wardrobe.

"She should let you keep it," Jane said. "Never mind."

The bellow of the steer in its death throes woke Doreen when daylight was streaking the sky with pink chalk.

She put on a kimono and went and sat on a tree stump with a cup of tea found hot in the pot.

She did not know if Frank saw her.

"I might take Martha back to Sydney with me, Dad," she called. She swallowed her tea and hooked the cup on her little finger. "A bit of a change for her!"

Frank spaded earth very quickly on a spread of blood, rust coloured the same as the blouse.

154

11 A Haircut on Saturday

Hardly anyone lived alone in Cobargo, except for old Mrs Williams.

She was widowed and childless, and with no relatives in the town.

Mr Williams had the town's first barber's shop, but this was long gone. Some former tearooms had been taken over as a newsagents and barber's salon combined. It was run by a family named Phillips.

The son, Cliff, was the barber, and the parents and the daughter, Grace, about twenty-five, looked after the business and the living quarters at the back.

There was not much work done there, plates and cups used for meals stacked in the washing-up dish, crumbs on the floor, the stove in need of a good clean. In the sitting room there were chairs at any old angle, piles of papers and magazines on a chiffonier and two little cane tables which threatened to collapse under the weight. There was dust on the mantleshelf and sitting thickly on the top of picture frames (not always straight) and dust at the edges of the mats on the linoleum. Askew on the table was the cloth, a thick green fringed one, never removed, for the family ate in the kitchen, seldom at once, mostly making up little meals of favourite food, like lettuce and cucumber for Grace, who used the cucumber peel on her skin, proud of her clear creamy complexion, and a thick slice of steak, thrown on the top of the stove for Mr Phillips.

Mrs Phillips was in the shop most of the time, putting little price tags on books and toys, serving customers mostly with newspapers (a day old from Sydney) getting orders of pencils and crayons ready for the traveller when he came, and making sure the school children did not steal a rubber, or even a pen nib from a flat cardboard box that should not be left on the counter, but often was, especially if Cliff was called from his barbering to serve.

Mr Phillips spent little time in the shop. One of the hotels in Cobargo was a couple of hundred yards down the street, and Mr Phillips liked to go there, mainly to yarn. He even sat on the steps when the bar was shut to talk to anyone passing by, or willing to join him. If caught in the shop he had difficulty meeting a customer's needs. He would toss things about on shelves to search behind them, and peer into the one showcase, all the contents visible to the customer anyway, and blame Mrs Phillips for her habit of changing things around, until the customer felt guilty and said not to worry, he would try and get the item at Rossmore's, at which point Mr Phillips would yell for Edna, who was most likely having a meal, for she was seldom in the living quarters for any other reason.

Customers saw the state of the Phillipses' sitting room and kitchen, for a door leading to them was behind the shop counter. A second door a little farther along opened into the barber's salon. It was an austere, masculine room with only a poster of a bullfight on one wall, and a fire-place and mantleshelf on which stood Cliff's shaving and hair cutting materials, most of them in jugs without handles, cast offs from the kitchen.

The mirror over the mantle was one left behind when the people with the tearooms left. It was badly spotted, and customers had to put their head at a certain angle to see Cliff's handiwork. Some ducked and jerked about trying to get a full view of their parting, in the end Cliff taking hold of their shoulders and steering them towards the left hand corner, sucking his teeth with irritation at their stupidity.

The salon door was almost always open. A fire there in the winter helped warm the shop and with two or three waiting at times to occupy the one chair, the place had a busy air even if the shop trade was quiet.

Mr Phillips, using the other door to pass through the shop, usually left it open, showing the untidy state of the sitting room and, beyond that, the kitchen even worse with perhaps a few dying embers in the stove, the door of the firebox which opened downwards, hanging like a hungry tongue.

Mrs Phillips didn't worry about the normal run of customers seeing, but she hated old Mrs Williams to see.

Mrs Williams's well kept house was a talking point for Cobargo. It was far too large for one, and so was the garden, but they kept Mrs Williams busy, for she did little else but work in both.

It came about that John Boyle and his sister Ella saw both houses on the same afternoon.

John had a haircut at Phillipses' when the Boyles could afford it, and each time Mrs Boyle sighed as she parted with the sixpence, giving silent thanks for her family of five girls (with long hair and no chance of anything else) and only John, and the baby Leslie with a great round silvery ball of a head, still a long way from Cliff's scissors at the rate of his hair growth (and times would be much better when he needed a barber, Mrs Boyle always told herself).

Ella, next to John in age, went with him for his haircut. She squeezed into a corner of the seat attached to the wall, fearful of strange men coming in and forcing her into conversation.

Grace found her there this day, with John in the chair, beginning to look different already, his neck whiter, the little stools of hair scattered over the piece of sheeting around John's shoulders like hay left behind when the Coady men gathered it in a hurry to stack in the great shed by the dairy.

It was an extra busy Saturday for Cliff with three men waiting, and he was snipping and frowning over John and thinking it typical of the feckless Boyles to send their kid for a haircut on a Saturday when there were hours after school days lying idle. He would put a notice up saying so (no children on Saturday) he said to himself, snipping around John's ear and sending a shower of hair inside it, causing John to shudder and lift his shoulders.

"Still!" Cliff called, and John leapt in the chair and turned bright red, seeing with terrible embarrassment Cliff take a step backwards, and hold his arms up in his white coat, like something about to fly.

Ella blushed as red as John and put her face into the corner, away from the waiting three, shouldering some of the blame for the delay inflicted on them by her brother.

Grace was in the shop behind the counter but not needed, for Mrs Phillips was there and she preferred to do everything herself. Since the space was restricted, Grace pressed her back to the shelves, hands behind her, as if they required curbing should they sinfully leap out and pass someone a newspaper or accept twopence for one.

Knowing her mother wanted her out of the way, Grace avoided looking her way, but turned her gaze towards the salon where Ella's white neck and a portion of scarlet cheek was showing over a shoulder with an old cotton dress half falling from it.

Grace felt a rush of affection for the innocence of that piece of neck and slid behind her mother to go into the salon.

She was pleased that Charlie Hanrahan was there waiting for a haircut. He and Grace had been lovers for six months and used to meet down the creek bed and make love under a ledge, lying on a slope, her body pressed into a bank of moist sand (she never felt or saw damp sand again without remembering).

Some children jumped heavily on the ledge one day and Charlie and Grace were discovered, both showered with sand and earth. Charlie pulling his trousers on plunged down into the creek, escaping into the bush on the other side, and Grace hiding her pants under her jammed together legs, called to the children to go on home without turning her head to see who they were. Unfortunately, one was a cousin of Charlie's.

Grace was so relieved to escape a pregnancy, she was not greatly affected when Charlie avoided her after the incident, and a couple of years later married Una Yates from out Bemboka way.

But as the years slipped away and there appeared no suitable suitor for Grace, she gave the romance an aura quite unworthy of it. She almost convinced herself Charlie was the one true love of her life, and she had discarded all others trying to fill his shoes. If they met in a barn dance, she held herself stiffly and looked coldly over his shoulder, and in the street, walked past him without speaking. He was uncomfortable, and she, with a churning of revenge that was almost pleasure, looked about for others to notice and think (so Grace believed) of the great tragedy of the broken romance and wonderful, beautiful Grace sworn off men forever.

Charlie, now twenty-seven, looked at his boots when Grace came in, she pleased to be in her white dress with the blood red coin spots that made her look (she thought), with her black hair scalloped around her face, wan and fragile.

159

Since she ignored Charlie, she brushed the others aside too, and stretched out both arms to Ella. This would show the born mother she was and look what he missed, nothing coming from Una as yet, and not likely after four years. She pushed a gold bangle up a white arm and pulled Ella's head down to lay it against her waist, made to look smaller with a wide red leather belt.

She tilted Ella's chin upwards and looked into her eyes, and John, wondering at this spectacle, swung his head, although he saw the reflection in the mirror.

"It's the same in there as it is back there!" Cliff cried, stepping back again with arms raised. He came forward to run the comb hard down the back of John's head and above his ears, then fling the sheeting from his neck, and John stood to climb down, only to be ordered to sit, for Cliff to lather at his neck and ears with a dry shaving brush.

Ella, given charge of the sixpence to pay Cliff, overcome by the display by Grace, kept it in her tightly squeezed hand, and Cliff had to extend an open palm in John's direction and sigh as if failure to pay could only be expected, and John had to pull at Ella's wrist, before the transaction took place and Cliff had slapped the coin on the mantle and began flapping the sheeting for the next customer.

"Come along dears," Grace said. "I've got something to show you, you'll simply love!"

The waiting two saw the back of Charlie's neck redden as he climbed into the chair. There was a softening of their faces and little smiles like baby rabbits scuttling from beneath bushes into the open, and eyelids dropped and idle, hoary hands opened and shut.

Grace had something to show old Charlie, no doubt about that! The only difference was he had seen it before. He'd love to see it again though, simply love to see it,

160

make no mistake about that! They got the story ordered and ready for the first group of yarning males they could join.

Grace bore John and Ella off through the back door of the salon which led onto a veranda, with doors opening off it to both kitchen and sitting room. All the Phillips clutter was spread out before the eyes of the young Boyles.

Not that they looked its way for too long. Midway down the veranda was a pine box on its side, and inside the box, on a heap of old blanket, a newborn, squirming pup.

It had a little, black, wrinkled face with eyes squeezed shut, a writhing pinkish stomach, marked with teats like press studs, and a coating of brown hair over the rest of its body. It turned over on its back, beating at the air with its feet, crying a thin cry with no urgency in it, as if no answering comfort could be expected, and it intended to cry on interminably.

Grace gathered it up and laid it near her neck, swinging it back and forth with eyelids lowered. John and Ella, feeling some sort of response was expected of them, each put a hand out and stroked the pup, Ella a sprawling hind leg and John its flattened back, letting the warmth of its flesh run into their fingers from under the wrinkled skin.

Grace moved along the veranda to allow the salon to see. For a moment her eyes met those of Charlie in the mirror. See this kind and loving person, they said. She pressed her face close to the pup's, which put a tongue out, then darted it back almost immediately, not liking the taste, and Grace wanted to wipe at her stiffened cheek, but didn't want Charlie to see, nor the others who bagged and drowned kittens and pups as fast as they arrived. Their bored and disgusted expressions said only fools of women smooched over pups. Old Charlie did better with Una Yates after all, barren as she was and with a

161

whine in her voice, not unlike a newborn pup's, but not so easily quietened. It would be good to see it piss down Grace's dress and give Charlie a laugh, trapped there in the chair and unable to look anywhere but at Grace and the two round-eyed Boyle children, who were automatically stroking the pup and looking as if they would like something a bit more exciting to do.

"We'll put him back to beddy byes, shall we?" Grace said.

Even Cliff, quite proud of his sister most of the time, sucked a tooth and moved his scissors faster, indicating irritation, and the two on the seat looked deeply on their boots in contempt of this feminine silliness.

With the pup dropped suddenly and quite heavily (to the surprise of John and Ella) back onto its bed, Grace brushed rapidly at her dress, picking hairs from the red spots with fastidious fingers and a frown.

"I know!" she said, squeezing at a shoulder of each child. "Some cake! What do you say to that?"

Ella pressed close to Grace's silk side and John tried not to rush. He thought of his mother who would have liked them to refuse, he was sure. Grace had to look about the kitchen for the cake tin. A red edge showed under a tumble of clothes at one end of the kitchen table and Grace seized it with triumph.

Unfortunately, Mrs Phillips had brought the clothes in hastily from the clothes line and dumped them close to a pot of axle grease with an old wooden spoon to stir it, and Grace, snatching the cake tin, tipped the spoon which smeared a fold of a cream silk petticoat, Grace's best.

"Oh, look what she's done!" she cried. "My best slip!"

She held it up to the light from the doorway, stretching the silk between her hands, watching with an angry face the greenish black mark spread even further.

162

"I'll strangle her, I will! Look at it, just look at it!"

The children tried to keep their eyes on the stain but slid them around towards the cake tin.

"Whatever will I do?" Grace said, sitting on a chair with her arms lost in the folds of the silk.

Ella saw an embroidered cluster of roses which would sit on Grace's breasts, and shoulder straps of the finest tubes of silk, and lace inches deep at the hem, and wondered at Grace's ugly expression when she owned such a lovely thing, grease marked or not.

She forgot the promise of cake in a wish that Grace would pass the slip across to her for Mrs Boyle (since it was damaged). She visualized the silk strained across her mother's stomach and Mrs Boyle's eyes lowered towards the embroidered bust, her face soft and pretty in her happiness. To bring the dream closer, she reached out a hand to finger the lace, and Grace, as if alerted to this, pulled the slip back into her lap.

"Would your mother know how to get axle grease out of a real silk petticoat?" Grace asked.

Grace's face became even more petulant the moment she spoke. Of course she wouldn't, it said.

John and Ella screwed their heads so as not to see the cake tin. Grace, both sulky and dreamy, and still clutching the petticoat, opened the lid.

Inside was the end of a plain cake and a mess of biscuits, clinging together as if they needed the support of each other to remain whole, currants falling away from their sugary tops, shining with dampness.

"That's her!" Grace cried. "She puts cake and biscuits together, and what do we get? A mess of mouldy crumbs! Just look at that!"

She took the cake out and cleared a place for it to sit like a little ant hill with a broken top. She looked at John and Ella with such a glitter of anger, she seemed cross-eyed.

"Your mother would know better than to put cake and biscuits in the one tin, wouldn't she?"

John and Ella felt great discomfort. At home there were few cakes and biscuits, and no real cake tin as far as they knew. They felt sure Grace knew this too.

Grace, still attached to the petticoat, got up from the table and slapped open the doors of a large brown cabinet which Ella would have loved for her mother. Ella saw flashes of china and groceries and papers and bottles of jam and pickles, the paper covers filmed with dust. That would be a wonderful job for Mrs Boyle and the girls, Beryl, Mary and herself, to clear out and put everything back in beautiful order. She saw her mother's face, even pinker than normal, and her blue eyes very blue, the way they were when she was happy. She longed for the doors to stay open to see more of what could be done.

But Grace was in search of cake, and nothing like it obvious, shut each door with an angry little bang. Ella had to be content then with a dream of wiping down all the outside and cleaning each of the glass panels in the top part, going right to the edge with a finger under the cloth, an old tattered singlet outgrown by all the Boyle babies.

"You simply can't eat one of these," Grace said, shaking the tin and seeing the clump of biscuits wobble, but fail to separate. "Could you?"

Her angry eyes glittered on them. They wanted to say yes they could, but understood they were expected to indicate that they couldn't.

Grace pulled a drawer open in the cabinet, and there was a loud rattle of the cutlery (so much Ella's mother would be in a constant state of joy). She took out a knife and cut the cake in half and, helped by the blade, passed a slice each to John and Ella. It was very dry and needed to be eaten fast to stop the crumbs escaping. Both children would have liked to take small bites and savour each slowly, but they followed the bites swiftly with the next, hoping for more flavour, but only succeeding in cramming their small throats to choking point.

Grace pinched a little pile of crumbs from the table and, putting her head back, dropped them onto her tongue. She buried her face in her petticoat, and coughed and slapped her chest.

"What vile cake! She'll choke us next!" She put the lid on the tin and pushed it along the table, bumping the can of grease and sending the stick wobbling, endangering the other clothes piled up.

Grace held her petticoat up, stretching the marked part against the light from the doorway.

"Oh, look at it, just look at it!" she cried, as if she had been hoping the mark would disappear. "I'm telling her!"

She charged towards the shop, and John and Ella wondered if they should follow, but thought better not, although they were greatly attracted to the idea of getting behind the counter.

Grace held the petticoat for Mrs Phillips to see, stretching the mark to twice its original size. Mrs Phillips looked from her end of the counter where she was talking to Mrs May, who was spending an hour in conversation after the purchase of a packet of envelopes. Mrs May looked too, and there were these two large, middle-aged faces with mouths falling open.

"You threw it down on the grease pot!" Grace cried. "My best slip! Ruined!" Mrs Phillips went red and tidied the box of envelope packs not yet returned to the shelf.

"I'm taking it to Mrs Williams to see!"

"Shut the door!" Mrs Phillips cried at the mention of Mrs Williams.

Grace put a foot behind her and dragged the door nearly shut.

"It'll never come out!" she cried.

Mrs Phillips put the envelopes away.

"Rubbish! Of course it will! Won't it, Mrs May?"

Mrs May shook a doubting, mournful grey head. "I wouldn't be sure," she said. She had no silk petticoat, and felt satisfaction in seeing Grace's ruined. "I don't know of anything that'd take it out."

"Mrs Williams will!" Grace cried, her eyes firing the two of them into a mould of incompetence. "I'm taking it to Mrs Williams!"

"Now don't be silly!" Mrs Phillips said. "There'll be a book in the cabinet saying what takes out grease!"

"I don't intend spending the next five years searching through that cabinet!"

Mrs Phillips went a deeper red and tossed her head. "Then give me more help in the shop. I'd dearly love to have the time to make the house look like Mrs Williams's!"

Grace hooked the door open with her foot and charged through.

"Did you hear that?" she said to John and Ella. "Everyone in Cobargo knows she won't let any of us sell a pin without she's looking on!"

She pushed the petticoat under an arm and seized a hand of each of the children, racing them through the back door and jumping off the veranda into the grass. The Phillips had no garden and this was quicker than using the steps.

A sagging wire fence ran across the bottom of the yard, separating it from the creek bank. A fairly narrow path was left beyond this, running behind all the properties, the hotel and other houses, Mrs Williams's the last before

166

Colburn's shop on the corner where the road turned towards Wandella.

Everything was different the minute you reached the Williams back gate.

Even outside the fence there were no great tufts of grass wedged tightly against the palings but ivy geraniums planted there (fancy garden *outside* the place, Cobargo said). The vines climbed up and made a great weight on the top of the fence like someone in a hat decorated with white, mauve and pink flowers.

Mrs Williams's gate was neat too, kept shut against straying stock. Sometimes the Phillipses found a cow munching at the grass against their back veranda. If all the doors were open into the house, customers saw the red, black or fawn back, and Mrs Phillips yelled to Cliff, who raced out with a razor raised, and Grace came out of her bedroom with her face striped with cucumber peel, and the cow was chased and the gate shut with a violent bang, and loud blame placed on children perversely opening it as they used a short cut to school.

Most of Mrs Williams's back yard was under flowers and vegetables and there were several fruit trees as well. All the front had flower beds, so many rose bushes so well cared for, the blooms were usually prize winners at the Cobargo show.

People tapped on Mrs Williams's door when there was a funeral, and she (not generous at other times) gave liberally, grateful that the body was someone else's, for she was past the age of seventy and worried from time to time about her own demise, and the necessary organization to follow.

She had only one nephew, a fifty-five year old bank clerk who visited her once a year. Her house was willed to him, and she wrote to him regularly as well as looking forward to his visit months in advance.

He was a poor correspondent, and the more one-sided the exchange of letters became, the more anxious grew Mrs Williams, fearful of something happening to Cyril before it happened to her, giving her the major task of finding another beneficiary.

Grace put her hand over the gate and released the catch, John and Ella in awe of the boldness of anyone approaching the Williams house with such confidence.

They were hesitant about following, but Grace held the gate open, her frown saying she would close it, no one else could be trusted.

"Mrs Williams!" she called, running quite eagerly up the steps.

The kitchen door opened onto a back veranda (what a place for the little Boyles on wet days and Mrs Boyle to hang her wash!) They waited there in full view of the kitchen for Mrs Williams to appear.

"Just look at it!" Grace said.

The Boyles were looking, no mistake about that. Ella had projected her mother there, on the linoleum which was like slippery glass, a beautiful brown colour with a pattern of fawn stripes like scattered fence panels. It would be wonderful to play on, to imagine there were real fences to jump sheep over. She saw the baby Leslie there on a hot day, his little legs sticking out from a clean nappy, the linoleum cooling them and his little fat round bottom.

There was a table in the centre, not big, for there had only been Mr and Mrs Williams, and the top was scrubbed white, with a brass bowl in the middle filled with oranges from trees along the fence. Around the walls were chairs and a big dresser crowded with blue china and white meat platters. Mrs Boyle would have loved to cut the roast on one when (rarely) they could afford meat.

Mrs Williams had a sink, gleaming white with a tap

over it, sending little sparks off the polished brass. Under the sink curved around the water pipe were shelves covered with blue checked paper and saucepans with their right lids on, and down the wide wooden part that supported the sink, wonderful shining things were hanging, a grater unlike the rusty old one Mrs Boyle used for the nutmeg, and different kinds of big spoons for stirring gravy and jam.

The preserving pan that took up most of the bottom shelf, and had jars with lids in a group beside it, showed not a trace of black or grease, and Ella thought instantly of their old one on its side by the stove with dents where Les had flung wood down, carelessly at times, not bothering to move the pan out of the way, even with a foot. Ella's eyes left the pan and jars to rest on a glass fronted cupboard near the door to the hall that led to the front of the house. Mrs Williams had her filled jars there, peaches and apricots, even lemons in one, looking like fat men doing a balancing act, rhubarb holding the shape of the stalk but looking ready to burst, quinces of delicate pink, and plump blackberries packed so tight there seemed far too much for one, even eating them over a week.

Soft steps were heard and Mrs Williams, who had perhaps been on the front veranda or inspecting her big round bed of roses between the veranda and the front fence, or her wallflowers, like strips of brown and gold carpet, came down the hall and across another smaller hall leading to a bathroom at one end and to the kitchen at the other.

She was a tall, spare woman with a lot of hair that had once been chestnut in colour but was mostly grey now, making Ella think of their old tank with rust invading the flat sheets of iron. She was broad of hip and flat of stomach, having never borne any children, and she wore black nearly all the time, not covering her dress with a cretonne apron like other Cobargo women.

"Mrs Williams!" Grace called from the doorway.

"Grace!" Mrs Williams answered, and quite a lot of severity went out of her face. "Come in, Grace!" Mrs Williams's eyes behind gold-rimmed glasses went severe again, looking on John and Ella.

"The Boyle children," Grace explained, "John has been for a haircut." She smoothed John's hair away from the parting. "They can sit on the back step."

"How are their feet?" Mrs Williams asked, peering at John and Ella's feet, sending scarlet into their cheeks and a fear of glancing down to confirm their vision of scarred toes and cracks, creeping from the soles to the uppers, threaded with ingrained dirt, which even a scrubbing brush failed to move.

There was no way of hiding their feet, they could only turn quickly and sit on the veranda edge, thankful for the top step that put them mostly out of sight.

But they turned their heads to make sure they missed nothing of what went on in the kitchen.

Grace held the petticoat out to show the mark at its best. "You'll know something to take it out, Mrs Williams?"

"Whoever did that?" Mrs Williams asked, the gleam in her eye answering her own question.

"Who else?" Grace said. "She dumped it on a pot of axle grease!" Grace gave no thought to blaming Cliff, who had used the grease on his Ford motor, and dropped the can on the first available space.

Grace kept the peace with Cliff, who was her means of transport to Bermagui on hot Sundays, to Bega races once a year, and events in Cobargo, even those within walking distance when it brought her great pleasure to

170

ride past trudging parties on their way to the showground or School of Arts.

Grace allowed her arms to fall heavily with the petticoat to her front and a deep sigh rose from her bosom. Mrs Williams came forward and looked closely at the grease mark.

"Eucalyptus, perhaps."

"We've got some," Grace said. "God knows where, though."

Men hungry for work set up a makeshift plant once in the bush towards Yowrie, a few miles from Cobargo, to distil eucalyptus oil from trees growing thick and wild. They brought samples of their product to Cliff when they came to Cobargo for a haircut.

"It might work," Mrs Williams said. "Sit down, Grace."

Grace sat and before she realized it, fixed her eyes on the stove, shining black as wet tar, unlit, with a primus with a brass belly bright as the sun sitting on top, and in its place a kettle of copper looking far too handsome for the mundane job of boiling water.

Mrs Williams looked too, and thought she should offer to make tea for Grace, except that the Boyles were there and would have to be given cake.

"Perhaps you little ones should run home now," Grace said, reading Mrs Williams's thoughts. (Everyone in Cobargo knew she had no time for children.)

John and Ella obediently but reluctantly stood, and looking down, made their way down the steps.

"Perhaps an orange!" Mrs Williams said and they stopped. She went to the bowl on the table, but the best ones were there and she didn't want to disturb the arrangement.

"We could find two on the tree," she said. All the work she did kept her agile and she went down the steps quite fast, Grace following only as far as the veranda rail over which she draped herself to watch Mrs Williams part branches, looking for oranges suitable for the young Boyles.

"I want the tree looking nice for when Cyril comes," Mrs Williams said.

Grace ran down the steps and sat on a garden seat and beckoned the children to come, for she was worried that they were standing too close to a bed of verbena trailing mauve flowers onto the brick path. They sat, glad of the reprieve, but not excited about the oranges because they had a boxful at home, given to their father on his first day clearing blackberries for Coadys (the job given to Les not entirely on his skills, but mainly for the sake of Doris and the children).

The Coady oranges were larger, smoother and a deeper gold, much superior to the two Mrs Williams pulled from her tree, each liberally spread with green on one side and spots like a rash of brown measles on the other.

"Say thank you to Mrs Williams," Grace said before John and Ella had a chance to. They rolled the oranges in their hands, rubbing a thumb on the spotted part, sad and ashamed they were unworthy of the superior fruit.

"I'll show you this new rose," Mrs Williams said. "I was hoping it would be out for Cyril."

"Stay there quiet and don't eat the oranges yet," Grace said to John and Ella, thinking of the peel thrown down on the lawn. "Save them to share with the brothers and sisters."

John wanted to say there was only one brother, the baby, who took his orange juice from a spoon lovingly administered by Mrs Boyle or Beryl, but was saddened again that the number and gender of the Boyle children was rated so unimportantly.

The rose was at the corner of Mrs Williams's house at the front, and Grace followed Mrs Williams down the

172

side where the garden was as carefully tended as anywhere else.

Grace thought unhappily of the space at home, similar to this, but filled with old tyres, garden tools gone rusty, wood and paper shavings used for packing toys, kerosene tins and cardboard boxes reduced to pulp by wet weather.

The rose was a cream one, the curled-back petals edged very faintly with pink, and Mrs Williams turned the one bloom on the bush towards Grace and it bounced proudly on its stem, sending a drop of water like a happy tear to slide across a leaf.

"Cyril will simply love it, Mrs Williams," Grace said.

She saw very little of Cyril, for he stayed with Mrs Williams for only a week in the year, and spent the time reading on the front or back veranda or taking walks along one of the four roads leading out of Cobargo. He did not go to the post office, or the newsagent's or Rossmore's or any other shop, unnecessary anyway for Mrs Williams did all her own shopping, and Cyril, smartly dressed in clothes bought in his home town of Ballarat in Victoria, would scarcely be looking for socks and ties in Cobargo.

The locals said he kept himself to himself, peeved a little that he did not attend dances or sporting events that sometimes occurred when he was visiting, for any new-comer sparked off interest and speculation, and in the case of Cyril it was well founded, for most people knew the Williams house was willed to him, and when she passed on he would either sell it, or move in, the latter most unlikely. His visits to Cobargo were seen as token gestures, merely acknowledging the inheritance.

"He doesn't give an owl's hoot for her, and she thinks he's the bee's knees," was the Cobargo summing up. "When she goes, we won't see his heels for dust."

Now Grace began to think about Cyril, the grey,

creased trousers he wore and his highly polished shoes and his haircut with a centre part which irked Cliff, who guessed (rightly) that Cyril got a fresh haircut for Cobargo, scorning the use of the local facility.

He would be thirty years Grace's senior, but she saw herself in white satin and tulle, clinging on his arm.

He'll never leave Cobargo now he's got Grace, she imagined people saying. He's absolutely devoted to her. She looked up onto the veranda with the white cane chairs and settee with plump, spotless cushions, and through the open front door down the hall, the afternoon sun slanted on the brown and fawn carpet runner, the boards at the edge shining like dark brown silk. She felt a rush of possession as if it were already hers.

"He's coming to see you soon?" Grace asked eagerly (me, really).

Mrs Williams stepped sadly from the rose as it had betrayed her. "He hasn't written," she said.

He's dead, Grace thought. He's dead, and I get the house! She wills it to me! She bent her body to see into more of the hall, a table finished handsomely with curved timber slats enclosing a bottom tier holding a brass jardiniere, with a similar container on the top, both filled with Mrs Williams's best ferns.

"It worries me half to death," Mrs Williams said.

Death! Grace thought with relish. (This time Mrs Williams's death.)

"August he always comes," Mrs Williams said, looking up the street to the post office where the mail car stopped every day except Sunday to dislodge passengers if there were any.

Grace looked too, growing dreamy. She saw Cyril standing with his suitcase staring at the newsagent's, watching for Grace to appear. (She would tease him, make him wait.)

Grace stood now on the bottom step, hoping this would encourage Mrs Williams to go through the house to the back. She wanted to see into the front rooms, the bedroom with the great brass bed and the towering wardrobe and dressing table shaped like a kidney, and the sitting room with the dark polished wood couch and chairs upholstered in pink velvet, and the mantlepiece with Cyril's photo, and the shepherdess figurines in porcelain, and twin crystal vases, each holding three or four of Mrs Williams's best roses.

Grace could also see into the bathroom, white tiles on the floor and halfway up the walls and the pedestal basin and thick white towels untouched, since Mrs Williams used a skinny worn one kept behind the door.

Mrs Williams did go the front way, allowing Grace to go ahead, which was disappointing for she had to hurry with Mrs Williams hard on her heels. In the kitchen Mrs Williams saw the chair Grace had occupied askew and the petticoat on the seat. She swept it backwards to Grace, straightening the chair and brushing at the seat as if Grace or her petticoat might have soiled it in some way.

Grace reddened and looked at the grease mark. "Eucalyptus, you said, Mrs Williams?"

Mrs Williams's face, Grace saw, considered the grease mark insignificant against the weight of her own problems. She went to the back door to see what John and Ella were up to, and although they were innocently rolling the oranges in their hands and throwing them up a little way to catch them, she frowned heavily their way.

"I hope there is eucalyptus at home," Grace said.

"I've got some but I'll need it if Cyril gets a cold while he's here," Mrs Williams said.

Grace made a face at her back and tucking the petticoat under her arm stepped past her onto the veranda.

"I should take them home, I suppose." She went down

175

the steps and John and Ella got up, then looked down to make sure they stepped in the right places to reach the path.

Grace turned to look back at Mrs Williams by the veranda rail. "I might come and say hello while Cyril's here," Grace said. Mrs Williams's rusted head shook once before she went inside.

"Oh, dearie, dearie me," Grace pulled the children with her down the path and pushed open the gate with energy.

"Oh God, I'd love to leave this gate open and let a cow in!"

The children looked up in disbelief and saw Mrs Williams back on the veranda, watching. Grace lifted the catch, opened the gate a little way, then snapped it shut.

"Shut tight, Mrs Williams!" she called. "Goodbye! Thank Mrs Williams again for the oranges, children!" John and Ella could find no words but held the oranges up, the gesture to be taken as an expression of gratitude.

Grace ran with them along the track. "Heave them into the gully! They're not fit for the pigs!" she cried. "She didn't even ask me if I had a mouth! 'I need the eucalyptus for Cyril's cold!' Cyril's dumped her, that's what's happened. She's got no one now to leave the place to. Serves her right!"

John and Ella tried to look at each other for help in interpreting these strange remarks, but Grace's red and white dress was beating and thrashing about between them, and little short breaths were whistling from her red mouth.

"Oh, stop!" she said suddenly and flopped down on the lower side of the track, sloping towards the creek. Some rocks, partly covered with a dried greyish moss, sat among the grass, and Grace leaned back on one. John and Ella found two the right size for sitting on.

Grace tipped her head back closing her eyes. "Oh that

house, that dreadful house!" she said in a little moaning voice.

Ella thought it must have been the Phillips house she was referring to and wanted to fly to the defence of the brown cabinet.

"Like a tomb, a cold and terrible tomb, don't you think?" She opened eyes first on Ella then on John, glinting in them a plea for agreeability.

Their faces warmed.

"No, you didn't see inside, did you? Less than four people have crossed the threshold of the Williams house, and I'm one of them.

"But I'll never return, never. Never." She rolled the petticoat up and stuffed it behind her head like a pillow and closed her eyes again.

"She's jealous of me, jealous of my youth. My looks." She kept her eyes closed, willing the Boyles to look at her profile. "Jealous of Cyril's love for me."

She opened her eyes to look for the shocked reaction. Then she hooped forward, pushing her fingers into the grass and twisting it about.

"It's a secret I'll share with you. No one else in all the world."

The Boyles tried to assume expressions worthy of this great honour but, failing to, stared at their oranges and turned them in their hands.

To their great relief on glancing up, they saw their father walking towards the opposite bank.

"Oh, look! Dad!" John cried, getting to his feet. Ella scrambled to hers. Les was carrying a sugar bag, bulging at the bottom with a vegetable marrow from the Coadys. Grace stood up too and smoothed her dress down, slapping at the parts where grass had stuck and frowning as if someone were to blame.

She smoothed her hair too and pushed her scallops upwards with the tips of her fingers.

"Here Les!" she cried, and the children were surprised to hear her use his Christian name. She took a hand of each and raised them, as if they had just won a race.

Even at that distance the children saw their father's face change, go softer, and the mouth stretch gently. He put his head down and ran like a boy down the bank and jumped some water strung out in patches on the creek bed, not looking for the narrow part, but leaping over the widest and landing with space to spare.

He jumped on the log too that ran through blackberry bushes up the bank to where they were. The log ended in more blackberries sending out long prickly stems which Les swept aside with his bag and jumped clear of, except for one that clung to his trouser leg, and he swung the bag and brushed it off as if it were no more than a twig.

"John had to wait ages and ages for his haircut!" Grace said, smoothing at John's hair as if proof were needed that he had been barbered by Cliff. "There were simply crowds of people waiting.

"Will Mrs Boyle be worried, do you think?" (Mrs Boyle, the children noted.)

Les smiled as if Mrs Boyle did not matter much. He sat on a rock, and the children did not obey an impulse to lean against him.

Grace sat on the grass and linked her arms around her skirt, covering her knees and showing only the pointed toes of her black patent shoes which she brushed clear of dust with her fingers.

John and Ella had the feeling they would be told to run on home and waited, wondering at their fear of hearing the words. When Les appeared absent about their presence, they sat in two little heaps like bent over mushrooms, almost behind Les and Grace.

John nervously let go his orange and it raced down into the blackberries, and Ella, startled to see it bowl away too fast to catch, let go hers too, and it raced even faster as if it were trying to catch up.

In a moment both were lost deep in the bushes and there was only a few trembling leaves to say what had happened. It seemed odd that neither Les nor Grace appeared to notice, particularly Les, since food of any kind wasted was just about the worst sin the children could commit.

Les saw instead the petticoat in a little silk ball nearly under the rock. He pulled at it and Grace took hold of it too, touching the grease mark wordlessly. Les laid the big brown stain of his hand over it, and the flesh of the watching children crept a little, as if their father's hand were on Grace's body. They thought he stroked the silk gently before he looked away, down over the blackberries. Grace folded the petticoat and laid it across her arm, filling her lap with a froth of lace. John and Ella did not want their father to see.

Grace's face, they thought, was sadder and prettier than they had seen it all day. There was nothing said at all it seemed for a long time.

Then John saw a thin column of smoke rising from the vicinity of their house, lazy and peaceful and beckoning.

"Mum's lit the copper fire," John said, and everyone looked that way.

"For our baths," Ella said.

They all stood, and Grace flung the petticoat over one shoulder and turned and walked off. Les flung the sugar bag over his shoulder and gave his free hand to Ella, who rubbed at the hard palm for a little while before it became warm.

She had been thinking all the afternoon of bed that

night, dreaming of the Williams house in its beautiful state for her mother, or the Phillips place brought to order by her mother's hands. She had savoured the richness of the choice.

But now she thought only of the round tub in front of the stove and the firelight dancing on the floorboards, making them appear cleaner and whiter than they really were, and her mother kneeling in her wet apron, lathering Ella's neck and shoulders with soap, and Beryl and Mary doing the washing-up until their turn came, and her father smoking on one of the kitchen chairs and talking about the way Coady's farm would be run if he had it.

She hoped that's what he would be talking about.

12 A Soft and Simple Woman

Dick was the first of the Laycock children to leave home soon after leaving school.

You couldn't blame him, Cobargo said, Albie Laycock was a slave driver and his wife, Sarah, too soft and simple to stand up to him.

Dick was the eldest, a nice looking boy with black curly hair and very good at drawing. He drew birds and trees, the farm animals, the creek that ran through the property, the heads and shoulders of his sisters Minnie, Ada and Harriet. He did not draw his brother, Dan, or the clump of pink climbing roses that grew over the wash house, although he started both.

Albie found Dick at a corner of the dining table making a drawing of Dan playing with a teaspoon while Mrs Laycock and the girls cleared the table, for the midday meal was finished.

Albie wanted both boys out clearing a paddock of saplings, ferns and blackberries. It had started to rain and Dick, who was nearly fifteen, and had left school only a few weeks before, thought he would be able to settle into an afternoon inside with Dan and his sisters, for it was a Saturday and they were not at school either.

In this self-imposed holiday mood Dick decided to draw Dan, to capture, if he could, his pensive expression. He was attracted to the idea of a composition of Dan with the spoon on the empty tablecloth and the heads of his sisters looking down on him, Ada and Harriet with plates and cups and Minnie removing a vase with a spray of roses.

He had to imagine the roses. The Laycocks never put flowers on the dinner table, and Dick thought if he was a girl he would snip a branch from the wash house blooms and put it in a jar or jug in the centre of the table. One big advantage would be the shield it would provide between him and his father, for they sat opposite each other.

Mr Laycock hardly ever spoke civilly to his family, even with other people around. If a visitor came, he sat him in the little sitting room with the seagrass table and settee and piano and hardly room for anything else and called out to Mrs Laycock to bring in tea. Usually it was one of the girls who brought it, mostly Minnie, the eldest, only eleven but already developing into a beauty, keeping her eyes down, watching that the tea didn't spill, then, when it was safely on the table, throwing her long bright hair back from her face and shoulders, a little shy smile starting to come, eyes anxious though, wondering if she should run off quickly or try and walk out like a grown up.

Albie only wanted her out, and showed this by pushing the sugar to his visitor and dumping the empty tray by the leg of the table with a clatter that took the eyes of the visitor away from Minnie (a soft, pretty young thing, the man would think, taking after her mother). The visitor would then look hopefully at the doorway for a sign of Sarah to confirm this before returning to Albie, his teacup, and the reason for his visit.

The farm was quite a prosperous one. Albie kept a good herd of Jersey cows and raised vealers and pigs. There was a good fowl run and an orchard, bearing oranges and apples in the winter and peaches, plums and apricots in the summer.

All this was hard work, and Albie looked forward to Dick's help full time and later Dan's, without wages, for he had fed, clothed, and educated them since birth and it was their duty to repay him this way.

There was no room in the arrangements for drawing in working time. And flowers! They did not belong to a man's world. Dick was so anxious to get Dan's expression, that of a wistful thirteen year old wanting more from life than farm drudgery, and looking into a teaspoon to try and find it, and the roses with their little frilled edges. He had Dan, Minnie and the flowers outlined, when Albie saw.

He picked up a tablespoon that had been used to serve the rice pudding and slapped it across the sheet of paper, dampening Dan's head and spraying some rice grains that had clung to the spoon over Minnie and the roses.

Mrs Laycock, holding a kettle of water to pour over the plates and cups in the washing-up dish, lifted it higher so that the steaming spout was pointed at Albie. The black iron kettle with the lid still jumping from the steam inside showed more expression than Sarah Laycock's face, which had the eyelids lowered as was mostly the case when she looked Albie's way.

Look at him, Dick cried inside him, if you can't tell him what a mongrel he is, look at him! He discovered with shame and sorrow he was angrier with her than with his father. He took the page and stuffed it in the stove, sending a flame flaring through the opening where the kettle had been.

"And so you damn well ought to!" Albie said, his eyes on the back of Dick's head. "There's a time for work and a time for foolin'!"

He snatched up his old tweed cap and pulled it on, waggling it with a hand on the peaked front to feel the joined seam at the back telling him it was straight. He had a white face and thick black hair and fierce brown eyes, and most of the time the children's eyes went round when they looked at him. Nearly always they looked away quickly as they did now, after a glance at their mother, checking her reaction. She always looked the same.

Dick put on his old felt hat and Dan found his under a chair. They went out to the slide hitched to Jacko, a rough-bred animal with a black brown coat, neither draught nor hack, for which the children had great affection and Albie scorn. Jacko had his head down too. The rain had eased but the slide was wet and the boys looked at it, wondering if they would please or offend their father by finding a corn bag to cover the damp. Albie decided for them.

"Get on!" he shouted. "Never mind a bit o' damp on your backsides! There'll be more than that before you're finished with livin', I can tell you that! Gittup, gittup, lazy, useless animals!"

The boys, believing themselves to be included in this general cover of all farm inhabitants, drew their knees up and tried to make themselves as small as possible.

Dick saw himself mirrored in Dan's position, with thin tense arms binding his legs and his chin wedged between his knees. So Dick put his shoulders back and rested his hands loosely on the space beside him and trailed a foot over the side, gripping between his toes the ends of shivery grass, only to have it torn away as Jacko walked at a brisk pace under the touch of Albie's whip, Albie standing legs apart, the vibration of the slide gently shaking his buttocks and shoulders, the black hair sprouting from his cap moving more than any other part of him.

I won't be frightened of him, Dick told himself, blinking away his mother's lowered eyes. The slide went sideways down the gully to avoid running onto Jacko's hoofs, and Albie parted his legs wider, exhilarated by the challenge to balance despite the precarious dip, and turned his head just enough to see if this impressed his sons and if they had to tighten their grip, which he suspected they would.

The clouds had rolled back like a grey eiderdown trimmed with silver. I'd like to paint it, Dick thought with his face upwards. Then he saw the back of his father's neck and thought about the shotgun hooked to the lumber room wall, steering his thoughts away from the barrel to the wood part, glossy like Minnie's hair, the part of the gun he liked to stroke, keeping his eyes from the barrel, especially the two eyes at the end, into which he avoided looking, because he could never convince himself of their innocence, even with the gun unloaded.

The slide stopped by the heaped axe, crowbar, mattock and tomahawks in the shelter of a clump of saplings, their leaves shining and trembling with wet. Albie tied Jacko to the stump of an old oak that had come down in a storm, kicking at the spreading roots as he did, causing Dick and Dan to wonder if he was going to order them to dig these up, believing anything of their father who flung their tomahawks towards them.

Dick watched Albie walk off with the crowbar in one hand and the axe in the other, trying to read what his heart said, and seeing only a piece of white cheek and a bit of bristly eyebrow. The day had gone cold too in spite of the sun parting the cloud. The silver was gone and there was a paleness in the gap, a washed out light reflected on the sweep of dying grass between the saplings, the patches of fern, and the blackberries coming up from the creek bank, seeming to stretch long prickly fronds to him.

In fact everything seemed to grow under his eyes, a new line of gums with tender-looking pale pink leaves, but he knew the frailness was deceiving. The roots were tough and to pull at them was only to strip them of leaves and to fill a hand with a woody, oily moisture, the stalk left embedded in the earth, resisting all efforts, as if sprouted from some steel-like growth far, far down, miles below the surface, some giant forest chuckling through the night, tantalizing human endurance, knowing its own power and the joy of morning, waving with triumph the flag of a thousand new trees.

Dick saw Albie raise his crowbar and send it deep into the roots of a tree. Then he flung the crowbar aside and took the axe and split the low forked trunk, and Dick thought of a tooth when he heard the crack and saw the bone-white wood weeping juice, and looked foolishly for blood.

"Get on with it!" Albie called, flinging a great branch onto the heap of others already with leaves shrivelling and browning.

The boys seized their tomahawks and beat at some ferns, stubbornness clutched strongly to their roots too while the foliage spread fan shaped, green and tender and vulnerable.

I will think of Minnie coming with the tea, Dick said to himself, knowing that was hours away, wondering how he could endure the time. He looked at Dan thrashing the ferns with his tomahawk and then had to steer his thoughts from Dan, remembering him at the table, and his excitement knowing in his head how he should look, and the white paper there conspiring with him, determined as he was that it should come out right.

His mother found him at bed time that night hiding the sheets of drawing paper his teacher had given him in the bottom drawer of the cedar chest in the boys' room.

"Keep up your drawing son," was all the teacher had said, putting the generous pile into his arms.

Dick had looked gratefully into the teacher's eyes, surprised to see them as dark as Albie's were, thinking of Albie then, and getting the paper quickly into his school bag as if Albie were looking on.

Mrs Laycock came in with the lighted candle, her feet whispering on the linoleum, her face oval like the flame, her hair darker than Minnie's, blended into the shadows, her white apron alone making her real.

Dick shut the drawer and got into his side of the bed, a large oak one, each of the four posts finished with a flat little shelf. Mrs Laycock rested the candle on one at the foot. Dan saw her sorrowing face and felt the familiar ache in his throat, and climbing into bed saw Dick curled near his edge and decided it was Dick's part he must take and burrowed deeply under the covers, not touching Dick but aware of the hard cocoon of his body, and sad enough for him to close his lips tightly on a goodnight for his mother.

"Sleep well," she said in her light and girlish voice, sweeping the candle to her and going out so light of foot, Dan peeped with one eye out of the blankets to make sure she was really gone.

"You've never drawn me," Dan said. "I was wondering what I'd come out like."

Dick moved, so Dan knew he heard.

"I'm running away," Dick said. "If you cross the mountain you get to Monaro and there's a railway at Cooma. You go from there to Sydney."

"You'd have to pay on the train," Dan said, seeing it flying and rattling and Dick borne away from him forever. He opened one eye on the room as if it too might disappear with Dick.

Dick made a noise in his throat and wriggled, impatient with Dan's naivety. "You tell the guard you've lost your money." He turned his pillow over, rubbing a cheek hard on the starched slip to warm it. "I'll go to night school and learn drawing," Dick said.

Dan thought of Dick as already able to draw and couldn't imagine what he would learn. He wanted to bring up the subject of living somewhere but felt Dick would have an answer there as well, and think him stupid. He began to feel deeply miserable, envying Dick, who seemed to have a future, an exciting one too, while he was left to endure a lonely life on the farm, doing double the work with Dick gone.

Adding to his misery was the fact that he would not fall asleep quickly because of the turmoil inside his head and Dick there only feigning sleep.

It was always a challenge to fall asleep at once, with the chance of waking perhaps an hour before his mother called him. He found great joy in hearing the clock in the sitting room strike half past the hour, knowing there was a half hour, or maybe an hour and a half to lie with his waking dreams, different now, seeing himself with Dick in Sydney, sleeping late, lemonade on hot days, bags of caramels, not just at Christmas but any time they wanted them, good shoes with punching across the shining toes, no more heavy boots, a job in a big shop for him (if Dick could cheat on the train he could pretend to be fifteen) and Dick drawing in a big high room with all the light he wanted, a wonderful kind man looking after them both. He brushed away a woman's image, someone with his mother's face which halted the dream and caused him to turn over, determined to fall asleep.

Sunday made no difference to the time for rising, Albie believing that lax habits would develop if a more leisurely pace was observed on any particular day of the week. He did not recognize Sunday as anything apart from other days, being an atheist, and reinforcing this attitude to

188

emphasize supremacy over Sarah, who had been brought up in an Anglican home with a relative a minister. Albie would often get up from Sunday dinner and call the boys to heel, as if they were dogs he had failed to train properly, and go off and prune fruit trees or mend pig pens or shell corn in the big shed if the day was wet, working until it was time for the boys to round up the cows for the afternoon's milking, and Albie to go to the dairy and put the separator together and dump the big cans in place to take the cream.

Mrs Laycock, in spite of Albie, tidied the three girls after the washing-up was done. It would be a big one, for she roasted meat and baked and boiled vegetables of every variety in the garden (she made the vegetable and flower gardens and maintained them), and made a special pudding, apples in a suet crust or blackberry pie in the winter, lemon tart or trifle in the summer. Sometimes the children mentioned Sunday dinner in Albie's hearing and he shouted a correction. "Dinner it is! Just dinner! You eat it like any other dinner!"

Mrs Laycock took the girls to the sitting room when the kitchen was tidy and brought out picture books for Ada and Harriet, and Minnie, who showed signs of becoming an excellent seamstress, was given a job from Mrs Laycock's sewing basket, like hemming a new petticoat, or, better still, putting a row of faggoting around neck and armholes, listening to Mrs Laycock's whispery voice promising her a traced afternoon tea cloth to embroider when she was older.

Sometimes Mrs Laycock would quite suddenly stick her needle in her sewing (although it was mostly mending) and snap the basket shut and lift the lid of the piano and play a hymn like "Lead Kindly Light", and the girls would look through the window surprised to see the day sunny and the flowers waving peaceful heads, not black clouds and thunder and night coming steel coloured, and the horses galloping for shelter with flying manes and frightened eyes.

Their father passed the window this Sunday afternoon, coming back for a forgotten tool, and not sending Dick or Dan, knowing they would find relief in the errand. Mrs Laycock saw him, as did the girls, who gave their mother breathless attention, as if she were playing out a part on the stage and they were a little fearful of what was to come. They saw her put her head to one side and thunder out the last few chords, then close the piano and tuck the stool back in place. She went and did something to the window curtain too, shaking it by an edge as if she shook the image of Albie's face away. The girls saw her put on her brightest face.

"As well as the raspberry buns, shall we make some little apple tarts too?" she said, for she always made something special for Sunday tea as well as dinner.

The girls sensed this had something to do with Albie at the window but brushed the thought aside to rush with her to build up the stove fire for the baking.

There was some delay in getting back to the kitchen for they had to chase the fowls back into their pen.

Ada yelled out when she went for a pinafore hanging on the line on the back veranda, and they all ran to see the white fowls making a beautiful picture among the green lettuce, new peas, and worse for Ada the long row of her strawberries with the first fruit like pale green gemstones. She ran, weeping wildly and hating the fowls, the way they jerked their heads back and forth, snapping the berries off, and their sprawling red feet crushing the plants. She wanted to kill them all.

"Shoo, shoo, you horrible things!" she cried, and she screamed at Harriet too, who was running and flapping her arms among the strawberries, doing as much damage as the fowls. Mrs Laycock was trying to save her young peas, the frail bushes collapsed under the weight of hens as they bounded from one to another as if competing in an obstacle race. They spread their wings like scythes slashing into the lettuce and squawked as they ran, which seemed to the weeping Ada to create more havoc.

When the fowls were back in their pen, Mrs Laycock closed and latched the two gates side by side and took a hand of Ada and Harriet to go into the house. Minnie, with a hand on her mother's waist, waited fearfully for one or the other of her sisters to ask how the gates were opened.

She had not much heart in putting the good starched cloth on the table, and the plates of buns and tarts in a line down the centre, but she smoothed the corners and swept her hands down the sweep of cloth almost touching the floor, although it was practically without a crease.

Ada put the knives and forks and bread and butter plates the right distance from the edge, judging the space with her head to one side, but with troubled eyes.

Harriet sat on a stool by the stove nursing her doll, a large celluloid one that had belonged to Mrs Laycock. The firelight deepened the pink of its face and limbs, making it glow like a fire itself, and Mrs Laycock was distracted from slicing the cold roast, half expecting the doll to burst into flames. But in a little while, when Harriet saw tea was ready and heard the clank of buckets on the dairy veranda, always with a special sound, pushed under the bench by the boys' feet, joyful feet, ready to race to the house with the work behind them and food and bed ahead for those blissful hours until the time came to start all over again, she took her doll to the bedroom and tucked it in its cradle. Then she came dancing back, an alien movement in the still sombre atmosphere and, aware of this herself, sat on her end of the long stool and wriggled only once before she was still.

The boys combed their hair as they always did for Sunday tea and made sure their shirts were buttoned and tucked neatly into trousers no matter how old they were.

Albie made no contribution to the occasion with his dress. He left his sleeves rolled up as they had been throughout the milking and separating. His old blue cotton shirt, one of the worst he owned, was only buttoned from halfway down and it showed his grey flannel which had the buttons undone too, and a generous growth of black hair sprouted through the opening.

He ate meat and lettuce salad and, when Minnie took his plate away, took a slice of bread and ate it with butter and melon jam. The girls looked pointedly at the buns and tarts wondering how anyone could eat bread in preference to them, watching in fascination the jaws working, knowing the lowered eyelids shut nothing out.

Harriet, barely aware of opening her mouth, said: "The fowls got into the vegetables and Ada cried."

Albie stirred the sugar round and round in his teacup and clinked the spoon on the rim before laying it in his saucer. He swallowed half a cupful at one go. Since she was not rebuked Harriet said more.

"Someone left the gates open."

Albie finished his half cup of tea with another swallow and got up, not putting his chair under the table as everyone else did on Mrs Laycock's instructions, but leaving it sideways with a piece of the tablecloth across a corner of the seat.

"I will," Harriet said, and got up and tucked the chair in, and with great care took up her father's plates and cup and saucer and carried them to the little table under the window where the washing-up dish hung. Albie's neck with a swatch of black hair resting on it was all Harriet saw as she moved very quietly.

She was about to trot back to her place at the table when Albie swung around.

"You've left the table!" Albie cried. "You stay away from it once you've left it!" He turned back to look down on the top of the stove. Harriet began to blubber. Albie turned his head again without his body.

"You sit down there!" He ducked his head to indicate the seat by the edge of the fire recess where Harriet sat a lot of the time.

She cried on, fairly quiet about it, causing the throats of the other children to thicken in sympathy and lose the craving for the buns and tarts untouched on their plates.

In a little while Ada took a bun, which gave her a feeling of theft, and with a warm face held it on her knee to break off little pieces and eat them as privately as possible.

Albie saw.

He crossed to the table and leaned across from his place, a big man, he could reach with ease Ada and her empty bread and butter plate.

"There!" he said, hitting the plate hard enough for it to bounce, the noise causing the other children to jump and straighten their backs. Ada lifted the bun to her chest. Albie picked up a big serving spoon and slapped her hand hard with it, then slapped the plate hard enough to break it. Crying now, Ada put the bun on the plate. Albie hit the blade of the knife lying across the plate and it jumped onto the bun.

"Pick that up!" he said. Blinded by tears and too dry of mouth to want to swallow the bun anyway, Ada's trembling little hand found the knife.

Albie picked up the carving knife that had cut the meat, and holding it in the air, pointed the blade downwards.

193

"Now cut!" he said. Ada raised her tear-washed eyes and fastened them onto the knife blade, now more menacing than Albie.

He drew strokes in the air, and Ada, swallowing and whimpering, and with more tears rolling down her cheeks, clumsily cut at her bun.

"Not neat enough!" Albie shouted, slapping her fingers with the knife blade. Ada howled now and dropped her knife and put both hands to her face. Albie slapped them away, his knife cutting the soft edge of her hand where the palm started. It stung and a little blood oozed out, and Ada saw and wailed louder but picked up her knife and sawed at her bun, abandoning all hope of cutting it to please Albie.

"Look at the mess!" Albie said with ringing scorn, flinging crumbs across the table when he slapped the knife among them. "Clumsy, useless, whingeing, whining thing! A rabbit in a trap. You wring their necks and shut them up! That's what you do!"

Ada, now as terror stricken as a trapped rabbit, picked up bits of her bun and put them in her mouth. It was already working with her weeping, and opening and jerking in an uncontrolled way so that crumbs escaped and she needed to press a hand to her chin to try and hold some inside her mouth.

Albie gave her hand another sharp slap with the knife, setting up a squealing, and he threw the knife then among the tea things and backed away.

"A rabbit, I said she was, and she squeals just like one!" He took a seat by the stove and laid his arms along the chair arms as if to relax and enjoy the warmth.

Harriet, hiccupping every now and again with accompanying shudders of her small chest, hemmed into her corner by Albie, tried to quell a new alarm. Albie glanced her way.

"Another rabbit in a trap!" he said. He raised his eyes to the ceiling, and adopted a reasonable, almost conversational tone. "Rabbits are for exterminating, and I'll be rid of them one day! One day I'll be rid of them all!" Mrs Laycock rose from her chair, and stretching her arms down the table, lifted them up and down to indicate she wanted empty plates. Dick and Dan and Minnie stacked theirs and passed them up. Ada, quieter now, was swallowing, largely to clear the crumbs from her throat, and hiccupping more regularly than Harriet.

"May I have a bun, please Mother?" Dan asked in a voice that was whispery like hers.

" 'May I have a bun please mother!' " Albie roared. "Talk like a man! Another squeaking, whimpering rabbit!" He got to his feet, sending the chair flying back, almost hitting Sarah on her way with plates and cups to the little table. She set them down with great gentleness and went back for more.

"What about saving them for your school lunches?" she said. "There'd be enough for all the week."

Albie leaned back against the mantelpiece, and little Harriet had to turn her knees to avoid the crushing with his powerful legs.

"Yes, do that!" Albie said. "Make every day a Sunday! A day of singing and praying and eating and loafing!" He dropped his voice to the reasonable tone of before. "That way you have the place overrun with rabbits in no time!"

Although it was dark outside, Albie found his cap and jammed it on and put on his coat which hung in a corner over Harriet's head. He swept it across her face, catching her eye with a rough edge, bringing forth a little squeal and a new gush of tears. Albie slapped the coat back on her face before putting it on. Harriet squealed a little louder and put her face on her knees.

Albie went out the kitchen door, which opened into the yard, and the catch rattled behind him and a blast of cold air blew in with the slamming of the door, and the tablecloth lifted a skirt with an angry air copied from him, it seemed, then settled down, making a few protesting ripples as it did.

Mrs Laycock took a large old tea tin with a fading design of Indian women shouldering baskets of tea leaves, arms and necks of exaggerated length, and brought it to the table to pack the buns and tarts in, handling the delicate pastry with such care she appeared to have fingers frail enough to break as well.

The children swallowed away their yearning as the lid closed. Dick stood with his hands on his chair back, long slender fingers like his mother's.

"All of you can go to bed," he said. "I'll wipe up."

"You will not!" Ada cried sharply as if she had not been weeping her heart out minutes earlier. She rubbed at the cut on her hand as if getting that out of the way too. "He won't order us to bed, will he Mother?"

Minnie gathered up the cruet and sugar bowl and brushed the bread board free of crumbs to take them to the dresser, adopting an industrious air, removing her from the realm of childhood.

But Mrs Laycock looked across at her. "Take them off," she said. "Make sure you all piddle well." The emotional upset, Mrs Laycock knew, could result in bed wetting, especially in Harriet's case, and she had not yet stopped weeping.

"Come on," Minnie said and pulled at Ada's shoulder, who wrenched it away and climbed from the stool and walked with her head up to the door leading to the sitting room, the bedrooms opening off that. She spied Dan still at the table, his chest against the edge, hoping to escape everyone's notice.

"Him too!" Ada said. "He has to go too!"

"Yes, Dan too," Mrs Laycock said. He slid off the chair, tucking it under the table, taking his time.

"Goodnight all of you and sleep well," Mrs Laycock said, looking on the little bunch in the doorway, her sad face saying she wanted to tuck them in and linger at their bedside with a few whispered words.

But she shut the door and Dick unhooked the tin dish from above the little table, rested the soap saver by it, and took the tin tray and put it in place ready to drain the china and cutlery. Dick waited with a tea towel over his fist while she poured the water into the dish, turned from the sitting room door, sad at the memory of Harriet's legs passing through, lonely, frail and thin enough to snap.

He watched his mother hold the knives by their bone handles to keep them out of the hot water and swirl the blades about, shaking them vigorously before placing them on the towel across his open hand. As he polished the blades he thought he would always remember the way she had of doing everything with meticulous care.

Albie had never beaten Sarah, and Dick worried that he might one day. Dick imagined her now with wounded arms, fumbling with the knives but keeping the handles clear of the water, her face not all sorrowful because of her concentration. He drew his breath in sharply and looked away afraid. He was leaving home, not here to watch out for her!

He was silent hanging up the tea towel, then said goodnight and went through the sitting room. "Sleep well," he said to the girls' room and Ada's head flew up.

"Did you have a bun or a tart?" Ada asked.

"Neither," Dick said. "Go to sleep."

"Goodnight, Dickiebird," Ada said.

Dan reared up too from his side of the bed, glad to

see him. "Did you tell her you were going?" he said.

"Not yet," Dick said and pulled off his trousers. Dan saw his backside, turning him into a child again. It was round and pale, and small too, not much bigger than Harriet's, unfit for a long walk across mountains. He had a vision of a cruel train guard kicking it and went back down under the blankets.

Dan saw Dick's face once more before he closed his eyes for sleep. Dick looked out across his pillow through the window at the silvery paddocks, the whitewashed dairy and a few of the cows not taking the trouble to move too far off, but standing with lowered heads, their posture saying why bother with distance and comfort when time is brief between freedom and duty. Dick's face was a man's face now.

Albie's black mood continued all week. Dick worked with Albie at the clearing job. He cheered himself with the thought of Dan's seeing on the next Saturday how much had been done.

"I found the main root of that blackberry today," he said to his mother on Wednesday when Albie left the kitchen after their midday meal. "I loosened it with the mattock after I'd cut my way in and pulled hard."

Mrs Laycock saw his exhilaration return to him remembering the earth fall away like fine flour from the thick stalk and the leaves turn limp while he watched. He rolled his hands one inside the other as if revering them for their skill. Mrs Laycock looked at them too, checking for injury.

"You drawing anything?" she asked.

Dick put his hands half behind him as though they were suddenly in shame. "Not these last few days," he said. "But soon."

She went to attend to the stove. He thought he would

say he was going to Sydney if he had only to address her back.

But when she turned her face he didn't need to. "It won't be easy," she said.

"Easy?" he echoed and gave a man's laugh.

She turned and stretched the tea towel on the little line in front of the stove, and he stood very straight and she was surprised when she looked that he had suddenly grown so tall.

He went out, for there was the noise of Jacko in the slide, and he thought about walking rather than riding on it, or running, for he felt more like that, but decided no, he would ride as usual and look at the back of his father's head. I will see it differently, he thought, and the sky overhead, my goodness, the sky would look beautiful now. He hooped over, bunched up as Dan travelled, and Albie turned his eyes with a flash of black, a contemptuous flash at the childish posture. Dick was about to straighten, then decided to stay the way he was, it didn't matter for the little time there was left.

He looked boldly on his father's back. Perhaps when I'm gone I'll never see him again, he thought, and unprepared for the sudden swerve of the slide going sideways down the gully, he fell backwards. Albie, startled by the noise, dipped his body, close to losing his balance and angry with Dick for causing it, yelled out "Get up!"

Jacko, thinking he was addressed, plunged forward, and Albie fell into a sitting position, and before he got to his feet flung his whip in Dick's direction, slicing into Dick's shoulder, not heavily, but reaching the skin through his old shirt and sweater with a sting and a sharper one on his bare neck.

Dick leapt from the slide then and ran past Jacko, stopped with a questioning head up, Albie's curse following him. He ran with the sting fading, not rubbing his shoulder or neck lest Albie see, panting in his speed and his anger, and actually glad to reach the patch of ferns where his tomahawk lay. He seized it and sent the blade deep into the earth, hearing the crack of broken roots and wondering at Albie's blow giving him extra strength, for the fern left the ground as a loose and rotten tooth leaves a jaw.

He had a fair heap when Albie came. Albie saw and was sorry he hit out with the whip, but didn't say so; rather he told himself he swung the whip when he fell and the young fool got in the way.

Dick left to bring the cows in when the sun was at the top of a great gum on the ridge that was the western boundary of the farm. He went without a word, as usual, running hard when he was out of Albie's sight, for once the cows were in the yard he went inside the house for tea. Only on weekends did Minnie or Ada bring it to the paddocks if they were working there.

Dick was not only anxious for tea. As soon as he was in the kitchen he turned and lifted his hair from the back of his neck and showed his mother the whip mark. She moved her eyes away from it fairly quickly and stared at the tea things set out at the end of the kitchen table, frowning a little as if she might have forgotten something, and touching the sugar bowl as if to assure herself it was really there.

His anger began to rise and he screwed his head to stare at the mark, wishing it were deeper and redder.

Suddenly she became brisk and energetic and made the tea and poured him a cup. She pulled a scone from a batch lying upside down and buttered the halves, swift and industrious as if this was the most important job in the world. Dick thought about going out and not having anything, letting the tea grow cold and the scone soak up the butter like a small yellow swamp, but his throat craved them and she was swirling a spoon in a little dish of her cherry jam and setting it by his plate.

He pulled his chair back and sat sulkily, and she too took a seat and her sewing basket with socks on the top, drawing one over her hand and sliding the needle under a hole, drawing her brows down with her fingers spread, the smallest on the hand that held the needle curled like a tarantula's leg.

Her sewing! Dick thought. That's all she cares about. But behind Dick she had the sock on her knee and the hand inside it curled so that the needle dug into her flesh, though she didn't feel it. She was watching the whip mark move with the motion of Dick's jaw as he chewed his scone. While she looked Dick's hand came up, two fingers working around the mark, turning it white. When his hand went away the weal, like a tiny caterpillar, flared red again.

Mrs Laycock peeled the sock from her hand and lifted the basket from her knee. "Finish your tea and saddle Jess for me and bring her to the back gate," she said, taking off her apron and looping the neck piece over the nail from which her oven rag hung.

She looked down, checking the respectability of her tweed skirt, and tucked her blouse neatly inside and rolled the cuffs down and buttoned them at her wrists. This kept her face away from Dick, who turned his head right around so that the weal was gone, and in its place his face, red and white like the weal, and as ugly and angry.

"I'm riding over to Parsons," she said. "Tell Minnie where I've gone and get her to start the vegetables for tea.

"I won't be long. Ettie's been in bed for a week, I suppose you know."

Ettie Parsons was old, past seventy. In Dick's eyes it was a waste of time visiting someone whose life was practically over.

He went out through the front of the house, crossing the garden beds, angry at her for their order. She did not care so much for him if she cared so much about her flowers, seeing the carnations tied to their stakes with blades of grass beautifully knotted.

He felt he hated her as much as his father and cried at this and was still crying when he had his face against the flank of Sybil, the oldest of the herd and privileged to be milked first. Dick thought of all the years he had milked morning and afternoon, and this was the first time his tears had wet the coat of a cow. Sybil lifted a back leg as if she had made the discovery as well.

Mrs Laycock went into the lumber room and took the shotgun from the wall. She took a sugar bag from a folded pile inside an old meat safe where she kept her smaller garden tools. She slipped the gun inside the bag and pulled the top together around the end of the barrel, holding it by that.

Jess was there tied to the gate, and farther away the cows were packed in their yard, close enough together to make their backs look like a creamy, folded blanket. She imagined Dick's head against a cow's light flank and saw the weal showing up more, stretched with his bent neck.

She rode Jess down the gully and met Albie coming up, Jacko straining to pull the slide and Albie, with a dark expression and curled mouth, slapped the reins on his back telling Jacko with his scowl that he should go up the hill as easily as he went down.

He jumped from the slide when he saw Sarah, and the surprised Jacko rushed on thinking this was expected of him with a lighter load.

"Woa!" Albie yelled, pulling the reins hard, then flinging them on the slide.

"What have you got there?" he said to Sarah, for he

got a good view of the bag-wrapped gun as Jess had jigged around in a state of agitation, reined in by Sarah, and wondering if Albie's shout was addressed to her.

Sarah pulled the bag back to show the end of the twin barrels, like a proud mother pulling a shawl away to show her baby's face.

"That thing could be loaded!" Albie said. "You wouldn't know!"

"I've been around guns for a long time, Albie," Sarah answered. "I know when one's loaded."

"You're mad," Albie said. "Riding with a gun wrapped up like a leg of mutton. It can shoot through a bit of bag, stupid woman!"

"Of course it can shoot through a bit of bag," Sarah said. "And through a bit of head."

"That horse'll take off when it goes off and break your neck!" Albie picked up Jacko's reins and jerked them. "Silly woman."

"I know what horses do," Sarah said, freeing the hand that held the reins by looping them over her elbow and patting Jess on the neck.

Jess looked back and stopped shivering and lowered her head as if she might crop at some grass if things settled down, but she would remain alerted until they did by turning her eyes back to take in Sarah's shoe in the stirrup and a fair view of Albie with his legs apart and a little wind blowing his trousers back the way it blew the grass.

"I've been around horses too, a long time," Sarah said. She straightened her back and held her head erect as she did when she was a competitor in riding and dressage events in the Cobargo show.

"Pass that gun over to me," Albie ordered.

Sarah shook her head, the lowering sun now burnishing the big tree on the ridge and Sarah's hair as well. Albie wanted to shout out to her that she should be wearing a hat.

"You used the whip on Dick," she said. "Animal." She patted Jess again, for she lifted her head at the last word and asked a question with her ears laid back.

"They don't want to work. They want to fool. I never got this good place foolin'!" Albie said.

"Dick doesn't want your place, good or bad. He wants to work somewhere where he can draw."

Albie jumped on the slide as if no reply to this could justify the ridicule it earned.

"Stop!" Sarah called, and raised the gun, pulling the bag back until her hands were in the vicinity of the trigger. The wind, tearing Albie's hair back, showed it blacker since his face was whiter.

"You crazy woman!" he said and stepped off the slide.

"You carry your money around with you Albie," Sarah said. "Put ten pounds of it under a stone there for Dick to go to Sydney with."

Albie stared at the gun barrel as if it, not Sarah, had spoken. Jess fidgeted and Jacko took a step as if testing Albie out on his intention of moving.

"Woa!" he yelled, and Jess lifted her head and shook it and blinked an eye on Sarah, looking there for direction.

"That's all you've got to do," Sarah said, using her soft and whispery voice. "Put that money under the stone there before Minnie and the others get home from school.

"I don't want to shoot you with them looking on."

"You fool of a woman," Albie said.

"Steady Jess," Sarah lowered the gun barrel to point at Albie's side pocket.

He took out a roll of notes fastened with a little elastic band, peeled one off and flung it down. The wind lifted it and it fluttered about for a moment before settling on a tussock. It had a different look there and Sarah wondered why. Did it seem worthless stuck at the end of a worthless weed, or should not the weed have suddenly gained a new status? She felt like a little smile at the thought of the children's coming upon it and their screaming surprise.

Albie was back on the slide, slapping the reins savagely on Jacko's back, the whip lying idle on the slide, Albie for a reason of his own not bothering with it. Jacko rushed forward, glad it seemed to use his stored up energy, and Sarah, quick and agile as Minnie, jumped from Jess and plucked up the note.

She knew it would anger Albie further but she had to gallop past him to get the gun away before the children saw. They were home from school and Dick, seeing them from the yard, remembered his mother's instructions to Minnie and raced up to tell her. Near the house he saw his mother climb from Jess and pull the bag from the gun, and he cried out at the sight, his face white like Albie's and his black hair blown about like Albie's was. People said how much alike father and son were and Sarah saw for herself now.

She pressed the gun against her side and tiptoed across the back veranda and, opening the door of the lumber room, hooked the gun back on the wall and folded the bag as neat as the others and put it with them in the old meat safe. Then she dusted off her hands as if something were clinging to them and, going into the kitchen where the children were, their school bags dropped on the floor and their eyes looking for food, she turned her sleeves back and told them to change into their old clothes while she buttered them some scones. She was surprised to feel the scones so fresh, it seemed such a long time since she had made them.

Three weeks later she went with Dick to the roadside cream box, helping him and Dan carry the two cans, then

205

sending Dan back to get ready for school. Dick was travelling in the cream lorry to Cobargo to take the mail car there for Nowra. Mrs Laycock's other hand not gripping the cream can carried Dick's suitcase of clothes.

Dick would live with his Aunt Bessie, his mother's sister whose husband was a storeman in a factory that made bedding. They lived in Camperdown. There were no children and Bessie was excited about Dick's coming. Sarah read the letter with a stretched mouth but sad eyes. This puzzled the children, who had been as anxious as she that Bess agree to Dick's coming. Sarah saw behind Bess's careful sentences that she was already looking upon Dick as the son she had always wanted.

Dick heard the cream lorry coming and went red then white. He looked like Albie again, and Mrs Laycock looked down and checked the catches on Dick's case, then back at Dick pleased to see his colour normal again.

"Were you going to shoot him?" Dick blurted out. He had wanted to ask her that since the incident, but had been afraid to. If shooting had been her intention, he would not have felt free to go. Now it was too late to turn back.

"No," Sarah said, straightening her back, remembering how she sat on Jess. "I was taking the gun to ask Alex Parsons to buy it, to get you the money for Sydney.

"Then when he came out of the gully I thought of another way."

There was only time to kiss him briefly, with the cream box shutting them away from the lorry driver, who well might have teased Dick all the way to Cobargo about the kiss.

"Alex Parsons used to be sweet on me," Sarah said. "Be a good boy, won't you?"

Dick got work as a storeman through the influence of his uncle but worked at the job only a few months. His

Aunt Bessie took his drawings to an advertising agency where they were placed on top of a pile of samples of other people's work who wanted to be commercial artists too. Aunt Bessie was told Dick was to watch the newspapers for advertisements calling for applications for trainee artists.

Bessie watched with him and when one appeared Dick applied and got a start.

His first drawing published was of a pair of women's shoes on slender feet and legs. He sent a cutting home. In private, Mrs Laycock looked at it and down on her own feet and legs and was sure Dick had drawn hers from memory.

Minnie pinned the cutting to the side of the dresser with a Christmas card Dick had made and sent. It was a drawing of their house with snow covering the garden and banked nearly to the windows and the cows sheltering under the big walnut tree, snow dripping from it as well. Santa Claus was on the roof about to descend the chimney with a bag of toys.

"The snow means Dick is cold and lonely at times, but Santa means there are some good things to make him happy," Mrs Laycock told Dan and the girls.

They looked at her, disbelieving at first, and not sure this is what they heard in her low and whispery voice, but always afterwards studying the card they saw it this way.

They all worried that Albie might pull it down and the drawing of the shoes as well.

But they stayed.

13 The Mission Priest

Every few years the Sydney diocese of Catholic priests sent one of their men to inject new religious life into the Cobargo flock.

It was a time for lax church goers to be rounded up, like the wayward cows who frustrated farmers with their habit of getting away into gullies and thickets of trees at milking time. Rebelling Catholic families with children at the public school were harassed into changing their ways, those who didn't support the church financially were told to review their budgets, couples with small families were asked for valid reasons why they were not larger if the wife was still of child bearing age.

The parish priest, Father O'Malley, shamefaced with his own failings, supplied the families' names and addresses, half hopeful the mission priest (as he was called) would do no better. There were church services on weekdays as well as Sundays, not only in St Joseph's, Cobargo, but in every outlying hamlet from Yowrie at the foot of the mountain to Bermagui by the sea, south-east to Dignam's Creek and northwest to Wandella. The mission priest's old Ford rattled over poor roads, uncertain of direction at times, but determined to take a satisfactory report back to his superiors in Sydney.

"The Lynches today," the mission priest said at breakfast in St Joseph's presbytery, with Miss Logan, the housekeeper, shuffling in with bacon cooked to a crisp and cold fried eggs.

"Latchetts," Father O'Malley corrected Father Ryan, not as gently as he might have done earlier in the week.

He was sorry for Miss Logan, flustered as she was with a guest in the house. Although she brought his meals to the dining room when he was alone, he never rang the little brass bell for extra service but hopped from his chair and went into the kitchen when he wanted something.

She merely gave one of her deep huffs when he came in to warm his cold toast at the stove fire and slap more butter on it.

"If you want Rossmore's bill to stretch to Bermagui that's the way to do it," she would say, stirring the fire with a rattle of the poker.

"Just in case I don't make it to the good place I'll get my fill of good Cobargo butter before I go," he would answer, looking over the jams on the kitchen shelf (given by Jane Cullen, various Rossmores, and other good Catholic families) and selecting a cherry or a peach, while there was half a jar of plum yet to finish off.

Like a school boy he speared the paper covering with a knife blade, the pop of air startling Miss Logan so that she dropped the poker. He roared with laughter, then put a corner of the toast into his mouth, taking nearly half of it in the one bite and went back to his cooling tea in the dining room.

Snapping the stove door shut with the poker, Miss Logan told herself she would rap his knuckles with it if she caught him opening more jam, and, not bothering to find a new cover for the jar (bearing traces of a buttery knife), hid it behind things in the bottom of the dresser.

"I will slap the great school boy of a thing next time!" she muttered, but ended up with a little warm smile at the thought. He would yelp, she knew, and thrust his big soft hand into his mouth to bite away the hurt, pretending it was much worse than it was.

He was forty-five and she was twenty years older. He could be her son. She often dreamed he was.

Father O'Malley, after four days of Father Ryan, was counting the remaining days of the visit. This was Tuesday and he would go on Friday. Two more days, he thought with rising spirits, cutting into his leathery eggs. He decided not to count today, although almost untouched, nor Friday, hopeful that Father Ryan would get away bright and early.

In no great hurry this morning, Father Ryan backed the Ford out of the presbytery driveway, and sailing down the hill swung into the main street, preparing for the climb up the cemetery hill, the Latchetts' place about two miles off.

The Latchetts rented a farm from the Quinlans, who owned two other district properties and had them all tenanted. The Quinlans lived in comfort in the Sydney suburb of Hunters Hill and made occasional visits to Cobargo, staying at one of the hotels that they owned also.

There was a tribe of Latchett children, the father, Len, a Catholic and the Mother, Esther, Anglican. They were struggling to feed and clothe their brood and sent them to the public school. They were never seen in church.

"I've got the lot there!" Father Ryan said aloud, the engine of the Ford making such a commotion, there was no chance of anyone's hearing. "The whole kit and caboodle! A man is likely to come away with a bloody big dog hanging to his backside!

"Well, never mind, never mind!" He changed gears to take the rise. "The Lord has sent me a good day to to it in. Thank you, you lucky old geezer up there with your harps and your good looking women!"

He saw on the post office side of the street a knot of school children and thought here is an excuse for a bit of delaying and stopped the car. The children halted, forming a tight little bunch and some waved school cases towards him.

"Father Ryaaaan, Father Ryaaan!" they called, establishing themselves as convents, not publics (in the local jargon) and setting Father Ryan free to beam his widest. He was a large, fat man, like a great mound of yellow butter dressed in black clothes. His chin was in folds and his plump, creamy yellow hand, stretched out to open the car doors, had a yellow ring on the little finger. This impressed the children and earned him greater awe. Cobargo men did not wear rings.

"Get in!" he said. "And the rest sit on the running board!" The boldest of the group, a large boy, fat too, and sweaty already on the warm summer morning, scrambled in with a girl close behind him, so close her cheek was squashed against his plump rump, which set her giggling and infected the others following her. Four got a seat, four others stood in the space between the front and back seats, two small ones were pressed together next to Father Ryan and three, all boys, stood on the running board.

"We'll have a little talk before school goes in," Father Ryan said. "There's no Latchetts here, is there?" He thought two or three had a foreign look.

The children shrieked at such ignorance. "The Latchetts go to the public!" yelled several.

"Public pimps!" screamed another and crushed a hand to a mouth too late to erase the outburst.

"It's very wicked, isn't it, to be a Catholic and go to the wrong school," Father Ryan said.

"Very, very wicked!" screamed the children.

"We'll have to do something to change those wicked ways, won't we?" cried Father Ryan.

Some of the children exchanged glances. They doubted the wisdom of Father Ryan's efforts, since the poor

Latchetts would scarcely be an asset to their classrooms. When Sister Joan made toffee, as she sometimes did on Friday afternoons, the warm hearted nun would be sure to give the Latchetts any left over after it was passed down the lines before dismissal.

"There's Mr Rossmore!" one of the children yelled.

Fred Rossmore, out of his store to check that the hose on the bowser was not leaking petrol, saw the priest's car and the children. He put on a broad smile and went across to join them.

"Mr Rossmore, Father Ryan is going to the Latchetts'!" said the fat boy.

Father Ryan was startled but kept his smile wide for Fred, notable pillar of St Joseph's church. Reared in the city, he was unused to the mental telepathy that appeared to operate in small country centres like this, even children able to tell what everyone was up to.

"Is he indeed?" Fred beamed on Father Ryan as if the priest's intended deed were of no lesser magnitude than raising Lazarus from the dead. "I might go back to the shop and get something for Father Ryan to take to the little Latchetts, eh? What about that for an idea?"

This could only mean lollies or shop biscuits, rare treats for most of the group. The thought of the Latchetts munching on them, probably with a day off school, free to swim in the creek, a regular past time, did not please the convents.

"They mightn't be at home," the fat boy said. "They could be at school by this."

The Latchetts did not take the road to school but crossed the paddocks of the property adjoining theirs (or the Quinlans') which adjoined the town, and that morning they had not been seen emerging from behind the post office to straggle their way, most of them bare footed, through the town to school.

"They mightn't be going," someone else said, aware of the truant-like habits of the Latchetts.

"The truant inspector went there once," said the fat boy, blowing out his cheeks at the importance of such tidings.

"But it didn't make any difference," said another voice.

Fred turned on his heel to go to the shop for the goods to send the Latchetts.

"Now I mustn't hold you up any longer," Father Ryan said to the children, with his smile that looked oiled from the grease of his abundant body.

The children removed themselves with an attempt at covering their reluctance and started down the road, watching Fred disappear into his shop, wondering about loitering on the chance of seeing what he had for the Latchetts. Father Ryan made them jump when he blew his horn. They looked back at him and waved in response to the large wave he gave them over the car door.

"See you in church!" he called with his uproarious laugh.

"Yes, Father!" they called back, their arms waving like a patch of corn stalks.

My God, Father Ryan said to himself, they don't know that's a saying. I hope for something better from the Latchetts!

Fred arranged biscuits in a cardboard box of the right size to take a row of banana creams, raspberry slices, honey jumbles, afternoon tea cake, ginger nuts, and butter oat cake.

Fred's calculating eye told him there was two shillings worth there, and a gift the like of which the Latchetts would not have seen in a long time. He bore it shoulder high on the palm of his hand to the car.

"From you now, not from me!" Fred said, laying the box tenderly in the middle of the back seat.

"From the church!" Father Ryan replied. Fred closed the car door with reverence.

"From the church, yes," he said, putting his dry shop-keeper's hand into Father Ryan's. It was like being plunged into a warm cushion. He stepped back and arms close to his side bowed slightly as Father Ryan drove off, the box sliding to a corner to make itself at home there. Fred saw it with some regrets.

I could have left out the raspberry slices and put in something plainer, he said to himself.

The Latchetts' place had the Tilba and Bermagui roads as boundaries on either side. The house was midway between the two. Either road meant the same distance for travel but the Tilba road was favoured, for the property was fairly level on that side, dipping in an ungentle slope towards the Bermagui road. Father Ryan was advised by Father O'Malley which direction to take, Father O'Malley telling himself he didn't want the trauma of taking his motorbike and side car to return Father Ryan to the presbytery in the event of a broken-down vehicle halfway up Quinlans' hill. (Owing to the tenuous nature of the Latchetts' tenancy, their failure to meet the rent regularly, and the widespread knowledge of this in Cobargo, the place was usually referred to as Quinlans'.)

The way in from either road was marked by tracks, not well defined, the grass invading those made in earlier times by Quinlan motors, the Latchetts without car or buggy and seldom using them. Len rode occasionally to town, but Esther, like the children, always took the way through the paddocks.

About once a month on a Saturday she cashed the child endowment cheque given by the government at Rossmore's, paying something off the bill there and a little to the butcher and baker as well, and coming home to a little army of Latchetts waiting at the edge of the last little gully she crossed. The eldest, Flora, would have the baby clasped in her thin but surprisingly strong arms, it bending forward like the others as their mother's head bobbed towards them through the bush, her arms full of parcels, and her shoes and stockings too, for she walked barefoot once out of town to save them from wear.

Sometimes Len went to meet her on the horse, hauling her up behind him and taking the baby too, and after a while the two year old as well, in response to the woebegone expression it started up, soon soothed away by the mother's free hand stroking a bare leg.

The children would run whooping and shouting behind the trotting horse, with Basil, the eldest boy, racing ahead to fix the stove fire so that the mother would be pleased.

Approaching the house, Father Ryan sat up as straight as his size permitted. He drove between the cow bails and the dairy, an abandoned tennis court just ahead, stopping the car by a gate swinging open in a hedge.

There had once been a beautiful garden around the house, for the Quinlans had lived there until they took their growing family to Sydney for higher education than Cobargo had to offer.

The move paid off, for there was a priest, a teaching brother, and a nun among the Quinlan brood, a state schoolteacher too and a nurse. The other child in the family was retarded.

Father O'Malley had briefed Father Ryan on this, giving rise to a small dream on Father Ryan's part that history might repeat itself with his influence on the Latchetts. There must be something in the air here, he told himself getting out of the car. Must be, must be, he addressed himself sternly, going through the gateway past some potted plants that had been upturned when the Latchetts moved in and never righted, and some stone surrounding something that looked like a neglected grave but had once been a bulb garden, the Quinlans' pride, now hollowed out by the little Latchetts at play.

The Latchetts were on the veranda. Mrs Latchett was sitting on a kerosene box, as it was known, the box containing the tin of kerosene used for lighting and splashing on stubborn wood in a fire slow to burn. The tin, when emptied, often found a new life with a wire handle fixed to the top and swung over a fire to boil water. The box made a handy seat or woodbox, or, if desperate for firewood, a good, crackling blaze.

Mrs Latchett had her bare feet and legs stretched before her and her thick fair hair on her shoulders. She was very freckled, as were many of the children, some of them with hair deepening to copper. Len Latchett was lean and his hair was dark, thick too, so that all the children had an abundance of rich hair that took on bright lights with the sun on it.

Some of the children on the veranda edge had school cases beside them but did not appear to be going to school. It was close to mid morning and unlikely that they would be setting out now. At the sight of Father Ryan, Mrs Latchett drew her feet up close to the box and gathered up her hair and held it at the back of her head.

This helped Father Ryan solve an identification problem, for the tall light-haired freckled girl (Flora) was on the floor near her, wearing a more serious expression, and Father Ryan felt he could easily mistake her for the mother.

Len, occupying a bursting seagrass chair, leapt from it and jumped over the veranda edge to greet Father Ryan. The two men shook hands quite heartily, the children impressed at their father's familiar manner with a priest and his ready use of his title of Father. He called for a chair for Father Ryan, and the girl who looked like the mother, being the eldest (Father Ryan working this out

216

swiftly), brought one from inside and placed it near the seagrass one, then joined her brothers and sisters on the veranda edge. Father Ryan was pleased at this since it isolated the mother and saved further confusion.

"This is my family, Father," Len said.

"A fine lot," said Father Ryan, running his eyes over them all, then over the mother last.

"It's our mother's birthday!" a child of about ten burst out. Reddening a little at his boldness, he stared hard at his school case, heavily marked with grease, the corner pieces missing.

"Her birthday," Len said, and the children's heads shot up, for it sounded like singing.

"I just happened to ask if anyone knew the date," Len said.

"Flora knew," said the ten year old, whose name was Claude, and the priest saw, or imagined he saw, Flora's small young breasts pout when her chin went up.

"She's thirty," said Roland, the seven year old.

The mother's smile deepened but the father put out a foot and moved it gently against the childish bottom. "You don't say how old a lady is, son. They don't like it."

"We were going to school and now we're not," said a girl of about six, smacking her case lightly as she was now in a position to feel affection for it.

"Well, it's good you're all home since I've called," Father Ryan said, putting aside a little wave of shame at his easy dismissal of the public education system.

"We might be going to the creek because it's our mother's birthday," said Roland. He looked down at the ground between his feet, knowing he shouldn't be saying this.

"That's a nice way to spend a brithday," Father Ryan said. "But what about Our Lord's birthday? How do we spent that?"

217

He looked at Flora and Basil for a response and Flora looked for help towards her mother, who was able to do no more than pull her lips into a smile, very small and refusing to dart into her eyes.

Basil gave his father a man's look. Come on, his bright brown eyes said, you're the Catholic.

Len shifted a little on his chair, sprawling the legs which held on bravely. "We don't have too much money Father," he said. He looked over the dairy roof. "Unfortunately."

Father Ryan reached out and tickled the bare leg of four year old Evelyn. "This is a nice little plump one," he said.

The thin Latchetts felt envy. Because the priest was fat, he would prefer fat people, they thought, wishing for means of hiding their stalk-like limbs.

"Plenty of milk and cream and eggs and fruit," Len said, looking away from the veranda to the orchard and the herd of cows, not long milked, some of which had so far only advanced as far as the tennis court, cropping there and adding to the liberal scattering of cow pads, ranging from the dry as dust to the fresh and steaming.

"We have all those good things in plenty," Len said, looking at his wife, as if including her in the bounty.

The priest saw her eyes understanding and believing and the shy glance downwards that followed. She got up quite suddenly and the eyes of all the children were directed through the kitchen door until she returned with shoes on and carrying a chair.

She set the chair down and sat on it and Father Ryan was puzzled that she suddenly seemed taller.

"I'm sure they all know how important the Lord's birthday is," Father Ryan said, looking mainly at Flora and Basil blushing in shameful awareness of religious knowledge resting mainly on them.

But it was Claude who answered. "Christmas is over

now!" he said, barely disguising his scorn that anyone could be so ignorant.

"Christmas isn't the only time for Our Lord," Father Ryan said. His voice was quite gentle and the children looked at his hands, one on a thigh and the other holding a knee and saw the sun strike lights from the ring on his finger.

They looked at their mother's hand gripping a chair edge, a ring on it too, a whitish gold, paler than the freckles, a little loose-looking, although it never came off. Their mother's ring, they knew, signified her marriage to their father. What did the priest's ring mean? Did he have a wife?

"Have you got a mother?" Claude said.

"The Blessed Virgin is my mother," Father Ryan said. "The Mother of the church. Our Lady. You've heard of her?"

The children felt it was less complicated to let it be assumed they hadn't. Father Ryan was smiling, he seemed happy with whatever was said.

The mother crossed her feet, and reaching down, brushed some dust from the toe of a shoe.

Evelyn, still glowing in praise of her plumpness, stroked the other shoe, her eyes asking the priest to admire them.

"Dad bought those shoes for our mother," Claude said. "He was going to buy a share for the plough, but he bought the shoes instead."

Father Ryan's lips remained stretched, but he lowered his eyelids and a coolness hardened the melting butter of his chin and jaws.

The mother had sent a small darting smile Len's way to thank him again for the shoes. The children looked at him too, anxious that his face remember.

But his face had hardened too, and his eyes were on the strained cloth of his old work trousers shaping his

219

bony knees. The mother put her feet under her chair, making creases in the shining leather toes as she lifted the heels from the floor. The shoes were right back under the back rung of the chair almost out of sight.

Len rested cool eyes on Flora, shutting out his wife. "We should be offering Father some tea, or a cool drink," he said. The younger children straightened up. Was there lemon syrup somewhere in the house they didn't know about?

"Tea then," said Mrs Latchett and got up and went into the kitchen.

They heard her heels for a while then a soft padding, hardly a noise at all, but they knew she was there for there was the clunk of a kettle on the stove and a grinding noise that said she was removing a stove lid to make it boil faster.

Claude got up and went and looked through the doorway, then returned to his place. "Mum's taken her shoes off," he said.

The priest's big shoes stirred on the floor.

"You should all go off somewhere," Len said, eyes on Basil, telling him to make the first move. Basil stood looking on his school case, undecided about it.

"Take it and the food out and put it in the safe till dinner time," Len ordered, giving the doorway a hard, unsmiling look as if chastising his wife for not organizing this.

Flora got up and smoothed her dress down, a thin old cotton with a speckly pattern, which made it hard to distinguish the cloth from her speckled neck and arms. The priest looking hard appeared to be trying to.

"They're like a brood of speckled fowls," Len said when they had all gone, Claude last, sliding his school case along the veranda into the kitchen with one foot.

"I apologize for their manners, Father," Len said. "I know the nuns would be good for them."

Mrs Latchett came gently to the doorway. "Better to go into the front room for the tea," she said. "The flies are bad everywhere else."

"Follow me, Father," Len said with dignity and went around a corner of the veranda and through a doorway to the room the Latchetts called the "front", although it was at the back of the house.

It was large and clean with two windows shut against the flies and a hallway opening off it leading to the bedrooms. The door to the kitchen was closed, and the room was quite cool.

There was no furniture at all in it, no covering on the floor either, and Father Ryan, feeling ashamed at doing so, craned his head in the direction of the hall, wondering if there were any beds in the other rooms.

The two men stood in the centre of the room and Father Ryan looked about him, checking in case he overlooked a couch or table or chair coming in from the bright sunshine.

But nothing.

In a moment the door to the kitchen opened, and the girl Flora put her head in first, and allowing herself just enough space, passed her body through with a kitchen chair under each arm. She set the chairs down near the men, and Len frowned heavily on her for a chair back had pulled her dress from her shoulder and there was a lot of it showing like a beautiful freshly-laid speckled brown egg.

"Fasten your clothing there," Len said sharply.

Flora lowered her chin and looped long fine fingers around strings to make a bow tie and restore the top of her dress to its rightful place. She went through the door, closing it, only to return very quickly with a tin tray of

teapot, cups, milk and sugar and some buttered bread.
Basil was behind her with the kerosene box Mrs Latchett
had sat on before she went for a chair and her shoes. He
put the box on its end and set the tray there, both going
out as speedily as they came in.

Len poured the tea. "Every Christmas I make a
resolution I'll send them to the nuns when school starts
after the holidays.

"I make the same resolution every year, Father."

Father Ryan got the impression Len believed he was
achieving something this way. He crossed his great thighs.
"You need to carry out resolutions. Do you pray for the
strength to do so?"

Len tipped his cup to stare into what remained of his
tea. "Women make it hard for you, Father."

There was the sharp uncrossing of Father Ryan's legs.
Women, said his face with terrible scorn.

"Those children are being deprived of the sacraments,"
Father Ryan said. "That's on your conscience. Or should
be."

"It is, Father," Len said in great misery.

"Then do something about it. The other alternative,
as well you would know, is to perish in hell!"

Father Ryan crossed his arms loosely on his chest and
leaned back just slightly in his chair and let his lids fall
down on his eyes. Len looked between the priest's legs,
his trousers tight there, bulges on the inner thigh, high
up. Nothing more complicated than that! He crossed his
own legs tightly in sudden shame and fear. Was the priest
praying now for Len's salvation?

A cry startled them both. It came from one of the bed-
rooms, a sharp child's yell, commanding and demanding.
No fear in it, no question that it would not be answered.
It trailed off and became a shout, half a laugh.

Then there was the noise on the other side of the door

222

to the kitchen, a rush of feet, some squealing, and bodies flung against the wood. The priest and Len heard Mrs Latchett's voice above the others and saw a little of her when she opened the door to let Flora through.

"Are there more?" said Father Ryan, not disguising his astonishment.

"Eight all told," Len said. "That's the baby."

They watched the hall doorway for Flora's return, carrying the baby, no trace of a scowl on its round sunny face, coppery hair in damp curls on its forehead, the mouth sweetly pursed, a singlet on the top half of the body, the bottom sitting in a napkin, loosely fastened, on Flora's arm, her other bound tightly to its back.

Flora stopped between the two doors for Father Ryan to see, not believing anyone apart from the blind could fail to love and admire such a beautiful baby. The child beamed on its father and appeared undaunted when Len did not respond. The priest looked only at Flora. The baby flung its head back in show-off fashion and beat both its feet quite frantically on Flora's stomach.

Flora shifted it to her other side to open the door into the kitchen. There was a scream of greeting from the children there.

Len lifted the tray to put it somewhere, and when there was no other place but the floor, turned it to another angle. The shouting from the children continued, and some noises from the baby, evidently pleasing the others for they shouted louder at the sound.

"Your wife?" the priest said. "She's — reasonable?"

Len looked down and turned the tray around thoughtfully.

"A little slow then — here?" And Father Ryan stroked a yellow finger across a yellow forehead.

Then he stood. "I'll talk to her," he said.

223

Len struck one side of his chest with a hand beating it until the priest understood.

He sat.

Len put his head in a listening pose, hearing the silence in the kitchen. They had gone, he knew, to the coolness of the little veranda, darkened by a shrubbery gone wild, that opened off the other end of the kitchen. There the mother would sit on the edge, her feet among thick rough geranium leaves, and lift a long pale breast from her dress. The children crushed against her would shriek at the baby's eagerness in fastening its mouth to her teat, flashing a look half surprise and half triumph on the others before closing its eyes to take the first long draughts, the children seeing it as a fresh miracle every time and lowering their cries to a reverent murmur.

The priest took a prayer book from his pocket.

"We'll pray then," he said. "The Our Father, the Creed, the Act of Contrition?"

"There's time for them all," Len said.

But when he went to the little veranda, everyone was gone.

In the kitchen the school cases were open on the table and empty, the baby's wet napkin on a chair, the stove door open looking for wood. Flies were running and darting and landing in the school cases, and massed around the door of the food safe not properly shut.

The mother's shoes were the only neat things in the room, sitting tidily side by side against a wall.

Len returned to Father Ryan. "They've gone to the creek," he said in an agony of shame. "She lets them take their clothes off if they want to. I couldn't take you there."

All of them, wondered the priest. He saw the big girl holding the child, the sun making a halo above the coppery hands, the water running from her speckled arms onto the white porcelain between the young breasts, and her elbows and knees and ankles like the pointed end of a bird's egg, so pale you could hardly call them blue at all.

He kept his eyes on the doorway where she had stood. Then he said to Len: "Keep up those resolutions, and keep praying."

Len shook his hand hard in his enormous relief, and when the car had rumbled off, ran from the house and over the orchard fence and down the hill where all the heads were like small bright suns, growing larger the nearer he got, and after awhile he heard them whooping and calling his name when one of them caught sight of him.

Father Ryan, turning the car into the road to Cobargo, looked back to see if anything was coming, a city habit, for there would be hardly any traffic that way at that time of day. He caught sight of the box of biscuits. He slowed the car to a stop under a great gum. A branch threw a pattern on the wind screen, making it look like a silvery coloured curtain with a pattern of leaves dancing about as the wind stirred it.

"They would have loved them," he said aloud, after a moment reaching back and sitting the box on his large thighs.

He thought about going back with them.

No, he said to himself, I believe my need is greater than theirs.

He took out a banana cream and ate it, barely getting the taste. Through the silvery curtain were clouds rolled about in the sky, soft and downy like a bed cover. He watched them part and saw a shape like a woman's hip, jutting provacatively, and a long stream of vapour like a woman's hair.

He ate another banana cream and near the end got the taste. He took a ginger nut and put the box under the seat, cheered at the thought of stopping and eating at intervals on his way back to Sydney.

He started up the car. Only two more days to go, he told himself, cheered even more. He decided not to count today since it was almost gone, and he would get away so early on Friday he needn't count that either.

14 A Long Time Dying

Old Mrs Faigen was always talking about dying. "I'll die soon," she said to her husband, Harry, as she had said many times before. "The time's not too far off now, I reckon."

Harry, noting the vigour with which she swung a bucket of hot water from the copper to a washtub, lowered his lids over his knowing eyes and pulled a serious mouth.

"You're dead right there, Mother. Won't be long now."

"Mother!" snorted old Mrs Faigen. "What a name to give me!"

"You are a mother. Twice over. Beats me how you forget so easy."

He bent down to lace up his old boots, which were whitening with age. Then he straightened and shuffled his feet to get his trousers to fall into place. He looked down quite proudly on the boots.

"I reckon they'll last to the funeral," he said. "A course I'd give them a polish for the occasion. Get a tin of ox blood 'specially."

"Ox blood! A new fangled name for plain old red."

Old Mrs Faigen turned on a tap to fill a bucket and replenish the copper. Harry sat again on a plank against the unlined wall and raised his eyes to the corrugated iron roof. It was the hotel wash house, and old Mrs Faigen was the hotel washerwoman. Harry was never referred to as old Mr Faigen, although he was seventy and his wife two years younger. He was the yardman, wiry and spry, with some of his original sandy hair among the grey crop, a tuft of which had stood up when he was among the first

227

pupils at Cobargo Public School. He put a hand up now to smooth it down as he had been doing as long as Cobargo could remember.

"Anyway, don't waste time on boot polishin'," old Mrs Faigen said, laying the washing board against the side of the tub to rub an apron. "There'll be nobody there to see what state your boots are in."

"Course there'll be somebody there!" Harry said. "The cove buryin' you!"

"Father O'Malley! He'll refuse the job. I haven't been to church for forty years. Not my fault either."

"Aw, I don't know about that," Harry said. "Nobody tied you up with a rope to keep you away. That I know of."

"There's more ways of keeping you away than tying you up with a rope!" said old Mrs Faigen, flinging the apron in the copper and jabbing it to the bottom with a copper stick, white with the constant bleaching of boiling water and caustic soda.

"None as foolproof though. Save for poppin' you off with a bullet.

"Now that might be just what you're lookin' for." Harry hung his hands between his legs, elbows supported by his knees. "Never thought of that.

"As you always say, I'm a selfish, thoughtless cove."

Old Mrs Faigen rubbed at a beetroot stain on a serviette. "You'd be thinking of your own skin. The skin of your neck! That's what'd decide you!"

Harry stretched his neck and rubbed it thoughtfully, bringing forefinger and thumb together under his chin, waggling the loose skin there. "I guess you're right as usual, Mother. I wouldn't favour a rope around the old craw."

"If you don't favour the axe at that woodheap, she'll be in here blamin' me for keeping you. As usual."

"Reckon I can afford another five minutes. The thing that keeps me goin' Mother, is these cheery little conflabs with you."

Old Mrs Faigen sat suddenly on a chair without a back, discarded from the hotel dining room and wedged between the copper and the tubs. She leaned her face on her hand with an elbow resting on the edge of a tub. Harry knew she wanted to cry, but was unable to squeeze moisture from the dried-up tear ducts behind her eyes of faded blue, stained tan on the whites, making you think of a dog's patchy coat.

"Them two 'ud never make it back, bet on that," said old Mrs Faigen.

"They might, given enough notice."

"I'd lie in state here in the wash house waitin' for them. Most likely for ten years or more."

Harry raised a wrinkled brow and twitching nose. "I can't promise to join you. Unless I pop off the day after you.

"Come to think of it, that could happen. The shock of seein' you go at last, might have a serious effect on me."

Old Mrs Faigen jumped to her feet suddenly and began to poke at the things in the copper, at the same time using a foot to push wood together in the fire, then with the same foot shutting a little iron door of the fire box. She was lifting a pair of men's overalls high above the water line in the tub and plunging them back in again when Mrs Rawson, the wife of the hotel keeper, came to the doorway. Old Mrs Faigen's sharp ears had heard the one step crunch the gravel as Mrs Rawson crossed the path that led from the hotel kitchen to the wash house.

She was a tall, dark haired woman inclined to bulkiness, but able to carry it with her good height. She had fine legs and feet, in beige stockings and tan leather shoes, splashed with damp where she crossed the flower beds.

229

Harry shook his head looking down on them.

"The path had a good rake-over yesterday, Lou," he said. "You should be usin' it, instead of sloppin' through the rose beds and messin' up your footwear."

He cocked a tufty eyebrow in their direction, grey and sandy, like a tussock the sun had partly dried out. Mrs Rawson's face warmed, partly at Harry's admiration of her legs and guilt at her attempt to sneak up on them. She looked at old Mrs Faigen's heavy legs flowing towards old slippers, stopping at the ankles as if an invisible string tied the flesh, separating it from the feet.

"You need more soap from the pantry, or anything?" asked Mrs Rawson.

Old Mrs Faigen held up a half bar of soap resting across the corner of the tub. It brought a frown to Mrs Rawson's face.

"It needs cutting into three," said Mrs Rawson. "It's wasteful putting a great hunk like that in the water all the time."

Old Mrs Faigen used the soap to rub a towel, then dumped it on the window sill. Mrs Rawson took it up, spreading the fingers that were free, and Harry got to his feet and, taking a pocket knife from his trousers, unfolded the blades, bowing his head as if it were a ceremony, and putting out a hand for the soap. He marked it into three, cocking an eyebrow for approval, then, balancing the bar on the corner of the tub, cut it and held up the first portion on the knife blade.

"Look at that!" he said. "A shame to wash clothes with that. Should go on the bar for counter lunch, Lou. They'd eat it for cheese!"

"My soap never crumbles, never dries out," Mrs Rawson said.

"A champion soap maker, Lou. Nothing less than a champion."

Mrs Rawson put the soap on a saucer and set it on the window sill. Old Mrs Faigen might have snorted or it might have been the noise of her plunging Mr Rawson's work trousers deeply into the suds.

"Well!" said Harry, calculating that since he was standing, he should not sit again, but go to the wood-heap, which he did, rushing with a show of youthful energy. After a moment Mrs Rawson, studying all corners of the wash house as if making sure there was nothing to keep her there any longer, looked carefully at her feet before stepping onto the gravel and sauntering to the woodheap too.

Harry seized the axe and swung it high, bringing it down to bite into the wood. His breath came out huh-huh-huh with each blow, and his back rippled under his shirt, and his buttocks shook, and he hardly paused between blows with his huh-huh-huhs growing louder, and a panting haw-haw-haw when he stopped to find a new piece, working fast as if every fireplace in Rawson's Family Hotel was crying out for wood.

Some chips flew down the path close to Mrs Rawson's feet, and she gathered them up in the crook of her arm pressed to her breast, and Harry stopped chopping and pointed the axe at an upturned basket near the clothes line post, there for a surplus of pegs (there was never any) and she tipped the chips into this, brushing her dress free of splinters with a fussy air and then seating herself on a log, holding the basket in a loosely bound arm as if it were a child.

Old Mrs Faigen, moving from copper to tubs, saw her.

She was angry at the wood in the woodbox, wishing the box empty. She wanted to call out for something to bring Harry into the wash house. She had nothing to go out for, her first copperload hadn't boiled, and there was the rinsing after that before she could take the first basket full to the line.

Mrs Rawson, old Mrs Faigen saw, settled herself on the log, arranging one arm along the top of a pile near her back. She might have been in the hotel parlour staring into one of Harry's good fires, except that she liked it better there, Harry not chopping but stacking a wheelbarrow, keeping the different lengths separate, and when the barrow was full, taking the basket of chips and shaking them on top of the load and tossing the basket away to watch, with Mrs Rawson, it roll and finally stop exactly where it had been before. Old Mrs Faigen brought a piece of worn towel from the wash house and ran it along the length of both lines, holding it out to examine the dust on it but Harry and Mrs Rawson not appearing to notice.

"Boil you bastard," she said to the copper when she was back in the wash house.

Harry lowered himself onto a pile of wood, looking at his boots stretched out before him, and Mrs Rawson stretched her legs too and took off a shoe and, turning it on its side, wiped it clean of some damp earth on young grass growing furtively almost under her log. It was large and tough, resisting an axe, bone hard and dry, worn by seated bodies, turned grey white among the ripe red wood, dripping blood, like an old familiar armchair. Harry watched Mrs Rawson put her foot back into her shoe, and she wriggled her toes longer than necessary to hold his gaze.

Old Mrs Faigen brought two sheets, screwed like great snakes, pale blue from the last rinse, and swung them over the line. When they flapped down, jigging about before they were still, they showed her feet and ankles and a shrunken head, like an enormous infant in a great nightgown. Then the clothes prop was jerked angrily upright, startling the two at the woodheap, as if their privacy were gone.

Old Mrs Faigen went into the wash house, and Harry took the handles of the barrow and steered it to the path where the wheels crunched the gravel, and Mrs Rawson's shoes and Harry's boots made a biting noise passing the wash house, and the other sound was the iron door of the copper flung shut and the hissing slither of old Mrs Faigen's feet on their way to the tubs.

She looked from the doorway when it was safe to see only their backs, Harry running the barrow off the gravel when the path narrowed near the kitchen steps to give Mrs Rawson all the room.

Harry stacked the wood under the steps and Mrs Rawson went inside. No one was in the kitchen, the one maid, Lottie Parsons, on her day off. The room was big and clean and cold, although the stove burned all day and half the night all the year round. It being ten o'clock, Mrs Rawson, who did all the cooking, began to set a tray for morning tea. The table was large and empty of everything else, covered with the same brown linoleum that was on the floor. Almost everything was dark brown, the cupboards shutting off the china and cooking utensils, a clock in a brown wooden frame on the mantlepiece, canisters ranged on either side, the once-gold lettering chipped away, nothing inside them true to the labels anyway, the flour, sugar, tea and rice in larger containers in the pantry, other groceries in smaller lots remaining in the brown paper bags filled in Fred Rossmore's store.

There was a bucket of freshly pulled rhubarb on the draining board by the sink, alien as a singing child in a stark deserted classroom. Mrs Rawson plucked it from there and put it in the pantry, closing the door.

"Him and his bloody rhubarb," she said.

Harry was almost at the end of stacking the wood. The

Faigens did not have meals at the hotel or live there. Their accommodation was former horse stables converted to two rooms, one with a stove set in one wall used as a kitchen and living room, and the other a bedroom.

Mrs Rawson had never created a precedent by giving the Faigens tea or anything cooked in overabundance for the hotel table (a rarity this). The arrangement was that they "did for themselves" when the Faigens gratefully accepted their respective jobs shortly after both children had left home.

Mrs Faigen had always been a washerwoman, Harry with no trade apart from fencing or clearing land, and until they moved into the stables, they had rented various houses in Cobargo while their son, Allan, and daughter, Lillian, were at school.

Allan had left school at fourteen and had gone with his father, trapping rabbits and cutting eucalyptus, camping out. Allan whined like their old mongrel dog, hating the cold and Harry's cooking, and in the end (at the last job), leaving after a row with Harry over a lost axe, and finding his way back to Cobargo, his mother and Lillian who was whining her misery because Allan had finished his schooling and she had a year to go.

Allan stayed around until she left, then unexpectedly made his escape one Sunday at the height of summer.

The Faigens had joined a big band of other townspeople without cars of their own for a day at Bermagui, the nearest coastal town, travelling in a cream lorry (given the name for the function of collecting cream from farmers' gates for delivery to the Cobargo butter factory) for the fourteen mile trip there and back.

Allan didn't make the return trip, joining the crew of a fishing trawler which had dropped anchor for a few hours before continuing on in pursuit of a catch in cooler waters southward towards Tasmania.

He went in the clothes he was wearing, although he was told by the owner of the trawler he could be picked up when the boat returned in a couple of weeks' time. That was an eternity off to Allan, and fearful of a change of heart by his new boss in the interval, he ran onto the boat while the man and Harry were engaged in conversation and sat in the middle of a great swirl of fishing net, and when the boat started out to sea, he was too shy to look back at his mother and father and sister in a short, sad line on the shore, and Mrs Faigen (she was not old then) felt a hatred for her son, believing (or choosing to believe) he wanted nothing more to do with her.

"They've netted him alright," Harry said, opening his tobacco tin to comfort himself with a smoke.

At his words Mrs Faigen ran for the lorry, although it was not time to leave for home, and she sat in the middle of the table top unconsciously imitating Allan on the fishing net, her eyes down while she plucked at some splintery boards. She was there by herself for nearly an hour until Lillian came.

"I'll never see him again," Mrs Faigen said. "I'll die and never see him again."

Lillian felt fear. She had been thinking, watching Allan sail off, how simple it was to get away. Her mother's face appeared to her as a steel trap, and she looked quickly from it to the first reluctant families straggling across the grass to the lorry, and beyond that to her father, boasting to two other fathers with sons Allan's age, pointing to the trawler, jet black in the sunset and about to slip over the edge of the sea. She heard the foolish cries of children, suddenly excited about going home, scrambling for the best places on the lorry, carrying sodden shirts and boots and bathing suits, wrapping skinny damp towels around shoulders, screeching about each other's sunburn, strange people, Lillian thought, hardly able to believe anyone could be happy returning to Cobargo.

Two years later she got away. Allan was working as a deck hand on a passenger ferry running on Sydney Harbour, and he wrote that he would get her a room at his boarding house in Annandale and pay her board for a week or two until she got work.

Mrs Faigen (beginning to look old now) refused to walk with her to the mail car on its way to Nowra and the train. Harry carried her case, not kissing her goodbye in front of the driver and the other passengers, but taking his cigarette out of his mouth and looking down carefully on it lying on the ground, just as carefully stamping out the lighted end.

Neither Allan nor Lillian came home again.

Sometimes they sent a card at Christmas, the last from Allan from Victoria, ten years ago at least. He had grown tired of the sea and was working in a factory canning fruit.

Lillian got married at eighteen, not successfully, and because she was three months gone was ashamed to write this in a letter.

She left her husband, taking her child to Queensland. After some weeks she found work on an outback cattle station, leaving her son behind with the woman running the rooming house, who had grown fond of the child while he was in her care and Lillian was out looking for work.

Lillian never went back for him. This was two or three years after her last letter home. Keeping dark her marriage and the birth of her child, she was even more reluctant to say she had abandoned him.

Allan "took up" with a married woman in the Victorian town of Hamilton and moved in with her when her husband left home. Allan and the woman talked of visiting the Faigens in Cobargo, but it was a long and costly journey and there were the woman's two children to explain (to Cobargo as well as the Faigens). Their ages made it difficult to pass them off as Allan's, he being the woman's junior by ten years. Allan did not send Christmas cards any more, embarrassed that he could not include greetings from Rose and the children as well as his own.

Mrs Rawson collected the mail for the hotel from the post office and saw there was never anything from Allan or Lillian. But this did not prevent her asking, fairly regularly, for news of them.

Hearing the threat of Harry's departure in the spit of gravel under the barrow's wheels, Mrs Rawson, moving to the doorway, asked again.

"Any word lately from the two?"

Harry dropped the barrow handles and in one step rested a foot in the doorway.

"Wait," Mrs Rawson said, "while I take this to the parlour." She made the tea and put a little stack of oatmeal biscuits by the pot, calculating the number with her head on one side, then put half of them back.

"There's only him and the tea man there," she said. Him was Mr Rawson and the tea man, a traveller in groceries, the main line a well known brand of tea.

She was back just as Harry settled himself across the doorway with his knees raised. She pulled out a rocker that could have brought an air of softness to the room, but being hard, and cushionless, and dark brown too, was unrelenting as a church pew. Mrs Rawson sat on it with her feet not too far from Harry's and made a few gentle little rocks. An old brown and white cat sprung onto Harry's knees. He stroked its back, which it arched more, looking about the kitchen as if Harry's friendliness might be connected in some way with scraps of food within reach.

"Out!" said Mrs Rawson, stamping a brown leather toe

237

near Harry's boot. The cat smacked Harry's face with its tail in its haste to be gone.

"Nothing from either of them?" Mrs Rawson said.

"Not via His Majesty's mail, as well you know, Lou."

"Only asking," Mrs Rawson said. "We worry about what's become of them."

"Good of you Lou, to do the worryin' ".

"Course you worry, Harry. I know."

"They'll turn up one day," Harry said. "Hullo, Grandad!"

Mrs Rawson's dark face stiffened. (She was childless.)

They both saw old Mrs Faigen through the shrubs, going up and down the clothes line, surprisingly swift on her heavy legs, the line jerking with an energy matching hers, bouncing away long after the last peg was driven in and old Mrs Faigen had the empty washing basket on her hip.

"I suppose I wouldn't know," Mrs Rawson said with a laugh that wasn't one. Harry started to look into her face then didn't, concentrating on taking his tobacco from a pocket, sorry he did. Rolling the smoke reminded him of putting one out when the round, young, innocent bottom of Lillian went inside the mail car.

Mrs Rawson sent the chair rocking again. Harry felt better with the cigarette alight and the faintly biting hot and acid taste in his throat and the burn in his nostrils. Old Mrs Faigen was back at the line with more clothes, the wire dancing quite crazily now. Harry stood.

"Must be funny having kids," Mrs Rawson said.

"I been laughing for forty years."

Mrs Rawson laughed this time, softly, nearly warm.

Harry ran down the steps and in the next moment was at the woodheap flaying the air with the axe. Mrs Rawson listened for his breathing, disappointed that the distance took it from her.

Mr Rawson came in with the tea tray.

Oh you, thought Mrs Rawson and got up to poke the stove fire. Mr Rawson looked around the kitchen. She knew he was wondering what became of the rhubarb.

Let him think I flung it to the fowls, Mrs Rawson said to herself. She took a plate of steak slices from the meat safe. The safe danced like the clothes line when she shot the little bolt home and went on dancing while she slapped the frying pan on the stove.

"A tasty braise," Mr Rawson said, and Mrs Rawson plunged a knife deeply into a piece of steak on the cutting board and drew the blade from one end to the other.

Mr Rawson winced and ran down the steps.

Old Mrs Faigen was back at the line pegging out socks. All of them were black and still in the cold air, and old Mrs Faigen's face went in and out behind them like a child dodging behind a fence.

"Not much of a drying day," Mr Rawson said. Old Mrs Faigen looked up at the sky and shook her head at it and went into the wash house.

Harry shook his head sideways too, while picking up a piece of wood to split, this a greeting to Mr Rawson, seeing him for the first time that day.

Mr Rawson looked from one to the other making up his mind. "Save me a bucket of them suds," he called to old Mrs Faigen. "I'll do down the back veranda."

Harry stopped his chopping. That was one of his jobs. The axe blade, lying loosely on its side a moment, seemed to be making up its mind too. Oh bugger him, it said, flying high in the air again.

Mr Rawson took a bucket of water from old Mrs Faigen, sitting it in the middle of the gravel, watching as old Mrs Faigen went over the wash house floor with a long handled scrubbing broom. She had restored the room to order, the wash board hanging on its nail, the

239

soap and caustic soda and starch and knobs of washing blue in a jam jar on the shelf above the tubs, the window sill wiped down and the ash pan below the copper fire emptied.

Old Mrs Faigen always left the wash house this way. When the door was left open and visitors to the hotel, wandering about the back yard, saw inside, some (women) became anxious to be at the wash tubs at home, resolving to keep their wash houses in a similar state, remorseful and ashamed if their habits were slovenly.

Old Mrs Faigen shook the broom free of water after rinsing it in one of the tubs, wiped the tub dry, and hung the cloth on its peg, then took the broom to Mr Rawson. She looked back on the ordered room, like someone who had made her former home ready for a new tenant, regretting her departure.

Mr Rawson looked too and would have liked to praise her. But Mrs Rawson would not like that, so he gathered up the bucket with energy and tucked the broom under his arm and went rapidly off towards the rear of the hotel, as if demonstrating in this way how she inspired him.

Old Mrs Faigen took some of Harry's wood to build up her stove fire. She had potatoes to peel, cook, and serve with a wedge of corned beef in the meat safe, smaller and more battered than the one in the hotel kitchen. The smell of the steak and onions cooking there reached her.

"I wish I was dead, truly I wish I was dead," old Mrs Faigen said, taking up a potato.

Harry came in with more wood for their box.

"I wonder when I finish that wash, will I ever do another," said old Mrs Faigen.

Harry straightened up. "Wonderin' keeps you goin', I always reckon."

"Wonderin' when them two'll show up," mourned old Mrs Faigen. "A waste of wonderin' that!"

240

She crammed the lid on the saucepan of potatoes and sat on a chair, making herself small in spite of her big, flowing feet by drawing her thighs together and crushing her hands between them. The saucepan was the smallest of a set she had owned since she was married. It was showing signs of wear now in spite of the high polish she gave it, tipping to one side and with the lid not fitting well, sending out steam with the potatoes starting to boil.

Harry felt hungry. He left his chair to close the door on the smells from the hotel kitchen.

"A whiff is all you'd ever get from them," said old Mrs Faigen.

Harry looked at her feet, then into the stove fire. Old Mrs Faigen put her feet under the chair. "Four pairs of shoes in her cupboard and me with hardly a piece of leather to me feet."

Three weeks later on a Saturday afternoon, Lillian came home. No one knew her when she stepped out of the mail car pulled up by the post office. It was late that day, and there was already a good crowd on the porch. The door was snapped shut for the sorting, Sandy Schaefer showing an important face briefly in the doorway after the bags were thrown on the floor.

Then the driver went to haul a suitcase from the roof of the car. It was the only one there, and the last passenger stood uncertainly in the middle of the road.

She was short, just missing overweight, but neat, her black hair bobbed with a fringe across the forehead and a black beret flopping to one side showing most of it. She did not look thirty-eight, which was her age, and Cobargo, remembering the year she left home, knew this, and when she was recognized, her youthfulness was not approved but scorned, as if she sinned in her efforts to preserve it. She wore a black crepe dress, trimmed on the matching short jacket with white, and black court shoes, very shiny. After only a minute on the street, a film of dust settled on the toes, and Lillian, attempting to stamp it off, sent more flying up onto her pale beige stockings. She began to feel depressed and partly sorry she had returned to Cobargo with the same rough old dusty street and the people staring from the post office.

Grace Phillips, who had been a toddler when Lillian left home, made a special crossing from the newsagents, something she did not usually do, scorning the practice of waiting while the mail was sorted then cramming inside to be served, many of those in first getting nothing.

Grace dressed carefully (never the same twice running) and sauntered across when the crowed had thinned out inside, but were lingering about outside, so no one would miss seeing her. She rarely spoke to anyone, Sandy Schaefer sometimes giving her the mail across others' heads. She would go through it frowning and biting her red lips on her way back to the shop.

"Dear me," she said, this time feigning surprise at the sight of the shut door. This gave her another look at Lillian on her way back across the street, Lillian holding her case now, uncertain what to do.

She had the name Faigen on the label, and the driver "twigged" (in Cobargo jargon) and pointed in the direction of the hotel across the bridge.

Lillian nodded as if to say she knew that much and set off, every head from the post office following.

Walking in the middle of the road, she said to herself. Just like the old days. Crossing the bridge, she tried to stamp the dust from her shoes but seeing it thick on the road ahead gave up. Inside the hall of the hotel she looked up at the staircase, wondering if her parents would live on the upper floor. (She had forgotten about the converted stables although her father, in one of his rare letters when they had first moved in, described the quarters in such a way, they sounded superior to the hotel itself.)

She was still staring when Mrs Rawson found her, coming from the kitchen to check if Mr Rawson was minding the bar, tending to blame him if there were no customers, her theory being that a show of activity like polishing glasses attracted them.

"I'm Lillian Faigen," Lillian said, and Mrs Rawson, who was wearing a cretonne apron, rolled her hands in the skirt in her shock. When she smoothed it out, she felt she should be removing it.

"I'm Mrs Rawson," she said, inclining her head towards the door where the sign said Rawson's Family Hotel. She was a trifle peeved that she might not be remembered. She removed the apron now, pleased with her grey crepe dress underneath, and hung it in the closet under the stairs, pleased too with the newly shined brass knob on the door.

"Are they alright and that?" Lillian asked, meaning were the Faigens still alive.

Mrs Rawson considered saying they were ailing to punish Lillian for her absence and long silence.

"Always on the lookout for word of you," Mrs Rawson said, drawing a long, mournful face.

The back door to the hall opened then admitting Mr Rawson. He had seen from the middle of the beetroot patch the flutter of a black skirt mounting the hotel steps and came to see. He knew it was Lillian.

"It's Lil," he said, his face going in and out of slanting sunlight, like broken prison bars. "I remember how black your hair was, and wondered why they called you Lily!"

Lillian swept off her hat and Mr Rawson ran his eyes right down her and picked up her case. "They'll be pleased to see you," he said. Habit made him look to Mrs Rawson for directions, but he removed his eyes quickly.

She's not going into one of our rooms for nothing, said the look Mrs Rawson gave back.

Chastened, he led the way down the hall, Mrs Rawson deciding to go to the kitchen but watching the twinkling movement of Lillian's shoes and decided she would get a black patent pair of courts for herself in Bega first chance she had.

Harry was rolling a new delivery of beer in barrels into the coolroom when Mr Rawson and Lillian stepped onto the back veranda. Mrs Rawson heard his cry from the kitchen and ran down the steps and towards the back to miss nothing.

Old Mrs Faigen, darning a grey woollen skirt she had worn since Lillian left home, threw it from her lap and rushed out. Harry was holding Lillian in his arms and laughing quite wildly with her, and Mr and Mrs Rawson, having forgotten themselves, were standing quite close together. When Mrs Rawson, unfolding her arms, touched Mr Rawson, she moved away.

Old Mrs Faigen came slowly across the yard. When Lillian saw her, she shrieked and rushed to her, pinning the toe of her mother's old slipper to the ground with her patent leather heel then jumping back when old Mrs Faigen winced, crying out that she was sorry and looking down at both their feet.

"Come inside!" cried Harry, his grey and sandy hair blowing about, hurrying ahead with Lillian's case.

"I remember now where you live," Lillian murmured, walking close to old Mrs Faigen.

Harry was disappointed the rooms were untidy. They usually were, for old Mrs Faigen did not keep them in the scrupulous order of the wash house. Lillian saw she would be sleeping on the couch and sitting on it tested the thickness of the matress.

"Not a bad bed," Harry said, sitting beside her. "And we'll keep the stove fire going."

There are no extra blankets, Lillian thought. I'll be getting away as soon as I can.

Old Mrs Faigen rolled up the grey skirt and put it on top of the sewing machine. She was ashamed she had worn it so long and fearful that Lillian would remember. She put the cloth on half the table, as was her habit, then moved Harry's shaving things to the machine too, and changed the cloth around to a diamond shape to cover most of the table.

Harry was pleased, seeing it as a gesture of celebration, and took hold of Lillian's hand. There was no wedding ring there, Lillian having sold it to a man buying gold who had called at the station property where she had been the cook, the money helping her get back to Brisbane. Once there, she decided against looking up the rooming house woman and her son, since several years had gone by. Best leave things as they are, Lillian told herself, boarding a train for Sydney where she worked as a domestic for more years. She saved for her rail and car fare home, only starting to worry that one or the other of her parents might be dead when the car was a few miles out of Cobargo.

Oh, my God if they are, Lillian said to herself then. She felt a great relief that they were not, now on the couch with her father, and squeezed his hand causing him to look down on its ringless state. He did not think she had never had a man though. He thought her body not a virgin's body, and was sad remembering her climbing into the mail car when she was sixteen. But he kept hold of her hand and she knew he was silently asking about marriage.

I'll tell them nothing, Lillian thought, withdrawing her hand.

They heard a step near the door and it was Mrs Rawson with a plate of sliced roast beef.

"Good heavens!" cried old Mrs Faigen in shock.

"You wouldn't be prepared," said Mrs Rawson, red running into her face so that it looked the same colour as the meat, the slices overlapping each other with a glistening yellow edge of fat to each.

Harry jumped up from the couch and took the plate from Mrs Rawson to make sure it wasn't refused. "That's real nice of you, Lou," he said and put it tenderly on the centre of the table. He moved the salt and pepper close to it and rubbed his hands together, eager to do more.

"I'll leave you to it," Mrs Rawson said, turning from the doorway. In a moment her face was back. "Did you bring the boy with you?" she said, making a little cackling laugh to finish the sentence.

Lillian caught both hands between her knees, jamming them tight. She looked upwards to the timber beams supporting the iron roof, only half realizing the rooms had no ceiling. She looked back to the stove where the kettle was rattling its lid, saying it had boiled.

She remembered the last time she had made a bath for her son, half aware then it was the last time. The rooming house woman hovered near, thrusting an elbow into the bath water, doubting that Lillian had it right.

"You finish him," Lillian had said, and went to the back veranda to pull some underwear from a little line there and in her room she finished packing her case.

The boy. He would be nearly a man now.

Old Mrs Faigen was watching her face as she laid a knife and fork on the table, looking down at last to check that the space between them was right.

"You heard from Allan lately?" asked Harry.

246

"Not lately," said Lillian.

Mrs Rawson left the doorway and they heard her shoes on the gravel growing fainter, and after that a rush of water into the teapot.

"One at a time," said Harry, getting up. "She'll do us for the present, won't she Mother? Where will we sit her?"

Mrs Rawson invited Lillian to go to Bega with her to buy the black patent shoes. They had a navy blue Rover car, which Mr Rawson drove, so he had to go too.

He was pleased about the trip and gave the car a polish.

"Ooooh, that's nice," said Lillian, standing near the Rover in the yard, wearing a ruby red wool costume and a cream coloured blouse with a frill spilling out the front of the jacket.

Mr Rawson, going red with pleasure, rubbed harder at the door handle, the back one on the side where Lillian would sit. Mrs Rawson watched from an upstairs window, where she had come from her bedroom across the hall to see what Lillian was wearing.

"My good black, I reckon," said Mrs Rawson in her petticoat, going back to her bedroom.

Mr Rawson took them to the best Bega hotel for midday dinner. He knew the owner of the Crown, who hovered about the dining room and came across to their table, and Mr Rawson was able to show off in front of Lillian, discussing with a knowledgeable air various brands of beer and spirits and the difficulty of getting good, hard-working staff.

He remembered then his help was mainly the Faigens and they were Lillian's parents.

"I been lucky," said Mr Rawson. "This little lady's Mum and Dad help me run the place."

247

Mrs Rawson had not been able to find black patent courts in her size. "I sit in the parlour all day and file my fingernails," she said in a little burst of a laugh with no smile in it.

Mr Rawson was not too put out, taking in big forkfuls of boiled beef and onion sauce. He stole a glance at Lillian, with her shining square haircut and her white skin and well marked eyebrows. She would look good behind the bar. He felt buoyant inside and said he would have the apple pie, and a beer for himself and the women, wishing he did not have to include Mrs Rawson.

All the way home in the car he pictured Lillian helping him serve customers in the rush times like Saturday afternoons. He would be there to make sure no one made passes at her.

Cobargo had never had a barmaid in either hotel. He would be the first. The Rover flew along the dusty road through Bemboka, nothing more than a post office and a couple of houses and a store that looked like another house except for an advertisement, grey lettering on white enamel proclaiming a popular brand of tea nailed above the roof of the veranda.

"A one horse dump if ever there was one," Mr Rawson said, turning his face briefly so that Lillian would know the remark was mainly for her. Cobargo, said the silence following, is the place to be! I'm taking you there, by jove I am, said the gear change in the Rover.

Mrs Rawson went huffily to her bedroom to change her dress, for not only was she without the new shoes but she had to get into the kitchen and start the tea at once. The fire in the stove was low, as you would expect, and the isolated item on the kitchen table an enamel dish of rhubarb, cooked by the Parsons girl (with far too much water) before she went off home at four o'clock.

"I could do with more help," she said aloud, rattling

248

the poker in the stove. She pictured Lillian with Harry and old Mrs Faigen by their stove recounting the day's outing. Tom had paid for her dinner, this rankling thought causing Mrs Rawson to slap the cabbage saucepan heavily on the table. You would think she would ask if there was anything she could do to help, since the trip was mainly for her benefit (Mrs Rawson had just decided this). She heard the back hall door open and two pairs of feet tapping the linoleum. Mr Rawson and Lillian stopped in the kitchen doorway, looking just a little sheepish.

"I'm going to be shown how to pull a beer!" Lillian said, her voice very bright.

In spite of her mood, Mrs Rawson felt pleasure. Lillian was vibrant, bringing the dark old hotel to life, like a bell someone decided to polish up, then pushed and it rang with a melody that surprised and gladdened. But Mrs Rawson did not allow any expression of cheer to show, rather she pointed her rear to the doorway as she threw potatoes and pumpkin around the leg of mutton, which the Parsons girl did manage to put in the oven to start roasting before they got home. When she straightened up, Mr Rawson and Lillian had gone, Mrs Rawson straining her ears but the bar too far off to hear anything.

Then there was the crunch of the wheelbarrow on the back path and a glimpse of Harry's back with his shirt pulled tight across it, as he stacked wood under the steps.

"Hand me up a few pieces," Mrs Rawson said, although the box by the stove was half full.

When she had shoved a piece in the stove, she swept potato and pumpkin peelings to a corner of the table and stood by them in view of Harry stacking the wood.

"She said how long she's staying?" asked Mrs Rawson.

"Seems dug in for awhile," Harry said. Mrs Rawson

saw how young and happy his face looked. She set a jealous mouth.

"Nothing on the other one though."

Harry moved a few pieces of wood to make an even side to the pile. "I'm not greedy," he said. "We'll hear sometime."

He picked up the barrow handles. "It was real good of you Lou, to take Lil to Bega for the trip. She liked it."

He started to go and Mrs Rawson did not want that.

"I been thinking I could give her something to do in the hotel." Harry dropped the barrow handles and came half way up the steps. "In return for a room," said Mrs Rawson hastily, in case Harry thought there might be wages involved.

"No question about it, she's cramped on the couch. Nowhere to hang her pretty things. That would be great, Lou!"

Her pretty things! bridled Mrs Rawson. In her view, Lillian's clothes were not as smart as hers and she was dumpy of figure too, without Mrs Rawson's height. Mrs Rawson ignored the age difference of twenty years.

Harry lowered his pleased face for a moment then wheeled the barrow off with a spurt of new energy, obviously hoping to be the first to tell Lillian.

I'm not sure I've done the right thing, Mrs Rawson grumbled to herself, swinging the mutton around in the oven, then throwing the oven rag down and going to the bar.

Lillian was enraptured at the idea of a bedroom in the hotel and a few light duties in return. Mrs Rawson almost changed her mind about the offer, having found Lillian on a high stool, showing a lot of leg. She was sipping a brandy and soda poured for her by Tom, who had his back against the shelves. He removed the smile from his face when Mrs Rawson appeared and leapt forward to

250

take the bottle from the counter and fussily put it back in its place.

Lillian hopped off the stool, and taking her drink followed Mrs Rawson to the kitchen. Without being asked, she picked up the cabbage from the kitchen table, and selecting a knife gouged out the stem without any waste. Then Mrs Rawson told her.

Mr Rawson hovering about the hall heard Lillian's joyful shout and looking in saw her hug herself with the knife pointed outwards, and pink running into her creamy cheeks in the most delightful way.

He smiled broadly at whatever it was, and when he was told forgot himself and stretched out both arms, moving them Mrs Rawson's way after a moment's acute embarrassment.

"She would get it soft," said old Mrs Faigen from her chair by the stove when Harry came in to tell her. "It's my poor boy I'm thinkin' of. God knows where he is, killed in some war, or in jail more than likely."

"There's been no wars lately that I know of," Harry said, filling the woodbox happily. Lillian might stay now for a long time. She looked years younger than her real age. She might get married in Cobargo and never leave.

"What future is there for a girl just slavin' for a roof over her head?" asked old Mrs Faigen.

"She'll be eatin' here, you can bet, there'll be nothing for her in their dining room, apart from the crumbs she shakes from the tablecloth.

"Lou Rawson'll be working something out to suit herself, bet your bottom dollar on that."

"Now come on Mother," Harry said. "We got her home and that's what you always wanted." He put the kettle on the heat, hoping Lillian would come in and have a cup of tea with them.

"Mother!" snorted old Mrs Faigen. "The way that one's carryin' on you'd think she was the mother!"

Harry went to say something, but didn't. He got a quick vision of Lou and Lillian and himself at the Bega races, looking at the ring events at the Cobargo Show, at the seaside with Lillian in the swimming costume she had shown him. He looked across at old Mrs Faigen, trying to find a suitable place for her. He blamed the fire for turning his face red when he couldn't.

"Hummph!" said old Mrs Faigen when Lillian did not come in for tea that night, Mr Rawson putting his head in the door to say Lou had two travellers arrive unexpected and Lil (Lil!) was staying on to help.

That night she moved her things into a guest room, three doors down from the Rawson's bedroom.

Harry helped carry her suitcase and shoes and hats and stood when he had laid them on bed and chair. He saw the little tableau Mr and Mrs Rawson made with Lillian between them, all leaning gently against the dressing table.

Mrs Rawson reached out and stroked a lace curtain, with pride in its immaculate state. "It's time the curtains in the other rooms had a wash," Mrs Rawson said. "That's something you can do tomorrow, Lil. Take them down and give them to Sal to do up."

Harry picked up the empty case and went back to his place and heard the hollow sound it made slithering under the couch.

Cobargo was outraged when the Rawsons sacked Lottie Parsons, who had worked for them since leaving school two years earlier (although she had a name in the town for slovenliness). Lillian was now given Lottie's wage. Lottie was seen red eyed during the following week, and her father gave out the word that he had taken his custom permanently from the Rawsons. Since he bought only a small bottle of brandy every third Christmas for his wife's

252

pudding, the Rawsons had a laugh over this in the hotel kitchen where Lillian was preparing some of Mr Rawson's rhubarb with hardly any water, brown sugar, orange rind and a sprinkle of nutmeg. Mr Rawson could hardly tear himself away to go back to cleaning a side wall of the hotel after cutting back an overgrowth of ivy.

It was not long before Cobargo forgave Lillian for taking Lottie's job and took to praising Lillian for her adeptness at the bar and the improvement in the hotel fare.

"By jove, she's pepped things up, no question about that," said Sid Farrington, a regular traveller in soft goods who stayed at Rawsons and had been considering making a change to the other hotel.

Lillian slipped some fresh milk into the oatmeal so that it went to the breakfast table white, not grey white, ran a little melted butter over the beans and gave them a garnish of parsley, and put a daub of whipped cream as well as custard on each serve of steamed jam pudding. On the days when Lillian was not in the kitchen (she had a day off a week) Mrs Rawson was inclined towards similar practices, not wanting to be shown up as too frugal, although she complained sometimes to Harry that she (Lillian) would put them all in the poorhouse if given a free hand.

They took to exchanging clothes, blouses mainly, for they were the same bust size.

"Bega hasn't seen me in this," Mrs Rawson said, getting ready for a trip to Bega, having established by telephone that the black court shoes in size eight were now available in a large general store. She handed over to Lillian a blouse in navy and white spotted muslin, just the perfect match for her navy pleated skirt.

In a moment Lillian was in Mrs Rawson's bedroom with a red felt hat, turned up jauntily at one side. "Bega hasn't seen this either," she said, and Mrs Rawson tried it on. She called to Tom to come from the bathroom and look. Mr Rawson had to train his eyes away from Lillian, wondering what she would wear, thinking briefly and gloriously of one day buying a hat for her.

As it happened Lillian went without a hat, with the idea of finding something in the shops, for she had money saved from her wages, low as they were.

Mr Rawson stood in front of a saddler's, two doors from the milliner's, while the women were in the shop. When they came out, it was all Mr Rawson could do to stop himself running towards them, Lillian in a beige coloured toque with a feather in a lighter shade, curling from one side to almost reach the other.

Mrs Rawson saw his rivetted eyes.

She didn't speak on the way home in the car. Nearly in Cobargo, she took off Lillian's red hat and without turning her head put in on the back seat in the empty corner. Lillian looked at it, her cheeks nearly as red.

Mr Rawson was bent over the wheel, willing Lillian to move closer to the centre of the seat so that he could see her in the rear vision mirror. He thought of her passing through the bar door back at the hotel, the swing doors that clapped to, caressing her breasts (the lucky things!). The bar was closed, it being Wednesday, and no one was likely to disturb them in there for a drink. Please God, Lil would leave the hat on, the tip of the feather teasing her cheek and a bit of her black hair.

He sensed the stolidness of Mrs Rawson beside him. She had the huff, despite her new shoes. Never mind, she was often this way.

Lillian took the red hat to her room and removing the beige one laid both tenderly on the shelf of her wardrobe. She clung to the catch of the door when she closed it, holding a chair with her free arm. It was as if she clung to a child that threatened to reject her.

She then peeled off the spotted blouse and put on her black maid's dress, and on her way down the hall slipped into the Rawson's bedroom to lay the blouse on a chair. Lillian had never been alone in the room before. The furniture was massive, the mirror in the wardrobe gave her back her reflection, very small. There was nothing on the polished surface of the dressing table but an ebony backed brush and comb set and a tall crystal scent spray. Lillian saw the blouse upset the starkness of the room and took it to put it somewhere else. She was holding it across her arm when Mr Rawson pushed the door open wider and found her.

"Putting this back," Lillian said, and Mr Rawson was puzzled at the pain in her eyes. She put it down on the chair and went past him quickly and down the stairs, almost running, so that when he went out of the room to watch her, he saw her head like something on a fast running current bobbing away, he with no chance of catching it.

In the kitchen Lillian began to do the beans. Mrs Rawson was making pastry for meat pie. The two of them had cooked steak and kidney early that morning in a glow of mutual satisfaction at their forethought and organization. It was on the table now, in a basin, the gravy grey, tiny corners of the meat standing up hard and dark. Lillian wanted to stir and smooth it, but Mrs Rawson had it close by her and was rolling dough with a hard, closed face.

"Just pull the strings out of them beans," Mrs Rawson said looking at the beans, not Lillian. "Cutting them down the sides like that you waste too much. I meant to say it before."

Her grey white pastry sheet, flung into the pie dish,

255

might have slapped coldly on Lillian's face. "People come here with their city ways. They don't always work."

Mr Rawson came in rubbing his hands, almost shy of Lillian as if they had been intimate together in the bedroom. "Anything from the garden wanted here?" he said. "Rhubarb?"

"Yes!" Mrs Rawson said. "I'll do a dishful and bake some rice if you'll bring it to me here, Tom."

Her pie was ready and she pointed her rear at Lillian as she put it in the oven. Mr Rawson wondered if there was time to screw up one side of his face in a wink at Lillian, but Lillian had her eyes on the beans and he could see she was going to keep them there. He was terribly in need of a look from her.

"Pity we can't use up all them beans out there," he said. "There's a paddock full of them."

"We could," Lillian said. "You slice them and pack them in jars with salt between the layers and they keep a long time."

"Hummmph!" snorted Mrs Rawson. "You'd use up a ton of salt then gallons of water washing them clean of it.

"Besides I'm not sittin' doin' beans till Kingdom come while others are enjoyin' themselves."

Mr Rawson went quickly down the steps and had the hoe in his hands in the lettuce patch, then flung it from him remembering the rhubarb, and almost laughed out loud at the thought of seeing Lillian again back in the kitchen.

Lillian surprised old Mrs Faigen and Harry by coming into their kitchen after tea and sitting with them by the stove. Harry was overjoyed at the unexpected visit and fussed about, filling the kettle and putting it over the heat, and opening the stove door so that it would be warmer for Lillian. Lillian put her feet on the fender with her shoes off and rubbed one stockinged foot against the other.

256

"She get her shoes?" Harry asked.

Old Mrs Faigen put her big slippered feet under her chair. Bet your life she got 'em, said her sniff. Five pairs now and me with hardly a scrap of leather to me feet.

Lillian put her feet into her shoes and looked at the door as if she should be getting back.

"When that boils we'll have a cup of tea by the stove," Harry said. "Nice and cosy."

"No mail come over there?" old Mrs Faigen asked. "Nothing from the boy?"

Lillian held the arms of her chair.

"Now Mother," Harry said. "If there was mail, you'd have had it five hours ago. Don't go pesterin' Lil. It isn't her fault."

No one spoke.

"He'll turn up the same way Lil did." Harry took hold of Lillian's wrist as if there was a threat that she would fly off. "She's here and got herself a job and doin' it well too."

He leaned forward and took a burning splinter of wood to light his cigarette. The flame deepened the glow on his face. "The way she does the mashed potato and the rhubarb is the talk of Cobargo."

He turned the kettle as much to remind Lillian that she was staying for tea as to encourage it to boil.

A moment later there was a small and hesitant tap on the door, and Harry had only to tip back on his chair to reach the knob and open it, leaving the caller to find his way in.

It was Mr Rawson. He took only one step inside, looking across at old Mrs Faigen, which was disconcerting, for he was talking about Lillian.

"We was wonderin' where you'd got to," Mr Rawson said.

We? wondered Lillian.

257

She stood and swept at the back of her dress under her buttocks where it creased easily, a navy crepe she had put on after tea. She always changed to sit by the fire in the parlour, sometimes making up a fourth at cards if there was a guest in the hotel willing to join in. Wondering why she bothered to change that night, Lillian wondered too if she would sit in the parlour that way again.

"I'll get back then," she said, and went out behind Mr Rawson, not looking at Harry's disappointed face.

The night was pitch black. Once the door was shut it swallowed them up. Lillian laughed, a gurgling sound like water from the spout of an overflowing tank. She did not know where to put her feet and realized now, with another little gurgle of laughter, how little attention she had paid to the layout of the yard.

Mr Rawson took her arm and jammed it to his side. "Put your leg against mine," he said. "And you won't trip over anyting."

"Oooh," said Lillian. "You could be leading me anywhere!"

In a little while leaves brushed Lillian's face and she jumped right into Mr Rawson's arms.

"It's the ivy on the back wall," he whispered, brushing it away. He saw her face very white, her black hair running into the ivy, blackened by the night. Mr Rawson pushed more branches away, leaving his hands pressed to the wall, Lillian's face between his wrists.

She moved her head, and when her lips brushed his skin, he put both hands around her neck and held her lightly. Lillian was not certain of the strength there. Perhaps he could crush her neck if he wanted to. She shivered, not afraid, exhilarated.

She had thought of him as a weak man, directed by his wife, but there was strength in his profile now she could see it outlined.

"I'd like to kiss you Lil," he said. "If you'd let me."

It had been a long time since a man had held her. He was twenty years older than she, but in the dark he seemed only her age, a hard body now she was close to it.

A window went up suddenly above their heads, screeching at the quiet night. He dropped his arms.

"Go up by the back stairs," he whispered. "I'll go round and in by the kitchen door."

She flew at his bidding and was up the stairs before she knew it. I'll see what he looks like in the daylight tomorrow, she said to herself, opening the bedroom door.

It was morning tea time before Lillian saw Mr Rawson. He is avoiding me, she thought, feeling terribly alone, although Mrs Rawson was opposite her, buttering currant bread.

But almost at once he came into the kitchen, rubbing his hands, and keeping his eyes from Lillian, who was setting up the tray to be taken into the parlour.

"Fire's burning up nicely in there," he said.

I can't sit by it, but he is saying he would like me to, said Lillian to herself, putting new efficiency into matching the cups and saucers and laying the teaspoons at the right angle.

"I'll take it in," Mrs Rawson said. "You bring the teapot, Tom." Looking after them, Lillian saw Mr Rawson was wearing different trousers. They were well fitting and of fine tweed, and his shirt was finely striped too and well ironed by old Mrs Faigen.

Lillian thought with a little stirring of pleasure she might iron it herself next time it was washed.

That afternoon Mrs Rawson went across to the wood heap to sit on the log while Harry was chopping. He slowed down a little, keeping the chips from flying near her by turning to chop at another angle.

After a while he stopped and looked at her face, holding

259

the axe by his knee. Then he sat on a pile of wood, looking down first, then across to the hotel, then back to Mrs Rawson's feet, pressed together on the ground.

He was surprised she had not changed her shoes, as she always did when leaving the kitchen, but was in an old bursting pair she must have put on for the long stand by the sink at the washing-up.

Old Mrs Faigen found something she wanted from the wash house. She went past them, between the two lines of washing, her old mauve coloured feet looking as if they did not belong to a body.

Mrs Rawson and Harry, watching the feet, saw them as something on a stage behind a half raised curtain. When they had gone, Mrs Rawson looked down on her own feet, and after a while got up quickly, ashamed and embarrassed.

"Excuse me," she said, and hurried down the gravel path.

"Chased her off, did I?" said old Mrs Faigen coming from the wash house (with nothing).

Harry stood, idly waggling the axe by the end of the handle, nothing on his face.

"Look at that wash!" said old Mrs Faigen. Her eyes flashed at one end where there were dresses and underwear belonging to Lillian.

"It'll kill me in the end. I'll drop dead scrubbin' and reachin' and bendin' and not a soul'll turn a hair!"

She went into the kitchen and Harry heard the noise of the irons dragged from the back of the stove to the hottest part.

He felt a great envy of her having no worries beyond the ironing and dying.

260

15   That Carrie One

Carrie Grant was the eldest of the three daughters of her widowed father, Hector.

He was also blind.

It was a natural progression that Carrie stay on in the house and care for him after her mother died. Carrie was twenty-five and not likely to marry.

The second girl, Hilda, was married to the town's baker. She was his second wife, and after two years of marriage she had a child and another coming, and there were the baker's three, aged twelve, eleven and eight, to care for as well. She had a terrible life as it was and could hardly take on the burden of a blind father.

The other girl, Nettie, "got away" as Cobargo expressed it. She was bright at school and was accepted by a Sydney hospital after taking nurses' exams. She was twenty-two now and a sister with a veil.

She sent a photograph of herself wearing the veil and holding her graduation certificate, and Hector sat for a long time by the corner of the kitchen table feeling the cardboard edges.

When the mother, Gertie, died with cancer of the breast (which she tried to cure with cabbage leaves), Nettie came home for the funeral, getting leave of a few days from her job, not so well paid but with meals and living quarters provided.

Nettie returned to Sydney the day after the burial, although she could have stayed another day.

It was very depressing, with Hector weeping from his sightless eyes, Hilda heavily pregnant, and Carrie aware that she was trapped forever as her father's housekeeper. The grief was already running from her face, taking the softness with it. The pupils of her tearless eyes had sharpened to arrow points.

In the mail car, Nettie took a cigarette from a pack in her handbag and lit it. Stares and frowns from other passengers followed. Oh damn them and their backward dull little towns, Nettie said to herself, lifting her chin and lowering her eyes under the flat black hat, trimmed with grosgrain ribbon, loaned to her by her close friend Elsie White, the nurse sharing her room at the hospital. Nettie did not think it necessary to tell her sisters the hat was not her own. She blew smoke now with a red underlip thrust out, watching it make a pale blue film on the underneath of her hat brim.

When she finished the cigarette, she played with the lapel of her black suit, trying to make her face sad to alert the car load to her bereaved state. ("That lovely girl all in black, she has lost someone dear to her.") She had not cried much at her mother's death. She had cried more at eleven, sitting on the tank-stand at St Joseph's Convent, reading about the death of David Copperfield's mother with a curious nun watching her from the school veranda. The other children were screaming and tearing about the playground, but she read and sobbed, imagining it was her own mother dying.

Nursing has hardened me, she told herself with a little shiver of pride.

Hilda did not stay long at the house after the funeral, leaving for home with her small child sitting awkwardly on a hip. The child's leg gripped Hilda's great mound of stomach, rubbing it up and down. Here is a new game, said the sparkle in bright brown eyes, something that hasn't always been there. She would make a horse of it and jig about.

262

Hilda moved her to the other hip and gave the leg a light slap, not so much in anger with the child but in trepidation at returning home.

Always there was the job of trying to appease her husband, to coax some civility to his face, greyish white like the dough he mixed in the room behind the shop, nearly as barren as the shop itself, not much more than the flour bins and the counter for rolling the dough and a few slits of light from the oven door, the fire hiding too in keeping with the gloom.

When customers came into the shop, Crusty (as he was known) looked sourly through the door on them, telling them with round hating eyes they were intruders. Hilda would rush in, over friendly to atone for Crusty's rudeness, and when the shop was empty again, Crusty would turn violent to punish her for daring to oppose his mood with pleasantness.

Hilda returned her child to the other hip. Perhaps he would be better today with Mum's death and the funeral and all. Since school was out, her three stepchildren, dawdling towards the bakery, rushed past it to meet her. They reached up to touch the baby, then pressed close to her for the short walk home. The eldest was shy of her face, expecting it to be even more sodden with tears than during the past two days. But it was soft and pretty, she saw, and was pleased about this and wondered if she should be. She put her school case to her other hand so she could take hold of a piece of Hilda's dress at the back.

They all looked back when the Grants' house was about to slip from view. It was on the opposite side to the bakery, sliced from sight by the School of Arts, which hugged the roadway while the Grants' house was set so far back, the front veranda was in line with the School of Arts lavatories, the high fence not much help in cutting off the stench, particularly bad after a ball on a Saturday night or a tennis match on a Sunday, for the town courts were on the same plot of ground.

Nettie waved from the veranda (not troubling to come to the gate) and they all waved back, the stepchildren tentatively, still uncertain of the relationship with Hilda's family, and Hilda, taking the arm of the baby, pumped it up and down, the relationship there unshadowed by doubt.

Nettie went inside to see to her suitcase and to detect through the movements of Carrie in the kitchen her resentment at carrying the full burden of caring for their father.

"Old Mumma Fox is gone," Nettie heard Hector say. The click of Carrie's heels on the stone hearth, where she was stirring the stove fire to life, said this should be obvious since she was buried at eleven o'clock that morning.

"Mumma Fox," Hector said. "You know why I called her that?" The sisters knew. Hector had only a couple of years formal education and he remembered for the rest of his life a story in a school primer about a family of foxes.

"Can you smell the flowers?" Carrie asked, for the front room was filled with the pungent smell of roses and stock, sent to the house by the nuns at St Joseph's, and she was ashamed that Hector might detect her ill humour.

Hector lifted up his head, rather like a fox alerted to a scent in the wind.

His face was remarkably unlined for a man of seventy. The skin was like fine brown leather, with a slight shine on it as leather has. It was drawn over his nose and cheekbones and outlined his jaw, as if it were a mask pulled tightly over his real features. He had been blind for ten years, losing the sight of his right eye first and telling his family for a long time beforehand he was "beggared if he could see a thing out of it."

264

They did not believe him, scoffing at his claims, telling each other he was looking for sympathy, Gertie worrying about the cost of seeing doctors. In the end he went to Bega and a doctor there told him yes, he had no sight in the eye, and it appeared the retina had become detached. There was further bad news about the sight in the left eye. An eye man came from Cooma to do several operations in the Bega hospital, one of them cutting the retina of Hector's good eye and sewing it back. The operation was what Cobargo called a botch. Hector signed his way into the hospital but Gertie had to sign for him coming out, foolishly grateful that he could not see her weeping.

Hector had been a telephone linesman, employed on and off up to the time of the operation.

Cobargo was greatly moved by the tragedy. A benefit night was held in the School of Arts, then after a few months Hector got a small government pension, mainly the work of Fred Rossmore, already a leading figure in community affairs, who wrote a great many letters to the local Member of Parliament on Hector's behalf.

When word was received that the pension would be paid, the letter borne triumphantly to the house by Fred, the Grants were so overjoyed they overlooked Hector's blindness, the reason for it all.

"Pass me the salt, Hec," Gertie had cried when they finally sat down to dinner. It was nearly two o'clock in the afternoon, Fred staying so long with the letter, steering them back to the subject of his persistence and talent with the pen when they got off it, the regular meal hour came and went.

Hector forgot his blindness too, and reaching out for the salt shaker, plunged a hand in a bowl of custard. They all rushed to his aid, holding back laughter in case he was offended.

Carrie brought a basin of warm water and a face cloth, and put it under his dripping hand, and swiftly dabbed up the blob of custard on the sugar bowl, flinging a slice of bread that received a coating into the fowl bucket. She removed the pickle jar to mop up some splashes on the table cloth.

"Good girl, Carrie!" Gertie said to the fourteen year old. "Dad, you should see the way that girl has cleaned that custard up!"

Hector put both hands out to grope carefully, triumphant when he found the salt and pepper shakers neatly together and located the bread, touching a crust.

He lifted his head and sniffed the air, then picking up a dessert fork (they had not yet been served the pudding), crashed it down on the table, catching only the edge of his dinner plate.

"That settles it!" he cried. "That girl leaves school!"

Carrie shrieked (they had all developed the habit of exaggerating sound as if Hector were deaf as well as blind) and Gertie said "Well!" and pressed both hands to her cheeks.

"Yes, she leaves school!" Hector said, feeling for the fork across his plate and using it to check his plate should anything be left uneaten, the news of the pension, followed by the spilled custard, of great distraction. Gertie swiftly dumped a large potato near the fork prongs, causing joy to run into Hector's face, then disappointment that he had missed locating it.

"Mum just put it there, Dad!" Carrie cried, and leaping from her place, trotted to his side to cut the potato open and lay a piece of butter in the incision, shaking pepper over it.

Hector raised his head again. "Looking after me is a full time job," he said. "A job for two women!"

Carrie held his chair, straightening her own back, pink running into her cheeks. A woman!

Hilda, a year younger, left school at fourteen too and went to work as a telephonist at the Cobargo Post Office, the job falling vacant when Merle Sharpe married a young man from the bank and went with him to Bathurst to live. Hilda was a natural choice for the job, Cobargo still enveloped in sympathy for the Grants' plight.

As she grew older, Hilda formed an attachment to the baker's wife, spending her free time helping with the children.

The wife died at the birth of the youngest, and when the child was about five, Hilda and Crusty were married.

Nettie was then in her second year of nursing, stoically adapting to the hard life, coming home for the wedding, envious of Hilda with a husband (who looked unfamiliar and smart on his wedding day and actually smiled, possibly for the last time) and a ready made family, quite pretty children and healthy too, Nettie thought, already conscious of her profession.

Nettie did not envy Hilda any more.

She could dismiss her now, she and the children were back at the bakery and there was only Carrie to endure until the mail car carried Nettie off quite early the next morning.

She went alone with her case to the post office.

"You can't leave Dad," Nettie said on her way out, and then went red, hearing a snorting sound from Carrie about to fill a kettle with her back to Nettie, who picked up her case and went without a goodbye kiss, but ducking into the front bedroom to kiss Hector, aiming at his cheek, but landing it on his nose since he turned his face too late to receive it.

Well, that's that, Nettie said to herself, safely in the mail car now, tearing towards Nowra. She snapped open her bag for another cigarette. She gave it everything, head back, black patent shoes with their high heels fidgetting to draw attention to them, skirt high enough for her knees to show in their fine silk stockings, a long white hand trailing over the back of the seat. A small boy in a improvised seat facing the car load rounded his eyes as she inhaled smoke and failed to exhale it. It's the drawback, she said silently and contemptuously, lowering her eyelids. These country clots have seen nothing. She leaned forward in her seat as if this would bring Sydney closer.

"Feels like time to get me up, Carrie one!" Hector called to the kitchen. There was nothing for a moment, then Carrie's swift hard heels brought her to the bedroom. She saw the side of the bed where her mother had slept, nearly as neat as when Carrie made it up the morning she went to hospital, only the pillow a little crooked.

She went around and tossed the pillow onto a chair and flung the quilt back over the foot of the bed. Hector felt the space the pillow left and his face mourned, but only briefly should Nettie be looking.

"I slept quite good last night," he said. "I didn't think I would."

Carrie had barely slept, sharing her bed with Nettie, the moonlight cruelly showing up in bright silver the lock on Nettie's case, standing upright near the door, anxious too to be away.

If Carrie looked away from it, it meant turning over close, too close, to Nettie's head on the pillow. She heard the grandfather clock in the front room strike midnight. Six hours to go before she could get up! She had to lie stiffly all that time, not moving lest she disturb Nettie. It had always been like that, Nettie the baby, favoured and pampered, then the smart little school girl, the best in history, arithmetic and parsing at St Joseph's. The nuns came to the house one afternoon to talk to Hector and Gertie about Nettie, encouraging them to keep her at school, suggesting a career in teaching or nursing.

Carrie (seventeen then) sat on the old cane chair on the veranda while they talked in the front room. The nuns dipped their hooded heads as they went past Carrie on their way out. In the years since Carrie had left St Joseph's, a new nun had taken charge who did not recognize Carrie, and the other nun did not like to, afraid she might appear to flaunt the authority of her superior. She lowered her eyes, watching the points of her black shoes flick at her habit, as she went down the steps. Carrie needed to grip the edge of her seat and rub at the rough cane to make sure she was real.

She swallowed now, releasing the tension of her jaws, moving her head slightly on the pillow. Nettie heard and flung herself over and gave a great contented sigh. The tears began to run down Carrie's cheeks. She will hear and think I'm crying for Mum, Carrie said to herself and cried without restraint until she fell asleep.

Here was Hector calling her. It did not sound different to the other mornings. (Gertie was three weeks in Bega hospital before she died.) I don't know why I think it should, Carrie thought, and went on solid feet but stopped in his doorway.

He was sitting up in bed, the covers raised to his chin.

His head sat as if unattached to a body. A child might have drawn the picture, the head egg-shaped, tilted unnaturally, eyelids down, features dead. Nettie made her feet loud going to him. He sprang to life, his face a question. Was she angry? She picked up one of his hands and laid it against his cheek. He clung to the cheek longer than necessary.

"Is it a nice day out there?" he asked.

"Nice enough for you to sit on the veranda." She laid a large white towel across the bedclothes. He stroked it, changing his expression as the texture changed from smooth to rough.

"Put on the shirt from yesterday," Carrie said. "There'll be people coming in."

He had only gone to the church, not the cemetery. He could not ride in a car since his blindness. "I feel like a cat in a bag," he always said.

She brought a dish of water, laid it on the towel, and when he was washed, removed the dish and used the towel to wipe him. Nettie had done the job the last two mornings, looking for methylated spirits to rub his buttocks and the backs of his legs, guarding against bed sores, she said, airing her knowledge of nursing and over-looking the fact that Hector did not spend more than the normal time in bed.

He was thinking of Nettie now, Carrie could see, feeling about for the second towel Nettie had used. All very well for her when she had only to throw the linen to someone else to wash.

"I heard the car go," Hector said. "I sang out but you were rattling them pans and things in the kitchen."

Carrie's feet, thudding around the bed, said she had no time for the luxury of listening to the mail car carry Nettie off. Hector's face was remembering the way Nettie walked, soft and slithery, like Gertie. Gertie had wanted to be a nurse and was happy to see Nettie become one. His words came out in tears, making a thin shiny line on his leathery cheeks. Carrie used the corner of the towel to wipe them.

"Old Mumma Fox," Hector said, as if he should explain his weeping.

Carrie flung the blind up and the sunlight slanted across the bed, making half his hand pale. He smiled as if he felt it. She was angry for a moment. He has no right to be happy, her heels said, going for his shirt in the wardrobe.

Nettie had put it away on a hanger, not straight, and the sleeves not unrolled, but just as it had been taken off. A great nurse I must say, if she is as thorough in everything else she does! Hector heard the air rush up her nostrils and the flapping of cloth.

"I'm going to iron your shirt," she said and saw his head go up and settle on the edge of the blanket and his features die as they did before.

In the kitchen she unrolled the ironing blanket and laid it on the end of the table, and took the iron from the back of the stove, wiping it clean with a hessian rag. The beeswax was on its saucer, glancing at her with its yellowish eye. Gertie always used it but the collar of Hector's shirt still carried its funeral shine. She moved the great black boiler a few inches and the beeswax eye was closed decisively.

She pulled the ironed shirt over Hector's head and he twisted about, helping it settle on his body.

"That Nettie one," he said. "Where would she be now?"

Carrie had never left Cobargo except for three days in Bega at the dentist's, staying with Gertie in a guest house, trying to imagine what it would be like with a job in an office or a shop, living all the time in a place like this, sliding in under the table at meal time, food coming

271

over her left shoulder in a pair of red hands, shutting her eyes briefly, then opening them to catch the full surprise, hoping for fat, pinky grey sausages, but not disappointed with whatever it was.

She sat on the veranda a lot of the time though, dabbing at her mouth where the two great teeth had left her jaw, Gertie getting impatient after a while, frowning at the constant dabbing and staring at the blots of blood and Carrie turning the handkerchief over to take a new blot.

"Surely it is done bleeding by this," Gertie said and Carrie, ashamed, held the blood and saliva in her mouth as long as she could, then rushed to the veranda edge to spit into a may bush, the tender white flowers trembling and scattering under the bloody onslaught, showing up so vividly Carrie was fearful that other people from the guest house would see.

"Come into the room," Gertie said and Carrie followed her stiff, cold back and sat there on a chair, carrying on the dabbing, suddenly hating the stiff, cold order of the room and longing to be home.

Hector was on the veranda having heard the mail car, and had lifted his head, the better to hear their footsteps on the road approaching the house.

Carrie ran ahead of Gertie and made a loud noise with the gate and saw his head go higher and his smile starting, then ran harder until she was on his knee and had hold of his hand, pushing his fingers into her cheek so that he could feel where the teeth had been.

"That old dentist man hurt you, Carrie one?" he asked. She lay the cheek on his shoulder and felt there would be no more pain there.

In the years that followed she frequently put her tongue into the hollows and rushed it onto the next tooth, relieved that it too had not disappeared. Sometimes, dancing with a new clerk at the bank or one of the Clancy boys, she

272

tried to keep her mouth from going full width in a smile. One side showed no gum, but the other, where the teeth were missing, did.

Carrie practised smiling before the mirror, allowing her mouth to reach only to the last tooth before the gap, but only occasionally remembered and then in the company of her sisters or other girls.

"See how *I* smile," Nettie said, drawing her lips back as far as they would go and showing all her teeth white and even with beautiful little picket edges. Hilda was there in the bedroom too, and made a great smile of her mouth, fingers in both corners to stretch it further. The strain made their eyes look crossed and cruel.

Carrie looked quickly in the mirror at her round tight mouth, then seized a brush and drew it down her hair in deep, hard strokes. The hair, thick and dark brown, crackled and hissed as it tried to cling to the bristles.

Nettie, who was sitting on the edge of the bed, rolled over, pulling the pillow from under its sham to bury her head in it. Hilda jumped on the bed and lay behind her, face in Nettie's back, both giggling.

"Carrie!" Gertie called from the kitchen and Carrie stared for quite a time at the bristles of the brush before laying it down to slide a clip into her hair to hold it from springing back from her cheek.

"Carrie!" Gertie called again, and the two on the bed rolled over in the one motion and sat upright with their cross-eyed, cruel look.

Carrie lowered her head and went slowly to the kitchen.

She went there quite briskly now, her heels clipping the linoleum.

She used one of them to drag the rug on the sitting room floor back a foot or two. Nettie of course! She had moved the furniture in the room to sweep behind it (a great show of thoroughness!) and had not put things back as they were. Hector would not know where he was! There was the little table with his and Gertie's wedding photo on it in front of the fender, not at the edge. Carrie lifted the table and set it down, Hector and Gertie wobbling and twisting the doily about. Carrie lifted the picture, smoothed the doily, and set it back in the centre, not at one end. She took the vase with violets in and put it on the mantleshelf; it did not belong on the little table.

The photographs were all wrong on the piano too. The baby photo of Hilda's first was behind the silver vase that had belonged to Gertie's grandmother, not in front where everyone could see it. The piece of Spode china Gertie always put the first spring daisies in was out of sight and in its place Nettie's graduation photo. The brass jardiniere, always in the centre of the chiffonier, had been moved to the end of the runner, and the pair of china horses, one with a flying tail and the other with a head against a foreleg, had been set apart. Carrie put them together with a grinding of porcelain.

The blind was raised high on the window. Nettie had left it that way after she hung the long lace curtains washed for the funeral. One trailed across the leather couch. Nettie had left the weights out of the hems. Where were the weights? She pulled open a chiffonier drawer, then rushed and lowered the blind to half way down the window, jerked it up then down again, sweat coming onto her forehead. Hector heard the noise the blind made like a tearing of cloth.

She went back to the drawer where the little stack of envelopes, the writing pad, and Hector's fountain pen, which he had won for taking out the most points in the

274

vegetable section at the Cobargo show when he had had his sight, had been disturbed by the violence of the tug. Nettie had been routing among them, of course she had! All that remained unmoved was the stack of Nettie's letters home, which Nettie had taken out the first day she was home and read through, then tied them up with a piece of ribbon from Gertie's sewing box, saying with a toss of her head that was the way her letters should be treated. Carrie seized the bundle and flung it onto the round table in the middle of the room, knocking over the picture of Hector's grandfather who had died in the Boer war.

The kerosene in a frail glass lamp sloshed about and the delicate mantle shook. Carrie set her mouth and looked about her, breathing in a strangled way. The sofa was not directly under the window, the rounded end too close to the front door. Hector could easily stumble against it coming in from the veranda. Carrie put a knee against it and sent it rushing towards the chiffonier, which was not flush with the corner but inches from it. What did she think you would do with the space left, nothing more than a harbour for dust? The chiffonier needed pushing into place but it was awkward with everything on it.

She began to take the things off with shaking hands. She piled them on the table, the lamp shaking again, the china horses upside down with the linen runner flung like a tent over their feet. Nettie had not ironed the runner very well; it needed to be done again. Carrie went to the kitchen and unrolled the ironing blanket again and dumped the saucer of beeswax beside it, staring back coldly at the yellow eye.

Hector coughed from the bedroom.

Oh, cough all you want, Carrie said silently, stretching the crochet with the point of the iron in a way that put an edge of pleasure to her anger. She smoothed it out

275

over the back of a black leather chair when it was done, her anger having risen again, for the chair was out of its place, too far forward from the fireplace. She sent it flying back to hit the bookcase and rattle the glass front.

"Carrie one?" Hector called in an anxious voice.

"It's that Nettie!" Carrie answered, laying the runner on the chiffonier and beginning to put the things back on it. The noise she made helped disguise her thick and choky voice. "She's got everything out of place in here! You'll fall over and get lost trying to find your way about!

"I'll see to you when I've fixed it up!"

"Take your time, Carrie one," Hector said, and began to feel about for Gertie's pillow, to put it back in place and get the feeling she wasn't gone.

He couldn't find the pillow and after a while rested his hand where she used to lie.

"Old Mumma Fox," he murmured under Carrie's noise.

16 Madge and Patty, Patty and Madge

Rene Rossmore wept a lot of the time in the latter part of 1935.

Stan did not go back to university and it was as if there were a death in the family.

Mrs Rossmore wept in the kitchen in front of the stove, watching for the milk to come to the boil, and on her way to the farm gate to collect the mail, which was dropped there with the empty cream cans from the butter factory, reminding her that there would be no more letters from Stan with the post mark of the university post office. She would start up at afternoon tea sometimes, seeing Stan in his old farm clothes and thinking of him in the neat trousers and shirt and jumper he wore as a student. Then her thoughts would turn to him in academic cap and gown, and she would turn her tear-blinded eyes to the piano where she would have placed his photograph, then leave the table and go without a word to her room, sometimes with the bad fortune of running into Jessie on the way, Jessie with a jug of water to refill the teapot.

Jessie would feel a rush of sympathy for her mistress, transferred to disapproval of Stan, so that her face in the dining room wore a drooped mouth for Mrs Rossmore and a heavy frown for Stan. Holding the teapot up, she would not look Stan's way, saying silently only Mr Rossmore was deserving of more tea and her services.

One of the great joys of Mrs Rossmore's life was visiting her family, the Murchisons, on their farm four miles from Cobargo, off the Wandella road. She could not drive the Studebaker and relied on Bert to take her and then her father to drive her home, or as was the happy practice in the first half of the year, Stan taking her there and back when he was home for holidays.

Mrs Rossmore was not so eager for the visits now. She went out of duty, not pleasure.

There was an unmarried sister of thirty-seven, Florence, with an inside soured like the small hard plums on the tree that grew by the Murchisons' farm gate.

Florence saw Rene well married, in a comfortable home with smart, good looking children. (Two years younger than Rene, she had thought of Bert as a marriage prospect for herself when they all went to the Cobargo dances.)

Florence barely hid her triumph that after twenty years there was trouble for Rene, a good dose of it too. But she kept up a pious look, bringing in the tea tray and a new marble cake, not missing the look Rene gave her in a moment of envy that she (Flo) had no trouble of this kind to contend with. About time, my lady, said Flo's navy poplin back returning to the kitchen.

"Flo's been in a black mood lately," Mrs Murchison said, by way of hinting at the troubles others had. She was disappointed Stan would not become a doctor too, but there was a time to stop grieving over it.

"She's real fond of the boy too." Mrs Murchison was not sure that Stan was the cause of Flo's mood, but glad she could place the blame somewhere.

"When Dad comes in I'll ask him to run me home," Rene said.

She had only arrived a couple of hours earlier, taking the cream lorry from Cobargo on its way back to Wandella where the man with the run, Cletus Campbell (more commonly known as Creamy Campbell), lived on his small property.

Rene found this an undignified way of travelling but she would not ask Stan to drive her, and she and Bert

278

were on distant terms, Bert beginning to ease out of his resentment of Stan, developing a grudging admiration of his work on the farm, and starting up a defensive attitude when Rene was on the subject of Stan's abandoning his career, or weeping about it.

Mrs Murchison did not urge Rene as she would have in former days to stay for the midday meal with them and have Vince drive her home before milking.

Enough's enough, she said to herself. Sprawled largely in her chair by the fireplace, she gave her attention to the crochet edge she was putting on a linen handkerchief (never forgetting her pleasure in needlework of this kind after the harsh early days when she was kept occupied darning and patching rough farm clothes) and not much to Rene, pressed to one side of her chair under the window.

She's got thinner, Mrs Murchison thought. My goodness, she did set great store by getting a doctor in the family. Mrs Murchison turned the corner of her handkerchief and smoothed it out on her chair arm.

"Flo!" she called in the direction of the kitchen.

Flo came almost without sound to put her frame, large like her mother's, but not yet running to fat, in the doorway. Her dark expression said you are not bringing me in here on some trivial matter like fetching you a new ball of cotton, I hope. Her hooded eyes, flashing once on Rene said there is the lady as usual, too full of her own importance to move off her seat. Well, she might think she is back in her own place with Jessie to order about but it's a different story here.

Mrs Murchison held the handkerchief well above the chair arm to study it, the needle a silver arrow threaded through her pudgy fingers.

"Bring a cup and sit in here for a while," she said.

"There's no need to rush dinner. Rene's going home when Vince gets in."

Rene a child again, being disposed of by her mother, tired of her sulks, fished between the cushion and the side of the chair for her handkerchief and snapped her handbag shut on it. Flo brought a cup and poured tea from the silver pot.

"You should use one of the pretty cups, silly girl," Mrs Murchison said.

Flo sat on the edge of a chair with a spoon shaped seat, a braid edge to the velvet covering. Hardly anyone used it. She sipped her tea and did not take any cake.

"The cake was very nice," Rene said.

"Wrap up the other half and take it for Stan and Madge," Mrs Murchison said. Her face went soft at the mention of her little grand-daughter. Rene immediately thought of Eric, the middle child, a plodding student, who would go to agricultural college from boarding school and then work with Bert. A new rush of tears had to be curbed.

"The farm won't provide work for three men," Rene said.

"Bert can do less," Mrs Murchison said, groping behind her for her ball of cotton. She had a genuine fondness for her son-in-law.

A spark lit Flo's dull, bold eyes. "You might be able to do without a sharefarmer," she said. That would bring you down a peg or two, said the tiny grind of china as cup met saucer.

Rene reached the window with a violent jerk of her body. She tapped the sill and frowned at the distance before sitting down again.

Mrs Murchison brought her crochet close to her eyes. "Flo should show you the new pansy out," she said. "Very dark brown and pale blue. Different to the rest. The beds were a great success."

Flo had most of the back yard under garden now, the recent extension of pansy beds encircling both clothes line posts. Her face though had a look as dark as the new pansy. She did not move and neither did Rene.

"Dad is slow," Rene said.

Mrs Murchison worked swiftly at the crochet. "Men! You can't depend on them!"

"Stan's a man now," Flo said.

"A child!" Rene said. "Nineteen, and doesn't know his own mind!"

"Vince was nineteen when we married, as you all know," Mrs Murchison said. "A pair of babes in the wood we were." The others did not speak. "And wood it was this place. We hacked a good farm out of it though."

We were always one step behind the Rossmores, said Mrs Murchison silently, stabbing hard at her handkerchief as if in punishment. But we caught up when Rene married Bert. She spread her big legs for comfort, contrasting with the slight discomfort inside.

If Stan had become a doctor there would be even pegging guaranteed. The first Cobargo born doctor and her own Rene's son. Her fat smooth face creased like a balloon going down. Her disappointment returned. Then she remembered Stan's round grey eyes, more watery than usual, swimming pleadingly towards her. Don't get on my back like the others Gran, they had said from the doorstep where he had sat in an old blue school shirt and worsted pants, once his Sunday best. It seemed that through wearing those clothes he was trying to obliterate the time at university, as if he had never been there, but stepped from boarding school in Goulburn to farming at Trangie. In a rush of compassion she had brought him a slice of lemon pie, one of Flo's best, the white of egg trembling on the yellow custard, soft and smooth, no dry skin to bite through, no teeth marks left in the gluey substance like the kind turned out by Rene and Jess, not the cooks Flo and her mother were.

Mrs Murchison thought briefly about asking Rene to send the boy across to visit her. Rene might have received some sort of signal, for she pressed her second best brown leather shoes together and moved her handbag to her knees, her eyes as cold and hard as its metal clip.

Dear me, that will have to wait, thought Mrs Murchison, knowing Vince was in sight by Rene's neck stretched briefly towards the window, and relief taking the glitter from her eyes, that said there was a long way to go before the end of Stan's punishment was in sight.

That was a signal too for Mrs Murchison. She rolled her needle and cotton inside the handkerchief and tucked them inside the sewing basket, moving it an inch or two with an expression that said, now don't give me away. And she brushed imagined fragments of cotton from her skirt. It was an old habit yet to die, for Vince had never approved of any occupation of a leisurely nature, like fine needlework or reading.

In a moment she rose and brought a cup and saucer from the sideboard, her movement doubting the errand was really her's, but the need to see to Vince's comfort given priority. She sighed deep in her heavy chest as she picked up the teapot. Flo sighed too, strangling the air in her throat and putting a hand there, going to the kitchen with mournful gait. She was back with a silver jug of boiling water, sighing too about its closed lid, when Vince came in.

He was a big square man with black hair hardly touched with grey, sweeping down on one side just missing an eyebrow, black too over an eye flicking towards Pearl, his wife, a little sullen, a little shy. Pearl gave him a look back, tender of eye, a little quirk of the mouth, not much different to forty years ago when he came in from clearing the land and she was making jam or pickles or bread, barefoot a lot of the time for they could not afford more than one pair of shoes, kept for best, her old dress strained across her stomach where he hoped a son was growing, but it was always another girl.

He reddened now and looked down, as in earlier times when the children were about and he was shy of showing his feelings in their presence. He sat on the unyielding chair Flo had used and twirled his old hat before capping it on his knee. Flo brought his tea and Pearl cut his piece of cake as if she alone knew the thickness to his taste. He was conscious of his daughters there, the only two left in Cobargo now, the others married, two in Sydney and two in Queensland. He remembered them as tiny children in this very room, leaving their game on the floor rug by the fireplace to climb on his knee for the brief time he was inside to drink his tea. He thought them a pair of beauties then, Rene in particular with that reddy gold hair and lips folded back showing the edges of her little white teeth and that light in her eyes giving the blue a glint like the sun through the wash house window on the blueing tub.

Her eyes did not shine now the way they used to. There was frost in them and the lips were rolled back in a small forced smile. The smile said she is ready to be driven home, Vince thought, picking up his cake.

"The cake did turn out well," Rene said to remind them she was taking some home. Madge would like a piece for school. But she saw Stan's teeth snapping greedily on the pink part.

"Oh yes," Mrs Murchison remembered and went to the kitchen. They heard the rip of greaseproof paper.

"There!" she said returning with the little parcel.

283

She felt Vince's eyes on her back. He was not pleased at the prospect of driving Rene home, taking time out from his work, a difficult ploughing job on a piece of land jutting into the creek where he would plant melons. He was taking a risk; heavy rain could erode a good part of it, bringing the crop to ruin.

He was inclined to blame Pearl when things went wrong. She was in favour of the melons, and it could all prove a waste of effort, and as it was they were late going in, spring being well on its way. Pearl could feel his eyes accusing her of arranging Rene's trip home, unaware she was being blamed for the melons too.

She went to the window where the new ploughing could be seen, an uneven piece of chocolate dropping into the blackberry and dogwood along the creek bank.

"Stands out now, Dad," Pearl said, bringing the teapot to refill his cup, then wondering aloud where Flo had got to, the answer given by Flo herself passing the back window with a bundle of sheets from the clothes line.

"Yes, it's coming up cloudy," Pearl said and sat on her chair again with her hands, pudgy and pale, hanging loosely from elbows resting on chair arms.

Useless, Vince thought, studying them. Pearl had given up working on the farm these twenty years. Once she would have seen the need to clear a good break around the new ploughing and would take a hoe and work among the rough growth. She would wear a big straw hat to protect her fair skin, which Rene had inherited. (Flo had been given Vince's dark, brooding looks but Ida, Stella, and Kathleen were light coloured too and the youngest, Edna, had hair streaked light and dark like toffee, as if signalling the end of the breeding programme and blending the genes of both parents.) A plump and pretty thing, Pearl would wield the hoe in tireless fashion, oblivious to blackberry branches pinning her by her dress, the sound of the hoe striking the earth like music to his ears when he stopped the plough.

There she was, stroking her fingers now, curling them and looking at the nails. That was something to come to, he supposed, admiring hands that did nothing.

He was getting on too, nearly sixty, but working on with no help, and she got it all, Flo gardening and baking and cleaning with a sullen passion. And Rene here who used to bring a sparkle to the place silent and sulky. Neither she nor her mother coming right out and asking him to drive her home. He was a good mind to take up his hat and just go back to the ploughing without saying anything either.

Of course it was the boy Stan. Giving up that doctoring business and wanting to stay at home and work on the farm. Then the next boy Eric home in a couple of years after studying (to be a farmer, God help us, when the earth and the rain and the sun and the wind were the best teachers). Overrunning Trangie with help while he was working like a dog running his place on his own, a gaggle of women (he chose to forget there was only Flo at home now) to be kept in their idleness.

He got up suddenly and picked up his hat, which had fallen from his knee. Pearl was startled, fluttering her hands as if looking for some occupation for them to appease him.

Vince pulled his hat on using both hands, momentarily obscuring his face so that the women did not catch his changed expression. By George, he might get hold of the boy for a week or two now and again! He would work well to prove he was right in giving up the doctoring. He would be especially good with sick animals. He was strong and healthy, in the prime of farming life. Vince saw him galloping off at his bidding to find a steer buried in the thicket of bush on the northern boundary of the farm where the mountain started, cutting the blackberries low with an expert hand on the scythe, then his foot steering the spade to the roots shaking every ounce of earth from them, setting up the dairy for separating, giving Vince more time at his afternoon tea.

He would be like the son Vince never had. He looked across at Rene, not able to keep from his face a look of triumph. Rene, unable to interpret it, got to her feet.

"As far as town will do," she said. "I can go to the stores for a few things." Or will I? Fred's face in Rossmore's store asking wordlessly about Stan, Frank Cullen throwing a mass of sausages on the butcher's block, reaching for his knife in the leather holder on his rump, eyes cast down, keeping from her the subject in them.

"I'll wait for you if you're not too long," Vince said.

Rene picked up the little block of cake, not really wanting to take it, no place in her life for anything sweet. "Drive straight through," she said. "There's nothing that can't wait."

Pearl raised her big face in gratitude to Vince. He was kind and good to the girls, despite their failing to be boys. She would have liked to kiss him before he left, but he didn't do that sort of thing if anyone was around.

She sighed but it was lost in her reach for her crochet. She was stabbing away with energy as the Buick was starting up.

Vince kept his thoughts on Stan on his way into Cobargo and over the bridge for the last mile to Trangie. Stan could ride across country and get to the Murchisons inside an hour. There were spare bedrooms if he wanted to stay. He would offer money, say, eight shillings for a day's ploughing. No, five would be good enough, seeing Stan was a close relative.

Here was a chance, too, for some new fencing, and a crop of potatoes farther up the creek on a flat he'd known would grow anything. He saw the waving deep green of the bushes and Stan pulling a pile of bags from the dray, ready for the digging and bagging. It might be worthwhile getting a small sized lorry, utility was the new fangled name for it, he had thought of it before but it seemed an extravagance unless it got a lot of use.

At odd times over the years he had employed men like Les Boyle and Barney Churcher for a week or two, but it was not successful, they couldn't work for any time without wanting to stop for smokes. They had no natural aptitude for farming. Stan would be different. Often he thought of getting a boy to work for his keep and a small wage, but he (the boy) would expect to be taken to the pictures and dances in Cobargo and would not be fit for early rising next morning, and after awhile, typical of youth, he would want to go to the city for an easier job, or start trying to tell Vince how the farm should be run. The growing girls would prove a distraction too. He could imagine them rushing through the milking to play rounders or hit a ball against the dairy wall, frivolous behaviour like that.

Stan was a different kettle of fish, anyone giving up city life and the chance to be a doctor would be in dead earnest about farming.

By the time the Buick was going through the Trangie gates Vince had Stan living permanently with his grandfather.

Madge flew across the veranda towards the car, looking for her grandmother in the back seat. When she wasn't there, Madge jumped back, balancing on the stones around a rose bed, concentrating on that activity, scowling towards her small feet in sandshoes.

It was the last day of the spring school holidays, a Monday, and Madge would have liked to have accompanied her mother to the Murchisons, but Creamy

Campbell sometimes had his young son on board, thus reducing seating space. Her scowl held the disappointment of missing the visit, and the discovery that her grandmother, who sometimes gave her threepence, had not made the trip to see her. Madge turned her little rump and ran with a flicking skirt into the house to sit on the kitchen step and watch Jessie, with her heavy hands in a basin of flour and suet, make a crust for the stew, which would be heavy too, unlike the tender feathery pale gold of her grandmother and Aunt Flo's pastry.

Jessie was ready as usual to discuss the mournful subject of Stan's giving up university.

"He's not goin' back then," she said, not bothering to disguise the relish, as it was only young Madge she was addressing.

Madge rubbed a cheek on a raised knee, her gaze on the top of the lemon tree. There were two lemons there, large and a rich yellow, pointing nipples towards the sky. Always the best fruit is high up like that, Madge thought, wondering if her father would take a ladder and bring it down.

Or perhaps Stan. Her face shot from her knees. She saw Stan's gingerish head with its tight curls up there, and staring at the tree she almost expected the head to bob out of the foliage and his strong and sure hand reach up and close around the fruit. Stan could climb to the top of the apricot tree and get the big rosy cheeked fruit before the birds, his reach would be the longest when they gathered blackberries, and his step the strongest, crushing the prickly branches, the ones that swung and gripped the hair and shoulders of Jessie and herself. Stan, at home now all the time, could do all of those things!

Madge stood imprisoning her energy in her skinny frame, hardly able to stop its trembling.

"Where is Stan?" she cried.

"Somewhere breaking his mother's heart," Jessie said, pressing the dough on the saucepan of stew, not laying it there lightly and tenderly as she should. She took her head out of the stove recess and turned a face, made darker with blood rushed to it, the hairs across her upper lip and her knitted eyebrows standing out more.

Madge wondered why Jessie cared so much about Mrs Rossmore's suffering as a result of Stan's behaviour. She had thought Jessie resented her mistress, and had once caught Jessie elevating her face and making a sniffing shape of her nose at Mrs Rossmore's back when Mrs Rossmore sailed out of the kitchen after ordering Jessie to do some extra work.

Madge dusted down her small backside and leapt with a giant step to the ground. Never-mind the steps, never mind Jessie, or her mother for that matter, she would find Stan somewhere in one of the paddocks, he wasn't riding his horse, there looking mournful under a poplar, so he couldn't be far.

Madge ran and climbed the house paddock fence, deciding to walk it from the gate down the dip which gave her a sight of the Jusseps' roof top and chimney with smoke trailing lazily skywards.

She had walked ten panels once without losing her balance. It would be good to do eleven or twelve and tell Patty Jussep when she saw her next day at school.

Beside one of the panels outside the house paddock was a heap of rubbish, rusted kerosene tins, some saucepans with holes in them, an old pudding boiler rusted through in several places, so long in the one position dandelions sprouted through the holes. There was a heap of bottles, a lot of them broken, grass muffling them so that glinting green edges could just be seen like sharp cruel teeth constantly parted, ready to cut into flesh and send blood spurting.

Madge stopped and stared on them, teasing her body, teetering it, thinking of her sandshoes losing their grip. She imagined hitting the glass and sharp edged tin with a cry, her back and shoulders pierced, great jagged pieces in her waist, her legs, her round little bum rapidly bathed in blood.

There she lay dying, looking up at the sky, ready for an angel to swoop from a parted cloud, to descend and lift and carry her off. The angel's wings would be like great harps spread out, and Madge's hair would be streaming out (in reality it was tight and frizzy). When she and the angel were gone, the hair would be left, swirling about refusing to dissolve, more beautiful than Mary Jussep's hair.

Perhaps she wouldn't die this way. She would be denied her mother's wailing and remorse. Patty would come upon her as she was breathing her last, and cry out for Stan, who would gallop up, and both would carry her in a desperate dash to the house. Madge looked at the empty slope surprised not to see the two figures, Patty crying in her wild grief holding one of Madge's hands while she ran, barely able to keep up with Stan's manful strides. She would live, only just, and whisper through dry pale lips that Patty was to stay at her bedside or she would surely die.

Madge looked down on the glittering teeth of the broken bottles, opening and shutting jaws (but it was the grass moving in the wind that gave the illusion) and she felt cold and her skin crept. Suddenly she made a great jump, landing close but safe. I fell walking the fence, she would tell Patty at school tomorrow. I prayed while I was falling and this angel turned the broken glass the other way and I didn't get a scratch.

Patty was wonderful. She never said you're a liar Madge

Rossmore or oooh aaah you'll go to purgatory if you don't confess that to Father O'Malley.

Exhilarated, Madge tore with great speed towards the creek bank. It's true, it's true, isn't it true, she said to the sky, daring a scowling angel's face to appear. She was sure she would find Stan somewhere, tightening the wire of a fence with pliers or walking at the edge of the young corn that seemed to grow while you watched, a green sea Madge often thought of plunging in, threshing her arms among the foliage, cool to her face, smooth as silk the way it was for a short time, before the leaves broadened and coarsened as the stalks grew taller.

She hoped every new season promising heat like this one her mother and father would ask Patty to come with them to the seaside at Bermagui after Mass on a Sunday. She had suggested it only once. Her mother had rolled her lips right back from her teeth and made her eyes round in a kind of frantic anger. To Madge's surprise she seemed greatly concerned about the feelings of the other Jussep children, if Patty went with them to the sea.

"All those other poor little things wilting in the heat would be so envious it would spoil the girl's day!

"It wouldn't serve any good at all!" Madge went red and felt deeply ashamed at her thoughtlessness.

"The big girl takes them to the creek, before the milking, I've seen them," Mrs Rossmore said, very comfortable in this thought. Her face went back to normal and she devoted herself briskly to folding the linen, smoothing the edges of the towels right out, making Madge wonder about the Jusseps' towels, whether there were enough for them all and where they were kept, since the Jussep house was so much smaller than the Rossmores' and there were so many more people in it.

"In my whole life I have only been to the Jusseps' once," Madge once told their grey and white cat, so old now its

291

sides were floppy, its coat hanging over its frame like a mat on a clothes line. It curled up in odd places, a hollowed out bed under the may bush, around the leg of a chair, not on it as it used to, as if preparing for death, and expecting certain discomforts, thought it wiser to prepare for them.

Madge stood now boldly in front of a young heifer standing in wind-blown grass, showing its unconcern and refusal to move out of her way by swinging its dark slobbery lips over a tussock, keeping its black eyes upturned on Madge.

"You wouldn't dare charge me!" she cried. "You wouldn't dare move a foot forward in my direction!"

The heifer flicked its ears and turned its eyes another way as if such a statement could never come from Madge, it must be another voice somewhere.

"Stan would kill you with one mighty blow!" she cried. "He could lift a fence post with one hand and" (she raised an arm and waved it above her head and the heifer's eyes followed the movement, surprise expressed that Madge was fitted with limbs) "and smash it across your neck and break it clean in two!"

The heifer gave its neck a shake as if to prove its intactness and its intention of remaining so.

"Oh you stupid thing!" Madge said. "Cows are stupid, all cows are stupid, and you are more stupid than the rest!"

She began crying as she ran, glancing back, half hoping the heifer would pursue her. She looked for Patty up the dry creek bed; perhaps she would be there looking for jacks and there would be this wonderful, accidental meeting.

The creek was almost dry due to little late winter rain, only a shallow pool at the bend quite a way up towards the Jusseps' orchard which ran down to the bank.

Madge's eyes enlarged the pool. It became a lake with little slapping waves, a boat there, she and Patty in it, oars idle along the sides.

Patty stands to save an oar from slipping into the water and falls in herself, sinking to the bottom, then the water parting to show a wild, frightened, pleading face. Madge dives in cleanly as an angel flies, and with an arm around Patty strikes out for the shore, Patty limp but alive and Stan running to wade out to meet them, lifting them both in his arms, carrying them to the shore. Mrs Rossmore appearing, wringing her hands, assorted Jusseps running down the bank from the direction of their house, her grandmother arriving with a big hamper of cakes and pies cooked as only she and Aunt Flo could, and this wonderful picnic following, races too, her father handing out sixpences to winners, little Jusseps clenching their fists on the first money they ever had to themselves, in the end Patty coming home to the Rossmores', staying the night and every night after that, yes, Madge's sister, a discovery made that they were full blood sisters (she would reason this out some other time).

There she was.

Up the creek bed there beyond the pool, a lake no longer, a stick in her hand prodding at the sand.

Madge felt her throat too tight to call out. When she began to, Patty turned her head to the bank where wattles grew in a low sprawl. Madge saw by the lift of Patty's head and the disinterested drag of the stick that Patty was watching for someone or something.

It was Stan.

He leapt across the end of the sprawl, bogging a little in damp sand, waving his arms about, pretending to sink. Patty twirled her stick and Madge sensed her laughter. Patty went to him while he was bent over and putting a leg across his back sat there holding a shoulder. He

293

raised himself, putting an arm behind him to hoist her higher. She twirled the stick as a whip is cracked and he jogged forward, sending her straight white hair flying up and down, the strands not parting, like a tiny sheet on some unseen clothes line bobbing away joyful in its pegless state.

Madge was very still, watching. Stan turned his jog into a run to take him halfway up the bank on the opposite side. There were taller wattles there and he caught hold of some fronds to help his balance. Patty dug her stick into the earth to help too. Near the top of the bank Stan turned, tipped her off, sitting her neatly down with legs dangling.

And saw Madge.

"Yoo hoo!" he cried, cupping his hands to his mouth, although there was no need to, she was only a few hundred yards away.

Patty leapt from her seat, her energy carrying her with great speed back down the bank, her body held back so that it wouldn't tumble over her feet, which slithered and slipped over stones and roots then pounded the sandy stretch to reach Madge. Her cheeks were blown out scarlet and moist.

"You look funny," Madge said, her eyes glinting the way her mother's did. "All red in the face and that white hair." She picked up a long stick like Patty's and drew some lines in the sand. She looked up and around the landscape but not at Patty. "If a bull saw you it might charge you, thinking your face was a red rag."

Patty's face blanched, some of the red slow to fade. "Now you're all spotted," Madge said. "You might have measles." She took a couple of careful steps backwards. "My mother wouldn't allow me near anyone with measles." She drew some marks in the sand, angry deep grooves. "Especially a Jussep." Then she examined the end of her stick, sand clinging to it.

Patty looked back to Stan on the bank with his boots off, shaking the sand from them.

"Mary went into town for more bread," Patty said. She swung her face, red again, back to Stan, ashamed that she was betraying him, who she knew had come to see Mary.

"You would need a lot of bread," Madge said, scorn as deep as the hole she made with her stick, waggling it to send it deeper.

"Mary didn't bake enough," Patty explained gently.

"Ten children is too many for the one family," Madge said. Then it was her turn to avert her face. Mrs Jussep had the ten children and died. It sounded like speaking ill of the dead, a venial sin, and needing to be confessed.

Patty was trying to imagine a smaller family, subtracting Bernie, Joseph, Nina and Peter, making her the youngest, but left still with the embarrassing number of six, twice that of the Rossmore family. The four young faces slipped into her vision, eyes hurt and puzzled, and tears came to her own.

Stan was now on his way to them, as if a school boy again, walking the log that lay halfway across the creek bed, sitting down and slipping both hands under his thighs. He smiled on sight of their faces. They're having a little fight, he thought, tenderness running into his eyes. Madge moved back and sat on the log too, causing him to question with his eyes the space between them. He patted it and looked at Patty. Madge moved down, jamming herself close to Stan, scratching the sand energetically with her stick as if this might disguise her action.

Stan patted his other side. Patty gave her head a little shake and this caused him to smile deeper. He put one

295

arm around Madge and hooked the other above the log. Patty seeing the hollow and feeling for the ache in Stan's arm rushed forward and wriggled close to his side. Stan squeezed them both.

Tom and Gordon and Malcolm were Patty's older brothers. They did not put their arms around her and neither did her father. He carried Peter about a lot and sometimes nursed Joseph or Nina. The others tried to remember if he had shown them similar affection, thinking it a great pity that Nina and Joseph and Peter would most likely not remember either.

It was Mary who sometimes lay with them on the bed in the good room and read, with a story book propped up against her raised thighs, Patty usually turning the pages, for Mary's arms were occupied in holding Nina, Joseph and Peter to her stomach and sides.

Patty almost cried at being in Stan's arms. She smelled his shirt, a clean soap smell that might have come partly from his body, the coolness leaving the shirt and a warmth taking over after her cheek had lain against it for a while. The flesh was just soft enough, the ribs just gently hard. This was how she could lie forever, she looked lazily up the creek bed, and turned her eyes without moving her head to the hills, the one gum tree on a rise with four of the cows under it, the wind blowing their tails. Ginger, Buttercup, Grace and Freda, she said to herself, loving them.

She loved everything really. Every single thing in the whole world, making sure her glance went nowhere near Madge. She pressed her cheek harder into Stan so that a warm little fire came back, and she was sure her cheek would be a deeper pink when she lifted it. Not that she intended to.

But suddenly Stan's body changed with the twitch he gave it. It was like watching a warm still pool, then a wind springing from nowhere and sending ripples on the surface, a thousand eyes glinting cruelly, saying see, things don't stay the way you want and there is nothing you can do about it, and the water goes on crinkling and lapping and slapping the edge of the sand, darkening suddenly, cold too, discouraging hot feet, threatening to bite and chill, rather than soothe.

That was like the space that rushed between her body and Stan's. Looking up she saw his face had left her.

It was Mary.

Mary on her horse Jock, having ridden through the sharefarm gate, as it was called. It was not really a gate, just a panel of the fence, one end bound around a light post, which could be lifted away when a hoop of wire was removed, attaching it to the sturdy post of the next panel.

Few took that way on foot, preferring to go another half mile to the main Trangie gate then around the base of the hill on the cartwheel tracks. But Jock took the rough, partly cleared land in his sure footed stride, flying over rocky patches sprouting saltbush in the crevices, spraying his body expertly around the clumps of wattles, snorting pollen laden branches out of the way, in the clear breaking into a gallop, saying here I go now at full pelt with my beloved Mary.

But Mary pulled the reins, Jock's neck curved like black rubber. She didn't want the bread flung about, still warm from Crusty's oven in the two sugar bags, their tops tied together hung across the front of the saddle.

She set Jock walking across the ridge above the creek, outlining her against the sky, her body straight, her old shirt and breeches given an elegance by the distance, Jock looking the thoroughbred he wasn't, as if at any moment he might rear up and paw the air with his forefeet.

She pulled him up and he turned and faced the creek,

tail and mane beaten about by a tugging wind, and she seemed exhilarated there, as if backed by a wave from a sea roaring behind her, darts of sunlight the spray, or perhaps it was sparks from her bright hair.

Stan was on his feet, already two or three paces from the log.

"Woa!" he cried, as if he should make sure Jock did not gallop off. Then his feet grew wings and he ran. Stones and sticks flew and crushed blackberries were too slow in raising quivering stalks to catch his clothes. The sun made a fiery ball of his head, as it did to Mary's. He vaulted the bank almost with a somersault and straightening up seemed very tall and walked not fast but with big steps until he reached Mary, stroking Jock's head and appearing to give all his concentration to that.

Patty thought this amusing, and forgetting, turned to Madge for her reaction. Madge with a tight little face put out an arm and covered the space where Stan had left. Patty dropped her stick and the two skinny little arms touched. They sprang apart as if the log were on fire.

Patty returned her gaze, hot and pink to Stan and Mary. Stan flung himself on Jock behind Mary, the raised saddle end separating their bodies, Stan beating at the rim with mock frustration, Mary putting a head back and laughing.

Patty wanted to, but didn't dare put her head back and laugh too. Madge stood on the log, looking down at her sandshoes.

"They're new," Patty said, keeping her eyes on them as if they would answer her.

"I got them 'specially for the holidays," Madge said. It wasn't easy for Patty to fit her bare feet under the log but she tried.

Both little faces wearing almost identical expressions, partly tense, partly disinterested, were directed towards

Stan and Mary, who were growing smaller as the distance swallowed them up and growing closer together as if Jock's saddle had been magically removed.

"Stan will be terribly late for dinner," Madge said. "Jessie has it almost cooked."

"If you like I'll walk with you as far as your place," Patty said.

The barely scuffed sandshoes turned on the log and balanced on their toes. They began to walk towards the end. Patty sprang up, her feet patting the log, softly but urgently. Madge climbed the big roots at the end to jump neatly onto a piece of rock.

Patty jumped too, landing beside her. The two little arms scraped together again. Neither pulled hers away.

17   The Wedding

Stan and Mary were married on the first Saturday after Christmas. It was very hot weather, but fortunately the time for the wedding was ten o'clock in the morning, so the day still carried the cool edge it began with, the roses in the bed near the church porch turning their faces, smeared with dew, on the bride.

Mary noticed the beds freshly weeded, guessing correctly it was the nuns who had done it, since school had been out these past two weeks for the Christmas holidays, and care of the church, convent and school gardens were part of gardening lessons for all but the very youngest pupils.

Mary's lovely stretched smile grew deeper at the thought of Sister Joan and Sister Paula working in heavy habits in all the heat to have it nice for her and Stan. They had filled the church with roses too, and maidenhair fern and asters of such a tender blue Mary wanted to cry at the sight of them. The nuns did not come to the wedding, and Mary wondered if they wanted to, thinking of this as she stepped from the gravel onto the wooden floor inside the porch. She had glimpsed Sister Joan dusting window sills on the church side of the convent. I think she was there to see me, Mary thought, a little ashamed of her vanity.

There was so much joy, everywhere she looked, down at her dress, at her brothers and sisters filling two pews, her father's profile as he waited to give her away (a handsome man still!). The women's hats were like flowers in a field, never were the colours more brilliant in the church windows. It was the sun of course, shining brighter than ever before.

There was too much happiness, she would have to temper it.

Think of Mum, think of Mum. But Stan was up there in a shaft of sunlight, making his hair quite red, sneaking his head around to make sure she was coming, and then she thought only of him, how young he looked, more like a son than a husband, and to save a rush of tears looked down on the satin moulded so perfectly over her young breasts.

"Flo excelled herself with that dress," a Parsons matron whispered to her sister Edna, widowed these ten years and living with her, justifying her keep by sewing for the family, occasionally making a dress for one of the towns-women, bravely trying to follow instructions on style and humiliated later on to see the dress in the town, altered and bearing only a slight resemblance to the original work.

But that wedding dress, Edna Fowler decided, the handiwork of Flo Murchison, renowned for her skill with cooking spoon, gardening fork, and sewing needle, would not be so perfect close up. When she got a chance she would study the neatness of the placket, and those pintucks, they would not all be straight and the same distance apart, and if you counted them there would most likely be more on one sleeve than the other.

She pulled her mouth into a smile of anticipation and looked bright about the eyes, causing her sister to think poor Edna is enjoying the wedding after all, and she thought it might have brought back memories of her Sam and their marriage in this very church, Sam still suffering war injuries after serving on Gallipoli, and dying a year afterwards. Mrs Parsons heaved a contented bosom, then had to straighten her lace jabot, Edna failing to get it to sit properly, and she decided that since Edna was going to be alright, she would enjoy every moment of the wedding and would start with a good scrutiny of the pews on the groom's side, notably Rene Rossmore in a green silk costume sent from Sydney by her sister Ida, seen passed across the post office counter by her Lorna, who recognized the handwriting, having gone to school with Ida, and this in spite of the great thick glasses Lorna wore and the general prediction that she would be blind before she was forty.

With the green, Rene wore a pale yellow straw hat. Mrs Parsons thought hard on the source of the hat, never having seen it in Rossmore's or the other general store in Cobargo, and decided it might be the fruit of a shopping trip to Bega, probably bought at the same time as the blue linen with the sailor collar on little Madge.

The shady brim of Rene's hat toned down the glitter in her eyes. Their expression worried Madge, who was looking up into her mother's face from time to time. Then she decided not to look when Mary passed and there was the back of her neck under her veil like thick cream with a gauze covering, and those wonderful high sleeves where the pintucks started at the shoulders like little mountains with ridges of snow, each peaked exactly like the other.

There was her Aunt Flo, sitting with closed eyes, lips moving in prayer, the dark wings of her hair more forward on her cheeks, not drawn right back as they usually were, on account of the importance of the wedding, Madge supposed. Aunt Flo wasn't looking at her handiwork, which Madge thought very noble of her. If she, Madge, had made those buttonholes and those beautiful, almost invisible stitches on the hem, whispering softly around Mary's ankles, she would not have been able to tear her eyes away for a moment.

Cobargo was surprised that Flo made Mary's dress, and indeed most things about the wedding surprised Cobargo.

That it happened only six months after the death of Mrs Jussep gave rise to speculation on Mary's physical state.

In town shopping for material for dresses for Joyce, Patty, and Nina, and with shoes passed down from the older boys to the younger ones to be given to Arthur Clarke for mending, Mary's face and body were studied for any sign of impending motherhood. There were none, but this did not satisfy.

"She'd have to be in a family way," Mrs Phillips said to Grace, wishing Grace was smart enough to snare a Rossmore. She had just served Mary with a little pack of invitation cards and was trying to work out whether or not Mary was intentionally keeping her stomach out of the way with the help of the shop counter.

All eyes were on Mary, in town now more frequently than before, noting her shy but authoritative air, especially when she went with Stan to the house in a street off the Bermagui Road where she and Stan were to live.

The house belonged to Harry Rossmore and there had not been anyone in it for more than a year. Harry was very pleased to get ten shillings a week rent, on top of his pleasure that Bert was brought down a peg or two with Stan's giving up university. Harry's children were much younger, his eldest slow, the nuns said, but good natured and honest, and he would go to boarding school anyway to see what the Brothers could do for him. Harry had great hopes for his youngest, who loved nothing more than copying words from his sister's primer onto a broken slate he favoured among all the children's playthings. He was not yet six and would be starting school after the holidays. Sister Joan, who taught the infants, was excited already at the prospect of having him in her class.

The house had four main rooms, a hallway and veranda back and front. From Rossmore's store Stan had bought a chest of drawers that Fred had kept in stock nearly as long as he had run the shop. Fred had used the drawers for storing short ends of material, and traced linen with complicated designs no one wanted to embroider, and some great heavy damask tablecloths no one could afford.

No one could afford the chest of drawers either, and Bert reduced the price to be well rid of it. Mary thought it beautiful, and it was the first piece to go into the house, and she laughed out loud when she came upon it against the wall in what was to be their bedroom. It was a lovely silky brown thing with two square drawers at the top, between them three smaller ones, and underneath three big deep ones.

Mary though it made the coming wedding and honeymoon and life with Stan real at last. It looked like a person, warm and solid and kind, there like a chaperone with legs like fat carrots that did not bother growing into the usual tapering shape.

Mary was holding one of the knobs when Stan came in.

She threw her face over her shoulder to him, smiling, asking him to love it as she did. Oh, please love our beautiful chest, said her eyes.

Stan's eyes passed over it briefly, holding both his elbows lightly, then looking everywhere else in the room and upwards to the ceiling.

Do I wait for him to come and put his arms around me, or do I run to him, Mary thought, stroking the wood around the knob and loving the perfection of the little brass keyhole underneath. The thought of locking their clothes from each other made Mary laugh.

When she looked at Stan she half expected him to be laughing too at the absurdity of it.

But he had turned his face to stare at some sunlight slanting from the window in bars filled with little gold flecks.

Once as a little girl she had put her hand in a bar of sunlight like that and when she took it away cried out to her mother to look at the gold dust there.

But her mother had taken her hand and rubbed it and showed her how the sun had just shown her freckles up, and there wasn't any gold, just dust, and she had better go and bring a broom.

If Stan believed there was gold in the sunlight, she would believe it too.

"Stan!" she cried, and he turned his face to her. No gold on that face. No sunlight. Round eyes watering, hungry, ungentle. A stretched mouth she wanted to rush up to and pinch at the corners to make it softer, kinder. The mouth was less soft, even when he ran his tongue around his lips. Like his mother's mouth, Mary thought, and looked back to the chest of drawers for comfort.

"Mary!" he said and held his arms tighter to his body. Then he half turned to where the sunlight was painting bars upon the floor.

We'll lie down there, said the little tilt of his head.

Mary shook hers just as lightly.

"You'll be mean with it! Mean! Won't you?" Stan said.

"Oh, no!" Mary said, shocked.

"You will!" Stan all but shouted.

Mary covered her face with her hands but the sound of Stan slamming down the window made her remove them.

The sill had pinned inside a branch of a fuschia bush. The little pink and purple bells bounced in protest. Mary rushed and lifted the window to free them.

"Oh, poor, poor flowers!" she said, touching the bruised stalk and crumpled leaves. "They'd be the first thing we'd see waking in the morning," she said, almost pleading.

She went to him and put her arms around him, and shut her eyes not to see his face.

Wait a little while. Wait for my sake.

She opened her eyes and saw the folded back lips like his mother's.

"For your mother's sake," she murmured.

He pushed her roughly by the shoulders.

"Who's she?" he said.

Mary stepped back from him. Who's she? A mother, Stan. I don't like her but I'll try. I'll be a mother too. Who's she?

"Words are such cruel things," she said and turned away so she only heard his angry steps ringing through the empty room and thudding across the earth outside.

She broke the branch of fuschia off at the bruised part. Some of the little bells had been crushed. They drew their purple skirts across their pink heads in shame and put out little dry and hungry tongues and licked her arm.

She ran to the back tank. There was Stan standing in a wilderness of grass near the fence where she had planned a vegetable garden. He turned his face at the rush of water but turned it quickly away again.

She had found a rusted jam tin on the tank-stand and put the fuschias in that and hurried into the kitchen and looked around to put them somewhere.

There were no benches and the window sill was too narrow for the tin and the stove recess too low to set them on the stove.

Is this the way I put the first flowers in my house, she thought, running to the front.

She dropped the tin at the edge of the veranda and sat near it trembling and gathered her skirt around her legs.

There was Stan's truck by the front gate, like a tiger crouched. She got up quickly seeing it ready to spring on her.

She ran along the veranda and out the side gate (a house with two gates had seemed such a wonderful thing) and set out down the road still running, then slowed to a walk since someone might be watching and think her behaviour peculiar.

There were a few houses to pass and old Mrs Hanrahan lived in one of them. She saw the blob of blue that was Mary in her old voile, which Mary intended to pass on to Joyce, with new dresses in her trousseau for the honeymoon in Sydney, but now Mary, looking down at the dress, was unable to imagine it anywhere else but on her.

Mrs Hanrahan came to her front gate, her face screwed against the sun and an effort to disguise her penetration of Mary's figure.

"Gettin' your dress and everything ready?" Mrs Hanrahan said, darting her eyes on Mary's waist and telling herself it was thickening.

A little grand-daughter, visiting for the weekend, ran down the path to press her face between the palings of the gate. "I sit near Patty in school," she said.

"You'll have to say 'Mrs Rossmore' to Mary soon," Mrs Hanrahan said, her tone suggesting that she would have the right to continue using the Christian name.

She was not going to the wedding, for in spite of the Irish sounding name she was not a Catholic Hanrahan. The grand-daughter was.

Earlier on when the first Hanrahan settled in Cobargo to farm, his only son married a Scottish girl, causing bitter family dissension, the Hanrahan "turning", as Cobargo said, under the influence of his wilful red haired wife. There were several sons of the marriage who founded a local Presbyterian church, then a younger one, born twenty years after his brothers, who married a Catholic, another strong minded woman who stipulated that he turn too, or there would be no marriage.

307

This caused a family split in the new generation, and there was no end to the wrangling and confusion, Lillian Hanrahan keeping the flag flying with her bitter outbursts against all Protestants, mainly her mother-in-law. She allowed her daughter Rachel to stay in town with her grandmother at weekends sometimes, or during a stretch of wet weather (the Hanrahan farm being two miles from Cobargo), making sure she had her catechism (which Rachel had not yet learned by heart), and instructions not to remove the scapular around her neck, even at bath-time, for once in old Mrs Hanrahan's hands it would surely be thrust into the heart of the stove fire.

"She'll burn in hell the same way it does, mark my words if she doesn't," young Mrs Hanrahan said to Rachel, who thought her mother must have amazing fore-sight to know the fate of her grandmother after death. Although she repeated the sentence to herself several times, she couldn't be sure whether old Mrs Hanrahan would burn or not burn, but was pretty sure her mother meant she would.

The grandmother would have loved nothing better than to be a wedding guest. But when it was a Catholic occasion, as in this case, it was usual to bypass all Hanrahans, Catholic and Presbyterian. Young Mrs Hanrahan blamed the defecting Hanrahans for her omission (she was a schoolmate of Rene Rossmore), in particular her mother-in-law who was perhaps the most tolerant of the non-Catholic Hanrahans, and who planned to dress herself neatly and stand outside St Joseph's, and watch the bridal party arrive and depart.

And indeed (the grandmother had just decided this) she would go through her china and glassware in the good cabinet and find a piece, something fine and pretty like Mary herself, and take it to the house before Stan and Mary returned from their honeymoon.

"That's something we can do now," Mrs Hanrahan said, hurrying back inside with Rachel following. Rachel jumped ahead on the veranda step and raised a questioning face.

"We can find some nice little thing in the good cabinet for Mary and Stan."

Rachel clapped joyful hands.

"Mary will need everything she can get, with all she'll have on her hands very soon," Mrs Hanrahan said darkly. "Life's no fairytale, little miss, as you'll find out for yourself one day."

Rachel looked up the street to the innocent house Mary and Stan would occupy and then the other way to Mary's blue back slipping out of sight.

"Don't let on to your mother," Mrs Hanrahan said, dipping into the big blue jardinere on top of the cabinet for the key. "I might give Mary something she has her eye on."

Rachel knelt in ecstasy before the cabinet. Silver and crystal and china so fine you could nearly see through it was heaped on the shelves. There was a jug, coloured gold with a deep blue band around the middle. The sun made it a fiery dazzling thing when it was held up, sending out darts from the scroll where the handle joined the body and making the little gold cottage, set on the blue, stretch out and run back as if it were alive.

But this wasn't Rachel's favourite. A mustard pot on three little legs of a paler blue covered with the smallest white daisies in the world, and salt and pepper shakers to match was what she wanted her grandmother to give Mary. Mary would love them. Rachel held her breath while old Mrs Hanrahan picked over the pieces, rubbing some against her skirt to free them of dust, looking for cracks or chips, though handling them so carelessly Rachel was surprised she wasn't responsible for a few herself.

She put a fingernail in a crevice of a cut glass jug scraping at dust there.

"It all wants a good wash," she sighed, sitting the jug inside a vase, also cut glass, and also marked with dull brown lines. She shut the cabinet door so suddenly Rachel had to jump back to save jamming her face.

"You should get into your room and learn that catechism," Mrs Hanrahan said. "Else she'll be blaming me if you don't know it."

Rachel sat back on her heels, staring at the little heap of daisy patterned china that would not be Mary's after all. She should have prayed for her grandmother to leave it out on the floor. She missed her chance while her grandmother was fingering it. But she was never sure about prayer involving her grandmother, whom her mother called a devil ridden Presbyterian. It would probably be a waste of time. She stood and straightened her old play tunic and went to get her catechism.

Mary started to cry when she was a short way from the Hanrahans. Then she broke into a little run and slowed to a walk again, thinking how foolish she would look if anyone saw her. She began to search her body for her handkerchief but she had left it in a little white heap beside the tin with the fuschias in it. More tears fell at the thought of the flowers there left to die.

When she had her eyes clear again she had turned the street corner and was in sight of Rossmore's corner.

There near the bowsers was a horse and sulky she knew belonged to the Murchisons. Either Mrs Murchison or Flo had come to town, neither drove the car, Vince not allowing any of the women to learn, Mrs Murchison because she did not have any sons, and the daughters because they were all girls.

Mary felt cold suddenly, surprising her on the hot November day, wondering at the chill rushing up the sleeves of her blue voile. When it's hot you want it cool and then the cool is too cold, Mary thought, watching the black, drooping Murchison horse and the baking sulky seat.

Flo came out of the store then with Fred Rossmore, who always treated anyone connected with the Rossmores in a special way. He carried a parcel of groceries and laid them almost reverently on the floor of the sulky. Mary, walking in the middle of the road, knew he saw her. He was giving a lot of attention to the parcel, moving it about and feeling that nothing breakable was in contact with anything sharp and hard on the floor of the sulky, and Flo's eyes were following its movements and giving it a few little pushes and pats too. When she stepped back to put a foot on the sulky stirrup, she stepped even farther back and put a hand on a hip to stare at Mary coming closer and putting on her stretched smile. Fred rubbed his hands together and turned, even more brisk and businesslike than usual, and went into the shop. Well, don't bother with me, Mary thought, hurt by the rejection, but glad there was only one to face.

She hastened her steps unconsciously, then slowed them. There I go, doing their bidding. Well, I won't. I'm blowed if I will! Flo's dark face was darker with her curiosity. The wider Mary smiled, the deeper Flo frowned.

And remembered. Those dances twenty years ago, trembling before the mirror at home, getting ready, thinking her eyes looked nice, bright brown under her good eyebrows, looking sharper too, the lamplight kind to her sallow skin. Bert would be there, asking her for the first dance. She lifted her arms, the better to show her waist, nipped in prettily (where his arms would rest). She didn't like the new fashion of loose bodices and long straight skirts. Rene had made herself a green satin with a sash lined with apricot. She turned sharply before the

311

other mirror on the wardrobe door, sending the sash flying out, flashing its apricot belly. Flo laid her hands lightly on her hips, lifting her chin and her bust too, pouting it a little, thinking of it teasing Bert's chest. She turned away to find her little tapestry evening bag, afraid the watching Rene might read her thoughts.

Bert danced nearly all night with the green and apricot.

Flo turned now from Mary's fine waist to fiddle with a footrest she had made by covering a light pine box with a bright cretonne.

"That's pretty," Mary said with her big, strained smile.

"You'll be learning to drive the truck, I suppose?" Flo said, pushing the little box as if it angered her.

Mary's eyes were fixed on the swirl of flowers on the material.

"I didn't bring my flowers," she murmured, looking back up the road as if considering going back for them.

Then she turned and dodging around the bowsers walked very fast towards the bridge that led to the Bega Road and home.

Fred, dodging too behind the drapery window, saw Flo climb into the sulky, and came out rubbing his hands and looking now without restraint at Mary's disappearing back.

"Get up!" Flo called, loud enough to startle Fred, who raised his hands and rubbed them near his chin, and watched Flo turn half her face, less sullen than before, even the half hidden eyes sending out a gleam of triumph.

"Get up!" she called again, the triumph vibrating the words and Fred, glancing again towards Mary on the bridge, called out Goodbye! his voice echoing Flo's.

The sound reached Mary and she turned her head and Fred, forgetting, turned towards her too, then hastily away and went with his brisk walk into the shop.

Goodbye to you then! Mary walked quite rapidly up

the road not looking towards any of the houses, surprising Mrs Schaefer on her veranda with several little Schaefers balanced on the rail (Sandy at an away tennis match that Saturday afternoon). Mrs Schaefer was disappointed Mary didn't stop to talk. She had travelled in with Stan in the truck (Mrs Schaefer had been on the veranda then as well) and here she was on the long hot walk to Trangie alone. Something must have happened and the older Schaefers read the puzzle on their mother's face.

"Why is Mary nearly running?" said one little Schaefer.

"She's running to her lover," the oldest said, the dreamy one who read books too old for her.

Mrs Schaefer gathered the baby from the veranda rail and, slippers slapping bore it through to the kitchen.

"Running away from him if she's got any sense!" she said, sitting the infant on the linoleum, and putting more wood in the stove, part of her glad about Mary's trouble (it must be trouble, Mary always stopped, or waved at least). Or else she was getting above herself marrying a Rossmore. That was more like it, Mrs Schaefer thought, moving the kettles over the heat for a good supply of hot water, for she suddenly decided to scrub the back veranda, and this helped offset a feeling of loss and depression that Mary, like most of the Rossmores and other superior Cobargo families, might not bother with the Schaefers after her marriage.

Mary thought how foolish it was to be crying with no one to see, trying to picture Stan's face, for she had never cried in front of him. Then she laughed at her foolishness and mopped her face with the hem of her dress, and ran most of the way after that, the removable panel of fence that led to the short cut through the farm coming up so soon it surprised and stopped her. Blow all the scratches and cuts, she told herself, feeling a certain relish at the thought of them, and such a loneliness at the thought of the Trangie gate and the big house, she plunged through the fence and ran quite wildly until she was in sight of the Jussep orchard and the five youngest up the apricot tree.

The first to see Mary shrieked her name, and the others picked it up, echoing it among the rosy fruit and trembling leaves, upon which they turned their young backs and slid down the trunk to the ground and ran to meet her. Nina expected to be lifted and carried, and when she wasn't, wailed, and Patty picked her up, struggling with the stiff body and with the effort to keep up with Mary's race towards the house.

"You're all so grubby!" Mary said, although it seemed she had barely looked at them. "You're not bathed yet! What's Joyce doing!"

"She's reading comics on the good bed," Bernie said.

Mary flew ahead of them and ran along the veranda through the sitting room to the good room.

Joyce rose from the bed like one of the less favoured farm dogs found making a bed in the young lucerne. She began to straighten the wrinkled counterpane. Mary swept her hands where Joyce's had been and put the pillows and shams straight.

"Pick up that rubbish and take it out of here!" Mary said of the comics on the floor.

Joyce went out with her loping tread. At the doorway she gave a great toss of her head. "Mrs Stanley Rossmore!"

Mary sat on a chair, screwed around so that she would not see the chest of drawers where the bottom drawer was filled with sheets and towels and pillowslips among crushed lavender her father had allowed her to buy on his store account. But she was seeing them in her mind so got up to go when Joyce returned.

"Dad's making the scones, so there!" Joyce said and rushed off again.

Mary found her father washing the mixing bowl in a tin dish, scraping away hardened dough, trying to make his expression pleasant above his annoyance with Joyce for her careless housework. Mary took a big kettle from the hearth, not disguising her annoyance, and set it over the heat. She had been making the scones mostly since her mother's death but she suspected her father liked the job.

She took a tin tub from the wall of what was known as the veranda room, where the ironing was done and the younger children bathed, and set the tub sharply on the floor. Her father, measuring flour, lifted his head as if someone had cried out.

A basket of clothes brought from the line sat on an old discarded dining table near the dish of soap and a rolled up ironing blanket. Mary picked through the basket for clean singlets and pants. They were few and thin and ragged and Mary went to the doorway to see if anything was left on the line, but there wasn't, and she was back holding the edge of the basket when her father put his head through the kitchen door. There was a shower of flour on his old grey flannel and some on his face, Mary thought, or he might have just turned pale.

"I'll look on the line for more clean things," she said and ran down the steps.

She passed Patty, Bernie, Joseph, Nina and Peter in a sad little heap under the pear tree near the fowl pen gate. Nina got to her feet to rush to Mary but Patty pulled her down and held her hard while she wept, and a small cruel wind came up suddenly and blew about them and bore Mary's hair backwards as she ran down the slope.

"Where is Mary going!" Bernie asked, as if one of them

should say this, and he rolled over and lay his face on the short soft grass, expecting no answer.

Mary was not sure where she was going, to the Rossmore's house she supposed to tell them she would not marry Stan. I can't be spared from our place, Mrs Rossmore. I'm needed there to see the young ones have their baths and get clean clothes. Joyce is not able to care for them all. She's lazy and should go away to work somewhere, but if she does the first boy she meets will . . . She won't refuse him, she's soft and easy, not like me. Stan works with animals and they . . . I know animals too, but I'm not an animal, Mrs Rossmore, though you probably think of me as one. And your sister Flo Murchison looks down on me, and so does Fred Rossmore, and Harry Rossmore is only polite because he is renting his old house at last.

She was stumbling through some dead ferns which stuck into her legs but she barely felt them, and hearing voices, listened and stopped and knew Eric was in the Rossmore orchard somewhere with a school friend from another farm. I won't go through the orchard and have them see me, Mary said to herself, seeing the sweep of peach and cherry trees, the fruit thinned out, some of the trees with only two or three peaches there, looking as if someone had stuck them onto branches. The proud arms of early spring were drooping now, and they looked like sad parents abandoned by their children.

The earth was dry around them, and Mary, feeling a corresponding dryness in her mouth, ran now to cross the road and plunge into the bush on the other side. This was part of the land belonging to the Gannons, where a few steers ran among the saltbush and she-oaks, and it adjoined the Murchisons. Stan rode this way to visit his grandparents.

Mary saw the indent in the earth near a panel of fence

where Stan jumped his horse, and the sight of the little cluster of hoof marks blinded her eyes again. She followed the thinned out marks to a log where they were grouped again, but skirted the log, choosing not to jump it, turning her thoughts from Stan's back in a billowing work shirt and his elbows flying up to the level of his shoulders and down again.

Mary ran fast until she reached the creek, crossing it by the great shelf of rock over which the water poured when there was a wet spell. The last thin stream was gone since she had sat there with Stan, both with bare feet, cooling them in the flow, making a miniature waterfall by stacking their feet, one above the other, pressing them so hard together Mary felt her thighs tingle.

Stan had put his arms around her and their feet came apart, and Mary scraped hers on Stan's shin and Stan pressed a knee so hard on Mary's shin, the rock hurt her leg and she broke free and ran like a fleet footed filly, her long streaming hair its mane, and Stan took after her and did not easily catch up, and then flung himself down, pillowing his head on some moss covered rock, breathing deeply to settle his lungs. Mary sat on another piece of rock, projecting sharply, a little cave formed underneath. Stan, with his eyes closed and the grass moving with his breath, stretched a hand out and felt inside the cave and smiled as if he were thinking of it as a little house for them both.

"I gotta marry you, Mary," he had said, not even reaching to touch her. "Soon. Real soon." He lay with his legs sprawled, crushing the grass as he might have crushed her body.

Mary walked quite slowly now, pushing her feet tiredly through the short pale grass that covered the slope between the creek and the Murchisons' house. She tried to decide which of the tracks Stan took but there were several, some made by dray wheels, crisscrossed with indents made by a slide, and bits of the track the Murchison girls had made as children going to the creek to play, showing here and there.

She began to feel bewildered as if she should have known Stan's tracks, and since she didn't, she did not know him. She lifted her head away from the confusion and saw Flo Murchison in a corner of their orchard by a nectarine tree, looking at her with the same expression she had worn earlier in the day outside Fred Rossmore's store. She wore the same dress covered by a calico apron. She had the apron gathered up in one hand and some fruit in there. Judging by the bulges and stains, Mary knew it to be plums, and was surprised Flo didn't have a bucket or a colander, she was such a meticulous person. Mary walked up and held the orchard fence. She fixed her eyes on the spreading plum stains and Flo untied her apron at the back and made a little bag of it, holding it away from her dress and inspecting that for any sign of a stain.

"There's nothing ripe yet." Flo felt among the branches where the fruit was bold and hard and glossy, green faces with blushing red cheeks.

"This is the early tree too," Flo said, frowning on the boat shaped foliage trembling in resentment at being disturbed. Although she had the back of her head pointed at Mary, Mary was sure she had missed nothing of her face.

"Stan's not here," Flo said, still groping among the branches.

"I'm not after Stan," Mary said.

Her voice was so gentle Flo shook the nectarine branch as if this would shake the voice to life.

"Not after Stan!" Flo said, and swung her eyes down Mary's old blue voile.

"No, Miss Murchison," Mary said, and turned and ran down the slope.

They were nearly done milking when she got back. Mary had eased out of the milking these last few weeks, ashamed of her vanity that she wanted her hands smooth and dry for the wedding, and no one disputing her decision, since they would have to manage very soon without her and it was as well to start and get used to it.

The younger ones were romping on the old couch in the veranda room and Joyce was peeling potatoes in the kitchen, her dress hanging from one shoulder, her feet bare, her expression sober. Mary took the big kettle of water and poured it into the tub.

"Don't go near that," Mary said, the flying steam mesmerizing the eyes of the children. She added cold water from the tank outside the door.

"You bath them, Patty," she said in the saddest voice the children had ever heard.

All five wore quiet faces. Patty pulled Peter's shirt from his body without unbuttoning it and he yelled inside the folds, and Nina rushed up to help and Mary did not seem to notice, but took her yard hat from the peg and crushed it on, making her face look different as it always did. But it was more different now than ever before. Bernie and Joseph left their game and sat together on the couch as if strange people were visiting and this was the behaviour expected of them.

The father, Joe, and Tom, Gordon and Malcolm were finishing at the dairy. Mary could not believe they had got through it all in such a short time. It seemed such a short while she had spent walking to Murchisons' and back, but it was more than four miles, she supposed, and she had walked home from Cobargo too, nearly another two miles, so that was six miles in one afternoon, perhaps the longest walk of her life.

"I went for a very long walk," she murmured to her father, catching the handle of the kerosene tin, full of separated milk, flies caught in the foam, struggling, but giving no warning to others landing alongside them until the milk looked like a white sea of swimmers doomed to drown.

Her father caught the other side of the handle and the two of them ran to the pig pens and tipped the milk into a trough, the squealing pigs jamming it, the milk running around their feet and rising to their knees. The big bristly heads grunting and pushing angered Mary and she pulled their rears from the trough, and kicked at their jaws, bringing a squeal of joy from a skinny pale pink half grown sow, who managed to fit her nose between the back feet of another three times her size.

Walking back to the dairy, Mary told her father she could not marry Stan and leave them all. She did not look at him saying it but down at her feet in the shoes that had tramped all that way, angry with herself that she had given them all that unnecessary wear.

In a moment she heard her father call to the boys to finish up without him. She saw their heads droop, a halting of their frantic efforts to get through scrubbing out the dairy to fit in a game of tennis before dark.

There was no real court, just an old discarded net from the town courts strung between the fowl pen wire and a tree stump and the players took turns with the two racquets, the others using bats shaped from pine wood.

Mary had eased out of the tennis games too, secretly looking forward to playing on the town courts on Wednesday afternoons when there were social games for the women, Mary blushing already at picturing her name as Mrs Rossmore on the slate hung on the end wall of the School of Arts. Mrs Andy Colburn, treasurer of the Cobargo Tennis Club, had extended her authority to take charge of midweek games and select players of matching strengths to make the games as even as possible.

These past few weeks Mary had gone riding with Stan after tea some evenings and on others sewed on the veranda room at two silk nighties for the honeymoon and two cretonne aprons for after it, pleased at the thought of abandoning at last the hessian apron she wore twice a day to help milk and separate.

"I'd be leaving you at the hardest time, Dad, all the cows in," Mary said, half pleading.

Peter came racing down the veranda to fling himself on her back, a tattered cambric shirt that was once Bernie's worn as a nightdress. Mary wrapped it around him since it was without fastenings and took him on her knee.

His skin was cool from his bath and his hair was damp except on the top of his head, where there were flakes of grime on the scalp giving off a sour smell.

"Look," Mary said, parting his hair to show her father.

"Joyce!" he cried, so loudly that Joyce, listening under her bedroom window, was shocked into jerking into sight. "There like a mongrel dog!" he said, and stood up not showing anyone his face and walked fast in the direction of the farm sheds.

All the younger children were on that end of the veranda by this time, some twining themselves around veranda posts, their bodies no thicker, like young plants glad of support. Bernie had a dreamy face pressed to the wood.

"Will we have to move from here now?" he asked.

Flo Murchison went back into the house after Mary left and tipped the fruit from her apron onto the bench by the kitchen sink (which Vince had put in when he saw there was one at Trangie) and took the apron to the wash house to soak the stain in salt and water.

Back in the kitchen, Mrs Murchison heard her movements and came to the kitchen door, checking the stage of tea preparations, but disinclined to do anything herself in the heat. Her feet had swollen and she was forced to wear a pair of old house slippers, unhappy about this, for she was vain about her feet and legs and liked to mince about in her best footwear and a fresh dress when Vince came in for tea, or fold her feet well out in front of her chair, pleased with the combination of fine beige hose and fine leather, a strap and buckle fastening to emphasize her good ankles (now unfortunately no more than a bump in a mound of flesh like a serve of pale blancmange).

She saw Flo's face now, not as tight and dark and sour as she expected but (given it was only a fragment of profile she saw) softened at the jawline, and ventured to mention the heat of the afternoon.

Flo was looking among the spices on the mantel above the stove, frowning and pushing the corners of her mouth into her sallow cheeks, dissatisfied with the powdered nutmeg Fred Rossmore had coaxed her to try, when she had always grated whole nutmeg onto her custards and rice puddings.

"God help us the day of the wedding if this heat gets worse," Mrs Murchison said.

Flo looked cruelly at her mother's feet, then wrapped herself in a sateen apron, keeping her eyes hooded. She broke eggs into a basin, for she was baking a custard, Mrs Murchison could see, and it would be warm for Vince's tea, the way he liked it. She felt the little familiar glow of pleasure when there were pleasures for Vince. She was almost ready now to offer to set the table.

"That is, of course," Flo said, "if there is a wedding."

Flo saw her mother's face and thought of laughing. It was like a pudding in its cloth, dragged from the water it was cooked in, the features washed away. It was a pale grey, pudding-cloth colour too.

"I saw Mary Jussep in town and again later," Flo said. I'll tell her nothing more, she said to herself, greasing an enamel dish with great vigour, pleased about this for her mother always said the dish only needed heating at the side of the stove. Mrs Murchison forgot to frown on the operation.

"Why don't you sit down and rest your feet?" Flo's tone was sweet as the sugar she measured carefully onto her eggs.

Mrs Murchison turned from the doorway moving fast on her heavy legs. Flo laughed and spoke aloud. "Straight to the telephone! Her legs will carry her that far and with a good dash of speed too!"

When she went into the dining room to set the table she saw her mother's impatient back at a window overlooking the dairy where Vince was using a broom to clean cobwebs from a window, swiping at the frame with great energy, his annoyance that even jobs like this were left to him reaching Mrs Murchison across the space.

He could leave that and come and hear what she had to tell him! She could call him, but she had never done such a thing in her life, even when her pains were coming on hard, and she needed him to get in the sulky and bring the midwife, a Miss Garson, who lived alone in Cobargo in those days, and attended to home births years before there was the cottage hospital, run by Mrs Patchett.

She decided to return to her chair, thinking that he would come quicker if she didn't watch, then got up suddenly and went to her bedroom to force her feet into new shoes she wanted to break in for the wedding. The leather pushed up a ridge of flesh on her instep and more flesh flowed over her heels, like boiling milk about to tip from a saucepan.

She tottered back to the living room and watched Vince at work on the other side of the dairy.

Flo put a glass dish of sliced tomatoes, well peppered, on the table. She looked down on the shoes. "Going ta-tas?"

Her mother sat in her chair again and joined her puffy fingers on her lap. "Rene's in a terrible state," she said.

Flo inspected a serving spoon, then rubbed it brighter on the corner of a tea towel slung across a shoulder.

"Rene has been in a terrible state these past six months," Flo said. "I thought that was plain to most."

She laid the spoon at a new angle. "The girl has called it off."

Mrs Murchison's hand flew to her throat like a giant moth beating against a great thick candle.

"The girl call it off? The girl wouldn't call it off!"

Flo's lip dug smugly into a cheek.

"Stan's thought better of it," Mrs Murchison said. "Like his mother said all along. He's far too young."

"But isn't she in a terrible state? A terrible state of joy, then?"

Mrs Murchison seized the lid of her sewing box and used it as a fan. Vince came in then.

"Our Rene's in terrible trouble, Dad," Mrs Murchison said, stretching a hand in his direction. He ignored it.

"We need to go to her straight after tea." She looked only as high as Vince's waist, then raised her voice for the kitchen to hear. "Give Dad his tea, Flo, so that we can get away well before dark!"

She got up and walked fast, though in pain, to take her place at the table and serve herself with tomatoes, leaving space on her plate for cold meat which Flo brought in, and though she reared back for Flo to serve her, Flo dumped the dish heavily on the table and went out heavily for bread.

Vince sat and Mrs Murchison clutched the arm he had ready for his knife.

"The wedding's off Dad, whatever will we do?"

Vince jerked his arm away to eat. He knew what he would do. Bring the boy to stay with them. The change would be good for him, Vince would keep him busy and that would be good for him too. He had known from the beginning that marriage idea was a mistake, for all Pearl's silly prattle about the two of them the same age as he and Pearl had been.

He would get the boy now! Flo could get one of the spare bedrooms ready and he could well bring him back with them that evening. That other boy, Eric, would be home for holidays soon from boarding school (a waste of money that, he would never have tolerated such unnecessary expense even if he had had sons) and he could work about Trangie, taking Stan's place. Then when it was time for Eric to go back to school, Stan would be so well dug in with him he would stay, perhaps going home occasionally when Bert and Joe Jussep needed a hand. Vince was glad he had not taken part in all the carry on about the wedding, all off now thank goodness. A son, a son at last! He flicked his dark eyes briefly on Pearl, reminded once again of her failing.

And he got briskly to his feet, for he was an athletic man still.

Pearl got to hers too and let out a little squeal of pain. "They'll be alright after I've walked in them for a while," she said, hanging onto the table edge.

And what walking is she likely to do, Flo asked herself, covering her scorn with a crashing of their dirty plates as she gathered them up to go to the kitchen.

Ten minutes later the Buick was backing out of the

shed, its rear bathed in pale blue smoke, and there were the two of them, Vince upright and square of shoulders and Pearl, Buddha like beside him, going without a backward glance.

Oh yes, Flo cried to herself, sending a rush of water over the plates in the sink, precious tank water that it was, aware that this would upset her mother, sorry she wasn't there to see.

Oh yes, they are off without a word of invitation to me to go too. I stay at home while they go to the euchre and the show meetings and any of the other big social events. I am left here to turn down their bed and make sure the jerries are emptied and the stove going in case she wants hot milk to help her get to sleep.

Well no milk would be hot enough to get me to sleep while I lie looking back on my life, their servant all these wasted years!

She left the sink and pulled down her sleeves savagely and wrenched her apron off and jabbed it on its nail behind the door. She slammed the door behind her and went along the veranda and down the stone steps, her climbing rose heaping a crust of pink icing along the railing which she did not even see.

The horse, Fried Scone, which Kathleen had named for its blackish brown coat the colour of a scone left too long in the boiling fat, was standing by the sulky having moved no more than three steps since Flo had unharnessed him a few hours earlier.

"Serves you right for not having the sense to get away, or the energy. Lazy like the other one! Well you won't be riding in state like her, but pulling me and fast too, that'll get some fat off you, worse luck we can't put her between a pair of shafts!"

Fried Scone gave only one surprised shake of his head when the harness was flung across his back and the shafts followed. Flo, like many big women, moved with brisk efficiency, and even Fried Scone, who should be well used to her, jumped in alarm as well as obedience when she slapped the reins on his back to send him trotting through the farm gates to the road, giving him the directions with a jerk of the bit and pacing him out on the way to Cobargo.

The Buick and the Rossmores' truck were in the Trangie driveway, but Flo tied Fried Scone to a telegraph post outside the gate. She was grateful to Fried Scone for getting her there before the Buick left for home.

"They'd pass me on the road," Flo said. "He would nod to me as if I was a stranger and she would say to him, 'Why isn't Flo at home stoking the stove for our supper?' ".

Fried Scone flicked an ear when he heard this, and ducked his head in turn, grateful to her for what in Flo's case was an amiable mood.

She rapped on the front door, although it was open and the hallway runner was noted to have some little pellets of fluff clinging to its edges, shown up in the slant of sunlight, one of the last of the day.

Jessie had run the mop down the sides of the carpet, not folding it back as she should, but there, careless as she was and incompetent, she received a wage, something Flo had never had in her life.

She knew they were in the sitting room by the voices and the way the sound was cut off by her knock suddenly, as a milking machine is stopped.

Bert came into the hall and called out "Flo!" as if she were the last person he expected to see.

There was her mother spread out on the frail little lovers' seat under the front window, Rene in one of the chairs turned to the fireplace in the winter and reversed for the summer, Bert obviously in the other one, Vince on a straight backed chair by the end of the piano. It was a darkish corner and his legs at first glance could be mistaken for a spare set for the piano. Stan was on the piano stool, his legs looked very long stretched out, his hat dangled from an elbow where his hand held both it and the elbow. The hat had not long been off his head, and there was the indent on his forehead, paler than the rest of his pale skin, matching the pale lids of his downcast eyes.

"You spoke to the girl Ma tells me," Rene said to Flo.

"Mary," Stan said and flapped his hat on his knee.

Flo saw, partly shocked, the tender little quirk to the corner of his mouth.

"Mary then," Rene said not seeing. She thought how few times she had used her name, and now she might not have to use it at all. She ran her tongue around her rolled back lips.

"What was it the father said to you again, Bert?"

She thinks we've all gone deaf, Flo thought.

Bert stared at his feet, then stood up as if they had ordered him to.

"Come on, son," he said to Stan.

Mrs Murchison forgot she wasn't at home and groped about her on her seat for her needlework. "Oh dear me," she said of her foolishness.

"Why didn't you come with us?" she quavered to Flo. "Poor Fried Scone!"

"Horses don't mind work, Mother," Rene said. It reminded her of Jessie.

"It's Jessie's afternoon off, or I'd have her bring in some tea."

My fine lady can't even manage a tray of tea, said Flo's briefly flashing eyes. Mrs Murchison found her smug look and put it on, as always when there was evidence of Rene's social standing.

"I wonder what will really happen?" Mrs Murchison said, looking down at her feet.

A lot of the puffiness had gone. There were no longer magenta coloured ridges where the strap crossed her instep, the boiling milk in its last heave over the saucepan edge shrunken to a wrinkled skin of eggshell blue. She stood fearing the flesh might rise again like scone dough in a hot oven. It didn't, and she stepped forward over two sprays of roses on Rene's carpet.

"These are the shoes!" she said, as if they had not been visible before.

Rene barely looked at them, and Mrs Murchison backed and sat on the settee again.

"Dear me," Mrs Murchison said. "I wonder what will happen next?"

Rene stood and smoothed down the green linen skirt she favoured with different blouses when she changed for tea. "We will simply go back to where we were before all the fuss."

Will we, my lady? Flo's brief bold look rested on the green lap. And where might that be? Somewhere where you are comfortable, you can be sure of that.

"I was never in favour as everyone knows," Rene said. "But I bided my time. Wisely." She looked over her mother's head through the window at a sweep of farmland, as if it had been threatened by a great flood, but the waters had receded in time.

She swept a hand under her rear to sit again, putting out her feet, wriggling them in her shoes, no puffiness, the feet and legs of a girl of twenty as she had been when Bert swung her into the Schottische in the Cobargo School of Arts.

A great sigh rose from Mrs Murchison's bosom. "I suppose we'll live through it somehow," she said, not disguising the moan that trailed the sentence off.

329

"You can return the shoes to Fred," Flo said gently, as was usual when her sarcasm was heaviest. "You've hardly taken a step in them."

Rene smiled, but not at this, giving the landscape through the window another glance, even more pleased with it than before.

Oh see her there, said the great wave swelling inside Flo. She took Bert, her son might have been mine! The wave was an ugly swell on a littered beach, with nothing to do but recede, taking black sand and slimy seaweed with it, gathering it up with a sucking noise, angry that it could not flow out sweetly on some fine white sandy beach.

Flo slipped from the room without a word.

She was nearly to the sulky and Fried Scone when she saw Stan and Mary at the rear of the truck.

Mary with a big, beautiful, aching smile on her face and the fuschias, drooping very badly now, still in their tin, in the crook of her arm.

"See Miss Murchison," Mary said. "I forgot my flowers. But Stan remembered."

Flo allowed Fried Scone to walk across the Cobargo bridge. She looked for Fred to bob out from behind his bowsers, although the store had been closed for several hours.

He rolled his hands one over the other near his long chin.

Fried Scone and the sulky dragged to a halt. Well? said Fred's big blinking glasses.

"Order in a bolt of white satin!" Flo cried. "Get up, Fried Scone!"